PC Must Die!

A Novel

By Wayne Baker

This book is for Jane.

And dedicated to anyone who's ridiculed for their crazy ideas. You never know, one of them just might get you in big trouble one day.

The Bold Harpooneer

So, be cheery, my lads! may your hearts never fail!
While the bold harpooner is striking the whale!

Herman Melville
Moby Dick or, The Whale

Part 1 - The Beginning

Morning

Morning! Which was what the now glaring sunlight was trying and failing to tell Philip Collins. Its increasingly persistent efforts going almost but not entirely unnoticed for the past few hours.

Phillip Collins, Phil, or more insistently PC, almost imperceptibly opened one eye, then kept pretending to be asleep. He decided to keep pretending until the alarm went off.

Phil liked, or more accurately demanded to be called PC for many very important reasons. The most important was that he thought it sounded pretty cool. The next most important was he hoped it was ironic.

Phil would draw the conversation away from what PC really stood for by saying, 'It's ironic that I'm called "PC", as I think "PC"', Phil always said PC with air quotes. 'Is a completely authoritarian, free speech censoring, judgmental, blame apportioning, total load of shit. Some sort of INGSOC, New Speak, Orwellian based thought control experiment I suspect. And don't even get me started on Woke...' No one ever did, but that didn't stop

Phil from pressing on regardless with a well-seasoned, and well-rehearsed monologue. If it wasn't ironic, he'd been making a bit of a wanker of himself for quite some time now.

The reason today for Phil's dozy procrastination was the pending 6am alarm. Phil hadn't had to set his alarm for a very, very long time. So long in fact, he'd almost forgotten how.

Phil hadn't set his alarm since that perfect day. That perfect day of his retrenchment. The retrenchment accompanied by a salivating, and totally demotivating payout. Phil put this hard-earned achievement down to his persistent, relentless, and completely non-negotiable efforts to not do the "smile, smoke, and laugh at my joke" thing with management. Fucking management! That's why they picked him, Phil would reassure himself.

He decided at that moment, with his newfound freedom, he would actually achieve something. Really achieve something. Completely unlike all his previous achievements, which up to that point had remained completely unachieved. The reason for that Phil suspected was because he always felt a little bit tired, a little bit sleepy. Ergo, with his newfound freedom, Phil created a new Philosophy. A Philosophy that also aligned perfectly with his new lifestyle. The Philosophy of getting up when he woke up, or "*Total rest. Gets total results.*" Six months into this new philosophy and unfortunately, Phil still had a lot unachieved.

During his Job Transition Phase. Which Phil thought sounded so much better than unemployed. He achieved all the little things that somehow should be done. All the things that somehow had to be done before doing something that really needed to be done. All the important movies and books that had to be watched or read, and all the important topics that required serious, and rigorous introspective debate.

Phil started the process by re-watching all his favourite Westerns. Through this exercise he was able to uncover, without any doubt at all, that the safest possible career path in the old west was to learn to play the piano. Ragtime was the preferred style. Nobody ever shot the piano player. He'd stop playing when the shooting started, and he'd simply pick it right back up when the shooting stopped. The old west was apparently very light on for entertainers.

He also devised an entirely new political system, found a major flaw in the fundamentals of mathematics, discovered a link between light, time and gravity, uncovered the unquestionable truth of the moon landings, that answer would make both sides happy, and he also figured out who really shot Kennedy. That one was a bit of a surprise. In addition to these revelations, he also worked out through extensive testing, and thorough research that he didn't need to watch any more pornography. Theorizing he'd probably seen most of it by now anyway.

Phil did, however, clean the house, which was totally unexpected even for him. Cleaning was normally so far down on Phil's to-do list it couldn't be seen by the naked eye. And this was not his usual half-assed, that's probably good enough effort. This was a proper under the fridge, kitchen benches and drawers, dust the bookcases and books, scrub the bathrooms, wash the walls, steam clean the carpets, and wash the curtains for fucks sake clean. A really, really proper clean. He'd also cleaned and organized the garage, even though none of the stuff was even his. He wasn't sure whose stuff it was anymore, or what most of it was. Although, that wasn't really the point. It too also took priority over doing something that really needed to be done.

BEEP! BEEP! BEEP! BEEP! BEEP! BEEP! BEEP! BEEP!...

Phil grasped onto that millisecond of blissful morning amnesia. 'Smoke alarm!' He hoped aloud, then remembered he took the batteries out of his smoke alarms to put in his remotes years ago. Then he remembered the alarm, and reluctantly rolled over.

'For fucks sake!' Phil moaned pitifully implying he'd just gone to bed, when the reality was he'd had a solid 10 hours sleep. Maybe even a bit more.

He opened his eyes wider, played revelry with a loud fart, then fumbled clumsily with everything on his bedside table before finally finding his phone. Phil's phone looked cool about ten years ago. Now he thought it looked retro cool. Not just retro cool, but reliable retro, built to *actually fucking work*. The reason it *actually fucking worked* was because it couldn't actually fucking do anything. He repeatedly pawed at it before mercifully putting an end to the clamour.

Silence...

Phil opened his eyes even wider, gathering his focus by examining a large dark stain on the ceiling he'd been looking at for years. He was often curious about the stain. However, to satisfy that curiosity he would need to climb a ladder.

Every time Phil had been to accident and emergency, there was always someone being stretchered in who'd fallen off a ladder. Phil planned meticulously on never being one of those someone's. The mystery of the ceiling would remain.

He sat up and blinked around the room admiring the freshly cleaned and able to be seen through windows, vacuumed carpet, clean curtains and neat, tidy piles of clothes on the floor and smiled with self-satisfaction.

'Let's get this started!' Phil shouted loudly as a motivational tool remembered from some corporate course he'd mostly slept through, except when everyone there actually yelled 'Let's get this started!', and in fucking unison no less. Today, Phil had an interview.

He leapt out of bed and into action, in his own leap into action and out of bed kind of way, then smiled again at the uncharacteristic and always unexpected tidiness. Phil had been a lifelong slob and was still having trouble adjusting to the change.

'Seems bright this morning.' He said absentmindedly thinking it must be the clean windows, while at the same time gathering up his neatly stacked clothes from the Floordrobe (Patent pending ™), then walked enthusiastically to the shower.

The Floordrobe™ was another one of Phil's new philosophies. This one was created out of necessity. The necessity was necessitated one morning when he was totally unable to open his wardrobe. It wasn't just stuck, it was irrevocably, showing no sign at all of coming to any kind of compromise, stuck!

Phil stayed calm. He used rational thinking and logic to try to uncover what could possibly be imprisoning his clothes. A very short time later he gave up on rational thinking and logic and used a broom. This resulted in the cupboard remaining unreasonable, and a snapped broom. At that moment any remaining strands of logic and rational thinking snapped with it. Phil started kicking it, which damaged his slippers and nearly ruined a good pair of feet. Then he tried swearing at it, then threatening it, which included a final countdown, before finally, tearfully attempting to bargain with it. The cupboard remained silently stoic.

Phil was forced to painfully dismantle it with a tire lever among other inappropriate tools before finally securing the liberty of his clothes. By the time he had achieved this goal, it was one thirty in the afternoon. He was cold, tired, and totally despondent. Basically, in no shape for anything. When he'd recovered, both physically and emotionally, he also decided there was no point at all in wardrobes. Why hang up your clothes and put them in a wardrobe anyway. Phil never ironed. This, as he learnt the hard way, could potentially ruin your entire day. Why risk it. Why is everyone so hung up about hanging up their clothes. They're only there for a day or two at best. What is the fucking point to this conformist tradition?

Phil decided to eliminate the complexities and potential hazards of the wardrobe entirely by simply folding and stacking his clothes neatly on the floor in two piles, clean and dirty. He briefly toyed with the idea of adding seasonal piles but decided it would ruin the Floordrobes™ simplicity.

This philosophy he realised would make the entire wardrobe concept obsolete. It had many, many benefits. It would save time, save space, discourage over consumption, improve productivity, help the environment by making coat hangers and wardrobes completely obsolete, plus it would reduce wear and tear on the carpet if you changed the location of the Floordrobe™ regularly. Another brilliant result of "*Total rest. Gets total results.*" Phil surmised.

He showered, dressed and walked downstairs, then looked out the window at the bright day outside 'Must be a fine day. Smooth sailing ahead.' He muttered to himself.

Smooth sailing ahead, Phil wondered why he said that, then stopped wondering and picked up his new backpack. Not the old one that was mostly gaffer tape, dodgy hand stitching, broken zippers, and had also now developed a not totally offensive, but off putting nonetheless, smell. Phil decided that one had earned an early retirement.

Phil's resistance to conform with today's disposable consumer society was legendary. If it wasn't broken, or totally, and Phil really meant totally worn out, it was definitely still good to go. Phil's collection of old T-shirts was also legendary.

He picked up the required paperwork for the day, along with his keys, cards, and change from the new "*Important Tray*", and put them in his backpack and pockets. He then performed a final pocket inventory before leaving.

The *Important tray* was another recent innovation. This innovation was also inspired through necessity. Whenever Phil couldn't find something important, the usual panic, accompanied by frantic searching, which was mostly comprised of throwing things in the air and swearing loudly, had inspired an anonymous handwritten note being slipped under Phil's door.

He assumed it had been slipped under his door as a

courtesy because all the swearing and searching wouldn't permit him the time to check the letterbox.

The note written in red, for dramatic effect he hoped, covered such topics as corrupting the youth, lowering the local property market, and a lack of respect for his neighbours, some of whom were apparently quite elderly. A poor upbringing, limited education, and a very, very, very, very, very limited vocabulary.

The letter was signed:

Shut the fuck up!
Your Neighbour.

Phil enjoyed the irony of the very's and pinned the note to the fridge with 'Shut the fuck up!' highlighted.

'Shit'! He said a little too loudly, then repeated 'shit.' more softly remembering the note. Phil's pocket inventory hadn't found his mobile phone. He patted down all his pockets again like he was putting out spot fires, then thought he remembered it was still plugged in on his bedside table. 'Fucking please!' He whispered. Which increased his audible swearing percentage for the day to well over 25 percent. Not bad considering he hadn't even left the house yet. Phil liked to swear, a lot.

He bolted up the stairs two at a time and looked at his bedside table optimistically. There it was, right where it should be, and it was fully charged. The sight of this fully charged Phil. Today was going to be a great day, no-no, a day of achievement! He swaggered downstairs, mobile phone in hand, checked the *"Important Tray"* again and then performed one last pocket inventory before swinging himself a hopeful look in the mirror.

The mirror? The full-length mirror next to the door, Phil assumed belonged to his new flat mate. He was almost certain he hadn't seen it before. Phil didn't think he owned a mirror. It was clean. Maybe he just didn't recognise it. Weird! But totally helpful, he thought maintaining his good mood.

Phil interrogated his reflection and lamented his body

shape that was almost completely devoid of any muscles, which reminded him he'd forgotten to go to the Gym for nearly eight years. He did a quick calculation in his head and worked out that he was coming up to three thousand days. Now that's real commitment he thought.

Phil's body shape made any suit he wore look like it was still on the rack. He bemoaned his almost but not quite average height and vampire pale complexion. Phil hoped the whole look would one day come into fashion. He did, however, think the suit he'd worn to only two funerals and one wedding looked pretty damn good.

'Not too bad at all.' Phil muttered to himself deciding to remain upbeat.

He checked the phone, wondering how early he was, and whether he'd have time to get a pot of tea and toast. No raisin toast, with this sort of controlled organisation. He'd earned it.

That's when it happened! It can't have happened, but it did. His phone read 9:37 AM. Phil froze in complete shock. Total disbelief. He remained frozen until the time changed to 9:38.

'FUUUUUCCCCCCK!!!' Phil yelled loud enough to lower the property values at least three streets away, while simultaneously putting any elderly neighbours into a permanent catatonic stupor. Phil's daily audible swearing percentage was about to go through the fucking roof.

'No, No, Nooooo!. Fucking Noooo!. FUCK, FUCK, FUCK, FUCK, FUCKing Christ. Jesus how the Christ fucking...' His increasingly creative, and even more increasingly blasphemous swearing continued until he heard a suspicious click from his neighbour's door. Phil dropped, and unnecessarily commando rolled back into the house. This sudden implied threat instantly and mercifully taking his mind off the latest catastrophic failure in his life.

Phil was hopeless when it came to confrontations. His approach to fighting was to run away as fast, and as far as possible, regroup, and when he thought it was safe, run further away. Phil boasted he won most of his fights by several kilometers. He planned on courageously kicking the door shut, and hiding until the threat passed, maybe even make an escape over the back fence if absolutely necessary. That was until he saw a very large, and very intimidating shadow looming up the driveway. The shadow ominously enshrouded him.

Before he even had time to turn and attempt a smile at the creator of the very large and ominous shadow, he saw a very large, and very red face less than a nose length away, open its mouth and shout.

'SHUT THE FUCK UP!' Then stomp away taking its ominous shadow with it.

I guess that clears up which one of his neighbours wrote the note he thought, trying to recover but looking and feeling extremely close to tears.

Then he remembered 9:38.

'Oh God.' Phil sighed and collapsed even further to the ground in complete acceptance of his fate. He staggered and stumbled through all the stages of grief, before arriving at his final destination. Hopelessness.

'How?... It's just not fair.' He moaned pitifully. 'This time I really, really tried. What the fuck happened?'

Phil then remembered. Well, kind of remembered last night at the pub, at the pub with his best and only mate Wil. He then remembered Wil's plan.

Wil and Phil had been mates for years. Wil liked Phil, or PC as he always called Phil because he knew Phil liked it. Wil and Phil had a bond. A bond built on mutual trust. A trust built on the ghastly secret they both shared.

When Wil found out PC's real name was Phil Collins, which Phil always expected to be greeted with a never-ending series of piss poor jokes. 'Another day in paradise mate'. Do you think there's something 'In the air tonight?' ha, ha, ha. Everyone's a fucking comedian. Phil had heard them all. He was ready.

Wil however, greeted Phil's secret with kindness, sensitivity and an optimistic view of sharing the same name as an Academy, and Grammy award winning artist. Plus, he could sing and play the drums at the same time. A genuine all-round entertainer. 'It's not too bad at all when you think about it.' Wil had said.

Wil sometime later, and many, many beers later disclosed in total confidence that his real name wasn't Wil at all. It was Wilma, and to never tell a living soul. Phil never did.

Phil slowly picked himself up off the floor, and stood motionless, unsure what to do next. The entire morning had suddenly turned into a dramatic anti-climax. He decided to fall back to his default setting. Procrastination.

This skill helped him come up with several plausible reasons why he should, no, must phone his prospective employers sometime in the afternoon. Even though right now, at that very moment he was less than fifteen minutes late. Phil needed to recover, that was obvious. He needed something to eat, something substantial to help him overcome the mornings series of unexpected, but not totally uncharacteristic mishaps. And also, help him recover from a bit of a hangover he suspected.

Phil walked to the fridge, then decided not to bother. The fridge had been cleaned to within an inch of its life. He checked it anyway.

The only things edible in it were a bottle of red sauce, a bottle of brown sauce, and two nearly, but not completely scraped clean jars of mustard. He decided it was time to start restocking with the essentials.

Phil closed the fridge door and sighed with disappointment, got a pen out of his pocket and wrote on a notepad dangling from the sturdiest fridge magnet 'Mustard'. If Phil didn't write a list, he was almost certain to come back from the shops with a bag of potting mix, a watering can, a pair of gardening gloves, a packet of magic beans and a copy of the Yates Gardening Guide.

He trudged back into the lounge room and pretended to think. Phil pretended he might come up with several alternatives. Then he pretended the only remaining real choice was to go to the pub. After all it was nearly 10. The bistro opens at 11ish. Wil's always at the pub in the morning. The decision really makes itself.

Phil changed into his best, I don't give a fuck about

clothes, clothes, walked out and closed the door cautiously and quietly behind him, in case his psycho neighbour was still lurking in his shadow.

The Pub

Phil walked out the driveway and strolled down the street following a well beaten path. As it turned out, today was a near perfect day, there was a slight chill under the breeze which took the heat out of the morning sun nicely. Far too nice a day to be at an interview anyway he reasoned.

He walked past the "way too close" Pizza shop. Wil thought Phil was the luckiest man alive to have a Pizza shop less than seventy-five metres from his front door. He'd measured the distance personally.

Phil crossed the road very carefully, as he thought getting hit by a car would not only really hurt, it would be an incredibly embarrassing way to die, runover like a cat on the freeway. Even more embarrassing than falling off a ladder.

He plodded on towards his destination. Phil passed and waved hello to the super friendly plumbing supplies shop guy he bought a single washer from about five years ago. The super friendly plumbing supplies shop guy waved a super friendly hello back, no doubt eager to sell another washer he thought. The last time Phil tried DIY plumbing it cost him nearly eight hundred dollars. Dream on super friendly plumbing supplies shop guy.

The Christian Op-Shop was the next attraction on his journey. Phil peered in and gave the suspicious looking prick at the counter the finger. They had history. The suspicious looking prick mustn't have had his glasses on and thought Phil was waving and smiled back broadly. Phil paused, not at all satisfied with that reaction, raised his middle finger on both hands, then waved them more vigorously. This only made the suspicious looking prick smile even more broadly, wave both hands back at him and excitedly start walking towards the door. Phil scurried away quickly. He wasn't prepared to test his theory that religion was actually spread by a highly contagious, and highly destructive neurological virus.

Phil walked up over the crest of the hill and was greeted by the stunning vista of the Pub shimmering through the morning sunlight like an urban oasis.

He arrived at the door, stopped and checked the time. 9:57am. Phil couldn't really remember whether the pub opened at 9 or 10 on Mondays and just couldn't cope with any more disappointments. He decided not to risk it, and walked around the block, then checked the time again. 10:01. Phil tentatively pushed the door which eased open invitingly.

He walked to the bar, and ordered a beer unnecessarily, Justin was already pouring it. Phil thought he could at least have had the courtesy to look a bit surprised.

'Starting early today PC?' Justin enquired with no malice at all.

'It's lunch time in New Zealand, and after 9pm in San Paulo Justy. We live in a global economy now mate.' Replied Phil.

'Of course.' Justin answered, in lieu of getting into Phil's International Standard Drinking Time debate again.

Justin had been Phil's barman for the past 10 odd years. He was a good bloke, a bit odd, but a good bloke none the less, and a truly excellent barman. Justin filled the most crucial requirements for any barman. He poured a beer efficiently, without judgement, and always, right to the top. Justin's only real problem was that he had a habit of getting involved in everyone's conversations. As an example, Phil and Wil could be engaged in a late-in-the-day discourse about the possible existence of reptilian overlords, the illuminati, why Kirk, who can root or shoot his way out of any situation, is so much better than Piccard, shadow governments etc., and Justin would somehow get himself involved. Somehow manage to take it too far, or even worse, get them completely off topic.

Justin once spent an entire afternoon trying to prove, with supporting evidence, that all British films made since Dame Judy Dench received her royal honour, must contain either an appearance, a cameo, a photograph, or at the very minimum mention her by name. Apparently, it was part of the deal. That one, they had to admit, had some credibility.

'Interview finished early, or cancelled PC?' asked Justin.

Phil forgot he mentioned the interview, while at the same time hearing the word cancelled, and scurried away.

'Yeah cancelled … More postponed really, some crisis, they'll get back to me next week …' Phil lied, scurrying away even faster.

He scoped around the bar unnecessarily, then spotted Wil sitting in the smoking area as expected. Wil always sat is the smoking area insisting the air was cleaner and healthier than the inside conditioned air. He already had an empty schooner in front of him balanced precariously on a ludicrously too tall, and far too small table.

They raised their glasses at each other as Phil walked over, opened the door, moved his own chair and ludicrously too tall and too small table next to Wil's and sat down.

'You're here early PC. How'd the job…..' is as far as Wil got before Phil put his hand up like a stop sign.

'Hey mate. Do you remember last night? Last night when we were discussing one of your all-knowing, fuck, I'm really sure this time theories?' Phil stared hoping for some semblance of recognition to appear on Wil's face. None did.

'The one you're so sure of…the mythical Lasseter's fucking reef?' Phil noticed Wil's eyes widen.

'You thought you'd figured out where it was, nobody else could, but you damn well did.' Phil said emphasizing his point by slapping the table lightly with his hand. 'We're going to be rich you said. I think you were pricing Armani suits, top hats and Swagger Sticks at some point during the evening.' Phil looked hopefully again at Wil.

'Yeah, I still do!' Enthused Wil, finally recalling.

'If I recollect, we planned to go to Perth first, and from there head directly to …'

Phil put his hand up again.

'Ok, but think back, what was your plan for getting us ready for this quest. I think you were referring to it as a quest at that point in the evening?' Phil said without any humour.

Wil looked skyward pretending to think deeply but was really just stalling for time.

'We were going to start wearing four T-shirts to acclimatize to the heat, and we changed our watches to Perth time to adjust to the time difference, and…' He was stopped mid-sentence.

'You changed my phone three hours ahead Wil?' Phil said accusingly.

'Yeah! That's right. And you made me change it back. You checked. Remember?' Wil said looking a bit nervous now.

'That is correct. But you changed the fucking alarm time instead.' Phil said in his very best stern voice. He was unable to get really angry with Wil.

'Oh, Fuck mate… PC. What can I say? I'm really, really, …' This went on for some time. 'Sorry. So, so, … very sorry. I was drunk. We were drunk. It was late, we skipped lunch again…I think it was a full moon as well.' Wil said, trying to lighten the mood.

'Can I get you a beer PC?' Wil said leaning forward looking sorrowfully at Phil.

'For fucks sake mate. I really needed that job.' Phil said, taking a large swig of his beer, nearly finishing it in a single gulp.

'I called in a lot of favours to get that interview. What the fuck! And where's my fucking beer?' Phil said trying to stay focused on being angry with Wil, but already failing miserably.

Phil was, if nothing else, resilient. He'd decided the day

16

was a total burn anyway and had already moved on. Then as expected, the next problem hit him like a cartoon Anvil. Only much, much harder.

'What am I going to tell Beccs?' Phil said looking very alarmed. He already suspected she had serious suspicions he was completely fucking useless. He didn't need this to finally confirm those suspicions.

Beccs and Phil had been friends for nearly as long as Wil and Phil had been mates. Their backstory was long and not very complicated at all. Phil had a serious crush on Beccs, and Beccs liked Phil, although neither of them would ever admit it. Especially not to themselves, and definitely not to each other.

'PC mate, it's not that bad, we can lie?' Wil said with his arms out giving two thumbs up.

'Won't work mate. She's got some kind of third eye, women's fucking intuition thing going on. She'll spot it right away. I'm absolutely, completely fucking doomed.' Phil slumped pitifully back in his chair.

'OK, I've got a Plan B. We hide at your place. With some beers, and a pizza of course?' Wil said giving it two more thumbs up. Phil gave it two thumbs down.

'And when she calls home. And then calls my mobile, and I don't answer. She'll know I'm hiding…, and I fucked up. Plus. I asked her to meet me for lunch. She knows I won't forget that.' Phil said shutting down Wil's plan B.

'Already thought of that mate.' Wil said, smiling confidently again.

'We ask Justy to say you left a message saying your ancient mobile finally packed it in. She'll believe that. And you got held up at your Interview, then we hide at your place. Justin loves a good caper. He'll do it for sure. Of course, we'll have to turn your router off, or just not answer the phone.' Will raised one eyebrow like he was an evil genius.

'Still won't work. Chris will turn it back on, or answer the phone probably?' Phil said explaining another flaw in plan B.

'So, you met the new flat mate then? The enigma?' Wil

17

enquired eagerly.

'Hell no! Still haven't, and I still know fuck all about them… It, what. And I mean nothing. I assume it's a girl as I found a mirror in the hall.' Phil said looking worried he might be being sexist. 'I can't be sure though. It could be a fucking budgie for all I know'.

'She, or he's been there a month now, haven't they?' Said Wil.

'I think so…' Phil said slumping again.

'How about my place then?' Wil said already knowing the answer.

'You live in the same building, on the same floor, next door to Beccs. You know she sometimes drops home during the day. And your place has walls like a Japanese apartment. You can hear your neighbours thinking. It's fucking hopeless. I should just face up to it.' Phil said, knowing he wouldn't face up to it.

'And where is my fucking beer!' Changing the subject back to procrastination.

Wil stood up immediately and left for the bar. Phil was left alone with his own thoughts, and they were all very depressing.

Wil walked back in, three beers in hand.

'PC. Got you an extra one, as an extra apology.'

Phil downed the first one and set to work on his extra beer already enjoying the buzz on an empty stomach.

'The bistro still opens at 11ish today?' asked Phil.

'PC, It's Monday. The bistro doesn't open on Mondays anymore.'

Phil nodded a knowing reply.

'We can get a pizza delivered. Justy won't mind, as long as he gets a slice.' Wil again looked impressed at his own idea. 'Maybe Beccs won't stop by anyway.' He added unconvincingly.

Phil looked at Wil and raised his eyebrows using his "You're fucking joking!" expression.

'No chance. I asked her to meet me at 1. You know, celebrate, commiserate as the case may be.' They both sat in the silence drinking.

'Listen mate. I've said I'm sorry, but I know that won't cover it. Not by a long way.' Said Wil.

'I'll throw myself under the bus PC. On the grenade so to speak. It's my fault anyway. I fucked up! I fucked your phone! Umm, I'll say I pocket dialled you at 4 as well....'. Phil again put his hand up like a stop sign, which Wil was now beginning to find a little bit annoying.

'Wil mate. We all know whose fault this is.' They both sat in silent thought again.

Wil was a good mate. A proper mate. It wasn't really important whose fault it was anymore. What mattered was keeping the beer flowing in Phil's direction and keeping his mind off the pending arrival of Beccs. Wil also knew how Phil felt about Beccs, not that he suspected. Phil thought he was a master of deception. He wasn't.

Four beers in and the time had spun around to 11:30.

'PC? What do you fancy mate?' Will said waving one of the many Pizza menu's he always carried with him.

'I can't do it.' Phil half whined, half moaned.

'You can't eat Pizza?' Wil said, without understanding the concept or the sentence.

'No. I mean. I can't be here when she gets here, I mean. I mean it. I just can't do it. It's not even that I let myself down I mean.' He said frowning, trying to remember not to say, I mean again.

'I just can't do it!' Phil sounded serious. Wil nearly interrupted but knew an important speech when he was about to hear one.

'She helped me get my suit dry cleaned, she went with me for a haircut, helped me pick my new backpack, and polished my shoes for fucks sake. I just can't face it!'. Phil looked like a Rabbit in the headlights. Genuine unrehearsed panic. Wil knew exactly what to do. Get him the hell out of there. Fast!

'Pizza sh...' Wil stopped knowing it was too close, and he'd just tried that. Wil had a bit of a problem with Pizza.

'How 'bout the Mall. She's on another health kick. No way she'll be at the mall. Food's disgusting, and she never goes over that side... Ever!'. Wil held his arms out again.

19

Phil still looked panicked, but nodded and downed the last of his beer, stacked it in Wil's empty glasses on another table and picked up his new backpack slumped on the floor and threw it over his shoulder.

They both stood up and simultaneously knocked their tiny tables over. Justin looked from behind the bar wearing his, I'm glad you're fucking off expression, then waved an unsubtle goodbye.

They strolled calmly over the railway bridge to the shopping mall. The conversation was light and as usual lent towards the ridiculous. Just the way it was meant to be. Wil knew exactly how to cope with one of Phil's all too common crises.

Phil felt a wave of relief washing over him. He could face the music some other time. He was only a little bit drunk, by his standards anyway, and he was with his best mate Wil. Plus, he wasn't going to make a fool of himself in front of Beccs, well not today anyway. He felt the cool gentle breeze procrastinators feel when they come up with a really good excuse.

That's when it happened. Again! And for the second time today. Total shock. Beccs was walking towards them in the middle of the bridge smiling and waving.

Phil thought about running, then he thought about jumping off the bridge, then he thought about faking a heart attack, but knew he wasn't that good an actor. Then he wished he'd decided to have pizza.

Wil leaned in and whispered in Phil's ear.

'Brace yourself PC.' Then stepped back a pace.

Phil braced himself. Waved, smiled and called. 'Beccs!' Beccs smiled back at Phil suspiciously.

The Backstory

Phil and Beccs backstory began at the park. The quaint little well-kempt park, opposite the police station, next to the library and adjacent to the local MP's office. This Park had a Gazebo, well-manicured flower beds, a statue, ornamental trees and even a little fountain. If it had a bird's nest with baby birds in it tweeting sweetly, Tim Burton could have used it as a set for his next movie. Location, location, location Phil always thought as he walked past.

The reason Phil and Beccs met, was because Phil decided that *"Work from home Fridays"*, which he'd fought Management long and hard to negotiate. Eventually successfully, although, not for the reason that he thought, which was because he was a brilliant negotiator. But rather that management were simply sick of having to listen to the same boring argument every single Friday.

Phil decided *"Work from home Fridays"*, would also include a working lunch at the park. The Park was fairly quiet, but not so quiet that he didn't think, or hope, someone would see him posing with his backlit hybrid laptop, Smart Phone, USB Hub, WiFi dongle, extra battery pack, and various other posing devices he didn't need, or use, but nonetheless all on full display. Phil was a bit of a wanker back then.

Beccs went to the same park on Fridays to get away from Ryan. Beccs was a legal secretary and Ryan was her boss. Ryan wasn't a bit of a wanker. He was a complete wanker, not just an amateur wanker, or even a weekend enthusiast, he was a hall of fame wanker. If wanking was a sport, every boxing day he would stride out onto the MCG to a deafening chorus of Ryan! Ryan! Ryan! from a jubilant packed house, all, who in years to come would be able to say. They saw the legend.

Beccs liked Fridays. Ryan had meetings in the afternoons on Fridays, which everyone knew was bullshit but didn't care, as they were all just really happy he wouldn't be there. Ryan was seldom seen after 11:45. Beccs wasn't taking any chances though and always left for lunch at 11:30.

Phil was set up in the corner of the park at his favourite picnic bench. Phil always started lunch early as he believed I.T. brain work burnt more calories than most jobs. It probably would have if most jobs involved sitting motionless for most of the day and daydreaming.

The bench Phil sat at was next to a statue he hoped looked a little bit like a distant relative. It was in the corner of the park, a bit out of the way, but still in enough view that anyone walking past could see him posing with all his techy stuff.

Phil checked to make sure everything was on display properly. Not overtly on display, but on display, nonetheless. He tore the wrapping paper open from his rissole and barbeque sauce sandwich, which was now also on display, then opened his can of Korean soft drink. Phil thought having a drink with geometric alien looking writing on it looked cool. Plus, maybe passersby would think he was multilingual. Phil really was a wanker back then.

He took a casual bite, started chewing, and caught a glimpse of a girl approaching out of the corner of his eye. He pretended to ignore her and stared intently at his laptop screen, trying to look like he was concentrating on something really complicated, and incredibly important.

'Excuse me?' Said a smart looking girl, in a smart looking business suit, with a smart looking expression on her face, holding a sandwich and a drink. Phil was pretending to concentrate so intently he was startled and involuntarily, and he hoped, inaudibly made a tiny squeak in surprise.

'Excuse me?' He repeated, clearing his throat. Phil always hoped girls would walk past looking impressed, not actually stop and talk to him.

'No. I said excuse me.' The smart looking girl said again. 'Can I sit here? Or, should I say, may I sit here?' She said gesturing to the seat on the other side of the bench.

'Of course. You can and may.' Phil said nervously thinking maybe his posing devices were finally starting to kick-in.

'You know they work better when you turn them on.' The smart looking girl said without any hint of sarcasm pointing at Phil's blank screen.

Damn it! He thought, thinking he should focus more on turning them on, rather than arranging the perfect display. He knew she was onto him.

'You sound like my genius Boss. He has that sort of deep technical knowhow. Gets right to the heart of the matter effortlessly. Why, one day he was able to deduce the power was out simply by falling over his chair!' Phil said matching her lack of sarcasm, and he hoped, upping the ante.

'Anyway, I don't need to turn them on. I'm really only using all this lot for posing.' Phil said confidently waving his arm around at his array of mostly unused and redundant techy stuff.

The smart looking girl giggled, accidentally spat out a bit of her sandwich, which Phil found totally charming, and put her hand out.

'Hi, I'm Rebecca, Becca, Beccs. How's the posing working out today?' she asked, leaning in looking genuinely interested.

Phil nervously held her hand, then shook it even more nervously, and looked surprisingly at their joined hands, then looked at Beccs who smiled a smile he imagined could raise an army, or at the very least an extremely

23

determined posse, then with superhuman effort composed himself.

'Not too bad at all. See that lady washing her bra in the fountain? Yes her.' He said, pointing unnecessarily. 'The one shouting at the tree?'. Phil pointed more obviously at her while nodding and frowning confidently.

'I think I'm wearing down her resistance. I've had my eye on her for quite a while now. I've definitely,' Phil emphasised definitely. 'Got a real chance there. Oh, I'm PC.' He said releasing the handshake apologetically.

'Nice to meet you PC. And I'd appreciate it if you'd leave my Aunty out of this. She's just been through a very difficult breakup with that smelly guy that lives under the bridge.'

'Oh, you mean Roger. Roger and I go way back. I should probably just step away if she's on the rebound from Rog. Well, he's a hard act to follow.' Phil said putting his hands up in mock surrender, trying not to laugh at his own joke, and increasing the sarcasm.

Beccs laughed and lost a little more sandwich, which Phil found even more charming. Then they both laughed, noticing they were both eating rissole and barbeque sauce sandwiches and drinking Korean soft drinks.

'Geonbae.' Beccs said opening and taking a sip of hers.

Phil smiled, raised his drink, took a sip and panicked. Christ! Pretty, smart, and multilingual. Maybe I should just give up now and go talk to her Aunty.

That was how Beccs and Phil spoke from that moment on. No bullshit, just total bullshit. Always parrying lightly back and forth until someone cracked.

Sure, Phil had had a few dalliances with girls in the past. Even some, who obviously had poor decision-making skills, had chosen to go home with him. Although most of them had come to their senses and realised their mistake by mid-morning. This was different. Phil would never admit it, not even to himself, but from that moment on, he knew he was in serious trouble. Phil never did manage to turn his laptop on that day.

Phil and Beccs met at the park every Friday for lunch

from then on. Neither of them admitted they were having a lunch date, but rather that it was just a convenient, persistent and happy coincidence that seemed to just keep happening. Totally weird, they would agree and laugh nervously.

Phil began to understand all of Beccs issues with her work and personal life. The problem with her work life was Ryan. The problem with her Personal life was that she didn't really have one. She'd only just moved into the area and didn't know anyone. The only people she knew were work people, and Beccs spent most of her days trying to figure out how to spend less time with them, not more.

Beccs got to know what PC's real name was, which she giggled over for a while, quite a long while. Then spent most of the day going through her repertoire of impromptu Phil Collins jokes, then softly humming Phil Collins songs, which also included air-drumming solos. Just to get it out of her system she insisted. You know, once and for all. Get it over and done with. It worked, eventually.

She also learnt that Phil did actually work in I.T., and wasn't just a poser, although he had little to no interest in the subject. What interested Phil was just about everything else.

They also found out they had two very important things in common. They both liked rissole and barbeque sauce sandwiches, and they both hated Ryan.

Phil really liked Beccs, and was totally loyal, and completely steadfast in his friendship. That's why Phil took his hatred of Ryan to the next level. He decided he hated all Ryan's. Ryan Reynolds, Meg Ryan, Ryan Gosling, Saving Private Ryan, Jack Ryan, Ethan Hawke (for singing Ryan's song), he didn't care, he hated them all. Beccs really appreciated it.

Mostly Beccs liked that Phil made her feel comfortable, made her laugh, never lied, always exaggerated, but never lied, and never intentionally made her feel like an idiot.

Phil liked that Beccs took him seriously, made him think, and made him surprisingly honest. Mostly because he couldn't lie to Beccs, he knew she would definitely know. He didn't know how she would know, but she would. You'd just be embarrassing yourself to even try.

Their friendship over the years moved on from lunch on Fridays, to drinks at the pub on Friday night, to stopping in at the pub for drinks with Phil and Wil most afternoons.

Beccs initially didn't like Wil, mostly because she used to see Wil in the corridors of the building they both lived in. Wil was big. He was big in a way that made other big people double take. And he had a no-nonsense goatee to match his no-nonsense countenance. He looked like trouble. However, after Beccs got to know Wil, she found out that he was actually no trouble at all. The main problem she had with Wil was that she thought he was a bad influence on Phil. She was right. But she had to admit that Wil did keep an eye on Phil, and was far too likable, in a big lost puppy kind of way to ever get seriously annoyed with.

Beccs and Phil also exchanged phone numbers and started texting each other. Beccs would text Phil with the day's unbelievable antics of "Ryan the Wanker", which they both promised one day to make into a comic book of the same name. And Phil used Beccs as a sounding board for his, this time I'm really right, I'm really through the looking glass now Beccs, theories.

They were both happy with the way things were. Well, that's what they told themselves anyway.

Showdown

Beccs and Phil walked up to each other cautiously, stopped at the centre of the bridge, then faced off. Phil felt like he'd just walked into a Sergio Leone western. It was high noon, and trouble was definitely a brewin'.' They stared at each other like two gun fighters. Phil, as usual, was completely unarmed.

Beccs smiled suspiciously, then smiled even more suspiciously at Wil with her "it's probably your fault." look, then turned her attention back to Phil.

'So, how'd it go? Where's the suit? Must have finished early?' She rapid fired, hitting Phil with each shot.

'Ummm' Phil started uncertainly trying to stall but already he knew she knew. The gentle cool breeze of procrastination changed into a burning Saharan sandstorm.

'You didn't even go did you?!'

'Ummm' Phil raised his eyebrows trying to look innocent but instead looked genuinely and suspiciously useless.

'I'm done! You are fucking useless aren't you Phil?' Beccs said, emphasizing Phil spitefully, then turned and walked away.

Phil briefly thought about correcting her by saying PC, but decided that would be the equivalent of asking, "Is this food Kosher?" at a white supremist meet and greet. He instead just stood there and watched her walk away.

What else could he do but stand there? He had no comeback, no real excuse and even if he did, he couldn't say it to Beccs.

Both Wil and Phil stood and watched her storm off over

the bridge shaking her head, mumbling and mimicking PCisms, whilst throwing her arms in the air at the same time crushing the last of Phil's spirits.

Wil immediately put his arm around Phil.

'It's not that bad PC, mate. She'll calm down. I'll explain it was all my fault, you know, the alarm...by the time I've finished she'll be too angry with me to have any appetite to take a bite out of you.'

'Not that bad!!!' Shouted Phil. 'Not that bad? I've never seen her that pissed off before, all I can remember is, "I'm done,... and your fucking useless."' He said in a piss weak Beccs impersonation that he felt bad for making.

Wil tried to usher Phil onward, but he was stuck to the spot.

'Come on Mate. PC. Let's go! Lunch, my shout. You can't just stand here, she's gone now, shake it off.' Wil smiled at Phil, doing his best Taylor Swift hand shaking improv.

Phil grudgingly started to move, looking a lot like Frankenstein's monster, only drunk and with much less poise.

'So, you don't think there'll be any... bad blood.' Phil said trying to shake it off, at the same time liking his upping of the Taylor swift anti.

'No mate, you need to ... calm down!' Wil raised his eyebrows knowing that was a passing shot.

Phil put his hands up in mock surrender and trudged on with Wil guiding the way.

They walked through the mall past the hearing loss centre where the person at the shop front always asked.

'Excuse me Sirs. Would you like a free hearing check?'

Which they would always reply 'Pardon?', cupping their hand to their ear. That joke never gets old, they thought. The person at the hearing loss centre thought it was getting pretty old.

They entered the food court and sat down at tables only slightly larger than the ones at the pub. They both ate in silence. Well Wil ate in silence, Phil mostly poked at his food.

Watching Wil eat always depressed Phil, and he didn't need any more depressing today. Wil was so good at it. Which always reminded Phil how bad he was at it.

While Phil continued poking at his sushi, Wil was already on to his second course. Six large spring rolls.

'Not hungry today mate.' Phil said sarcastically still poking.

'Watching my figure.' Wil mumbled through chews. 'Bikini seasons just around the corner PC. A bikini body is built in the off season.' Wil said smiling while patting his belly.

That was it for Phil. The thought of Wil in a bikini had finished him off. He pushed his now deconstructed sushi aside and stood up.

'I've still got two spring rolls to go.' Wil said before swallowing his fourth one.

'Think about your figure mate.' Phil replied, trying hard not to.

'You're right PC, I'll just leave it.' Wil said, at the same time stuffing the spring roll bag in his jacket pocket.

They both started on the return journey to the pub on autopilot.

Phil stopped at the supermarket to pick up some essentials for his starving refrigerator. He bought four types of mustard to try and cheer himself up. It didn't cheer him up very much.

Wil walked on enthusiastically with Phil lagging, trudging aimlessly on behind. As they neared their destination Phil stopped.

'What the fuck am I doing. I mean the pub won't help. Instead of being hopeless, useless and depressed, I'll be drunk, really drunk, hopeless, useless and depressed. How will that help?' Phil looked on the verge of an epiphany.

Wil stopped and stood shaking his head with his, your definitely wrong shake, then proclaimed.

'This is not a trip to the Pub mate. This is a meeting of the minds. This afternoon PC.' Wil said, pointing a finger skyward.

'We will identify and fix the problems in your life…. Including Beccs.' He finished.

Wil smiled and raised his eyebrows hoping Phil might just, for once actually acknowledge something and put everyone out of their misery. He waited, staring at Phil, then realised, he, like everyone else, would have to keep waiting, then changed the subject.

'Plus, I brought *The Book*.' Wil said taking a tatty spiral notebook out of his bag holding it out in both hands like a holey relic. Phil gave Wil that, just leave it look, then decided in his weak-willed way. Fuck it, may as well.

They walked back into the Pub both pretending not to, but nervously keeping an eye out for Beccs. Just in case. So far, so good. They moved back into the smoking area, sat in the same seats, picked up the tables that were still lying where they left them, and smiled and waved at Justin. Justin rolled his eyes, shook his head in resignation, then started to pour two more beers.

'You stay here PC. I'll get the beers. Draw up a new chapter in *the book* and we'll get started.' Wil said with purpose.

"*The Book*" is the combined work of Phil and Wil's musings on subjects ranging from Atlantis to Zombies. It's in its third volume, and as Wil says, when published would change the world forever. Neither of them could really work out how or why this would happen, either the publishing or changing the world, but pressed on regardless.

Wil returned with the Beers, put them down carefully and took "*The Book*" off Phil who hadn't moved. Turned it upside down, turned over the last page and wrote the heading "Fix PC".

'Right! Now in order to fix the problem we need to find out what the problem really is. You know. Define it'.

'What time is it?'. Phil said trying not to sound panicky, but not completely succeeding.

'Why?' Do you have a meeting?' Wil replied, immediately regretting how cruel that sounded.

'Sorry PC. We have the whole afternoon. It's only about

five to one.' Wil then remembered the cause of Phil's panicked look.

'She won't come to the Pub mate. She didn't look like she was in the mood to talk. Not just yet anyway.' Wil smiled.

'Who?' Phil said trying to look dismissive.

Wil looked at Phil with an almost hurt, it's me expression and turned another page over in "*The book*" and wrote the heading, <u>Beccs</u> underlined.

'I thought that chapter should have a page too itself.'

Phil blushed almost, but not imperceptibly and turned the page back.

'Can we just get started. We're here to fix my problems not yours.' He said knowing that sentence didn't make any sense at all.

Wil picked up his pen looking confused.

'Right... Let's start with what caused today's problem,' then wrote "*Today's problem.*" with a bullet point at the front.

'We know what caused today's problem. It was you, you dopy prick.' Wil ignored that and wrote under Today's problem another indented bullet point. "*Problem 1 - Faulty alarm.*"

'It wasn't a faulty alarm,' Phil said exasperatingly.

'Listen PC, we'll never get this done if we start out by pointing fingers.' Wil said, smiling broadly.

Phil took the pen, and "*The Book*" and wrote. "*Solution 1 – Get a better friend.*" Smiled at Wil jokingly, crossed that out and wrote, check the time and alarm time when the alarm goes off. Under that he wrote, buy a wind-up alarm clock.

Wil took "*The Book*" off Phil, took a glasses case out of his bag, opened it and put on a pair of very weak glasses. Phil thought they were probably just clear glass, and he only used them for effect. Wil adjusted them unnecessarily on the bridge of his nose and read what had been written.

'Brilliant PC, that covers a phone failure, power failure and a friend failure. Redundancy! Now you're working through the issues.' Wil said holding up his empty glass. Phil nodded and downed the last half of his beer. Will returned to the bar and returned with two more beers.

'Think about it. Phil. That's it. That's the entire problem. If you'd got up on time. No wait, you did get up on time, it was just the wrong time. So, motivation isn't your problem. Stop being so dramatic. With a new clock your problems are solved!'. Wil looked totally convinced and implied it was time to start some serious drinking and some serious thinking. Phil didn't look quite so convinced.

'I'm pretty sure I have more than one problem.' He muttered meekly.

'Alright then,' Wil grabbed the book, turned the page back to the one titled <u>Beccs</u> and hovered with his pen ready to write. Phil stared blankly at Wil for about 10 seconds and finally spoke, unfortunately breaking the awkward silence. Phil loved awkward silences.

'Did you see the latest Bigfoot video?' He knew exactly how to steer Wil's conversation away from the minefield topic of Beccs.

'Yes!!! Looked like Chewbacca too me. I mean why so blurry, why so far away, he was only walking, why didn't they run after the furry fucker.' Phil new immediately, mission accomplished, subject changed, procrastination complete. He laughed loudly and very casually leant over and turned the page back.

Wil was away. He was already reaching into his bag for Volumes 1 & 2 of "*The Book*" to check his notes.

Wil and Phil took turns as custodians of "*The Book*" nightly. Wil would summarise the days topics one night, and Phil would file and update his expanding folders the next. Phil was at least one or two books behind on that task. Plus, they would also have a valid excuse to meet at the pub daily.

Will said it was essential to meet at the pub as "*You do your best thinking, when your drinking,*" and some of the world's greatest minds were drinkers. Benjamin Franklin, Alexander the Great, Billy Joel, Winston Churchill, Nikola Tesla, Bob Hawke, Elizabeth Taylor, Oliver Reed, Jim

Morrison, Boris Yeltsin, the list just went on and on. Although he did have to admit that Oliver and Boris probably took it a bit too far.

'Before you run dry mate, my shout again.' Smiled Phil, standing up to buy his first beer not quite stumbling to the bar. He returned with two beers to a concerned looking Wil.

'What's up mate. You look like you've just seen a ghost or found a major hole in our who shot Kennedy hypothesis,' Phil laughed. 'And I know you think we've solved that one.'

Wil didn't laugh, he just changed his expression from concerned, to very concerned and said, 'Put the beers down PC.'

Phil put the beers down and stared at Wil. He then traced where Wil was looking. That's when he saw it, her he corrected himself. Beccs was walking from the bar, drink in hand smiling at them.

'See, it's not that bad PC, she's smiling.' Wil said, smiling, talking without moving his lips like a ventriloquist.

'Yes, it is.' Phil said doing the same thing.

'I know that smile, that's not her. It's good to see you smile. That's her sarcastic it's time to really let loose smile.' Phil said, still not moving his lips.

Beccs walked in, dragged a chair across to their tiny tables, which Wil and Phil both sat down at obediently. Beccs smiled again and said, 'I see you didn't forget to go to the pub today PC? And you didn't forget our date?'

Phil smiled keenly at being called PC again and at the "*our date*" remark.

'But you didn't, did you? You thought I wouldn't come, that's why you're here.' Beccs said spitefully.

'Otherwise, you'd be at Wil's house doing your "*research*", hiding'. She said using sarcasm, and air quotes.

Phil could already feel his smile fading, and the atmospheric change foreshadowing an oncoming category four storm. He tried to show as little fear as possible.

Beccs then turned to Wil to make sure he didn't think he was excluded and said, 'I'll get to your sidekick later.' she waved her hands around feigning forgetfulness 'Tonto, Igor, Robin, Barney, or is it Silent Bob? I shouldn't really compare you with those sidekicks as they at least had jobs, and kind of a purpose.' she said dismissively. That's when Becca really let loose.

Beccs Lets Loose

'I have a job. It has a purpose.' Wil said meekly immediately regretting the decision.

'A job! Is that what you call it, you're the night guard at the Mall, why do they even have a night guard at the mall, what exactly do you do? Has anyone ever tried to break in? No!' she said not waiting for a response. 'Has anything even remotely exciting ever happened?'

Wil was about to mention the time he caught a "*rogue*" brushtail possum, single handedly no less. A story that gets even more dramatic, and more dangerous every time he tells it. Then decided wisely against it.

'And I don't want to hear that fucking brushtail possum story again either.'

Phil laughed. Big mistake! Beccs turned her gaze purposively towards him.

'PC'. She said glaring.

'I'm not even going to yell at you. I mean what's the point, it doesn't seem to help, you can't get your shit together, or do you just not care. I bet you haven't even called to apologise for missing the interview yet have you? What is it?' She said, calculating in her head.

'4 hours. That's top shelf procrastination PC.'

Phil shook his head feeling a degree of shame.

'You know. When you got retrenched from that shitty job, I thought maybe he'd lift this time. But I was wrong, you fell further, you just settled into a rut with your idiot mate'.

'Hey, I'm right here.' Protested Wil.

'I know Wil, you're always right here.' Beccs said not

35

bothering to turn.

Phil looked close to tears for the second time today. Unrelenting, she continued.

'All you seem to concern yourself with is "*The Book*". Well, I've seen "*The Book*", and it reads like the drunken ramblings of two unmedicated, tin foil hat wearing paranoid schizophrenics.' Really rolling now.

'It's even worse than a James Joyce novel'.

That one hurt. Phil hated James Joyce. Beccs paused to take a gulp of her drink. Her victims paused and gulped as well.

'PC, did you even think that maybe today you should have called and apologised. You know, as soon as you knew you weren't going to make it. You might have got away with it. A bit of PC charm. But no, you thought it better to go to the pub, didn't you?'

Phil wasn't sure whether he was meant to answer the question or not. He decided to just open his mouth and wait.

'Don't say anything PC. I'm not close to finished yet.' Phil nodded in silence.

'You just keep putting things off. Why?' Beccs said staring at Phil. He wasn't falling for the rhetorical question again. He just listened.

'Not just things but people, anything, remember when you "forgot" to mow your lawn for two years. Do you remember your fish? Poor bastards didn't know what they were getting in for. It's been going on forever. Remember your drumming career. Or should I say drum career. You only had one drum to play, didn't you? One ANZAC day march. Your drumming career, as you boast, is best measured by distance, rather than time.' Beccs paused to let her remarks sting.

'Oh! What else. Your vegetable garden, how many vegetables did you get? Three tomatoes, two carrots and a zucchini from memory. You don't even like zucchini!' Beccs said, sounding really frustrated.

'I believe you and Wil were thinking about building a little stall to sell them from at some point. Didn't you even check the council by-laws'. Both Wil and Phil tried not to laugh.

'We did get a nice little salad.' Said Wil.

Beccs chose to ignore the comment and pressed on with her point.

'Well, what else is there,' Beccs said knowing she was cutting Phil to the bone.

'Oh, that's right. You were going to solve the world's problems by publishing your World manifesto or whatever it is. That I have never even seen. I think you promised to have that done two years ago. Fuck!' She said as punctuation.

'The list just goes on, and on, and on,'.

Beccs paused, smiled and took a deep breath, then looked intently at Phil.

'I don't mean to be a bitch. But in this instance, I think I'm justified.' She said with a pleading look.

'I try to help PC. I try to understand you. But I'm beginning to wonder why I bother.' Beccs looked desperately at PC.

'I like you PC. We've been friends for a long time now, and do you know why? Because I thought you were worth it. I thought you could be something or do something. You have such big ideas. You have such energy.' She said regretting saying energy and stared at Phil checking for any condescension in his expression. If there was any, it was well masked by terror.

'But that's all they ever are PC. Ideas.'

Silence...
More Silence...
Even more silence...

Phil and Wil both looked at each other hoping it was over. It wasn't.

'Now let me turn my attention to you Wil.' She said with a menacing look and tone.

'Leave me out of it Beccs.' Wil said with his hands up.

'If you don't shut up and listen Wil, I'll call you by your

real name from now on.'

'Dirty Pool Beccs.' Muttered Wil glaring at Phil accusingly.

'Your big secret Wil, was not told to me by PC, your faithful companion. We live in the same building Wil. You're on the strata tenancy list, and I'm the president! You know those meetings you never bother to go too. Everyone in the building knows your real name. Wilma! They've known for years!'

Wil was too shocked to say anything. Oh God he thought. I'll have to move.

'I know what that look is Wil. It's your I'm thinking about myself look.' Beccs smiled spitefully.

'That's all you do Wil. Did you ever think to help, rather than encourage your apathetic weak willed drinking buddy?'

She waved both hands in Phil's direction like he was part of a showcase.

'No.' She said answering her own question.

'FUCK! she yelled loud enough to get a look from Justin.

Beccs put her hand up to Justin to apologise. He nodded back with his "I totally understand" look and returned to what he was doing. Nothing.

'Listen Beccs.' Phil almost whispered. I know I'm a fuck up, but I am really trying.'

'It's really my fault this time Beccs.' He said trying to look as contrite as possible.

Beccs sat silently downing the last of her drink.

Again, Phil and Will did the same, not wanting to appear to show any kind of nonconformity.

'So.' Beccs said suddenly looking very tired.

'What are your plans for the rest of the afternoon, as if I didn't know. Harry, Lloyd? She said looking directly at each of them in turn.

They both just stared at Beccs for an awkward amount of time and then said almost in unison....'I get it. Dumb and dumber...Nice one Beccs'.

'For fucks sake guys, all you do is make jokes and talk about global issues. Both of which neither of you is qualified for. PC, I'm going to talk to you as I think Wil here is a complete lost cause. You need to actually do something. Anything, just prove you can finish something.' Beccs stopped, seemingly too exhausted to continue.

'Alright. You're right as always Beccs.' Phil picked up his mobile phone, scrolled through the directory and dialled Andre's number. Andre was an old workmate, they always got on well, had lots of laughs together. Andre will understand. He'll see the funny side.

The phone rang three times, which Phil took as a hopeful sign, then it answered to his great disappointment.

'You'd better be dying in a fucking ditch, in hospital, held hostage by terrorists, Mormons, something really fucking good PC.'

'Andre, mate. Funny story.'

'Funny story you say. Two months scheduling, senior management, and two fucking board members waiting to see you because I talked you up big. We waited for an hour and no word. Just answer me a few questions PC?'

'Ok.' Phil answered now not totally sure if this really was his old mate Andre.

'Were you too sick to even call?'

'No.'

'Was there a death in the family?'

'No.'

'Did your house catch fire?'

'No.'

'Did your dog or any other pet die?

Phil thought briefly about mentioning the fish but

decided not to and repeated.

'No'

'Was there any sort of reasonable excuse I could tell anyone?'

'Ummm, No.' Phil decided that Andre wasn't in the mood for a funny story.

'Can you fuck off and never contact me again?'

'Yes.'

The phone went dead. Phil pressed the end call button unnecessarily and put the phone down.

Beccs stared at Phil, eyebrows raised in hope, more than anticipation.

'Well?' She said.

'He'll get back to me to reschedu…..No he won't, it's fucked, I blew it.'

'So, what's next PC?' Beccs raised her eyebrows even further.

'PC shrugged and sipped his beer.' Too scared to hazard an answer.

'Aaargh!!' she shouted and unexpectedly started to cry.

'Christ Beccs don't get upset. This is my problem not yours.' She looked up at Phil.

'I'm beginning to think you're right. You know what PC, I've got to get away for a while. Call me when you've done something, anything, in a week no earlier, and actually finish something this time. I mean it. Really finish something!'. Beccs almost pleaded.

'Got it?' She yelled in a teary voice and briskly walked away.

Wil and Phil both sat in shocked silence.

'I've never seen her like that before.' Phil said.

'OK Mate. PC, we really need to fix this. This is serious. What's our next move?' Wil said looking very concerned.

Our Next Move

Obviously, the next move was to get drunk. It didn't help, but it did take your mind of what you should probably be keeping your mind on. They drank through the afternoon and well into the evening. Phil's look of shock and panic slowly started to submerge.

When Wil thought enough time had passed, and Phil was drunk enough to talk, he decided to broach the subject.

He leaned in and said. 'So mate. What are you gonna do?'

Phil looked blank, seriously blank, totally checked out.

'PC. Mate, don't panic, we can work through this.'

Now his blank look had a hint of resignation about it.

'It's over mate, I'm done. I think I'll just move to Tasmania and be done with it.' Phil said going straight to the dramatic.

'What, and look for the Tassy Tiger? Wil replied completely missing the drama, and the point.

'No! For fuck sake. To get away, maybe I am fucking useless. Down there I'd fit right in, probably become premier or something.'

'Hey that's hurtful.' Wil said. 'My Auntie's from Tassy I think.'

'Sorry Wil. I'm sorry I mentioned Tasmania, let's just forget about it and move on.' Phil said, hoping to put an end to the topic, but not before Wil could recite a fairly comprehensive list of noteworthy Tasmanians.

'Ok, but let's not forget Richard Flanigan, the Luca Brasi band, Errol Flynn, Princess Mary of Denmark, soon to be queen, David Boon, Laurence Olivier, Elizabeth Blackburn, Umm...' He paused thinking.

'Ok. Drop it.' Implored Phil interrupting.

'Simon Baker.' Wil announced sharply as a full stop.

'Hold on. Laurence Olivier wasn't Tasmanian.' Phil said.

'Uncle Laurie. Sure he was. He lived next to my Aunty for 20 years. He was a handy off spinner for the Glenorchy Magpies in his day.' Wil said looking offended at Phil doubting his knowledge of noteworthy Tasmanians.

Phil just stared at Wil knowing he couldn't win that argument and decided to get back to the problem at hand.

'So, tell me Wil. How are we going to "work through this"?' Phil said sarcastically using air quotes instantly regretting it as a barfly on the other side of the room made a wanking gesture in reply.

'Well let's take this back to the only method we know that works.' He reached down and picked up volume three of "*The Book*" and opened it to the page headed Beccs.

'Right let's break this down,' Wil said, poised ready to write.

'Really? Do we really have to do this now?

'You're right PC. I'll get a fresh round and some nuts, then we'll be set.' Wil stood up and walked briskly to the bar like a businessman heading to an important meeting.

'Right.' He said, returning with the beer and nuts.

'Now we can avoid having any sober thoughts on the subject, which as I have said many times before don't lead anywhere.' Wil paused briefly on the page, then wrote in slurred handwriting while saying out loud 'Becca is pissed off. Why?' Then stared directly at Phil in anticipation.

'Because she thinks I'm a fucking useless prick.' Phil said, stating the obvious.

Will clicked his pen to a different colour, moved to the next line and spoke and wrote 'Thinks PC is a fucking useless prick. Why?' Phil spotted the tried and tired method of Socratic logic and sighed.

'Well because I fucked up on the job interview, I guess.'

Wil didn't bother to write that down, instead he leaned back precariously on his chair with his hands behind his head.

'I think there is an underlying issue here. The reason I'm saying that is well, you've fucked up so much worse before and she never reacted like that. She could always see the funny side… eventually.' Wil said nodding knowingly at Phil.

'Remember when you forgot to meet her at the airport, she waited, no money, you convinced her to only take cash, avoid painful shopping spree regret. Leave the cards at home you said. Don't worry I'll be in a state of cat like readiness the moment you need me you said, … Remember that one PC?' Wil cringed.

'As I recall, you turned up two hours late, drunk, riding a bicycle and broke. Now I think that is more fucking useless than missing a job interview. Oh, and the time you …'.

'Yes, I get the point.' Phil interrupted not wanting to walk down that memory lane.

'And it wasn't even a tandem.' Wil said laughing.

'But then again, when she broke her ankle, who was it that delivered her favourite takeaway for breakfast, lunch and dinner every day? Stupid vegetarian hospital. How are you supposed to get better eating fucking tofu?' Grumbled Wil, remembering his own experience in the Adventist Hospital.

'You!' Wil answered his own question more loudly. 'So, it must be something else…, or maybe a combination of things, or a compounding of things, or a conglomerate of things.' Knowing he couldn't think of any more relevant words starting with C, he stopped talking.

'I think the issue is that Beccs expects a lot from me, maybe too much?' Lamented Phil.

'Bullshit! The reason she expects "a lot"' Will said using air quotes with his middle fingers directed at the guy who made the wanking gesture at Phil. 'Is because you're always banging on about how the whole world is completely fucked up, it's just so fucking obvious. You

43

write ideas down in your manifesto, whatever it is, folder. And they are good ideas PC.' Wil said nodding genuinely.

'And you talk about publishing something that could change the world, then you never get around to it.' Wil nodded his head acknowledging his own point.

'This is the one thing you have talked about, focused on most of the time, with me, with Beccs, even with Justy when your drunk enough. This is your thing PC.' Implored Wil.

'Remember, she was really impressed when you worked out the environmental saving of your Floordrobe philosophy.' Wil smiled.

'At about 500 million cupboards per year, 750 million trees used in manufacture, 2 square meters per tree, it equates to an area roughly the size of Mongolia,' Phil said knowledgably. 'And Keep your voice down Wil, I haven't patented that one yet.'

'Exactly.' Wil said ignoring the joke. 'She said you should send that one to the newspapers, the environmental groups, make a statement, show them a simple example she said. Plus, she thought it was pretty funny. Typical PC. That was an easy win. And you just let it slip, sure she forgot about it, but it's still another thing.' Wil sipped his beer, sighed, then continued.

'For Beccs it's one more thing that you haven't gotten around to yet, over, and over, and over again.' Wil looked again impressed with this train of thought.

'What I'm trying to say is how many times have you said I'm gonna do it this time. That's not just one disappointment, it's thousands?' Will said, really impressed with his emphasized extrapolation.

Phil looked like he was having trouble focusing, and like Wil was making sense.

'You're right!' Phil enthused, then slumped again.

'But I can't get anything published in a week, or even finish it in a week, and she did say, well yelled really, not to call until I'd finished something.' Phil mumbled from his slumped position.

'I may never speak to her again.' He added only half-jokingly.

'PC mate. You're just making excuses, do it electronically, everything is electronic these days, use social media. I'll help you.' Will said, remembering Beccs comment about not helping, then put his arms out again in revelation.

Phil looked genuinely horrified. He'd been avoiding social media like he avoided light beer.

Social media. Phil thought. Should I? He'd been calling it anti-social media, and bemoaning everyone's loss of privacy, loss of social skills ironically and its general purposelessness. Could he?

Wil stood and looked as sternly as he could muster after drinking most of the day and said, 'Think about it?' then walked to the bar for another round.

Phil thought about it. Mostly he thought about it as his last chance.

Wil returned unsteadily with two more beers that had lost some of their load during transportation. 'Well?'

'Fuck it!' I'll do it. We'll do it.' Phil said looking determined.

'Bullshit!' Will replied confidently.

'How long have I known you. You'll wake up in the morning, with a hangover and an I can't be bothered, what's the fucking point attitude and another opportunity will slip by. And this might be your last opportunity PC.' He said, sounding the most serious he'd sounded all day.

'No, no I mean it this time.'

'Bullshit! The only way to get you to actually do something is to force yourself to commit.' Wil said pointing his finger down hard on the table.

'Remember the trip we went on, the only trip we went on to Nambucca Heads! Checking out the latest Yowie sightings. Remember? How did we achieve that miracle?' He asked not even pausing for an answer.

'We booked and paid for the tickets and the hotel when we were drunk. Ergo we had to go. Commitment!' Wil again put his arms out looking like he was stating the extremely obvious.

45

'Ok, well I'm pretty pissed now. So, we should be good to go.' Phil said with total honesty.

'Wrong! That's not a commitment.' Wil crossed his arms over his head in a large X to labour the point.

'Yes, it is.' Phil immediately stood up and put his hand over his heart preparing to make a statement but was stopped by Wil.

'PC, you're forgetting where this whole topic started. Beccs. You don't care about breaking a commitment to me, and I don't care if you do. I'm your mate. You need to make a proper commitment. An, I can't get out of it now, commitment.'

They both sat again in silence.

'I know!' Wil said eagerly.

Phil looked over fully expecting to see a lightbulb over Wil's head.

'Beccs said don't call until you've got something done, right?' Will scratched his whiskers like he was on to something.

'She didn't say not to text her.' He said raising his eyebrows up and down vigorously.

They both looked at each other. Wil felt like a legal genius who'd just found a loophole in a big case cracking it wide open. Phil thought fuck it, why not, and pulled out his phone.

Will turned a new page and picked up his pen.

'This is not a casual message PC. We need to make a draft first.'

'Dearest Beccs,' Wil wrote.

'Not Dearest, it sounds like her grandmother's sending her a birthday card.'

'Dear Beccs…,?'

'No.'

'Dear Beccs.'

'Ok. Give me the pen.' Demanded Phil. He repeated.

'Dear Beccs,'

Then he started to write with one eye closed to help with his worsening double vision.

Dear Beccs, I'm very, very sorry I upset you. I know

I'm useless. I can't argue. I know what you think of me which explains why you were a bitch. Which was totally justified! Please have lunch with me on Friday as by then I will have really finished something. I promise, or I'll move to Tasmania! Last chance, no let down. Your caring friend PC.

Phil showed it to Wil who also read it through one eye and nodded approval.

'I like it. It's straight from the heart, it lets her off the hook for any guilt about the rant as she was justified, it also shows that you were listening, and you mention caring. Brilliant. Type it up and send it.'

'No wait, it's 11:50, don't send it now!'

'No, it's OK, we normally SMS each other at about midnight with something helpful, you know, "What's that noise coming from the cupboard?", "Are you sure you locked the front door?" She'll be awake.' Phil started to key in the message and pressed send.

'FUCK!'

'What's up?'

'Just sent the message to Andre by mistake.'

'Fuck!' Reiterated Wil giggling.

'Oh God, the phone's ringing, It's Andre.' Phil dropped the phone involuntarily and let it ring. He waited until it stopped ringing and heard the ping of a voicemail alert. Phil listened to the message getting paler with each passing word.

'All good?' Asked Wil sarcastically.

'Yeah, it's not really repeatable. Needless to say, I think I should start running the next time I see Andre.' Phil said looking a bit sad about losing a friend.

'Don't lose momentum PC. Send the message now! Before it gets too late, and this time try to not send it to a psycho.' Wil smirked.

Phil read the message again and felt happy with it. He handed the phone to Wil to proofread. Wil gave it a nod of approval and handed the phone back to Phil. He pressed send and committed.

Phil thought that ought to fix it. Now to get an early

night, well kind of early.

'Come on Wil, drink up. Time for me to go home and pass out ready to face a new day.'

'Time for me to go to work.'

They both stood up unsteadily, shook hands agreeing to meet at the pub tomorrow, and made a vow to get the job done. Then they stumbled in opposite directions into the night thinking they were on the right track. Things couldn't possibly get any worse.

Things Get Worse

Beccs was sitting up in bed with a nice warm fresh cup of tea. The shitty day almost over, but not forgotten. She finished the last of her tea, leant over, turned off the bedside lamp, rolled back over, got comfortable and tried to go to sleep. She lay in the darkness tossing and turning, still annoyed with PC. Not sleeping at all.

Maybe she'd been too hard on him. Sure, he was an unreliable, not quite making it, but on the cusp of making it, wannabe. But he was always there if you needed him. Just not always there when you wanted him. And with all his faults, which nobody could ever possibly have enough time to mention. Was a likeable wannabe, and has never ever yelled, name called, or generally ever made her feel like an idiot in any way. PC deserved another chance. She always knew she'd give him another chance. Beccs couldn't imagine her life without him.

That meant a lot to Beccs. She'd been yelled at and called a lot of names by a lot of men most of her life.

That's when her thoughts were put on hold as her mobile pinged a message.

She reached over instinctively to check it and then stopped. No! I'll make the useless bastard wait, teach him a lesson.

She paused and thought, what for. I've been trying to teach him to put his beer on a coaster for nearly 10 years with limited success. Just open it, might be funny, a little cheer up, all forgotten all forgiven. She flicked at the phone, opened the message and started to read.

A feint smile appeared on her face and then very slowly melted away. Her jaw dropped open, then she shouted.

'You Bastard!' and hurled the phone at the floor which bounced, hitting the wall hard making a terminal sounding crack. She pulled the blanket over her head and tried to mutter herself to sleep.

Unfortunately for Phil, the message was too long for the single message it was intended. The poorly bisected break in it came right after the word 'Bitch'.

Beccs woke in the morning still angry, still muttering, still pissed off. How dare he. The prick. The only time 'I!', she said out loud pointing to herself, ever yelled at him. He chose that time to call me a name, and not a clever or witty name. Just Bitch. 'What the hell! Really!'

Her internal monologue went on like that right through the alarm, through the shower, in ever angrier and angrier circles. She muttered her way through her entire morning routine and then left her flat still muttering.

She paused her angry thoughts briefly while walking down the stairs. That's where she broke her ankle. Phil had told her from that day onwards always, focus on roads, stairs, and never, repeat never climb a ladder. The rest doesn't really matter.

'Aarrghhh!' Break's over! Time to maintain the rage.

'Bastard!' 'Bastard!' 'Bastard!' She repeated with each step, as she approached the gate. 'Bastard!' 'Bastard!' then stopped.

'You Bastard!' she yelled as she looked up and saw a smiling and waving Wil, who slowed his approach and waving down nervously.

'Hi Beccs.' Smiled Wil, unsure if that was the right thing to say.

'Seem a bit upset this morning.' He raised his eyebrows even though he was trying not to. Better off looking blank, keep still he thought, no sudden movements.

'Don't think I would think that you, for one moment. That you wouldn't have "proofread,"'. More bloody air quotes thought Wil 'the text message!' yelled Beccs in conclusion.

'Text message?' Will said confused, then remembered.

'Oh. The text message, that's right.' He said recalling last night's details without any concern.

'Yeah, the early bird gathers no moss.' He said confidently. Wil loved his mixed metaphors.

'Yeah, so what do you think of the new PC? The committed PC?' he said smiling.

She seriously thought about slapping him, but decided that he definitely wouldn't notice, and it would probably not make him any smarter.

Instead, she just walked up calmly, gave him both fingers in the face and said 'Bitch?', and stamped off muttering 'Bastard!' with each step again, shouted 'Fuck', then stopped muttering.

Fuck me, thought Wil. Wish people would be more polite in the morning, I only just woke up. He shook his head, walked into the building, pressed the elevator button sarcastically as the elevator hardly ever worked. What was his strata for anyway, what do they do with my money? He really had to go to one of those meetings one day. Walked to the stairs and uttered 'Bitch?' still sounding confused.

What did I do, I mean if she took it the wrong way, how's that my fault. I'm only the proofreader, he thought innocently. Wil stamped up the stairs and on to his door thinking again, Bitch? That's an odd out of character quip he thought. Fumbled with his keys, opened the door, sat on the lounge and turned on the telly.

'Dopey big bastard!' He said out loud, that would have been better, less confusing, straight to the point. She must be upset. Beccs insults which are rare, are normally clever, cutting or at least accurate, he thought. I'm just not getting the Bitch? And why as a question?

Wil forgot all about the incident in his usual, I'm sure it'll blow over way, made dinner and ate it hurriedly. He resumed his position on the lounge, then fell asleep. Two hours later he moved a little, rolled over and went back to sleep again.

He woke up again in a further hour or so and

remembered Bitch? He was still confused. Then he remembered Phil and his legendary ability to procrastinate and decided to send him a message to get him up and going.

Wil put the phone back down, then picked it back up again after an alert and read the message, smiled and went back to sleep.

He woke up again this time feeling like he'd had enough sleep and also feeling pretty hungry.

Wil checked the time, 12:28. Not too bad. Time for a quick shower and at the pub by 1.

Wonder how Phil's going he thought in the shower, more to the point, what seriously well thought through excuse he's made. Good old reliable, unreliable Phil.

It's A Start

BEEP! BEEP! BEEP! BEEP! BEEP! BEEP! BEEP! BEEP! BEEP! BEEP! BEEP! BEEP! BEEP! BEEP! BEEP! BEEP!

'For the love of God.' Phil moaned pitifully, this time with what he believed was a high range Class 3 hangover, bordering on a class 4. He rolled over, picked up his phone and hit dismiss, then checked the time. 8am, what the fuck was I thinking, two alarms in two days.

Phil leaned over to put his phone down. A few more hours sleep, and he should be ready to face the day. As he put the phone down, he noticed a piece of paper Wil ran back to give him before stumbling again off into the night. In green pen it simply read.

1 of 4

Underneath that, written much larger, and in very threatening red, underlined twice, also in red.

Last Chance. Clocks Ticking! You're committed!

Phil sat bolt upright remembering the SMS. God, why did he send the SMS. He stared at the piece of paper and read "*last chance.*" over, and over again. Last chance rang in his head overriding all other thoughts, even his hangover. He got out of bed and walked to the shower uncharacteristically, without any procrastination or complaint. Showered, put on his, you can't leave the house in those clothes and started walking downstairs.

Phil's can't leave the house in those clothes looked like he stole them off a homeless person who'd been living rough for quite a while, possibly even been runover a few times.

He paused at the top of the stairs and opened his mouth preparing to ask Chris, his mysterious housemate, if he or she wanted some tea, then decided not to bother. They, he or she were never home. They, he or she may not even exist he was beginning to think. But then who was changing the toilet rolls. Who cares? 1 of 4.

Phil walked to the kitchen repeating 'Last chance, last chance, last chance.' out loud, then made a healthy, no time-wasting breakfast. Some washing up was calling to him from the sink. He resisted the temptation and started to cook, and on high for a change. Bacon, Eggs, Tomato, and some toast for presentation. Perfect!

He walked to the lounge room and turned on the Telly for background noise, then started eating with determination.

Phil finished breakfast, sipped his tea, took the dishes to the kitchen, again completely disregarding the mounting, and now mouthwatering distraction of the washing up, then went back to the telly, frowned at it, and walked upstairs.

Phil stood and looked at the broken wardrobe ominously. The wardrobe looked back threateningly. He reached out and grabbed the handle causing the door to fall off at the hinges, which he just narrowly dodged, then watched it crash to the floor. Phil leaned in and peered through the dust cloud. Two overstuffed expanding files labelled Part 1, and Part 2 emerged out of the cloud. Phil stood and stared portentously. He scooped up both files at the same time creating an even larger dust cloud. Sneezed, initially uncontrollably, which soon escalated into a full-blown convulsion. This caused him to drop both files, making the dust cloud even worse. Great start. He thought through a few final sneezes. Blew his nose to clear the years of dust he'd just inhaled, gathered up the files again, with loose papers and newspaper clippings dangling precariously. Then walked back downstairs.

The telly was blasting an infomercial about a completely new and advanced technology in filing cabinets. It's dustproof, fireproof, waterproof, soundproof and has an uncrackable locking system. It's more like a safe really, the constantly smiling salesman spruiked. Plus, if you order now, you can get a dustproof, fireproof, waterproof, soundproof briefcase, at no extra cost valued at … Phil turned off the TV and thought, who needs a soundproof briefcase?

He placed both files and loose papers on the dining room table, that was now always clear and clean. And as far as Phil could remember, had never actually been used for dining. He thought he should probably stop calling it a dining room table and just call it a table. He took a seat at a chair, formerly dining room chair, and focused on the task ahead.

Phil's phone pinged a message breaking his focus. He got up and walked back to the lounge to check it. It was from Wil reminding him to get up and get started. Phil proudly messaged back 'Already on it mate. Pub at 1?'

Wil replied 'Of course! Look forward to seeing your progress. Remember the clocks ticking. Tick tock.'

Phil walked slowly back to the table, sat back down, picked up the first piece of paper out of one of the folders, paused dramatically, then actually started. He read the heading off the now yellowing foolscap sheet.

"Who really killed Kennedy!!!?" Both sides of the page were covered in writing, diagrams, even a few drawings. At the top of the page, it had the number 1 circled.

Phil put that calmly aside and picked up the next page, also headed. "Who really killed Kennedy!!!?" with the number 2 circled at the top. He flicked through the next pages until he reached the final page on the topic, 8, calmly stapled the pages together, then put them aside without comment.

He picked up the next pages, conveniently paper clipped, and read the heading. "The undeniable truth of the Moon landings!".

Phil put those aside on the same pile and again moved on. Still without comment.

He repeated the process, this time with papers headed "9/11 What really happened", then "Where is Harold Holt?", then "Bigfoot" then he realised this was his conspiracy and cryptid folder, and Beccs was right, it really did read like the drunken ramblings of unmedicated tin foil hat wearing paranoid schizophrenics.

Phil thumbed through the rest of the file with controlled enthusiasm, embarrassment and some disdain at the ludicrous randomness of each topic. He put the papers back in each file and put the folder on the floor to use as a footrest.

What the fuck was I thinking, I mean, where was I going with that, how much time had it wasted. He decided it had already wasted enough and picked up the other file labelled Part 2.

Part 2 looked more promising. It was thicker to start with, at least three times as thick. And all the pages were mostly in their little pockets, and most of the pages hadn't started to go too yellow yet. Although he thought that might have given it more credulity.

The folder was titled "Aphorisms on a better future." He remembered writing that but couldn't remember what Aphorism meant. Something to do with Tuesdays with Morrie, he thought.

'This looks a lot more promising.' Phil said aloud, trying to keep up his spirits.

He again thumbed through the dividers noticing some ideas and topics he thought weren't too bad. He hoped.

Phil gingerly picked the first piece of paper out of the divide labelled A. And hoped his memory was correct.

The first pages were headed Alcohol/Drugs. It covered taxation, warning labels, prohibition, advertising blah blah blah...That's a keeper he thought. The next page was Anarchy. It was bullet pointed with slogans and question marks, and it didn't seem to make much sense at all. He put that in the maybe pile.

The remaining pages were headed with topics ranging

from, Air-conditioning, Addictions, Animals, Apple, Axioms etc. He read and sorted all these into three piles. Workables, maybe's and unusables. He preferred to think of the unusable pile as ahead of their time. Most of Phil's ideas were, unfortunately, still ahead of their time.

The next divide was predictably labelled B. The first pages were banking, mentioning deregulation, bailout packages, foreign share ownership etc., Phil thought another keeper.

He then read and flicked through all the other B's from Backlash, Balloons, Books to Buzzwords and found a good smattering of workables, a few maybes, and still a lot ahead of their time. He decided to merge the workables and maybe's piles together.

Phil pressed onward through the file and onwards through the alphabet, selecting topics he deemed worthy of further discussion. The list was optimistically compiled and contained the following:

Artificial Intelligence, Air conditioning, Airline ticket pricing, Balloons, Books, Cash, Celebrities, Cemeteries, Charity, Coffee, Conspiracy Theories, Cryptids, Dams, Daylight Saving Time, Drugs, Education, Fitted sheets, Flightless Birds, Freedom, Freud, Gambling, Garbage, Giving Up, Government Perks, Hair Regrowth Treatments, Instant Democracy, Junk Mail, Lobby Groups, Makeup, Mainstream Media, Mis/Disinformation, Motor Sport, Negative Numbers, Political Correctness, Phonetics, Plates, Politicians, Protests/E-Protests, Reality TV, Recycling, Redacting, Religion, Sportsmen, Superannuation, The Pope, Tolerance, Treason, Weapons and The Zoo

Phil looked at the pile of papers on the table, now neatly held together with a series of paperclips and felt reasonably satisfied with the start he'd made. Well at least satisfied he'd made a start.

He decided it was time for another cup of tea. After all the British Empire ruled the world fuelled by tea Wil said.

He then remembered Wil and the pub and checked the time on his phone without any concern.

'Fucking hell!' He really had to start checking the time more often, or stop being so surprised. It was 12:48 already.

'Christ!' Phil said, then quickly changed into slightly better clothes. Put his notepad, the folder containing his papers and notes from the possibles list in another folder and into his backpack, gathered up his phone and keys, grabbed some cash out of the wall safe, which was just a hollowed-out book. Ingenious! He always thought. Then walked out, closing the door behind him with unusual determination. Phil walked at a brisk pace. He was running late. He Wasn't sure why that mattered, but today Phil felt like he needed to be on time. He picked up the pace.

Meeting of the Minds

Phil and Wil entered the Pub through separate doors simultaneously, exchanged nods and hand signals, also simultaneously which went by completely unnoticed, so, the moment was unfortunately lost.

Phil walked to the bar. Wil walked to the smoking section then unnecessarily secured two chairs and two tables. The Pub was practically empty. The mood felt very serious for a Tuesday. They sat down, stared at each other and exchanged serious nods.

Wil decided after Beccs cutting remarks, that he would lift his friendship game. He was definitely going to put in a concerted effort.

'How's the morning's work PC? Hope you've made a start. Friday's coming.' Wil said using his best serious tone and serious face.

'On top of it Wil.' Phil said, reaching into his backpack to retrieve the folder with his notes, list of topics and the fading not quite yellowish originals he brought with him for reference.

'Tackled the wardrobe then?' Wil said, looking surprised. 'Did it give you any trouble?'

'No mate. Broke its spirit the last time I opened it.' Phil said looking pleased with himself.

'You broke more than it's spirit.' Added Wil

Phil stood up, put his arm in the air and made the following proclamation.

'Like Steve Guttenberg said in Can't Stop the Music.' Phil's all-time favourite B movie. 'My time is now!', then handed the list over. Wil put on his superfluous glasses and read through discernibly.

'It's a good start.' Wil said, handing Phil his own folder.

Phil opened it and read the heading on the first page. "Project Plan." Which was in a large font, underlined and centered. He then turned the page and read the second page. "This page left intentionally blank." in a slightly smaller font, also centered.

'Looks confident and professional.' Phil muttered, admiring the headers and footers, which included a copyright component.

'This will work. A real plan. Let me lead the meeting of the minds today PC.' Wil said, taking back the folder, opened it and read the next subheading.

'Day Planner:'. He looked up and read the following:

Day 1. Tuesday

    Point 1. - Acknowledge the time left – 4 days.
    Point 2. - Understand what we are trying to Achieve.
    Point 3. - Start.

Wil then handed the folder back to Phil who opened it and took out the page with the most writing on it, then turned it over hoping for more. He rubbed the page, thinking some pages must surely be stuck together, then blew at it in a final and desperate attempt to find another page, without success.

'Is that it?'. Phil said, looking a bit disappointed.

'How about thanks for putting in an effort.' Wil answered, feeling a bit hurt.

'It's three lines, over three fucking pages Wil.'

Wil thought about correcting Phil and pointing out that it's really 29 lines over 3 pages if you count the headers and footers, but decided to just let it go.

'Well, they are big points, and Day 1 is meant to be easy. You know first day on the job and all that, so let's fly through them. Plus, I am also a day's planning ahead of you. That's all you need to be to be a good project manager. Right? You always say that PC.' Wil smirked, thinking. Check mate!

'Right!' said Phil, knowing he had little choice but to agree.

'I'll fill in the Day 2 agenda at the end of Day 1. It's really the only way to keep it current.' Wil said nodding again confidently.

'Point 1. We have four days left PC. Today is Tuesday. Are you prepared to get a framework sorted out at close of play or close of the pub. Whichever comes first?'

Phil instinctively placed his right hand over his heart and said 'Yes'.

Wil paused and unnecessarily wrote, yes, next to Point 1.

'Point 2. What are we trying to do?' Wil asked, looking perplexed.

Phil stopped and thought about it.

'Well...I guess I'm trying to get people out of the somnambulistic state of compliance everyone is locked into today. Make people stop shrugging their shoulders at the insane decisions being made on our behalf, with our money. To create a world, we don't want and definitely didn't ask for.' Phil paused watching Wil squiggle frantically.

'I want to provide everyone with the knowledge there is something that can be done. You don't have to be manipulated by government and media mass hysteria. You are being lied to. You are caught in your own prison. You have the keys to your own cell. You can set yourself free. You have a right. No, an obligation to think for yourself, without fear of being accused of wrong-think, or being censored.' Phil eased back in his chair and paused, happy with his warm-up rant.

They both allowed the silence to resonate.

'Beccs always said I should take aim at the big targets. She'll be impressed.' Phil said, forgetting himself and slightly changing hues.

'Ok. You have a cause and a field of expertise.' Wil paused. 'And motivation.' He looked at Phil smiling with unsubtle subtext, of you're not fooling anyone.

Wil put his hand in his bag and brought out some more blank paper and an antique looking box that he opened displaying a feather quill, different size nibs, a stylized stand, and a small ink well.

That confirms it Phil thought, Wil is definitely a time traveller.

'This will give the project a sense of historical importance.' He said waving his quill around before dipping it in the well.

'No doubt. Nice touch.' Phil said genuinely impressed.

Wil then wrote effortlessly in a Dickensian style font, centered perfectly on the first page, complete with embellishments.

Then put the Quill, and Ink Well back in its box carefully, and put it back in his bag.

Impressively weird Phil thought.

Phil always suspected but now knew that he'd taken Wil for granted. Not only was he a really good friend. He would really help, take the time. Stay there right to the end and if he did fuck up, as Phil always expected. He would help shoulder the blame.

'I'd like to add if I may?' Will paused waiting for confirmation. Phil nodded approval.

'It seems like you're trying to hold a mirror up to society. Be that little voice inside everybody's head that screams out for justice. Rally people to fight for reason. Fight for the truth. Fight for their right to be wrong. Sound right? Need to make sure I have my own 30,000-foot view of the project.' Said Wil.

Christ! Makes me sound like a cross between Erin

Brockovich and Keanu Reeves Phil thought.

'Exactly!'

'Do you have a title?'

'Well. Tentatively, "Aphorisms on a better future." Phil said not liking the title one bit now.

'Wasn't that from Tuesdays with Morrie? P-hew. Aphorism sounds like a muscle spasm, and the rest sounds like a daytime soapy PC.' Wil said very, very unsure of the title.

'Yeah. It sucks. The title will right itself at the end anyway.' Phil added. 'Worry about it later.'

Wil noted down "Aphorisms for a better future." anyway and surrounded it with question marks. Then crossed it out and left the question marks.

He checked his project plan and announced 'Point 3. Time to start PC?' And made ominous eye contact with Phil.

Phil grabbed the paper titled possibles and laid his notes on the table.

'Wil. You ready to take notes mate?' asked Phil.

Wil nodded.

Wil's note taking ability was renowned. For reasons he never adequately explained. Wil was able to write in shorthand. Seriously! Shorthand. It was like looking back in time. If you add that to the Quill and Ink Well. The evidence that Wil is, or should that be are, tense with time travel is practically impossible Phil thought, were, or was really stacking up.

Wil stood up and stared sternly and seriously at Phil like he was about to make an important announcement and whispered.

'Need to have a piss first PC.'

'I'll get another beer.' Phil said also standing up.

He returned with the beers and put them on their respective tables. Wil took a big sip, picked up his notepad, cracked all the knuckles on both hands, and looked at Phil earnestly.

Phil picked up his list and was about to say Air Conditioning when he was interrupted.

'Do this arbitrarily, not alphabetically. Start with something to get you rolling. On a rant. That's when you articulate at your best PC. Oh, and drink up.' Wil raised his glass and gulped down at least half. 'Something that really pisses you off.'

Phil scanned through the possibles list and made a start confidently announcing.

'Artificial Intelligence.'

'Who the fuck thinks this is a good idea? Have these people never seen Terminator?' Phil said, as they alternately ran through a list of doomsday movies involving robots or AI.

'Westworld.'
'The Matrix.'
'WALL-E.'
'Transcendence.'
'I Robot.'

'Wait. Wil, WALL-E was a good guy, wasn't he?' Phil said confused.

'Not if you extrapolate the plot of the film. He will inevitably turn on humanity for being the source of all waste and come to the only logical conclusion. I find it quite a dark story.

'Interesting. I must see it again. Anyway, nobody could possibly believe that AI will end well.'

'Nice one. It's obvious but needs to be said. Pressing on PC.

'Motor Sport.'

Wil eagerly scratched some squiggly lines down that apparently read Motor Sport. Phil eased back in his chair, took a deep breath, exhaled, then moved forward again. Phil hated motor sport.

'Well! If we're supposed to be dealing with the biggest crisis in world history. The Greenhouse Effect, Global Warming, Climate Change, Climate Crisis... whatever its currently fucking branded as. It all started with the Charney Report, back in 1979, and fear mongering pseudoscientists have constantly been predicting the end of the world ever since, and constantly rolling the date conveniently forward, but not too far forward that it loses its doom and control factor. It's a fool's errand. Anyway, whether you are for, or against the hypothesis. Not that any voice or debate against will be allowed to be heard. You must surely be against the blatant discrimination of allowing one of the most pointless and destructive sporting endeavours to continue.' Phil paused for a sip.

'While at the same time we're all paying some outrageous tax. A tax that's not used in any productive way to actually address the "alleged" problem.' Phil said, while scanning his notes.

'Why do we for the love of God allow motor sport to continue! Why do we do that? For the love of all things sane. At least restrict it to one type of motor sport, what do we have now. Open Wheel,' Phil flicked through his notes again and continued.

'The list includes F1, IndyCar, Sports Car, 24hour races, La Mans, Daytona, Touring Cars, Production Cars, Stock Cars, Rally, Drag, and I'm sure a fuck load more I've missed. Or aren't even aware of. And they do all of these for cars, trucks, monster trucks, motorcycles, motorcycles with sidecars.' Phil said making Will snigger.

'Seriously!' He continued. 'I've seen it. Motorcycles with sidecars and go carts for kids. Which I guess guarantees the indoctrination of the next generation of petrol heads. And, ...and, all this takes place in almost every country on earth. Everyday.'

Wil scratched at his note pad frantically feeling the high-speed conclusion was on its way.

'Nobody can even calculate the total number of resources wasted. And that doesn't even mention the social impact.' Phil paused to wave away a bar fly who was moving in to proffer an opinion.

'These wankers set a fucking disgraceful example at every level of society. At least put warning labels on it like "Don't try this in your own Car Dickhead!".

'This has to stop! It needs to stop! There is nothing good about Motor Sport.' He finished satisfied.

Phil really, really hated Motor Sport.

He picked up his beer again and then remembered he'd finished it and looked at Wil who had also finished his note taking, and his beer.

'Your thoughts Wils?' Phil smiled looking happy with that one.

'Well, it's flawless, it's hard hitting. And polarizing. All the Environmentalist will agree with you and want to hug the nearest tree. And all the petrol heads will want to do burnouts on your front lawn. It opens the discussion up nicely.' Wil said nodding approval.

'Maybe something a bit more controversial now PC? Something on a broader spectrum.' Will stood up. 'I'll get some drinks while you have a think. You know, something that impacts everyone at some point.' Wil turned to walk to the bar.

He returned with the beers and picked up his notepad in readiness. Phil smiled mischievously and announced.

'Cemeteries.'

'What is the fucking point in having these perpetual memorials in place at all. After a hundred years nobody is even alive who remembers, or little own even knew the person the memorial was for in the first place. It just seems so egotistical, such a waste of time, a waste of space, a waste of money, and so damn depressing.' Phil stopped, referred to his notes, and continued.

'Take for instance a small country like Monaco. Which is roughly 2 square Kilometres in area, I Know this is a skewed example, but let's run the numbers anyway. It's roughly 2 million square metres. It has a population of about 40,000 people. 40,000 people represents 80,000 square metres of modest burial plots. Which means, when everyone there today is dead, about 4 percent of Monaco will be a cemetery. And that doesn't include any of its already existing cemeteries, or anybody who wants a fucking mausoleum, or wants to decorate it with big ass angel statues and a little fucking garden.' He paused with a look of disgust.

'Can't people see that if it's allowed to continue, eventually we will literally bury ourselves into a corner. Every population turnover creates a burial plot roughly the size of Kuwait. How long should we respect the dead? How long should we respect people's religious rights to burial?' Phil pressed on through all the noteworthy points on how stupid cemeteries are and finished satisfied he had made his point. Irrefutable.

Wil was still trying to figure out what Phil's problem was with cemeteries. Wil regularly enjoyed a quiet lunch at the local one.

'Maybe we should review that one later to see if it makes the final edit?' Wil said looking quizzically at Phil.

'Yeah Maybe?' Phil agreed and moved ahead.

'Drugs.'

'Drugs!' Phil said glancing and shuffling through his notes while noticing he said that a little too loudly, attracting a raised eyebrow from a dodgy looking guy who always seemed to be sitting in the corner for some reason.

'Legalise all drugs... Now hear me out!' Phil said shushing imaginary naysayers by waving his hands up and down.

'The drugs that cause the most harm, and by harm, I mean up to and not limited to death, are both legal. Smokes and Booze. They are also the Government's top money spinners. This is hypocrisy at its most extreme!' Phil paused again, unnecessarily waiting for Wil.

'Most of the money generated from taxation of tobacco and alcohol sales is not used to reduce or prevent the use of these drugs in any way, or even to treat the sick. It's used on something else. Most likely upgrading Government offices, or wasted on some frivolous project that nobody wants, or even asked for.' He paused.

'They don't really give a fuck about our health and well-being. If they did, they would ban them entirely, which I entirely disapprove of. Smokers and drinkers currently pay more taxes and die younger, which means they won't need as much support from the Government as non-smokers. Less pension. Less medical. And that's their choice. Everyone knows what they're getting into. The least they can do is stop putting pictures of dead people on their packs. How long will it be before they start putting pictures of fat alcoholics with yellowing eyes drinking their last beer on my schooner.' He paused to gather his thoughts.

'It's also a form of racism. I bet some third world countries with struggling economies would love to get a fair price for their drugs. But all they get is blame. The blame for not stopping the supply. Stopping the supply! Isn't that hypocritical when we're the one's creating the fucking demand.' Phil said, looking frustrated.

'The drugs they crack down on, and by crack down on I mean penalties up to and not limited to life imprisonment or execution, start at, and range from marijuana, opiates, amphetamines, cocaine etc., right through to the newest drug meth.' Phil leaned forward to emphasize that one.

'I mean have you met meth heads, they're fucked up and dangerous. And this is where the evolution. The endgame if you like of prohibition is taking us. I have some news for the prohibitionists, the war on drugs is over, you lost. It should be legalised now. Before they make, the next worst thing.' He paused again.

'People in society will always find a way to alter their reality. They'll spin around in circles in their front yard if there's no other alternative. Surely, it's better to have lower risk options available, with appropriate warnings. People who aren't taking drugs before legalisation will not rush out and think, Mmm, maybe I should try some heroin. Who do these authoritarian figures think they are to treat us like children?'. Phil stopped again and went to take another sip of his beer, then remembered he'd already finished it.

Wil picked up his empty glass and said, 'Another PC?' Already heading to the bar not bothering to wait for an answer to what, he assumed correctly to be a rhetorical question.

Phil looked at the notes Wil had been scratching down in utter amazement. It looked like something ancient and historically important you'd find inside a pyramid that Egyptologists would argue over for centuries.

Wil returned with the beers, took a very big sip, picked up his pen and notepad, raised his eyebrows and stared at Phil.

'Right.' Phil said, already looking tired.

'Right, anyway, to finish off. Just Legalise all drugs and let people exercise their freedom of choice.'

Phil glanced at his list, decided on the next one and continued.

'Charity.'

He didn't need to refer to his notes for this one. Phil hated the evolution, or more accurately, the complete dissolution of charity.

'When did this become a fucking business? It's not all that long ago, a couple of times a year, a couple of little old ladies, or boy scouts would knock on your door, they'd have a little tin, with a little slot on the top for coins, and a little label that read Salvation Army or Vinny's or whatever, and you'd give them 40, 60 cents or maybe nothing. They'd smile then fuck off. They didn't offer you a receipt, no big guilt trip, no professional chuggers chasing you down the street, no lock in contracts, no direct debit and definitely, no fucking Eftpos. And these little old ladies, or boy scouts weren't on commission. They were doing this on their own time, out of the goodness of their own hearts. Really trying to help. Fuck me! When did it become OK for a charity to behave like a business? Why are charities allowed to have paid staff?

Aren't they all supposed to be volunteers?' Phil took an angry mouth full of beer and referred back to his notes.

'The average salary of a CEO for a Charity is around $250,000 per annum.' Will rolled his eyes skyward and whistled.

'This, they justify by saying if they worked for a profit-based company of a similar size they could be paid more than twice that amount. Does anyone buy this shit? Isn't it supposed to be charity? I think someone is missing the point, or more likely the point has been completely obscured by a huge pile of cash. Why is this allowed to go on?' Phil held out the palms of his hands in dismay.

'If you look at the balance sheet of all these so-called charities, in there somewhere, generally right at the bottom is the percentage that they really give away to the needy. Spoiler alert!' He looked disgusted at saying spoiler alert and corrected himself.

'Guess what? It's only between one and five percent, sometimes even less. They try to say it's higher, but they hide junkets, conferences, and any other perks they can get away with as administration fees. How do they fucking sleep at night?' Phil paused looking genuinely disgusted.

'Don't get me started on the amount of money that gets siphoned off to dodgy politicians at best, and war lords at worst.'

'What happened to all that Live Aid money? Didn't a lot of that end up in the wrong hands.' Wil added.

'Exactly. When the money goes overseas to a country the charity knows little to nothing about and in reality, cares even less about. That money generally never ends up in the hands of the people who need it. The food is eaten by the Army. And the money is used to buy weapons. Basically, it makes the problem a whole lot worse.' He paused again looking even more agitated.

'Why do you get a tax deduction when you give money to charity? Sounds like it encourages money laundering to me. And don't even get me started on dodgy political, celebrity and billionaire charity foundations. Most of these never achieve anything, apart from making the politicians, celebrities and billionaires even richer through highly questionable "Philanthropic" practices.'

Wil finished taking notes almost at the same time Phil finished talking.

They both took another sip of their beers.

'This too has to stop. And I haven't even mentioned the Churches farcical role it plays in this appalling industry. And it is, an industry.' Phil and Wil both paused to catch their breath.

'That's a good one PC. You can't argue.' Will said tapping the list to keep Phil rolling, who obliged by saying.

'Gambling.'

Phil launched straight into his argument against some forms of gambling, and totally for other forms of gambling. Phil separated gambling into two types. Non-productive gambling. Poker machines, casino games, keno etc., and productive gambling. Greyhound racing, horse racing, sports betting etc., At least they create jobs, Phil said. He also outlined a strict set of rules for the regulation of both.

Wil dutifully noted everything down, although he didn't feel enthused about this one as it also rightly mentioned all the harm gambling causes, and at the same time justified its existence. Wil thought that's another one they'll definitely, need to work through.

'Junk Mail'

Phil said confidently after glancing through his notes again. This one Phil nailed. It was undeniable. It had to stop. There was no sane argument for its ongoing existence. It also highlights the hypocrisy of all politicians who talk a good green game, but when it comes down to touting for their jobs. They stuff our letter boxes with propaganda. It is just so last century. It is the last roar of the letter box marketing dinosaur. No one could argue against its total abolition. He finished the topic off with a rousing 'Fuck junk mail.' to a few muffled cheers from a couple of drinkers who had come out for a smoke.

Phil and Wil pressed on through Public Transport, and how it should be free, Freud, Education, Flightless Birds, if you can't fucking fly, then you're not a fucking bird. Surely, it's a prerequisite. The unbridled aphorisms flowed from Phil as fast as the beer flowed, and the time passed.

They both looked at each other happy with how it was going. They were both also pretty pissed.

Again, with an almost psychic connection, they both said 'Lunch.'

'What's the time PC?' Wil said, wringing the shorthand out.

'Good fucking Christ. 5:30. How'd that happen. No wonder I'm pissed and starved.' Phil smiled.

'Good timing though. The Bistro's opening again soon.' Wil said, looking optimistically at the light coming from the kitchen.

'Let's move in. If it's not open. If we stand there awkwardly long enough, he's way too polite to say no.'

They both stood up and walked into the bistro. Glanced around and saw Becca sitting at the corner table staring at them. She looked like she was still unfortunately, maintaining the rage. Phil and Wil then raised an arm each to wave.

Beccs stood up and gave them each the middle finger on both hands as a reply. She stormed off and tried to slam the door behind her, but the door had one of those gas door thingies and completely ruined her dramatic exit.

This made her even angrier. She slammed the flat of her hands on the outside window to make her point, and yelled THPPTPHTPHPHHPH, followed by BRAAAP as a car sped by, that was clearly fueled by Barito's. She threw both her hands in the air in frustration thinking the world must be a simulation specifically programmed to favour idiots. She thought that was something Phil would say, which made her even angrier and shouted 'Bitch!' loud enough this time to drown out any combustion engine regardless of its fuel source. Phil and Wil stared at each other looking confused.

'Why would she shout Bitch?' Phil said, looking a bit worried.

'That's what she yelled at me this morning too.' Wil added.

'What! Why didn't you tell me that before? Really?' Phil said, annoyed.

'Forgot. These things always blow over PC.' Wil said, looking unconcerned. Phil looked, completely not unconcerned.

'We need to order, and we need to find out what just happened.' He said, handing Wil a menu.

What Happened

Phil and Wil sat patiently waiting and thinking for the 10 minutes before their food arrived. Phil was worried Beccs was seriously, seriously angry, not just a little pissed off as he expected. Wil was worried he hadn't ordered an entrée. Their food arrived.

Will ordered a Chicken Schnitzel nearly the same size as his plate, complimented by a Kilimanjaro sized mountain of chips struggling to surface through a lake of mushroom sauce. Phil had Mo Mo dumplings as usual. The heavily overburdened waiter arrived at their table and put their plates down in front of them.

Phil ate Mo Mo dumplings as often as he could, or as often as he wasn't too embarrassed to order. Phil thought Mo Mo dumplings were the epicurean equivalent of crystal meth. He'd paid for them with coins, he'd bought them on credit. He even planned one day on travelling to Nepal to "*Try the real thing.*" Mostly he wondered what he was capable of if he couldn't get his regular supply.

'No dessert today mate?' asked Phil.

'No PC. Keeping the extras in hand. Didn't even cross my mind.' Wil lied, still regretting the decision.

They ate in silence. Phil didn't watch Wil eat to keep his morale up.

'So, what was that about?' Phil asked, scraping up the last of the sauce.

'What was what about?'

'Beccs. The fuck you fingers. The Bitch through the window.' Phil begged.

'Steady on with the bitch PC.' Wil sternly said, as always

75

ready to leap to Beccs defence.

'No, for the love of God! She yelled Bitch.' Wil immediately stood down and looked skyward thoughtfully.

'Not sure PC.' He mused.

'Well, why would she call me...'

'Us.' interrupted Wil.

'Us.' continued Phil 'Bitches.'

'Well, you did mention Bitch last night in the SMS, didn't you?'

'Bullshit! I wouldn't call Beccs a Bitch. She called herself a bitch, remember, a justified bitch.' That's when they both stared at each other with apprehension.

The SMS Phil thought. He fumbled for his phone and handed it to Wil. He opened it and checked the message.

'Seems OK to me mate. You said Bitch, yes! But it was justified, I thought it highlighted your listening skills.' He tossed the phone back across the table at Phil.

Phil searched for some other meaning and drew a blank. He'd never even contemplated thinking the words Bitch and Beccs in the same thought. Never.

'Forward the message to me PC. I'll check it again.' Wil said staring at the dessert bar looking fidgety.

Phil picked up the phone and forwarded the message to Wil. Wil's phone pinged its arrival. He got straight up, pulled it out of his pocket and walked to the dessert bar.

Phil looked on in astonishment, then realised it was hopeless, possibly even dangerous to get between Wil and dessert and waited patiently. Wil arrived back at the table with dessert and phone in hand.

'That looks good.' Phil said as small talk, pointing at Wil's phone vigorously with his eyebrows.

'Oh, the message. I'm sure it's fine.' He fumbled with his phone and opened the message, read it, flicked at his phone a few more times and put it back on the table, then grimaced at Phil. 'Bit of a problem PC.'

'What do you mean a bit of a problem? Just fucking tell me. You're killing me Wil?' Phil said looking close to a panic attack.

'Well. The message was split in two. Bisected as it were.' Wil pushed the phone over to Phil. Phil picked it up and stared at it in disbelief.

'How? Why the fuck does this shit keep happening to me. I mean. Fucking why?!' Phil exclaimed with exacerbation.

Wil began to snigger, saw Phil was not in the mood and stopped.

'PC, mate if you had a phone less than 10 years old, or maybe used SMS speak. You know b4 instead of before, u instead of you.' Phil looked at him with non-comprehension. 'lol instead of laugh...' He stopped when Phil nodded and when he realised, he wasn't helping.

'PC. I'll talk to Beccs in the morning. I see her most mornings at the letter box anyway. If not, I'll knock on her door. Explain everything. She'll have a laugh. It'll be sorted.' Wil said in his best calming voice. Phil still didn't look calm or convinced.

'Come on PC, lighten up. Stop looking so worried. Time to get back to business.' Will said having mysteriously already finished his dessert, then stood up pointing to their makeshift office. Phil just sat there, still in a depressed state, still wondering why these things did seem to just keep happening to him. Was the universe specifically designed to make his life difficult.

Wil for the second time in two days, guided Phil back to their respective workstations. Wil insisted on their tables being called workstations. To give the project a "*Business feel.*" he said. Wil had also made name plates that Phil had insisted on not using.

Phil tried to regain his enthusiasm but was unable to get the latest all too common mishap with Beccs out of his mind.

'Maybe we should just pack it in for the day?' Phil said, sounding completely disheartened.

'PC mate. I'll fix the SMS thing. There is nothing really to fix. It's a technology fail. Trust me.' Wil leaned in closer to speak in an even more serious tone.

'It will all be sorted out by this time tomorrow.' He

emphasized.

'Except by this time tomorrow you'll be stressed out that you didn't bother to get anything more done today. There is nothing we, or I, can do about it now, so let's just get on with it.' Wil stared intensely at Phil, knowing it was time to get stern as a proper friend should.

'You could call her?' Phil said thinking of something Wil could do.

'Fuck that! Did you see how angry she was. You call her?'

'I can't call her.' Phil replied now thankful for the restriction.

'I'll talk to her in the morning. In the meantime?' Wil said waving his notepad and pen at Phil.

Phil tried to look more enthusiastic and read through the list of possibles, found one, then glanced through his notes on the topic.

'Fitted sheets.'

'Fitted sheets.' He mumbled. 'They seem like a good idea but they're not! They don't stay on the bed like they show in the picture of the perfectly fitted bed on the packet. Plus, and most importantly, they're practically impossible to fold, unless of course you're an origami master. Fuck that! They are a sham product and should only be sold on late night television to the lonely and or drunk. They deserve this quality of product. They expect it. They won't even be disappointed.' Phil said a bit lacklustre.

'Quite right. However, they do make a good motorbike cover.' Will added.

'Well sell them as that then!'

'I think they already have those PC?' Wil added.

'Not really the point, or the purpose of the advertised product.' Phil added.

'You'd expect to buy this sort of shit off some dodgy backpacking geezer at the railway station, or at a popup shop in the mall, not at reputable Manchester outlets.

How is this even classified as Manchester.' Phil paused to gather his thoughts, then realised he didn't have any more.

Wil finished his note taking, looked at Phil a bit concerned and said, 'Not so sure how important that one is. I know you hate fitted sheets PC, but do you think you should let your own prejudice give it a platform.'

Phil nodded in agreement and said 'OK. Maybe that one won't make the final edit either. But I'm still right!' He insisted.

Wil nodded, not wanting to get into PC's pros and cons, mostly cons of fitted sheets once again.

'Something a bit more relevant to today's society this time PC.' Wil said, trying to get Phil a bit more enthused.

Phil looked through the list, found a topic and read his notes.

'Garbage.'

Wil picked up his notepad and looked happy Phil had picked something a little less personal.

'Yes. Garbage! There lies in the cause and only real solution to most of the world's problems. Less garbage helps everyone, helps the animals, fish, fishes, and us. Nobody likes garbage. Nobody likes waste!' Phil paused and extended a finger in the air to make another announcement.

'Garbage collections should be cut from weekly to fortnightly, then monthly.'

'What with bigger bins?' Will asked nervously.

'No. That's the point. The bin size would remain the same. And in addition, all public and private tips would be shut.'

Wil gasped in mock shock, while at the same time knowing he couldn't possibly cope with only one garbage collection a month. The takeaway boxes alone almost filled his bin weekly.

'This would definitely work. Seriously! This would cut the amount of garbage and waste we currently produce dramatically. It must. Everyone from that point on would be forced to consider how much garbage they were bringing home with their consumables. Market pressure would force the manufacturers to reduce the amount of garbage they sell with their products, and at the same time save money. Eventually you'd be bringing home only the product in a bring your own bag, or having it delivered naked. And at a packaging free price.' Phil paused.

'Sure!' he said, loaded with sarcasm.

'At first people would have a problem with monthly garbage collections, but we had a problem with seat belts, random breath test, no brown paper bags, then no plastic bags, which one are we up to now? No smoking indoors in pubs, and every other restriction I've probably already forgotten about. And now all have simply become a daily part of life.'

'Sounds a bit like a slippery slope PC. Just one other thing we will get used to, like a frog in hot water, isn't it?' Wil interjected.

'I see your point. However, if you add a financial incentive, like cheaper products. People will see the benefit.' Phil finished.

Benefit! Wil was sceptical about people giving a fuck about the benefit when their garage was full of rats and garbage. But couldn't fault the logic, smiled at Phil and nodded approval.

Will put his notepad down, stood up, stacked their empty glasses, and went to the bar to get another round.

'Be back in a minute. Pick another one, we're making great progress.' Wil said walking away.

'You pick one Wil.' Phil said pointing at the list.

Wil picked it up and pointed one out to Phil, then continued to the bar. Phil read through the notes waiting for his return.

'Sportsmen.'

'Good pick.' Phil said enthusiastically.

'Sportsmen, and I mean men. In the most part anyway.

Sportswomen don't generally appear in pixelated photos taken in a night club bathroom at 3am groping someone or pissing in a pot plant or poker machine change tray, before being politely shown to the door, then escorted less politely into a paddy wagon.'

'Give them time PC. I'm sure the girls won't disappoint.' Added Wil.

Phil nodded agreement. 'How the fuck did they all become such assholes!' He was worked up about this one. He'd met a few so-called sportsmen in his time.

'I know how.' He said answering his own rhetorical question.

'It's because the mainstream media and social media treat these wankers like they have something important to say on every topic. Instead of only asking them questions on the only topic they are qualified to talk about. How to catch a ball, how to throw a ball, run fast, or fall over without hurting yourself. Anything else is way above their pay grade.' Phil took a big sip of his beer.

'The real problem is that these one trick ponies, actually believe the sycophantic media that fawns over them and they start proffering their opinions on politics, world issues, even medical advice for fuck sake... And the worst part about this is not that they offer their advice, but rather that people actually follow it.' Phil said throwing his hands in the air in dismay.

'If a sportsman condemns something or someone, through either the mainstream media or worse, through social media. An army of their vacuous followers will attack without mercy and more particularly, without any thought. Hellbent on destroying that person's life. It's rabid pack mentality at its worst. You expect that from the despicable media, not from the general public.' Phil leant back on his chair satisfied, then started again.

'And as if that isn't bad enough, they are also deemed role models. What? A role model for doing something for a living that most people consider a bloody past time or simply gave up years ago, as they were beginning to feel a bit like a man child. They also cost us all a bloody fortune. Even the so-called professionals get subsidies, either directly or indirectly from the government. Or should I just say from us.' Phil gulped at his beer.

'Don't even get me started on the amount of money wasted on faux sporting events. The biggest waste of all being the Olympics. All the sports in the Olympics are sports that in the most part you wouldn't go to see if you got a lift, free tickets, and an open bar.' Wil nodded his approval of that one.

Wil hated that every couple of years his regular TV viewing was interrupted by gymnastics, or fucking figure skating, or something even worse and even more pointless.

'Every four years.' Phil continued

'Every two years if you count the winter Olympics.' Wil corrected.

'Yes, and you can also add the world championships to that list.'

'Doesn't really interrupt the telly though.' Added Wil.

'Anyway.' Continued Phil.

'Every Government in the world has to spend several bridges, a suburb's worth of public housing and a few fully funded hospitals funding this fucking scam. And all so a bunch of wankers living on the public purse can inspire us. Inspire us to what? Being one of them. If a sport can't pay its own way either through ticket sales, sponsorship, volunteers, chook raffles whatever., then it shouldn't exist. Sport is meant to be, well sport, not a lifelong fucking career. Not some, win at all costs international pissing competition. Sport has completely lost its way. There's no more sport or sportsmanship anymore.' Phil lamented.

'Thus forth.' Phil announced, pointing his finger skyward again.

'The word sportsmanship should be removed from the dictionary until some sportsmanship can actually be found.'

'In summary. Stop listening to, idolizing, or using these dickheads as role models kids.' Phil finished his beer and said, 'That'll do on that one.'

They were on a roll now and pushed through 'Education', 'Freedom', or how freedom is only a temporary right that can apparently be taken away if the government deems it to be for the greater good, or for some imagined media driven crisis. 'Cryptids', 'Lobby Groups', 'Recycling', 'Phonetics' and why the word Phonetic is not spelt fonetic ironically, and 'Freud'. Phil had already covered Freud but hated that intellectual charlatan and his self-made mumbo jumbo profession so much, he couldn't resist revisiting the subject.

They both looked exhausted, most likely caused by alcohol consumption than mental overexertion. They'd been daisy chaining the beers since 1 o'clock.

Phil checked the time and was surprised it was already nine. Stood up, pointed at his wrist where a watch would have been 20 years ago, and said 'It's 9 Wil. Time to head home I reckon. Good start though I think?'

'Yes. But we need to keep up the pace tomorrow. I'll take the notes and type them up at work. It's been a long day.' Wil said wobbling to his feet.

'Right. I need to eat something and get some sleep too. Same time tomorrow Wil?

'Absolutely. It's all falling into place now PC.' Wil said encouragingly.

Phil wobbled to his own feet as they left the Pub in different directions.

Phil was still worried about Beccs, and worried about the whole project. Had he bitten off more than he could chew, or maybe more than anyone could swallow.

'PHIL!' Wil yelled out now from a distance away. 'DON'T WORRY ABOUT BECCS. I'LL SORT IT OUT.' And gave Phil a thumbs up.

'WE'LL REGROUP TOMORROW!' He shouted before finally disappearing into the night.

Tomorrow's Regroup

BEEP! DING! DING! BEEP! DING! DING! BEEP! DING! DING!...

The regular sound of the morning alarm was added to by the clanging of an alarm clock, making the cacophony of noise particularly annoying. Phil decided which one was the most annoying, then shut the alarms off in their respective orders.

Wil gave Phil the clock as an unnecessary apology for the whole resetting of his phone incident. Phil had already moved on, deciding it was most probably his fault anyway. Wil still felt it was important to make a gesture.

The alarm clock was black and retro, with twin silver bells at the top. It had a classic key winder and two tiny dials for setting the time, both requiring Zen like patience to set with any kind of accuracy. Phil loved it. And it could wake the dead.

The clock had an added feature which allowed you to replace the picture on the face with "*A picture of your choice.*", the box proudly displayed in luminous electric blue font on the front of the box.

Wil replaced the stock photo that came with the clock, with a picture of Ryan Reynolds. He knew that would fire Phil up.

It was well documented how much Phil hated all Ryans, particularly Ryan Reynolds. Phil thought it was just not natural that anyone could possibly be in a good mood all the fucking time. Phil was an unapologetic Ryanist.

He bounced out of bed. Looked at the clock and

shouted. 'Fuck you Ryan Reynolds.' Gave him the finger and walked to the shower with now characteristic determination.

Phil got out of the shower thinking he heard the spare room door click shut. He quickly dried, dressed, and walked into the hall.

'Chris. Is that you?' Phil asked tentatively. Nothing returned from his/her's room.

Phil bravely knocked on the door. 'Chris. Do you want a nice cup of tea, coffee maybe?' Then remembered he didn't have any coffee and whispered. 'Sorry, no coffee.' And waited patiently for any sign of life. Nothing.

He decided it must have been his imagination, the wind, or hopefully a ghost. Wil was very eager to try out his new EMF Detector and K2 meter somewhere with a confirmed sighting. Phil gave up and resumed walking down the stairs only to be stopped mid step.

'No thanks Phillip. I've been out all night. Catch up tomorrow hun. Thanks heaps though. Muah, Muah. Goodnight. Love Ya.'

Catch up tomorrow! Hun! Fucking air kisses. Who is this crazy person? They've been here for, Phil did a quick calculation. Over a month and I've never even seen they/him/her. Never spoken. Wait, was that a girl's voice. Phil continued downstairs thinking. Yes, definitely a girl's voice. One piece of the puzzle solved. Sounds like a hippy though he thought, feeling a bit worried.

He prepared the same breakfast not wanting to risk throwing a working schedule into chaos and ate it, with now typical efficiency. He flicked on the telly. It was showing the usual morning TV. A nice mix of piss poor, not really their journalism, interspersed with thinly veiled infomercials masqueraded as news stories, and of course, sycophantic political interviews. It cut to commercial in idiosyncratic fashion with the talking heads dancing their way to the break.

An in-studio infomercial started with a maniacally smiling host beaming about a "*Simply can't live without*" product, like he'd done more cocaine than Robin Williams in his prime.

Phil ignored the telly effortlessly and looked at the list of remaining possibles. He started scratching some notes only to be stopped by the ringing of his phone.

He walked over to the telly, turned it off, picked up the phone and looked at it in disbelief. It was Wil's number. Wil never called in the morning. Will never called at any time. Wil used his phone strictly for SMS communication only.

'Hello.' Phil said tentatively with the grave expectations of someone answering an unexpected 3am call.

'PC. Beccs has gone to Melbourne until Thursday.' Announced Wil without introduction.

'What?'

'Beccs has gone to Melbou...'

'I heard that. You spoke to her this morning then?' Phil interrupted.

'No mate. Spoke to her neighbour.'

'You're her neighbour.' Phil said sounding a bit frustrated.

'No. The other neighbour. The little old lady with the crazy orange hair. Lucy, Judy, something. Just listen. She had to go to Melbourne with Ryan.'

'Fucking Ryan.' Muttered Phil.

'She gave her number to Lucy, Judy in case of an emergency. Lucy, Judy then told me, presumably because she must realise by now, she can't possibly have much longer to live. Although I've lived next to her for 20 years and she's always looked around a hundred.' Wil said getting off topic.

'Anyway...' Phil interjected.

'Anyway...,Beccs told her not to bother to call her until after lunch because her old phone is broken.' Wil explained already hating how long this conversation was taking.

'Lucy, Judy's phone is broken?' Asked Phil, getting confused.

'No. Beccs phone is broken!'

'Listen mate. You know I hate talking on the phone. I'll

see you at 1. We'll call her then. Gotta go.' Wil said hanging up abruptly.

Phil listened to the dial tone and remembered how much he hated Ryan, and how he never got any sense out of Wil in their rare phone conversations.

'Wanker.' Phil said out loud 'Ryan the Wanker'. He added, not wanting to implicate Wil by association.

Phil had only met Ryan once at Beccs' office Christmas party, and that didn't go all that well by his hazy recollection.

Poor Beccs. Stuck in Melbourne with Ryan. It combined two of her most hated things. Melbourne & Ryan.

Phil decided to stop wasting time and get back to the task at hand. He skimmed through his list of possibles, jotted down some notes without much interest, and pressed on trying not to worry. It was hopeless.

Phil had been a lifelong worrier and just couldn't kick the habit. He decided to take his mind off it by procrastinating. Well, it's only Wednesday morning. He was still on schedule, he'd earned this time he thought, knowing he hadn't.

He put the telly back on and watched the lifestyle channel. Unashamedly time wasting.

Phil couldn't focus on the tiny houses show he loved. The baking show he hated, and his favourite show where people make clothes for their pets. Couture Pets.

He decided a quick vacuum would aid his procrastination but just couldn't be bothered getting out and assembling his ancient vacuum cleaner. It was just too much effort. Phil wanted to replace it, but his policy of not replacing anything until it was broken failed him badly with anything made in the 1970's. Nothing made in the 70's ever broke.

He had to find out what was going on with Beccs. Phil decided to stop procrastinating like an amateur and do it properly. He went to the pub early, arriving about 11. Only a bit surprised to find Wil already looking over some papers.

Phil walked out, beer in hand and took a seat.

'You're here early Wil.' Remarked Phil, clearly pleased to see him.

'You can talk PC. Shouldn't you be preparing for today's meeting, not that drinking at the pub is not good prep.' Wil added seriously.

'Couldn't concentrate, you know, get into the whole vibe. So why call about Beccs this morning. I didn't think your mobile made calls?' Phil said half seriously.

'Yes mate. Found the feature this morning. The reason I called was to tell you about the note.' Wil said, raising his eyebrows.

'You never mentioned a note! What note?' Phil said a little too panicky, then repeated the question more calmly.

'Well, I don't think notes should be discussed over the phone.' Wil said, with a logic only he could understand.

'Ok.' Phil said not wanting to get into that discussion in any way.

'Sooo...What note?'

'The note under my door mate. Keep up.'

'For fuck's sake tell me about the note, give me the note, or read the fucking note. You're killing me again Wil.' Phil said, completely forgetting to be calm.

'Well, it wasn't so much a note, more of an instruction really.' Wil leaned in to tell Phil more closely.

'Leaning against my door this morning was that book you gave her, you know.' He said, clicking his fingers trying to remember.

'Frog and Toad Together.' Phil added desperate for Wil to just get to the point.

'Yeah, that one, and a post-it stuck to the front that read, and I quote, Give this back to PC. It's time he reread it. And it was signed Bitch!' Wil said and leaned back in his chair in consternation.

'For fuck's sake this has gone on long enough. I'm calling her.' Phil said picking up his phone.

'Oh! And it had a PS.,' Wil interrupted.

Phil just stared at Wil in amazement. 'It's like pulling teeth with you Wil. Just read me the entire note, including any PS's, PPS's, anything written on the back, or anything you might have found encrypted.' Phil said unashamedly panicking now.

'Tell that <u>bastard</u> he owes me a new Phone. And not one of those "*Retro*" phones like he has, a proper one!' Wil added emphasizing bastard. 'Bastard was also underlined PC'.

Phil wasn't listening anymore. He was dialing Beccs' number and getting the not available message. He tried another four times then stared at Wil for help.

'How is it my fault her phone is broken?' Phil said looking confused.

'Don't know. But it's only about 11:00. Let's just pick up where we left off yesterday.' Wil said, getting his notebook out.

'Can't concentrate with this hanging over my head. Let's wait until after lunch, call her, get this sorted.' Procrastination complete and justified. Phil was practically a grand master.

'Nice try PC. Remember it's Wednesday, tick tock.' Wil waved his finger backwards and forwards like a pendulum to help make his time's running out point patently clear.

'Wasn't it you that said worrying only makes things worse. This is a perfect example. While you're worrying, you're not working. And it'll all be sorted out by 1 anyway. Beccs will have got a new phone, and you will have just pissed away two hours. Right?' Wil remarked, looking sternly at Phil.

'Right.' Answered Phil a little annoyed at having his own logic used against him yet again.

'Oh, before we start, I've got some news. Chris is a Girl.' Phil said, without too much interest.

'The new flat mate. Right. What are they like.' Wil said genuinely fascinated.

'Still not sure, only spoke through the door. They … She said we'd catch up shortly.' Phil stressed she.

'Been there for weeks haven't they? More of an introduction than a catch up really. Keep me posted.' Wil loved his gossip.

'No worries. I know you love your gossip Wil'.

Will Pulled the project plan folder out of his bag and turned it to page three.

'Day 2' He announced, and slid the project plan across the table to Phil.

Day 2 - Wednesday.

- Acknowledge the time left – 3 days.
- Press on until the second third is complete.

'Second third?' Phil said out loud looking concerned.

'Yeah. Second third. I've formatted yesterday's work into a document that constitutes the first third of the project. I'll take you through it after lunch. I said I'd made a plan to get this finished. And we will get this finished.' Wil said again remembering Beccs remarks.

Phil picked up his beer and took a large sip to prepare himself.

'PC.' Phil announced.

Wil looked at Phil concerned he'd started referring to himself in the third person. Something he simply would not tolerate.

'Political Correctness.'

Phil unabbreviated to Wil's relief.

'Political Correctness is one of the most divisive concepts ever created by humankind.' He announced getting a raised eyebrow from Wil.

'Fuck government censorship. PC endorses public censorship. It allows anyone without any thought, to correct, or in other words be blatantly judgy, condescending, or just plain rude to people who may use a different or out of date turn of phrase to what is deemed acceptable by a PC lynch mob.' Phil continued.

'It's Newspeak. If George Orwell was alive, he'd fucking sue. Even the PC insensitives must surely be able to comprehend that there is no absolute and correct way to speak. No absolute truth. We live in an evolving truth. It's brutal mob censorship.' Phil paused to look adequately disgusted.

'May God help you if you have a different opinion on anything that is the current truth. Or hold what is regarded as an unacceptable opinion. You will be crucified by a PC lynch mob, spurred on by a media whose job seems to have devolved into trying to create division.' Phil paused for a sip.

'You won't when you have a different opinion in most cases, even get the chance to defend that opinion before everyone shouts you down with name calling, like the "C" word. Conspiracy Theorist, Contrarian or just plain Cunt.' He pointed at Wil in an almost threatening way to finish the point.

'When what you should be called is the other "C" word. Critical Thinker. It's vicious labelling, and herd mentality at its worst. Not because the correction or change is worse. In most cases it's a genuine improvement. It's the way it's policed without mercy or consideration that frightens me. I guess it's just easier to thoughtlessly be on the side of the majority.'

'And safer.' interjected Wil.

'And it's policed retrospectively for the love of God. I mean today almost everything is recorded in social media or wherever, which means that at some point, we're all fucked!' He paused to take a sip of his beer, changed his mind and continued.

'If someone has a bad day, 10, 20 years ago, and by bad day I mean said something that was OK then, and we know it was OK then as no one gave a shit about it at the time. However, by today's standards doesn't comply with accepted views. Even if the person being persecuted genuinely apologizes and learns from the experience. Life is a learning experience I thought. Well, that's not good enough. You're cancelled! The poor bastard may not even remember the incident, but none the less is hounded and hunted down by a PC lynch mob, or worse the next evolution of PC, Woke.' Phil leaned forward looking at

Wil's weird scribble, nodded knowingly and continued.

'Based on that line of thinking, at some point, all of us will go under the bus. Today's opinions will always be antiquated by time.'
Phil stopped and put his notes down.

'I noticed you aren't covering Woke as a topic PC? Any reason? Wil enquired.

'Woke is where common sense, facts and reason go to die. Fuck that! Woke people are seriously crazy Wil.' Phil said with alarm.

'Good point.' Agreed Wil. 'Next'.

'Plastic.'

'Fucking plastic. We've all seen those poor fish and sea turtles choking on the shit. Seals being strangled by some kid's toy, discarded tent or something else that should never have been made from plastic in the first place. Don't do it because of some media driven crisis. Do it for the fucking animals. Just stop using it. With the following exception.' Phil paused for dramatic effect, thought about doing a drum roll, then thought better of it.

'Medical use. That's it! We can literally, not figuratively live without everything else. Everyone seems to have forgotten that before 1907 it didn't even exist. And it was only commercially mass produced in the 1960's.' Phil paused to take another gulp of his beer.

'For fuck's sake we have individually wrapped cucumbers, and that's only what I've seen myself. I imagine somewhere, you can guarantee someone is at least thinking about individually wrapping grapes. Why is all our food wrapped in so much plastic? Why does it feel like I'm opening a present when I'm opening my fucking lunch?' Phil paused, trying to remember what other food he had seen wrapped, then didn't bother thinking. He'd made his point.

'Every week we all drag home new plastic bottles of shampoo, conditioner, orange juice, dishwashing liquid, laundry detergent, the list goes on, and on. Why don't supermarkets at least have an option to bring your own bottles. The product could then be metered to the right amount and sold cheaper because you have your own reusable bottle. It's just fucking ridiculous.' Phil proclaimed.

'And don't waste anybody's time talking about recycling. You can only recycle plastic 2 or 3 times at best. After that, it's either burned or ends up in landfill. At the end of the day when the oceans are basically full of microplastics, and it's permeated the entire food chain. We'll all keep blaming someone else. We'll protest, and hurl abuse at politicians. Like they're the ones using all the fucking plastic not us. And even when we eventually admit that it is us, we'll still blame the politicians for not forcing us to stop using it like we're little kids that need to be forced to do the right thing.' He picked up his beer and put it down again untouched.

'I'm sure nothing will change. We'll all just keep having totally non-productive meetings where we fly our so-called leaders around the world on expensive private jets, both financially and environmentally, on some pointless sojourn to an exotic location so they can all agree, to maybe someday do something about it. Or worse, sign some fucking pointless agreement to meet in another year, to talk about maybe doing something about it then. Sanctimonious fucking hypocrites!' Phil said a little too loudly.

He followed through by listing all the things that are currently made of plastic that could be easily made of something a little less aquatic life dooming.

'Another?' Wil raised his empty glass.

'Definitely.'

Wil returned with the drinks, picked up his notepad and nodded for Phil to continue.

Protests, E-Protests.

'Protests are an essential part of any free society. Everybody complains, but it's only when people come together and make their presence felt that change actually occurs.' Phil took a sip of his beer and continued.

'The problem we have with protests now, and it's a really big problem that will one day affect everyone, is that authoritarian Governments across the globe are legislating against them. Apparently disagreeing with the government should now be illegal.

Police are being given "All means necessary" powers to quash protests and protestors without mercy. And instead of the people being supported by the media, they are ritualistically lampooned by them. In a lot of western countries, you now even need a permit to protest. Doesn't that defeat the purpose?' Phil glanced back at his notes.

'Protestors are now being greeted with tear gas, rubber bullets, water cannons, pepper spray, sonic weapons, and all dispensed by their own governments endorsed thugs. How are they allowed to do this to peaceful protestors? Isn't it part of our Public Sector Guidance sheet.' Phil held his notes up to read verbatim.

'The right in article 19(1) to hold opinions without interference cannot be subject to any exception or restriction. The right in article 19(2) protects freedom of expression in any medium, for example written and oral communications, the media, public protest, broadcasting, artistic works and commercial advertising.'
Phil paused and looked seriously at Wil.

'How often are these rights denied? Don't even get me started on Covid policies. The social media. HeadSpace in particular, guided by the sociopathic hand of their freedom hating robot impersonating CEO Adam Socliea, threaten or suspend anyone who disagrees with whatever current narrative is being pushed by their authoritarian overlords. And let's not forget Clay Siliolvnee the software stealing scumbag who hides behind a mask of philanthropy, which surely nobody is buying any more. Now, not only wants to control computers, but just about everything else as well, including what we eat, and what medications he wants to force upon us. Oh, and then of course theirs Wal Sleter, the sweatshop running, slave driving prick who is planning to be the world's only retailer at the expense of every small business on the planet. Although.' Phil interrupted himself.

'They are not the real problem. They are just the money behind the World Treasury Forum (WTF).' Phil smiled to himself and thought, you should always think about what the acronym is when naming an organisation.

'They are all simply puppets of Schultz Dauber. The bald unelected bond super villain doppelganger who thinks he runs the world, and as it turns out. Just very well might soon. This is the most important point Wil.' Phil said with vehemence.

'The censorship industrial complex are about to implement complete control over what we say and what we hear. The final stages of censoring any kind of contrary opinion or allowing free debate is nearly upon us. Our last chance is rapidly approaching.' Phil paused looking angry.

'Protests, which previously were the best way to get your point across are now completely pointless. They are made pointless as they are purposefully ignored by the mainstream media and as such rendered meaningless. It's time for protestors to evolve. Become more dynamic, move with the times. Of course, I'm talking about a new method of protest. A new way to stick it to the Man!' Phil said making the piece sign with both hands.

'E-Protests!' He announced with an air of importance.

'Instead of hitting the streets and risk being brutalised. You can now protest in the safety of your own home.' Phil said smiling.

'Boycott Wal's mail order products. Don't login to HeadSpace, or any other social media sites that promote censorship. If everyone got together and stopped watching the mainstream media, stopped listening to them, and stopped buying their ironically named newspapers from these paid for pathological liars. They would starve to death and die. We have the power to stop the unelected global elites from taking complete control. Stop them from spreading fear. We can cut them off at the knees. Together it can be achieved. We can regain our freedom and truth. Let them know once and for all we have had enough of their propaganda and lies!' Phil finished.

Wil leant back in his chair with them both feeling satisfied that this one is important.

Tirelessly they worked their way through the morning. They got through Coffee the topic, not the drink. Phil was completely convinced that if all the time and money wasted on coffee was reclaimed. World hunger would not exist. Cancer would be a thing of the past, and humans would have travelled to the stars by now. Phil had done the math to back this point up. That should piss just about everyone off Wil thought.

Weapons, why the fuck are weapons banned for all citizens. Surely women, who are the victim most of the time, and at the same time the lowest perpetrator of violence, should be allowed to at least have something to fight back with.

Reality TV and why it's not OK to torture down on their luck people, or down on their luck celebrities in the name of entertainment. If you paid someone to do the things they get away with on those shows you'd be charged with coercion.

Airline ticket pricing and why it should be priced per kilogram, not per person, after all its weight to lift ratio isn't it? Why are we subsidizing fat people.

Plates and why they should all have handles and lips, which reminded them they were both hungry, so they stopped for lunch.

Phil ordered his usual. Wil ordered two courses. Phil checked the time. One O'clock. Better try Beccs, get the all clear.

The All Clear

Phil dialled Beccs' number which rang out and then went to voice mail. He hung up, still scarred by the SMS, definitely not prepared to risk a voice mail. Phil hit redial knowing it took Beccs at least two calls to find her phone at the bottom of the bottomless abyss that is her handbag.

The phone answered.

'Beccs. It's PC. Hi.' Phil beamed a smile at the phone knowing she would know.

'Oh. What do you want? I thought you weren't going to call until Friday. I'm not in the mood... Phil.' She emphasised Phil in a hurtful way.

'Plus. I'm in Melbourne with Ryan. Needless to say, you called at a bad time.'

Phil jumped in 'Understand Beccs, but please check the last message I sent. There's been a serious technical failure.'

'I read the message PC and...'

'NO! Read the second part!' Phil almost shouted, sounding desperate.

'What second part. Hold on.' Beccs said fading away to check her phone.

There was a pause, and then another pause, and then more rustling sounds and then there was Beccs.

'Fuck. I broke my phone because of that message.' Beccs said in a calmer voice to Phil's relief.

'I'll buy you a new one Beccs.'

'I have a new one. That's what I'm talking to you on.' She said with playful sarcasm.

'Oh right. Of course.'

'So, what did you want PC?' Beccs said even more light heartedly, Phil smiled keenly at being called PC again.

'Nothing really. Just clearing the air. Oh, and I've, we've.' Phil said nodding at Wil.

'Started the manifesto, document thing, you know finish something this time.' He said fishing for recognition.

'Seriously! Good for you.'

'Yeah.' Phil said, worried that sounded a little condescending.

'No. I mean it PC. I'm sorry I yelled like I did, but sometimes you can be more frustrating than a dodgy shopping trolley. Oh God. Here comes Ryan.' Beccs said, sounding tired.

'So, is he still trying to get out of the friend zone.' Laughed Phil.

'Friend zone! He's never getting out of the friend zone, even with a map, compass, tour guides, and a team of porters. Anyway, gotta go PC, he's here…'

'OK Beccs. See you on Fri…' Phil rushed to say but was cutoff.

'Phil is that you.' Said a disturbingly familiar voice.

'Umm, who's this?' Phil said, already knowing the horrifying answer.

'It's Ryan old buddy.'

'Ryan. What happened to Beccs.' Phil said instantly getting annoyed.

'I think the last time we met we got off on the wrong foot.' Ryan replied ignoring Phil's question and annoyance.

'Yeah, umm, forget it Ryan. It's all good. Is Beccs there?' Phil asked again, trying to sound casual thinking that may help. It didn't.

'Well. Let's not worry about that now. As Beccs and I are such good friends. I'm sure she's forgiven you.' Ryan said.

'She talks about your funny little quirks all the time Phillip. It's time we were friends too.' Ryan said still being annoying.

Fucking awesome, thought Phil thinking back to the office Christmas Party Beccs invited him to. The one where he got really, really, really proper drunk, and called Ryan a narcissistic prick and yelled "you've ruined Christmas for everyone" then pissed in one of his office plants before picking up a six pack and stumbling out with Beccs apologising behind him, saying something about drinking on medication, and he's not normally like this at all. Not normally.

Beccs later that night said it was the most fun Christmas party she'd ever been to.

'Right. Ok Ryan. Is Beccs there?' Phil said, trying not to start a conversation.

'Yes. I've spoken to her, and she agrees we should all do lunch.' Ryan said winking at Beccs who was now apologising to someone he'd offended without even noticing.

Was this guy talking to me from the 80's? Has Gordon Gecko made a fucking comeback. Do lunch?

'You know my shout. I hear it's your birthday Phillip. Dinner, a few drinks. People are still talking about your theatrical exit from the Christmas Party. Funny stuff Phillip.' Ryan said laughing.

'Yeah. Good times. Can't wait for next Christmas Ryan.' Phil tried not to sound confused, but his birthday was months away.

'So, Friday dinner. I'll bring Beccs and you can bring that friend of yours. Wil. I think Beccs said his name was?' Ryan said this with Phil imagining him waving his hand around dismissively, which he was.

Phil was just about to tell Ryan to go fuck himself, then thought of Beccs, then thought of free food and drinks.

'Sounds great Ryan. Free food, free drinks you say. Put Beccs back on, new friend Ryan. Talk to you Friday. Bye.' Phil said really trying to get Ryan off the phone now.

'Hi PC. So, so, sorry. I thought he was joking. He really wanted to take me out to dinner on Friday night, and I was running out of excuses and panicked. I said it was your birthday, and I was having dinner with you and Wil.' Beccs said apologetically.

'Good idea Beccs. Christmas was so much fun. I can't wait for the birthday do. Not sure how I can top my last effort though.' He heard Beccs giggle down the line.

'Anyway, any chance of guilting him into a birthday present?' Phil said only half joking.

Beccs laughed 'I'll mention it. Maybe he'll get something good to impress me. He just landed a big client so he should be loaded.'

'So, were all good again?' Phil smiled overtly again at the phone.

'Of course PC. We're always good. Can't wait to see how far you've got on Friday with the thing.' Beccs said instantly lifting Phil's spirits.

'How far we've got. It'll be finished by Friday. I said I'd get something finished by Friday, and this is it, and ready for publishing.' Phil said confidently, now fully, and totally committed to the project.

'Wow publishing, now I'm intrigued, anyway gotta go PC, your birthday date's headed this way. Talk to you tonight from the hotel after I've ditched Ryan. Bye PC. Can't wait to see you.' She said before hanging up.

'Bye Beccs. Oh, and I'll get Wil to put the book you returned back. And I'll pay for your new phone Beccs.' Finished Phil.

'Ok PC. Really gotta go. Bye.' And with that Phil ended the call and ended his stress.

He sat back in his chair and breathed a sigh of relief. So did Wil. Wil's sigh of relief was because their food finally arrived.

Phil thought about Beccs, and how he didn't really need to give that much thought anymore, then decided to focus all his energy on the task at hand. Really try to impress.

'PC. As far as I see, we're a bit ahead of schedule. But we need to keep focus. Everything OK with Beccs now?' Wil raised his eyebrows in hope.

'Yep! All good. Really good.' Replied Phil eagerly.

'Oh, and we've got a dinner date on Friday Wil. With

Ryan and Beccs. Ryan's shout apparently.' said Phil.

'I'll starve myself on Thursday. It'll cost the wanker a fortune.' Wil said between bites.

Wil pulled some pages out of his bag then slid them across the table to Phil.

'Have a read of these PC. And look at the format.' Wil said between swallows.

'Of course, I have these electronically, so feel free to scribble on them.' He added.

Phil looked carefully at each page in turn. Fuck me he thought. Wil could really make a document look professional, really professional. It had a Title Page, Abstract Summary, Table of Contents, List of Figures, Table and Terms, Annotations, Acknowledgements, References, Appendix, Glossary, Index, Christ and it was already about thirty pages.

'Your thoughts PC?' Said Wil as Phil flicked through.

'Well. Firstly, it looks good enough to have been produced by the UN security council. Nice job Wil.' Phil paused.

'Something bothering you PC? Is it the font?' Wil asked a little surprised.

'No, the fonts fine. Palatino if I'm not mistaken?' Said Phil.

'Yeah Palatino. Nothing better for a technical document. If it's something with the format, speak up now PC?'

'No. It's fine, it's well. It's already about thirty pages, you don't think it's getting too wordy? I mean, for a social media type thing, it's way past most people's attention spans these days don't you think?' Phil said, feeling some doubts creeping back in.

'PC, the communist manifesto was 156 pages long and that had people's attention.' Wil said and continued.

'Not in a good way though!' Phil added looking concerned.

'That was published in 1848. Right?' Wil continued unconcerned trying to get to his point.

Phil nodded, having absolutely no idea if that was right and no idea where this was going, but felt like he really needed some of Wil's wisdom.

'Well let's say approximately, and I mean very approximately 5 to 6 generations have passed since 1848, right?' Said Wil. Phil again nodded.

'Assuming, let's say every generation's roughly 30 years. Right?'

Phil nodded again.

'Current thinking suggests that every generation's attention span drops by roughly 10 percent, you know, since radio, TV, smart phones, two-minute cat videos, and what not. Right?' Said Wil. Phil nodded, now totally lost.

'Well. If you do the math on this, a document of about 80 to 100 pages should be just about right for today's lesser attention spans. It's simple mathematics.' Wil finished confidently.

'Right.' Phil said still not sure exactly what he was saying right to but liked the sound of only 80 to 100 pages.

They both finished their lunch, waved and smiled a thanks to the chef, then headed back to their workstations stopping on the way for another beer.

'What are you blokes up to?' Justin looked at them suspiciously.

'Not finally putting pen to paper?' He added.

'No Mate.' Phil said quickly shuffling Wil away, who paused and stopped.

'We should give a copy to Justy. Get the vibe of the average Joe on the street. Plus, it would make his fucking day. And nobody is more average than Justy.' Wil said not joking.

They both stopped and turned around, seeing Justin looking a little hurt.

'Hey Justy? Wanna read something for us? That is if you're not too busy.' Wil said, getting a big laugh from anyone listening including Justin.

Wil handed Justin a copy and asked him to give it back when he was finished. Justin took it tentatively but eagerly.

'Sure guys.' Justin said trying to not appear too excited about being included and having something to do this afternoon, apart from watching people's beer evaporate.

The afternoon moved them through a few more topics. But mostly onto their favourite subject, just to refresh their minds. Get them thinking laterally. Out of the box thinking Wil said. So basically, conspiracy theories. As Wil said, the difference between the truth and a conspiracy theory is only time. And that time is rapidly getting shorter.

Phil was in a buoyant mood because he no longer had to worry about Beccs. He was full of confidence and beer and thought fuck it, I will finish this thing the very best I can, and I will publish it. Whatever the fuck it is. What's the worst thing that could happen?

Day 2 and Wednesday was going better than he could have hoped. They left the pub before 6:30pm with uncharacteristic common sense.

Wil headed home to get a few hours' sleep before work, and Phil went home feeling better than he had for a few days. And feeling oddly optimistic about life. It was a refreshing change.

Day 3

BEEP! CLANG! CLANG! BEEP! CLANG!

'Fuck you, Ryan Gosling!' Phil shouted at his alarms.

Wil, in addition to giving Phil the clock, also gave him pictures of assorted Ryan's to swap in the face. He chose Ryan Gosling this morning. It was a tough call, he nearly went with that smug bastard Ryan Seacrest.

Phil turned off the alarms and launched himself out of bed enthusiastically. He showered, dressed and walked downstairs to start breakfast, flicking the TV on as he passed, then glanced at the dining room table and paused seeing a note on its usually pristinely clear surface. Phil walked over and picked it up.

Dear Phillip,

Sorry I haven't seen you for a while.

'A while! How about fucking never.' He muttered to himself.

Hows bout we catch up 4 a drink on Fris' nite at the Bowlo ☺?
Rite ur answer b low case we don't x paths b4.

Chris xxx ooo ☺☺☺ Luv Ya!'

Who the hell is this crazy person Phil thought not unconcerned. xxx ooo, catch up! Luv Ya! Bowlo, 4 instead of for, and what's the fucking point in b low. And Rite isn't an abbreviation, it's either bad spelling, or the wrong word entirely. Phil always found sms speak incredibly annoying.

Below the note were two boxes with accompanying illustrations. The first one headed 'Yeah!' followed by a beaming smiley face wearing a party hat. The second box headed 'Sooo very, very depressed', alongside a sad face crying profusely holding a gun to its head.

'Christ! I don't want to be responsible for a suicide!' Phil thought aloud.

Why not! He ticked the 'Yeah!' box, then wrote beside it. *At the pub down the road. Not the Bowling Club.* Refusing to encourage abbreviations.

Phil hated the Bowling Club, not just because everyone there would probably fossilize if they stood still long enough. But mostly because everyone was always spouting opinions from books they'd read in the 1970's, written in the 1930's by someone born in the 1890's. Fuck that! The cheap beer was just not worth it.

Hold on. I can't go Friday. I have a birthday dinner. Phil smirked to himself and thought. Would it be fair to push Chris under the Ryan bus? Could be fun, and she didn't even bring any furniture, apart from the mirror, which Phil hadn't positively confirmed yet. He also knew Wil would never forgive him if he didn't invite the enigma. Decision made. Time to return to breakfast.

He finished breakfast and read through Wil's typed notes. Wil was definitely a savant when it came to documentation. He was, without any doubt, completely wasted chasing possums around the mall.

He made a few scribbles in the margins, put the notes back in his bag and picked up his list of topics, underlining today's. Phil's concentration was broken hearing the theme song for Couture Pets. He was determined to ignore it, but then heard the enthusiastic host announce today's challenge was swimwear. Totally irresistible. He sang along with the theme and watched fervently. The show finished in a literal catwalk. Best one Yet! Phil agreed with himself.

He restarted working but stopped, feeling hungry again. Phil walked to the kitchen to check the fridge. The fridge now boasted milk, eggs, sauce, bacon and four types of mustard, but not much else. He decided it was time to make a shopping list.

Phil took the list pad off the fridge and started to list. Since Phil took Beccs' advice and started making lists, he simply couldn't go shopping without one. He was either completely paralyzed by choice or panicked and bought a whole lot of stuff that he should probably just put straight into the bin when he got home. That would at least eliminate the pointless exercise of putting it in the fridge, waiting a few months, then putting it in the bin.

When he was happy with the list, he picked up his old backpack and turned it upside down causing a book to flop to the floor gracelessly. It was the last book he'd been reading before his retrenchment. *The Catcher in the Rye*. Phil thought he should probably finish it one day. The problem he had with it was it was supposed to be so very controversial and profound, but he found it self-indulgent, boring, and none of the characters were terribly likable. He picked it up thinking he must have looked like someone who should be on a watch list. He put the book back on his bookshelf and decided not to finish it later.

Phil put a pen and the list in his pocket, picked up a reusable shopping bag, put it in his backpack, checked that he had his keys and phone, and left for the supermarket on foot.

On foot was pretty much the only way Phil travelled. He hadn't driven a car in more than 20 years and decided early on that driving was simply not for him. He didn't like the environmental impact he would tell himself and anyone else who would ask. Plus, it kept him fit, and what bloody business was it of theirs anyway. Basically, this was just another thing in Phil's life he hadn't quite gotten around to. Phil did enjoy the quiet time he spent lucid dreaming on his walks, and he lived within walking distance of everything he needed anyway.

He strolled in the supermarket and zoomed around the isles efficiently, checking everything off his list systematically. Phil always went through the self-serve checkout so he could steal the garlic and weigh a few items light. Phil wasn't proud of his stealing, but he justified it by saying all the big supermarkets at some time or another had been fined for price fixing, false advertising, operating as a cartel, or some other dishonest practice that indirectly cost him money. If these businesses were people, they'd be doing twenty to life, have a police record as long as your arm, ripped bodies and bad prison tatts. He was just getting some of his own back. Besides, what's the worst thing that could happen.

Phil arrived back home and put the cold stuff in the fridge, and the rest in his completely empty pantry. A new start. He walked into the lounge room and saw the note was still in the centre of the table, but now it was folded into a paper plane.

Does she actually wait until I go out? Phil thought unfolding it to read. It said PTO at the bottom. He PTO'd and read on.

'Dear Phillip,

Fries night at the pub sounds gr8. Look fwd to catchin up with u.'

Again, with the catchin up. Phil immediately regretted answering the note at all.

'Love Chris xxx ooo ☺ ☺ ☺'

'Ps., Just bumped into our neighbour. He seems soooo nice. I invited him on Fries 2. He's very eager to catch up with u Phillip. The more the merrier. ☺ ☺ ☺'.

Byeees again.
xxx ooo ☺ ☺ ☺'Luv Ya!'

He instantly, and angrily, started to write a reply. How dare you! You have to uninvite the fucking neighbour... Phil stopped, took pause for thought and re-read what he'd written. Then remembered the suicidal stick figure, screwed it up and tossed it in the bin.

Phil picked up a fresh piece of paper and wrote a new reply, folded it into a more impressive paper plane, not wanting to be outdone, and put it back on the table.

'Fantastic!

Looking forward to catching up on Friday.

PC (Not Phil or Phillip).'

Why was he saying catching up now? It's contagious. Phil decided to try not to worry about his neighbour, Wil would be there and say what you like about Wil, he was hard. Plus, it was beginning to sound like a memorable evening. He checked the time. 11:51, then remembered he'd agreed to meet Wil an hour earlier today. This time he really might be late.

Phil scurried off as fast as he could, arriving at the pub at 12:02. Went directly to the bar and exchanged money and beer wordlessly with Justin, walked out, sat next to Wil, then apologised for being late. Wil checked his watch. Who wears a watch Phil thought, more evidence he was a time traveller, it was really stacking up now.

'It's 12:03. You're pretty late PC. What happened?' Wil said with no hint of sarcasm. 'Got caught up making a swimsuit for your neighbours' cat?' He sniggered, then accepted Phil's apology while at the same time, insisting they start at least three minutes earlier tomorrow.

Wil's intolerance to lateness was well documented. Phil quickly apologised again before Wil had a chance to run through the numbers highlighting the global impact of tardiness.

Justin followed Phil out and handed the notes back to

Wil. 'Read through them yesterday. Looks good. I've added some of my own ideas for a different perspective. You know, a different tangent.' Justin smiled.

Wil had a quick look and was startled by all the writing in the margins and smiled back.

'Always interested in another opinion Justy.'

Phil smiled at Justin then changed his gaze back to Wil. 'Don't mention my neighbour, my neighbours' cat, or my flat mate.'

'The Enigma! Chris the invisible flat mate. Did you meet her? Was it a her or just a bloke that sounded like a girl?' Wil asked.

'No, and Yes. I'm pretty sure it's a girl. But we're going to meet both of them on Friday... Fuck!' Muttered Phil.

'What's up mate. Awesome! Finally meet her and your neighbour. Sounds like a top night.' Wil rubbed his hands together with unconscious enthusiasm. 'Might even get your mind off Beccs.' He let slip.

Fortunately for Wil, Phil wasn't listening. The reality of what he had been mentally ignoring since this morning was beginning to sink in. He would have to see Ryan again. But worst of all, he would have to meet his psychopathic, note writing neighbour.

Wil knew that look on Phil's face. He knew Phil needed reassurance.

'Relax PC. It'll be fun. Ryan's just an annoying little prick. And I don't give a fuck about you're pathetic, slip it under the door neighbour. I'll be there. It'll be fun.' Beamed Wil, confidently with two thumbs up.

Phil smiled and did feel better.

'Anyway, to more pressing matters. Did you see that guy trying to put the wetsuit on that poor fucking cat? That's award-winning TV.' Phil insisted.

'Yes. Did you see how many band-aids he had on when they came back from the break?' Wil laughed loudly.

They both discussed the finer details, and more technical aspects of pet fashion, and agreed this episode was even better than the lingerie one. When everything that could be said was, Wil changed the subject.

'So how did all this Friday night thing happen?'

Phil ran through the whole story in painful detail. All Wil had to say was. 'Cheeky. Can't wait to meet her.'

'Time to press on PC.' Phil finished his first beer, got up, walked to the bar for two more, then returned to their tables and took his seat. They both got out their notes.

'Books.'

'Books. They are why civilization has progressed to where it is today! They are the foundation stones. The very building blocks of all learning, knowledge and wisdom. They are time capsules of truth at their own particular point in history. They are important at all levels of society. That's why there are libraries in every city, every school, college, university. Just fucking everywhere.' Phil said passionately.

He was a big fan of books. Not only did he like reading them, he also liked collecting them. Phil currently thought he had around three thousand.

'I know everything is electronic today, and I don't want to sound like a luddite, but books can't be changed. Well not retrospectively anyway. They can't be rewritten on our bookshelves. They are a static pillar of an ever changing and ever manipulated past. It's vital and cannot. No, must not be corrupted.' Phil slammed his hand hard on the table and regretted it immediately. Their beers pirouetted precariously causing Wil to rush to steady the ship.

'It's not like it hasn't been done before.' Phil continued completely ignoring the narrowly avoided catastrophe.

'Has everyone forgotten the destruction of books by China's Qin Dynasty in 200 BCE, the destruction of the House of Wisdom during the Mongol siege of Baghdad in 1258, the destruction of the Aztec codices by Itzcoatl in 1430.' Phil paused, thinking. Of course everyone had forgotten them, then referred back to his notes to cite more recent examples.

'Let's not forget the 1940's obsession with book

burning. The Nazis, Fascist regimes, Communist regimes…They differed politically but all had that in common.' Phil paused again.

'This might sound like a history lesson. But unfortunately, it's not. Right now, we have the Chinese Communist Party censoring anything that doesn't reflect positively on their failed political system. North Korea of course, are taking it to the next level. Although at least with North Korea people don't applaud them, unlike the WTF's Klaus Dauber and his billionaire sociopathic benefactors, and the mainstream media who practically slaver at the amount of control the CCP has over their citizens and are now championing global governments to legislate similar censorship controls under the guise of misinformation, disinformation and public safety.' Phil looked disgusted.

'Why does the world do business with this regime. Have we all got collective amnesia and forgotten the Tiananmen Square massacre. For fuck's sake, less than 20 years later they hosted the Summer Olympics. And the Winter Olympics, not long after that.'

'I think they're getting them again soon too.' Wil added.

'How many atrocities do they think they can get away with? Why does the media even cover these events when free press will be any communist regime's first target.' Phil stopped knowing he'd gone off topic.

'Books!' He announced again. 'The reason they need to be protected is to protect freedom and truth. By definition, if someone is trying to censor, restrict or destroy a book, it's because it contains some inconvenient truth or inconvenient opinion. Why else would you censor something if it was a lie, when it could easily be discredited by the truth.' Phil stopped short of thumping the table and testing Wil's reflexes again.

'With everything going electronic, all they have to do now is a bit of typing, some search and replace, and the damage is done! Or better yet, simply remove its availability and redirect your search to their new truth. Complete and thorough censorship. It's especially easy when most of our social media and search engines are controlled by a few elite WTF bastards, who have cornered the market. Books can't easily be changed. Sure, they can be changed and reissued, but the original will always exist.' Phil ran out of steam, looked at Wil, nodded to confirm he was finished with that one then pressed straight on with the next topic.

'Celebrities.'

'What the fuck is that all about. I don't mind them showing off how nice their clothes are. What I do give a fuck about is that they actually believe they're experts on everything. They even get asked to speak at the U.N. for Christs sake. WHY!' Phil threw his hands in the air to Wil's relief.

'It just shows how busy they are at the U.N. And all they have done to earn their so-called Celebrity status, in the most part is showing their ripped bodies, their tits, umm, or have been on a reality show which permits them to do both simultaneously.' Phil continued.

'On the same day Kim Kardashian started her reality TV show KU-WTF or whatever the fuck that pointless shite's called.' Phil leaned forward and continued.

'In southern Afghanistan a woman stopped her bat shit crazy son from a suicide bombing. She triggered the bomb in the family's home, killing herself and four brothers and sisters. Including the crazy prick with the bomb.' Phil downed his beer looking really head-up and swallowed.

'I remember the news that day. There was a 10 second bulletin on this courageous woman, and a 10-minute forum style discussion panel on the Kardashians. You know the ones. The ones where they split the screen in four and fill each panel with the dumbest politicians, pundits, and social commentators they can find, who obviously have nothing better to do. Then they all gush about how inspirational, stunning and brave, and what good fucking role models they are. Talk about bread and circuses!' Phil looked confused.

Wil looked relieved the tirade was over. The problem was, it wasn't.

'Do you know how many celebrities have been UN goodwill ambassadors?' Phil asked.

Wil shrugged but looked curious.

Phil looked through his notes frantically without success.

'Neither do I. But it's too many, that's for sure. From memory, Nicole Kidman, Angelina Jollie, Jackie Chan, Orlando Bloom and David Beckham for fuck's sake, just to name a few. How do they have time to listen to these wankers, and what could they possibly have to say of any value? It just proves what a fucking joke the U.N. really is.'

Wil raised his eyebrows at Phil unsure if he was finished this time. He still wasn't.

'What could these vacuous fucks possibly know that world leaders don't. They are all spoilt, out of touch, uneducated in the most part, morons, and should stick to play acting and leave the serious jobs to people with more knowledge, education and experience. You know, just about anyone else.' Finished Phil.

Wil stood up at the pause.

'Another beer PC?' He said, hoping to change the topic knowing Phil could spend the entire afternoon hatcheting celebrities.

Phil ignored the question. 'And God help us if one of them dies. Suddenly any wife beating, and rape charges are all forgotten or forgiven. And we're supposed to all feel sad. Such a great fucking loss.' Phil said sarcastically. 'I don't know these people. I don't give a shit!'

Wil was shaking his empty glass at Phil now.

'Yes mate.' Phil said, finally taking the hint.

Wil arrived back with the beers. They both decided to take a break.

'Did you see the guy with the blue hair parading his cat in the one piece? They won't be on speaking terms for a while.' Wil laughed returning the conversation back to couture pets.

'The real victim here is the cat. And it wasn't even a flattering swimsuit.' Phil added.

They both discussed the undeniably dangerous game they were playing with evolution. And it's almost certain endgame. Planet of the Cats.

Phil checked the time. 'One more before lunch?'

'Definitely.' Wil said, picking up his notes.

'The Pope.'

Phil spat. 'The Pope. And I don't just mean the current pope, I mean all those gold leaf, dress wearing paedophile apologists. And we're only focusing on that particular sin at the moment, don't get me started on their many and varied past crimes.' No one was.

'How committed is this prick. If he really believed. And I mean really, really, believed in the whole thing. Heaven, Hell and all that. Why would he drive around in a bullet proof budgie cage? It shows a certain, dare I say, lack of faith.' Phil laughed at his own joke.

'The bastard also demands money, abstinence, dietary restrictions, hair styles for women, and other intrusions on our personal lives. While at the same time raking in the cash and turning a blind eye to all the sins his organisation racks up.' Phil skolled his beer.

'Does anyone really, truly believe that the entire universe is created, owned and run by a family from five square kilometres in the middle east, then administered by an old man in the Vatican. What is his real title anyway. CEO?' Phil scoffed.

'If someone walked up to you in the street, as one adult talking to another, and read the bible too you, and insisted it was all real.'

'You'd be standing there for a bloody long time.' Wil interrupted.

Phil ignored this and continued. 'Then he showed you a picture of the Pope in all his weird faux drag outfits, and said he was in charge. And he spoke directly to God. You'd laugh your ass off. That is until you realised, he was being completely serious, then you'd back away not making eye contact.' Phil paused and ironically looked skyward for help.

'Let's not even talk about their disgusting paedophile problem. Which no one seems to know how to address. Well, I do. Make churches and all church groups restricted premises. Stop letting minors in. Parents should be responsible for any religious education. That would definitely help.' Phil stopped, looking tired and disgusted.

'That'll do on that one.' Phil said showing incredible restraint as he hated religion, not personal beliefs which he had respect for, but organised religion. And he saw the Pope as a doddery harmful creep.

'The opiate of the masses.' Phil said in conclusion.

'Religion is the Opium of the people,' Wil added correcting the quote.

They finished their beers and walked to the bistro, stopping at the bar at Wil's urging, ordered the usual and when it arrived started eating. Wil took out a folder from his satchel and handed it over containing the latest document update, then unfolded a piece of paper from his top pocket and handed it to Phil.

'PC. I've reviewed the document and mapped out Day 3, and Day 4. I should have shown you this before we started today. But I was put off by you being so late.' Wil said. Phil picked it up and read the following:

Day 3 - Thursday

- Acknowledge the time left – 2 days.
- Press on until the second third is complete.

Day 4 - Friday

- Acknowledge the time left – 1 day.
- Finish.
- Review final draft.
- Publish.

Phil flicked through the update incredibly impressed.

'What do you think?' Wil looked at Phil hopefully.

'Nice. We've come this far, may as well press on.' Phil said half-heartedly.

'PC. Mate, a little more positivity please! You've been banging on about this for years. Now you might actually finish. This is getting exciting. How impressed will Beccs be? But let's not get ahead of ourselves.' Wil said trying to reign in Phil's non-existent enthusiasm.

Phil immediately picked up on how much effort Wil had put in. It wasn't just about him anymore, or Beccs.

'Just lost focus for a moment. We're going to finish.' Phil said confidently and rhetorically.

'And publish.' Wil added.

The thought of that caused Phil's heart to skip a beat. He still wasn't quite ready for that reality.

They finished eating, with Wil lapping Phil as usual, then strode back to their tables with renewed vigour.

The Second Third

They arrived back at their tables and noticed they were uncharacteristically clean and had fresh new coasters.

'It's not Friday? Justy normally only cleans on Fridays, doesn't he?' Enquired Wil without any hint of derision.

'Thought so. Wasn't he missing last Friday? Probably just catching up.' Phil replied unconcerned.

Justin was a master practitioner of the art of minimalist customer service. Phil thought, no doubt there's a woke university somewhere offering a doctorate in that very business principle.

'We're scheduled to finish the second third PC.' Wil said in his best business tone.

Phil glanced through the list of remaining topics hastily, selected one, and announced.

'Daylight Saving Time.'

He leant forward and started speaking with after lunch exuberance, forcing Wil to lunge for his notepad, this knocked his pen to the floor which rolled between their tables. They both bent down to pick it up at the same time, bumping their heads together hard, making a disturbingly hollow thud. They looked around hoping nobody noticed. Nobody did, then sat back rubbing their heads. When they'd recovered, Wil nodded to continue.

'Daylight Saving Time, DST. I guess if it has a TLA it sounds credible. Well, it's not credible. It's just another dumb idea that's been normalised. Just another one of those things we accept without question, or worse. If we do question it are mocked into silence. It will one day, eventually, inevitably come back and bite us on the ass.' Phil flicked through his notes.

'What's a TLA.' Wil said interrupting.

'A three-letter acronym.'

'Shouldn't it be a TLI. A three-letter initialism? An acronym forms a word from the first letters of a descriptive name.' Wil said knowledgably.

'Quite right Wil.' Phil replied impressed.

'Anyway, the idea was originally thought up as a joke by Benjamin Franklin in 1704. Where he proposed in a satirical letter stating that it would save on candle wax. Well, this joke has gone on long enough!' Phil declared, referring to his notes.

'It was first implemented in 1908 by Canada for some reason. Probably something to do with hockey I suspect.' Phil said only half joking.

'And it was then adopted by Germany during the first world war to save energy. Does this sound like something we should still be doing over a hundred years later? The environmental and financial impact alone should convince people it's a bad idea'. Phil referred back to his notes again.

'Why get people out of bed in the summer early when they've only just gone to sleep because it's finally fucking cooled down. Then, we keep everyone up an extra hour at night when you just might be able to get some sleep. It's completely ludicrous.' Phil downed his beer and continued.

'Plus. You know at some point, a dam, a nuclear reactor or something really fucking important will fail to turn on, or off at the right time. Most likely because the work experience kid, who was left in charge over the holidays will forget to click the apply Daylight Saving Time checkbox, or probably just fall asleep. In summary, fuck Daylight Saving Time.' Phil put a full stop on that topic and looked satisfied.

'Don't forget it also takes you a week to adjust to the

new time at the beginning, and at the end. Plus, heart attacks significantly increase as well.' Added Wil shaking his head with dismay.

'Quite right. It's a drain on productivity and a detriment to personal health. Did you know heart attacks increase at the start and end of DST as well. Add it to the notes Wil.'

Phil was impressed with Wil's input and his motivation throughout the entire project and felt he should be credited accordingly.

'So, are you going to put your name, or alias as the case maybe to this thing Wil? You've done most of the work anyway. Shorthand, documentation, influence...'

'I'm only a conduit Phil.' Wil said in a philosophical tone.

'I beg to differ. At the very least I'd describe you as a muse.' Phil said smirking.

'I don't want to be a muse. How about "Creative Influence."' Offered Wil in air quotes.

'Creative Influence.' Phil repeated, concerned. 'Influence makes you sound like one of those vacuous do nothings that recommend fake tans and take pictures of their lunch. How about "*Creative Director?*"'.

'Creative Director.' Mused Wil. 'Ok. I'll add it to the Front Matter.'

Phil wondered what Front Matter was, and then decided not to ask, and just leave those sorts of details to his Creative Director.

Apart from Phil and Beccs, nobody ever really included Wil in anything. For some reason everyone seemed to simply not notice him.

When they sold raffle tickets, nobody ever asked Wil. When they ran a tipping competition, nobody asked Wil. He was even locked in the pub once because nobody noticed he was still there. Wil really did blend seamlessly into the background.

Phil walked to the bar to get another round.

'Right-e-oh. Hydration sorted, let's keep at it.' He said upon his return.

'Redacting.'

'A definition for this one might be in order PC?' Wil said stopping Phil before he got started.

'Redacting is the censoring, or obscuring of part, or all of a document for legal or security purposes.' Phil paused unnecessarily waiting for Wil.

'It sounds kind of Ok, right? However, it can so easily be manipulated. Who defines what is a legal, and what is a security purpose? Currently almost all redacting, or at least all the stuff we really want to know about, is enacted by Corporations dealing with Government contracts. Or Government Departments themselves, directed by politicians with a vested interest in keeping the secret.

How is this acceptable? The very concept of keeping something a secret from the people who pay for a government that is meant to represent them is abominable!' Phil paused to think of an appropriate example of corrupt redaction, checked his notes and picked one of the too many examples he had available to choose from. It was also the most ridiculous.

'One of the worst examples, or at least the most blatant example of self-interested redaction was the UK parliamentary expense claims fiasco of 2009. Initially the MP's won the right to redact information which they, and their corrupt parliamentary buddies all agreed was a security risk. Well, a security risk to all their fucking gravy trains.' They both laughed, then tempered their laughter remembering, it wasn't really a laughing matter.

'It was only because someone in the process of redacting the documents, slipped some of the more extravagant and comical expenses to the media. Only then did the truth come out.' Phil said smiling. 'I bet it was a temp. Those smug bastards always fuckup on the small details.' Phil smirked.

'If it wasn't for that public minded person, nobody would know that their elected officials were spending their money claiming back mortgage payments, rent, gardeners, you name it they claimed it.' Phil hesitated, flicking through his notes.

'The most Pythonesque of these claims was made by Conservative MP Peter Viggers who claimed £1,645 to build a 5ft duck house. What cost the money was because it was made as an exact scale replica of Skogaholm Manor in Sweden.' Phil said holding his hands out in horror.

'Seriously. Check out the list of claims. It would be hilarious if it wasn't everybody else's money they were spending. Even the UK's former Prime Minister Gordon Brown was involved, and they didn't even sack him, let alone charge him with theft. I think he was shamed into paying it back. Which apparently makes it all OK.' Phil threw his hands up in horror again.

'Apparently that privilege is only extended to those in power. Does nobody give a fuck anymore, or do we just not have any other choice.' Phil leant back on his chair to further consider the problem. Made some notes to add to his comments on politics and pressed on.

'Redaction! Is a political and corporate get out of gaol free card. No, a get away with anything card, that's always up their sleeves. The entire concept should not exist. Underline that.' Phil pointed at Wil.

'We're paying for these bastards. We have the right to know what exactly they are spending our money on. Every cent! Underline our as well Wil.' Phil finished and then started again.

'And what is the deal with redacting, or withholding information for 20, 50 and in some cases 75 years. Or handing over documents almost completely blacked out, apparently for our own safety. Well, that's what the pharmaceutical companies tried to do with their Covid vaccine data. Why do the Government not only allow but support such practices. Mmm, I wonder?' Phil said sarcastically.

'The entire concept must be abolished. We pay for everything. We have the right to know everything!' Phil finished succinctly.

He looked pleased with that one, checked Wil had finished his note taking and his underlining, then moved straight on.

'Negative Numbers.'

'Negative Numbers?' repeated Wil.
'What's wrong with negative numbers. Sounds more like a hypothesis, or maybe even a conspiracy theory rather than an aphorism.' Said Wil, adding his creative director's influence.
'I agree Wil. However, I believe everyone knows there is something fundamentally wrong with mathematics. And I believe this is one of those meta problems and therefore, worthy of consideration.' Phil argued.
'Besides. If it doesn't fit in, we'll piss it off later. Wil still didn't look convinced but nodded for Phil to continue.
'They just don't make any sense at all, and I'm sure it's why the financial system doesn't make sense as well, and probably why we can't figure out some fundamental laws of the universe.'
He picked up one of the fresh coasters and created the following:

Definition: Multiplication is a concept, or symbol used to describe a series of additions. The repeated addition of groups of equal sizes.

Example:

-2 + -2	= -4	=	(-1,-1) + (-1,-1)	= -4
-2 x -2	= 4	≠	(-1,-1) + (-1,-1)	= -4

Phil slid the coaster across to Wil who looked at it with curiosity.
'That doesn't make sense.' He said scratching his head, then stopped scratching as it was still a bit sore.
'Exactly. But we are supposed to believe that's how negative numbers work when you throw multiplication into the mix. Bullshit I say.' Phil proclaimed, stopping his

hand from slapping the table again just in time.

'Do you know why?' Phil said rhetorically looking at his notes.

'It all comes down to an Indian mathematician named Brahmagupta who in around 600 AD wrote the following axioms.' Phil handed a piece of paper to Wil with the problematic axiom underlined:

A debt minus zero is a debt.
A fortune minus zero is a fortune.
Zero minus zero is a zero.
A debt subtracted from zero is a fortune.
A fortune subtracted from zero is a debt.
The product of zero multiplied by a debt or fortune is zero.
The product of zero multiplied by zero is zero.
The product or quotient of two fortunes is one fortune.
The product or quotient of two debts is one fortune.
The product or quotient of a debt and a fortune is a debt.
The product or quotient of a fortune and a debt is a debt.

'What's this?' Wil said copying it down then handed it back to Phil.

'It's the reason I failed Math.' They both laughed.

'No really. How can a series of additions not get the same result as multiplication? The definition of multiplication is a series of additions isn't it. And don't ever use negative numbers in geometry or algebra. You'll be completely fucked!

If multiplying two negatives together created a positive, couldn't we multiply our credit card debts into a fortune. It can't be right.' Finished Phil.

Phil all these years later, still harbored a serious grudge against his high school math teachers.

'And why do we still teach right to left mathematics,

when we should be doing it left to right.' Phil at this point realised he had gone completely off topic. 'Maybe your right Wil we should leave that one out.'

Wil nodded. 'Good idea. Some wanker with a doctorate in mathematics will just write a 4-page incomprehensible equation pointing out to an accuracy of 9 decimal places why you're an idiot.'

Wil kept the notes regardless. Read through the first part again and thought, does that mean 1 multiplied by 1 is really 2? The square root of minus 1 is zero, he thought with existential concern, then remembered Mathematics was definitely not one of Phil's strong points and stopped being concerned.

They both eased back in their chairs in a contemplative mood.

'Beep, Beep!' Phil's phone pinged an SMS. He picked it up, fiddled with it for a bit, then read the message.

'Groovy. Beccs is coming back early. Thursday now.' Phil said looking pleased.

'Why have dinner on Friday then?' Wil Said.

'I imagine she has to recover from the last few days with Ryan. Christ it'd take me a month.'

Wil stood up, made the signal for another beer and walked off.

'Same again Wil?' Justin asked unnecessarily.

'Yes mate. Oh, and a packet of plain chips too please.' Wil pointed at the chips unnecessarily as Justin knew Wil only ever ate plain chips. Anything else simply ruined the potato flavour he insisted.

'How's the Great Manifesto, or whatever you call it, progressing? Need any help?' Asked Justin.

'Well Justy. Thanks for the offer, but we're right on track. Don't need any help with the project, or the chips thanks.' Wil winked at Justin.

'Right on track for what?'

'Right on track to publish.' Wil said gathering up his chips protectively.

'You're going to show it to actual people! I don't see anything good coming from that. You'll probably be chased out of town by an angry mob, complete with flaming torches, laughed out of town, or assassinated.' Justin said looking genuinely worried.

Wil smiled at Justy walking away thinking. No one's going to read it.

Phil took his beer off Wil, said cheers and took a sip.

'Well, it's getting on for four. One more and we're done for the day. Right on schedule.' Wil said checking his notes and looking at Phil's mostly crossed off list.

'Cash.'

'Cash is an essential part of any democratic economy. It allows people the freedom to save money without the risk of financial institution entanglement. It means you can perform personal transactions without encumbering fees. Currently, if you buy almost anything with an electronic transaction the bank will put their hand in your pocket and take a minimum of 1 percent, sometimes up to 10. And that's for using our own money for the love of God.' Phil paused to look disgusted.

'Without cash we are at the mercy of financial institutions, and we all know how reputable they are. And let's not forget authoritarian Governments who now seem to think they have the power to freeze people's bank accounts if they don't do what they are told. I'm looking at you Canada, and you too UK!' Phil said with raised eyebrows.

'Let's not also forget that it's confidential. Why should a bank or Government know everything we purchase. Oh, and let's not forget all the incidental uses like pocket money, boot sales, homeless people, the list goes on and on. And why is no one cracking down on shops that refuse cash. It's legal fucking tender. By definition, they shouldn't be allowed to refuse it.' Phil paused looking tired.

'That'll do for today I reckon'. He said stretching.

'Same time tomorrow PC?' Asked Wil cracking his knuckles.

'Yep 12:00. Get another early start. Why not?'

'11:57 PC, and how about we meet at your place? You know work from home? Reduced travel time, help the environment, increase productivity and all that.' Wil said.

'Excellent idea. Do you want me to let Justy know? He can come around for lunch. You two can share a bowl of chips.' Phil said deadpan.

Phil knew Wil and Justin's relationship was OK, but still a little strained since the now infamous chips and fire escape incident.

The incident took place a few years ago now, but not long enough to be forgotten by Justin. Phil had just achieved one of his greatest accomplishments. Finally getting retrenched by his know nothing non-technical manager. With no small effort on his part either. Phil and Wil were in high spirits.

Wil knew how hard Phil had worked at this. He ordered a plate of chips to help him celebrate. A really big plate of chips.

'It's who you know.' He said, pleased with the serving.

Chips were one of Wil's major weaknesses. All types, hot, cold, standard cut, waffle cut, curly, shoestring. He ordered chips with everything. He'd order them with dessert if it was culturally acceptable.

The huge plate of chips had three condiments. Wil thought Phil had earned it. He'd worked hard for this retrenchment and Wil had travelled vicariously along on his journey. That's when *The Incident* happened.

Justy strolled in, congratulated Phil, nodded a greeting to Wil then helped himself to a handful of chips. A big handful!

Sure, Justy had known Wil for years. But everyone knew it was not polite to help yourself. But absolutely everyone knew that to help yourself to Wil's chips was basically a cry for help.

That's when Phil, who had heard a lot of Wil's *back in the day* stories about his time as doorman at some pretty rough pubs, saw firsthand what he was capable of.

Before Justin could even start chewing, and even before

Wil knew it himself, Justin was spun around, arms behind his back, caught ungainly in a proper full nelson and given the bums-rush face first through the fire escape. It all happened so fast Phil could only watch as the fire doors closed automatically putting an abrupt end to the scene.

'Fuck me Wil. That'll teach him to take liberties with your chips.' Is all Phil could manage to say.

Wil had a look of, what the fuck just happened on his face?

'Better come with me PC. See if he's Ok.' Wil said warily.

They both opened the doors nervously and saw Justin standing, looking a little shocked and dazed.

'You OK Justy? Mate?' Wil said walking over to steady him.

'Yeah. I only wanted a few Chips Wil?' Justin muttered, looking confused, and a bit unsure of what had happened himself.

'Don't make this my problem.' Wil said remembering his conflict training.

'You touched. No! You stole my Chips. I could sue you know. Or call the police?' They both laughed and left it at that, well that's what Justin thought anyway. Wil from that point on always kept an eye out for Justin whenever he had any chips.

Working From Home

BEEP! BEEP! BEEP! 'Fuck you … ' Phil paused, feeling something wasn't quite right, picked up his phone, dismissed the alarm then picked up the alarm clock, wound it, reset it, and waited patiently.

CLANG! CLANG! CLANG! '… Ryan Seacrest!' He shouted for completion. Phil changed the clock face yesterday.

He woke up in a good mood today. His issues with Beccs were well and truly behind him, Wil was happy and motivated, which meant Phil was happy and motivated, and his neighbour could go fuck himself, because Wil and Beccs would be there on Friday night. Plus, it was only Thursday morning! He could see some well-earned procrastination loitering on the horizon.

Phil strode to the bathroom, showered, dressed, and went downstairs to get some breakfast. Walked into the kitchen and stared at the inviting pile of washing up. The inviting pile of washing up stared back at him seductively. Phil smiled to himself. This time he had an excuse to do the dishes.

He finished the washing up, made and ate breakfast in his new efficient approach, then did another mini washup for the sheer pleasure of it.

It wasn't very often Wil came over. Mostly only for birthday celebrations, which were now held at Phil's house since it had been cleaned to Beccs birthday standards. He also came over on Labor Day, because it was a day off and no one really knew what the fuck that was for anyway, they thought it best to celebrate it before someone worked that out and cancelled it. And of course, whenever Phil really needed him.

Phil decided today's culinary delight would be his Italian Thai Chicken fusion, in seven easy steps. The recipe is as follows:

Step 1. - Fry thinly sliced Chicken breast fillet in hot butter until browned. Set aside.

Step 2. - Crush five cloves of Garlic and a few large sliced chilies into a hot frying pan. Melt in a fuck load of butter.

Phil was absolutely convinced Gordon Ramsey had a measuring cup with "Fuck Load" engraved on the back.

Step 3. - Add sundried tomatoes, sprinkle in Thyme and Oregano to taste.

Step 4. - Return the Chicken to the pan and increase the heat. Stir continuously until ready to serve. Take off the heat.

Step 5. - Microwave yesterday's left-over rice from the Thai takeaway and serve in liberal amounts.

Step 6. - Pour the chicken and garlic sauce over the rice.

Step 7. – Serve and savour.

Wil would be impressed, and not just because he was going to make heaps, but because it was going to be good. This was one of the only recipes Phil had truly perfected.

He fussed around the house, then decided to look at what was left on the list. There still seemed a lot, but he had confidence he was going to get it done. Why not.

What harm could it do anyway, and it would impress the people that mattered. Also, at this point he'd put too much work in to not finish.

The television flickered into life and presented Phil with the morning news. Phil had a love hate relationship with what the mainstream media laughably called news. He hated that the talking heads pretending to be journalists editorialised every story. Why do we give a fuck what they think. But he loved watching the acute bi-polar suffering sycophantic presenters switching gears.

Phil was also enjoying a rare feeling of calmness. Everything in his life was under relative control. He felt so serene he even applied for a few jobs. What a week! He picked up his shopping list, checked he had all the necessary ingredients, then added snacks in large letters and underlined it twice. A large variety was essential for bric-a-snacks. Wil liked to browse.

Phil will never forget the time Wil came over and he didn't have snacks. Needless to say, it involved a long walk to the service station and in the fucking rain too. Wil couldn't function when he was hungry, and Phil needed Wil functioning today.

Time to do the shopping. He flicked the telly off with the remote, then remembered he still hadn't replaced the batteries and walked over to turn it off, old school. "Old School!", where the fuck did that come from! Phil shook his head with disgust.

He checked his pockets, put on his old backpack and slammed the door shut, then scoped around nervously for his neighbour. All clear. He power-walked to the shops with a strange feeling this might be the last time he'd do this, or at least the last time it would be the same. Just a weird feeling. Normally he missed these moments. You know, the last time you see a friend, or the last time you go to a job. Normally he just didn't notice. Phil felt like this time, he wasn't missing it.

The time was 9:30 when he arrived back home. Not bad! Plenty of time to make lunch and a nice spread.

Phil turned on the telly and watched the last episode of

Couture Pets and was left feeling flat. Casual wear! Really, everything Cats wear looked casual. Phil turned off the telly and started to make the snacks while at the same time wondering what the reality television geniuses would come up with next week. Mental health counselling for pets? They've probably already done that he thought.

Snacks required precision. Wil loved his canapes. They were prepared with great care and put in his near empty refrigerator looking enticing and vulnerable.

Time for the lunch prep. Wil would be starved by the time he walked up the hill. He always said it took longer and required more effort to get somewhere than it did to return. Wil hypothesized a theory on the subject. Phil presumed it was merely a personal observation and didn't show much interest. That was until they went on a road trip together. Wil of course drove. They were both shocked to discover it took half an hour less on the return journey, even though the odometer showed it was 5km further, and the average speed both ways was the same. Weird! They documented the phenomena and filed it for further investigation.

He checked the time again, 10:18! Peaked too soon. Phil felt like he'd procrastinated long enough for one morning and decided to review the list and make some notes. The time moved around to 11:30. Time to start lunch. He brought out the Canapes and arranged them on the tea table. Phil hated coffee and everything associated with it. It was definitely, a Tea table, not a Coffee table.

It was now about 5 to 12. He had a final nervous fuss around and glanced at himself in the still slightly mysterious mirror. Phil plugged in his retro record player, then put on some vinyl. Business casual vibe complete. Phil knew he didn't need to go to any trouble, but he also knew at the same time, Wil would appreciate it. Plus, it would set the tone. The tiniest knock was heard on the front door.

'Whooo isss iiiit?' Phil said in a high-pitched piss poor impression of a Greek dowager he thought was a bit funny. It wasn't. But it was a bit racist.

136

'It's your neighbour. Turn that music down or I'll rip your fucking ears off.' Came a gruff scary reply.

Phil was momentarily rattled, then re-checked the time. 11:56. He was certain it was Wil, but slid off the lounge and duck walked cautiously to the front door, raised himself up slowly, and peered through the spy hole.

'I knew it was you.' Phil said seeing Wil's face looking back at him and opened the door relieved none the less.

He escorted Wil to the lounge room and gestured towards the Canapes.

'Don't be shy.' Phil said unnecessarily as Wil was already contemplating his second.

He walked back to the kitchen to finish lunch closely followed by Wil.

'Nice spread PC. What's for lunch?' Wil asked sniffing the air.

'Italian Thai fusion.' Answered Phil.

'One of your classics. Can't wait. I'm starved after walking up that hill.' Wil said, then turned around in a rush. 'Nearly forgot the beer. If your neighbours pinched even one.' Wil said, looking serious. 'of the beers, you won't need to worry about him on Friday night.' He said knowing Phil was still a bit nervous.

'Plenty of room in the fridge PC.' Wil said returning with the carton to distribute the beer.

'It looks like you've been robbed.' He said, staring into the cavernous interior. 'At least they had the decency to leave the essentials.' Wil remarked, noticing the sauces and mustards.

'Yes mate. Thieves today have no sense of real value.' Phil said shaking his head in mock dismay.

'Love the music.' Wil said air drumming to one of the best air drumming tracks ever created. Kiss Dynasty, Track 1.

Phil finished step 4 and got the plates out ready. Plates with handles and lips. Phil also posited a theory which surmised that plate manufacturers were conspiring to make everybody fat. He couldn't figure out why, but he had the proof. Phil had dinnerware given to him by his grandmother dating back to the 1950's, then compared them with today's and discovered a 1950's dinner plate was smaller than a present-day dessert plate. At this exponential rate of increase, he calculated in about 30 years' time a dinner plate would be roughly the same size as a toilet seat. He also presupposed that if you wanted to lose weight, you should buy antique kitchen ware.

He put in the rice, added the Chicken and sauce, then carried out lunch.

'Just in time PC. I was feeling a bit faint.' Wil said, taking his eagerly.

'That hill is definitely getting steeper.' He commented between bites. 'We need to buy an altimeter.' Wil paused for another huge mouthful. 'I'm sure of it.' He said looking at Phil seriously.

Phil nodded agreement, as he was also finding the hill steeper as the years went by. Strange. But then Wil also thought his suits were shrinking. Phil tried to keep up with Wil but decided he didn't stand a chance and settled into his own pace.

'Sorted out the last topics for today PC?'

Phil handed him the list with the remaining topics left uncrossed.

'Piss easy. Be finished by five I reckon. Beer mate? It won't drink itself.' Wil said already finished, already walking to the fridge.

'Does the pope shit in the woods?'. Phil replied, knowing Wil would like the mixed metaphor.

When Phil finished eating, they cracked their beers and took a sip. Wil raised his notebook and eyebrows eagerly, then nodded for Phil to continue.

'Superannuation.'

Phil said too loudly, then remembered it didn't matter. He was home, and Wil would answer the door if his neighbour's screws got any looser.

'Superannuation.' He repeated even louder. 'Was made compulsory for employees in 1992. It was specifically designed to save the government money on old age pensions. Well guess what? It's hardly made any difference at all. And it's been around for over 30 years. If it was going to make any difference, it would have done so by now.' Phil paused for a canape.

'All it seems to achieve is to cost the Government a fortune in lost tax revenue, not only that, but it also reduces the amount of real money going around in the economy. Guess who has to make up for that lost tax revenue? We do.' Phil said, answering his own question.

'With increased fucking taxes?' He slammed his hand on his very sturdy tea table confidently to emphasize the point.

'It's almost like a reverse pyramid scheme. No! It is a bloody reverse pyramid scheme. Except it's not just the gullible or stupid that get involved. Everyone is forced to participate.' He thumped his hand hard on the tea table, then decided not to do that again as his hand was really stinging now.

'The only people who benefit from this failed concept are the financial institutions. And why is it compulsory. Why do we have to give our hard-earned money to a financial institution for forty or fifty years for them to do whatever the fuck they want with it, and at the end of the day if they lose our money, we suffer, not the banks, they just get a, *Bad luck. Better luck next time*. They don't subsidise our losses from their obscenely large profits to make up for their incompetence.' Phil threw his arms out looking genuinely distressed. He knew how much money he had sitting precariously in his super.

'It's my money. Most of the time my mortgage interest rate is higher than my superannuation rate of return. It's a complete failure.' Phil paused to gather his thoughts.

'If I could get my super now, or whenever I choose, I'd be much better off. It's my money after all. I should be able to do whatever I want with it. How dare they quarantine it. I earned it. They have even put the retirement age up recently and are planning on it eventually being capped at 70. Well, that's what they say now. Who knows what age in the future they will decide on. How is that fair. If the system was as good as they keep trying to tell us it is, then it wouldn't need to be made compulsory. Everybody would be clambering to get on board.' They both paused to take a big swig of their beers.

'How many times have superannuation funds been fined for doing something sneaky like adding a compulsory and illegal life insurance component. Or something else you didn't ask for that erodes your balance or charge higher fees than permitted. I remember getting a credit in my super when they got caught and were begrudgingly forced to pay it back. But not with accrued interest of course. And of course, no one was jailed... And how can they charge fees when your balance is going down. Fucking outrageous! You wouldn't pay a plumber who couldn't unblock your toilet? Or made the problem worse!' Phil raised his hands again in frustration.

'How many royal commissions into these thieving immoral miscreants will it take before they stop forcing us to invest our hard earned in an industry everyone knows, if you take your eyes off, for even a moment, will rifle through your pockets. They'd steal your gold teeth if they could get away with it.' They both finished their beers and crushed the cans.

'And do you really trust the Government to even give it to you at the end of the day. I imagine they are already planning some imagined crisis which will regrettably require part of our superannuation to fix it.' Finished Phil.

'They've already done that in several European countries I think.'

Wil finished his note taking and nodded at Phil in agreement.

'Hair regrowth treatments.'

'How, or why do people keep falling for this. Everyone knows they don't work. They give you some bullshit tonic, combined with some dodgy technology backed up by some equally dodgy doctors who are, no doubt, on the payroll. Then you do it religiously for however long, and at the end of the day, the normally ironically bald consultant says that for some reason it hasn't worked for you. How fucking odd and put on their best, I don't understand it look, then sell you a wig or a weave. I thought false advertising was illegal. Apparently, this is such an obvious scam that the consumer protection, or whatever they call themselves now do nothing about it. They just don't give a fuck. Probably because they can't believe people keep falling for this shit. Or maybe it's just too funny, which is why it's allowed to go on.' Phil paused and thought that'll do on that one as he really didn't give a fuck about it either.

'Not sure how important that one is to include PC?' Wil said.

'Probably right. However, it does highlight that in today's society, apparently, it's OK to mislead your customers, if it's really, really fucking obvious.' Phil finished.

'Pressing on PC.' Wil said, still not convinced of its virtue.

'Instant Democracy.'

'Hold up PC. I'll just grab some more canapes out of the fridge.' Wil said darting to the kitchen returning with the remaining plate, then mumbled 'Continue.' spitting a few crumbs in the process.

'Instant Democracy would finally give us not just a choice of which of the two basically identical parties we vote for, but it would provide us with the opportunity to vote on actual policies. That way we at least can make them keep their promises. That would be a novelty.' Phil said caustically.

'Remember the covid lockdowns, mask mandates, illegal vaccinations. All of that was based on rhetoric not science. How many people died from the cure. How many elderly died alone and scared. Remember the weapons of mass destruction or should that be weapons of mass deception. Nobody voted for that.' Phil skimmed through his notes.

'How many people died chasing that rabbit down the hole. Between 100,000 and 200,000 is the answer to that grisly question. George Bush, Tony Blair and John Howard all received honours after that lie.' Phil said annoyed.

'Don't you mean Sir Tony Blair and John Howard AC, OM.' Wil added cynically.

'Everyone knew they were lies. Which is why the largest protests in recorded history, at those times occurred globally in a vain attempt to stop this injustice. Guess what. They did it anyway. That is only after a prerogative police force, who probably also disagreed, but were able to justify their immoral actions by "Just doing their job" tasered, pepper sprayed, and water cannoned valiant, and totally legal protestors... With Instant Democracy that fiasco could not occur.' Phil really believed in this.

'If we had instant and pure democracy, that decision would have been voted down. What do we have to lose, you can't really fuck up a system that is completely broken already? Anything is better than the current two-party dictatorship we're forced to live under. These people need to look at Aristotle's concept of the wisdom of the crowd. The crowd is always more accurate than any individual.' Phil looked through his notes and continued.

'There's proof of that hypothesis in guessing the weight of a cow I believe.' He said, unsure of how that sounded.

'I think it was a pig PC.' Wil interjected. 'Anyway,' He added trying to get Phil back on topic.

'We have the infrastructure to handle it right now. The TAB would eat this alive. I mean on Melbourne Cup Day everyone has a punt on the so called "big race" and it handles that just fine. The results and payout are available in five minutes. And more people would probably vote, plus you could have the added bonus of having a few dollars on it at the same time. Truly back your opinion. The Government would make more money and save a fortune by getting rid of a lot of politicians or at least pay them less as they really have fuck all to do now. Even the policies we vote on could be decided by Instant Democracy'. Phil checked his notes and added.

'I do understand the need for secret ballots. But why do they have to be secret to me. I should be able to login to an electoral web site and make sure that my vote is allocated correctly. If we had this power, we could all get together and check the election result was correct en masse. That way there would be less likelihood of rigging.'

'I like the idea of having a bet on your vote.' Wil said. 'The revenue alone would probably pay for the election process and there are Tabs in every pub. Fuck going to some scout hall, or Primary School. When you get there, they represent about three electorates which are not even named after your suburb. They don't even have a map which would solve the entire problem. I generally waste about half my time in the wrong queue. And if that's not bad enough, they then give you a couple of bedsheet sized pieces of paper to fill out with a tiny pencil that's normally blunt.' Wil said looking annoyed.

'Good point Wil. I hadn't thought of the waste it causes either.'

'What about those cardboard booths. They can't even hold the weight of a long neck. You know they are not reused either.' Wil said remembering his ungainly juggle on election day.

'Exactly. You could insulate your house with those fucking things.' Said Phil.

Phil heard Wil's stomach make a mournful groan and decided it was time to take a break, make more canapes, and bring out the snacks.

'Let's take a break Wil.'

Wil flicked on the telly and watched a daytime talk show materialize, then changed the channel in a fumbled frenzy. He just couldn't abide seeing the currently fawned over, holier than thou host dance down to the stage sprouting some politically correct bullshit, followed up by an array of unfunny jokes ridiculing anyone who opposes their views or political opinions. Then watch them pause dramatically zoomed in tight and stare imploringly into the camera with dewy eyes pleading us all to be kind to each other.

Wil was sure if you zoomed out, you'd see them grinding a kitten into the carpet with their offensively expensive Jimmy Choo stilettos without mercy.

Celebrities preaching you morals is like a pharmaceutical company teaching you ethics. Utterly ludicrous.

Phil returned with fresh canapes, beer and cleared some space on the table.

'What's on the tube?' Phil asked.

Wil flicked around the channels before finally hitting the jackpot. Classic 70's James Bond.

Still Working from Home

The movie finished as expected with a groan worthy double entendre.

'Not bad.' Wil commented. 'But totally unrealistic.'

'Not bad!... Unrealistic! What is it exactly that's unrealistic. The radioactive lint, the swallowing sofa, the bagpipe gun. They're all-doable Wil.' Phil added looking and sounding astonished.

'Granted. But do you really believe even Sean Connery could pull, wearing a powder blue terry towelling play suit? I can't suspend my reality that far.' Will added and then picked up his notepad.

'You're right. That was a bit farfetched.' Phil agreed, now perusing the list.

He started in a flurry running through 'Air conditioning', and how the entire concept is upside down. Followed it up with 'Balloons', which are really just inflatable plastic bags. Trillions are made each year leading to the death of over 100 million marine animals. Not much of a party for them. And helium is in short supply. It's not a renewable resource, plus it's a necessary component of scientific research, medical tech, and other really important stuff. Which is a little more important than a party favour. He then powered through 'Dams' and the catastrophic damage they cause, and that's not even taking into account when they fail.

'Hold on a second PC. Gotta get another beer.' Wil went to the kitchen and brought out a six pack, then nodded for Phil to continue.

'Giving Up.'

'Giving Up is a completely underrated concept. The reason being, every time and I'm talking in the high ninety nine percents, when you try to give something up you statistically have roughly one chance in...' Phil paused, held up his hand and tapped away at an imaginary calculator frantically.

'Exactly one chance in fuck all.' He said holding up his imaginary calculator to Wil, who leant in, and nodded agreement.

'Wasn't it Einstein who said that every action has an equal and opposite reaction. Therefore, doing nothing is really doing something. Doing nothing is in effect very efficient, and isn't life about making things easier! Basically, if you're trying to give something up, or trying to achieve something, just stop trying and you immediately increase your chances of success. And you won't have the constant aggravation of knowing you failed over, and over again.' Phil finished.

Wil nearly stood up and clapped realising Phil had perfectly, and succinctly justified apathy, and procrastination.

'Makeup.'

'Why!' Phil said in a voice raised loud enough to bother his neighbour he hoped.

'What exactly is wrong with women that they are trying to "make up" for? Whom amongst us' Phil said. 'Doesn't mind seeing girls without make-up on?' Wil underlined mind looking concerned.

'How is this helping equality? Men don't disguise themselves, apart from sucking their guts in when the girls go by. Why do women make-up themselves? Do they think they only look acceptable when they're in disguise? How is this helping equality both physically and financially. The whole concept is driven by the cosmeceutical industry, which is owned by the pharmaceutical industry, who work in tandem! Or should that be collusion. They push their products through a cartel style image campaign using every subliminal dirty trick, and vacuous celebrity to force you to change your face to their expectations of how they believe you should look. It's disgraceful manipulation.' Phil paused to snatch and eat the last canape.

'I just can't understand it. I can understand men being stupid enough to fall for this. I thought better of women. Lift your game ladies. Rise up against this self-imposed oppression.' Phil stressed.

'The worst part is most of the brainwashing is being carried out by women's magazines imposing an unrealistic image of how they are supposed to look.' Phil said spraying crumbs. 'Aren't they meant to support women, not bully them into spending a large portion of their salary on expensive beauty products. It creates gender financial apartheid.' Phil finished noticing Wil looking sadly at the empty plate and stood up to go to the kitchen to bring out the remaining snacks.

'That's enough on that one.' Phil said upon return, then caried on.

'Mainstream Media.'

'Well, they lost relevance and credibility years ago. It doesn't even deserve to be called the media anymore. Definitely not journalism anyway. When was it OK for the so-called media to call politicians by nick names? And don't even get me started on the ironically named morning news. Have you watched it lately?' enquired Phil.

Wil smiled, laughed and said 'Fuck no! I watch the shopping network in the mornings. You can pick up some real bargains!' Phil gave Wil a concerned look, then got back on topic.

'Morning Toddy, K-Dod, Noddy, or whatever the latest, most likely unelected usurping douche bags name is. Then he replies with Morning Dicky or Smithy or whatever that corrupt lying sycophantic journalist's alias is. When did it become ok for Journalists to be such close friends with politicians? When did morning TV and radio become a pseudo advertisement for the major political parties?' Phil looked annoyed.

'It's so rehearsed. And the interviewer, I won't say journalist, as these talking heads are not journalists despite their claims. Surely you can't become a journalist by simply reading the news. I thought it required a University Diploma.' Phil really hated these frauds.

'And if you look at their Website or Wikipedia pages, they all claim to be journalists. Based on that thinking, when I worked at the Ponds Institute.' Phil took every opportunity he could to mention his brief, but glamorous contract. 'I should be able to call myself a dermatologist, or at least a skin care specialist.' He returned on topic.

'When these talking heads interview the Prime Minister. He or she should not look so damn relaxed. The reason they're so relaxed is probably because they know they're going to be asked the easiest, and least relevant preordained questions, that have all the impact of being hit with a very small, perfumed pillow. Where have all the hard ass political journalists gone? I can't watch it anymore.' Phil said at the same time turning off the TV avoiding the so-called news update, that Phil had no doubt will be amplifying the latest agenda of lies and propaganda in an attempt to try to frighten us into compliance, and surrendering more of our freedoms.

'The media use psychological manipulation, fear, and guilt to control us. Isn't that a form of terrorism?' Phil said thoughtfully.

'When did the standards drop so low?' He paused scooping up some dip with a biscuit.

'I'll tell you when.' He said chewing.

'When the mainstream media lost its monopoly on news and advertising. Everybody must know the mainstream are being soft on both sides of politics, so they don't endanger their highly lucrative advertising dollars. I thought politicians were supposed to be scared of journalists, or at the very least a bit intimidated, or at the very, very least a little bit nervous. Not look like they're meeting an old army buddy at the pub. You used to see politicians sweat. When was the last time you saw a politician sweat, and I mean really sweat under a good grilling? The mainstream media are just a bunch of suit and tie, good haircut wearing sycophantic models pretending to be "across the issues" Winkers' Phil said.

'Wankers?' Asked Wil.

'No. I mean Winkers. It seems to be part of their protocol that at the end of the news they give us a wink. I guess that's a tell, or a nervous tick letting us know that it's all been total bullshit.' Phil said angrily.

'When the reality is they don't have a fucking clue what's going on about anything'. Phil looked increasingly disgusted.

'And I'm not letting the newspapers off on this one either. Most of the world's newspapers and electronic media are owned by media, or mining magnates, or some other billionaire cunt who manipulates our opinions so they can continue to rape and pillage us for their own profits. Or worse still, for some other evil fucking reason that it's probably best we don't even know about.' Phil slammed his hand on the tea table forgetting again how much it hurt.

'The mainstream media will always sell out to the highest bidder regardless of the consequences to us, or to our freedoms. This has to stop! We, all of us need to stop focusing on the good, or bad job our politicians are doing, and start focusing on the bad job our journalists and media outlets are doing. They're the ones not calling our politicians to account. We need to stop watching this propaganda until they lift their game. Until they stop saying what they are supposed to say and start saying what must be said. Most countries seem to be on their knees, or at least, have the staggers. The journalists should be the heroes of the piece not the court jester.' Phil stopped and looked introspective.

'To be fair though. It's really our own fault. We get bad politicians, because we have bad journalists, and we have bad journalists because we collectively continue to watch them.' He threw his hands up in dismay. 'If this doesn't change, we're all fucked!'

They both paused and had a reflective beer.

'It's nearly 4:30 PC. When does that Pizza shop open?' Asked Wil breaking their reflective consciousness.

'It's open now.'

'Now!' Wil said, sounding as surprised as if he'd just seen someone walk out of a room in his house he didn't even know was there.

'Yeah. He's trying to pick up some extra business since the lockdowns.' Said Phil.

'Remember that ludicrous weapon of mass bullshit.' Wil said, shaking his head.

'Everyone was in on that pharmaceutical, corporate sponsored political lie.' A frustrated look appeared on Phil's face.

'How many people died from the cure for which there was barely a disease.'

'And we couldn't buy socks and undies for months.' Added Wil.

'Never forgive.' Phil said with his fist clenched over his heart.

'Never forget.' Returned Wil.

'Pizza PC?' Wil said, successfully steering the topic back to his appetite before Phil started sprouting statistics from government websites that proved the whole thing was a complete lie.

'Supreme with everything?' Answered Phil.

Wil dialled the number from memory and ordered two large pizzas. Wil provided strict and complex topping instructions.

'Should be ready in 10.' He said eagerly. 'How many left PC?'

Phil counted. 'Nine.'

'No problem. We've still got plenty of beer.'

Wil stared down the clock in anticipation. Phil stared into the horrifying abyss of the finishing line. After watching the clock for nine minutes Wil stood up and left for the Pizza shop returning two minutes later.

They ate and mumbled through 'Population' and 'Religion'. Religion was a soft target and a pet topic for both of them. They practically write themselves. Then moved on.

'Tolerance.'

'Why is tolerance now such an aggressive word! It seems like one of the worst things in the world these days is to be intolerant. Isn't tolerance also a synonym for endurance, which basically means to endure something, or put simply, to put up with it. Why should we have to put up with it? This is apparently the only thing we just won't or shouldn't even ironically try to tolerate. Tolerance behaves like the bratty love child of Political Correctness and Woke.'

'It enables selfish rude people to get away with anti-social behaviour without any risk of impunity. God help you if you ask someone to stop their children playing hide and seek around your table while you're trying to have a quiet dinner.' Phil said.

'Or asking someone to watch where they're going when their zombie walking glazed over their phone.' Wil chipped in with his pet hate.

'Exactly! If you politely mention that you would like someone to modify their behaviour when they're in public. Not modified forever mind you. Just for now, while they're in society. The society we both have to share. Suddenly you're the selfish bastard who should just "Tolerate" it and go back to trying to mind your own business as you most likely were already'. Phil stopped, stood up, walked to the fridge and collected another six pack.

'I'm not talking about just plain bullying and douche bag behaviour. Like wankers that randomly attack a group of people because they're different. That isn't intolerance, that's criminal. However, if a group of people affect your freedom. Now we must tolerate it. It's all very confusing.'

151

Phil said swigging his beer.

'Time to move on PC. It's really a societal issue, without a clear definition that can't be expressed by any individual.' Wil said.

'Yeah.' Phil agreed.

'Political Perks.'

'Also known more appropriately as the trough. Everyone knows about it, and nothing is ever done about it. They occasionally catch a shady politician getting a helicopter ride on the taxpayer's money, then claim they're cutting down on corruption. Well corruption is almost beside the point and pales into insignificance compared to the completely legal perks available.'

'Let's just run through a few off the top of our heads, shall we?'

'Travel allowances' Wil kicked off.

'Early superannuation payouts.'

'Indexed superannuation.'

'Cars and driver.'

'Overseas travel.'

'Domestic travel.'

'That dodgy Parliamentary Contributory Superannuation Scheme.' Phil said referring to his notes.

'Why do politicians even have their own rules? The PCSS ensures percentages of salary are indexed to the CPI, or whatever smoke and mirrors statistical number they come up with. Some of these leaching parasites will be getting paid more than 100% of their salary only several years after they retire. Even if they're not even retired. I think the whole thing costs close to a billion dollars a year.' Phil guessed, fairly accurately.

They both pressed on naming more perks.

'Severance Travel.'

'Life gold pass travel.'

'And that includes their bloody partners and families too.' Phil added with scorn.

'The list just goes on, and on, and on, and the worst part of all this is that with all these benefits available, they still try and rort the system.' Phil was speechless with indignation.

'They're allegedly overworked, yet they somehow still manage to find the time to be corrupt. How low are the moral standards that exist in our houses of power? Even if they do get caught rorting, or should I say stealing, what happens to them? Generally, fuck all. They get demoted to the backbench, where they have even less to do, or leave parliament in disgrace comforted by the soft landing their taxpayer funded superannuation will give them.' Phil held his arms out feeling nauseated.

'If we nicked items of similar value from the public, or our employer, or got caught with a similar value of contraband, we would get sentenced to prison. Why do we put up with this? Why does this double standard exist? Phil added very frustrated.

Neither of them had the answer to that ridiculous question and sat silently until Phil's phone rang breaking the silence. It was Beccs.

'Hey Beccs. How's Melbourne?'

'Hi Beccs.' Wil yelled.

The sounds coming from Phil's phone sounded like classic one-sided cartoon phone speak.

'Right. Sounds like you're enjoying yourself.' Phil said with a wink.

'Soooo how's Ryan?' Asked Phil holding the phone away from his ear in anticipation.

More tiny squeaks from Beccs' end came down the line. He then heard Beccs running out of steam, then grind to a complete stop.

'Sounds like you two are really hitting it off.' He said knowing that would start her up again.

A few more angry tiny noises came out of the phone before finally a laugh.

'Were at home, keeping our heads down over the project.'

'No! The pub didn't burn down.' Phil said indignantly.

153

Wil immediately went outside and looked down the street to check.

'Really. We're in site of the finishing line. The rough draft is nearly complete. Then the final edit tomorrow, then it's time to put it out there. Can't wait.' Phil said trying to convince himself.

'Thanks Beccs. Oh, and what time tomorrow. I'll book a table. Apparently, there's six of us coming now.' Phil paused.

'Yeah six. I'll tell you more later. It's going to be bigger than my real birthday.' Phil said excited at the thought of seeing Beccs again.

'OK you book the table then.'

More squeaking sounds came out of the phone as Beccs found more to complain about.

'It's nearly over. Just get home safely, drink a bottle of wine, go to bed and maybe you'll dream of Ryan running for his life from a ravenous pack of zombies.'

Phil ended the call and put the phone down.

'Come on PC. Let's finish this thing.' Wil said encouragingly.

The Finishing Line

The finishing line was definitely in sight. Phil checked the list and fired off the next one.

'Treason.'

'Treason is the crime of betraying one's country or trying to overthrow the sovereign government. Right?' Asked Phil rhetorically.

Wil nodded rhetorically in reply.

'In Australia we had the death penalty for treason up until 2002. Most countries still have the death penalty for treason. But for some reason no one ever enforces it. Which is peculiar because world leaders have been committing treason almost continuously, from recent memory.' Phil stated.

'Everywhere, in every country, politicians and leaders accept cash or other pecuniary bribes from overseas diplomats, property developers, mining companies, just about anyone from anywhere who wants a free, or discount piece of their country. Do any of them get executed or go to jail? Generally. No.' He answered his own question.

'What mostly happens, is exactly fuck all. They either get demoted in parliament, or publicly disgraced. Big deal! It's an insult to everyone.' Phil said.

'Everybody knows Bill Clinton. That dodgy pervert president had a net worth of under 2 million when he took office, and a net worth of over 200 million when he left 8 years later. Does nobody care where that money came from?' Phil said desperately. 'All world leaders engage in that type of conduct.'

Phil then went through a long list of local and foreign politicians that should have been executed. The list included names like Sam, Joe, Eddie, Bill, George, Tony, John, etc., Wil put his hand up to pause while he went to the fridge for another beer, handing one to Phil.

'Wil. This is it, the last one before the edit. Let's take a moment to reflect.' Phil stared down the list that now only had one item remaining.

Phil looked down at the growing pile of notes and ran through a lot of emotions. Has he simply wasted another week of his life, will he be a laughingstock, will anyone even bother reading it, Will it impress Beccs?

Wil punched Phil in the shoulder as a gesture of "nice one." but only succeeded in knocking him off the lounge.

'Sorry PC.' He said helping him up.

'It's just now's not the time to take a moment to reflect. Fight your natural urge to procrastinate and finish.' Wil said sternly.

'Right! Thanks Wil.' Phil nodded, rubbed his shoulder.

'Zoos.'

'Zoos try to hide behind a mask of altruism and cuddly animals, when in reality zoos have perpetrated some of the worst acts of animal cruelty. Do you know when they built the chimp enclosure at Taronga Zoo? 1981. So basically from 1916 they lived on cement and swung on rubber tyres, if they were lucky that is. The 1981 enclosure had some grass but was way too small and was still mostly designed for people to look at the animals. Not for their benefit at all, but of course, for ours. Now they have the 2011 version which is a little better but still not anything like where and how they are supposed to live. And this is a pretty good zoo. Can you imagine how bad the worst ones are?' He cringed at the thought.

'Zoos put down an awful lot of animals every year. Over thirty percent of sea life exhibits die most years. Most of the animals are stressed and bored all the time. Just like criminals in jail, except that these poor bastards didn't commit any crime. Contrary to the PR the zoos put out, most animals have shortened lifespans compared to their wild counterparts. You only have to look at the elephants and tigers for proof of that. And God help any animal that happens to encounter a person who stupidly or clumsily gets into an animal's cage. Yes, I mean cage not enclosure or exhibit. Has everyone forgotten Harambe the Gorilla getting shot dead, or some poor orca that just didn't want to balance some fat sea hippy fuck on his nose around the pool anymore and inevitably lost his temper? They got murdered without trial, without mercy.' Phil looked horrified.

'Why do Zoos even exist anymore. The breeding programs have little to no success. They barely manage to keep the animals they have alive, let alone breed a surplus. If they are successful in their breeding programs, the poor innocent bastards are born and die in a prison. It must be purely for the tourist dollars. Or more likely for the private owners. Currently there are roughly 10,000 zoos in the world. If each zoo has roughly 10,000 individual beings, then this makes 1 million animals out of their environment and suffering.' Phil was really distressed with his own facts.

'Don't even mention their so called conservation efforts. Most of the animals at zoos aren't even endangered. And even those that are, if they miraculously manage to breed them, are rarely, if ever released back to the wild. That's if their wild even still exists. It most likely has already been cleared, probably to build another fucking zoo.' Phil said disgusted by his own sarcasm.

'Then they have the gall to say they are educational facilities. Yeah right, only if you want to educate our children on what a bored out of its brain animal looks like. And they say that the money they make goes towards the animal's welfare. Well, that's clearly bullshit, as while I sit in a five star restaurant at the zoo having my lunch, some poor animal doesn't even have any grass to sit on while he has his. Put an end to this travesty now! Once and for all. Don't make this like circuses where we banned them having wild animals way, way too late. Don't make this something else we will be ashamed of and will be saying one day, can you believe they still had those in the 21st century.' Phil said.

He paused, took a sip of his beer, looked at Wil who was reviewing his notes and said. 'That's it?'

A reverent silence fell across the room.

'I can stay here until 11 and help you with the editing and finishing the beer. Or I could go to work early, get some stuff done and then do the editing there?' Wil said.

They both burst out laughing at the thought of Wil going to work early and started working on the editing and the last of the beer.

Editing Process

By 11 Wil decided he was way too pissed to go to work. They'd drunk their way through the beer, then Phil found an old bottle of suspiciously too yellow wine and they were grimacing their way through that too.

'What time are we meeting Beccs tomorrow? Can't wait to hear what's worse. Ryan or Melbourne? She keeps a tally you know. Seriously, she writes it down, scores all the things that annoy her about each one, then declares a final winner or loser, as the case may be.' Wil said.

'Seriously?' Asked Phil.

'Seriously!' Replied Wil.

'I've seen her writing in a notepad after I've talked to her.' Phil said with concern. 'You don't think….'

'No mate. She's always writing on one of her lists. She even has a list of her lists. A master list if you will.' Wil said with raised eyebrows.

'Bullshit!' Phil said sceptically.

'Seriously. Ask her tomorrow. She's not even embarrassed. Doesn't even think it's weird. You've heard her talk about her lists. It's the reason you have a shopping list on your fridge mate.' Wil said pointing in the general direction of the kitchen.

'Well, yes of course, I know that. But a master list? That's a little weird.' Phil said thinking maybe he needed a master list himself.

'Anyway. What time tomorrow?' Wil repeated.

'4:30. A few drinks, then dinner'.

'Sounds like fun.' Wil said with his usual optimism.

'Sounds like a pending catastrophe if you ask me. My

mysterious flatmate sounds like a hippy, and my neighbour is a total fucking psycho.' Phil said with his usual pessimism.

'Like I said, sounds like fun.' Wil restated.

They edited with fervour and ardent debate, making changes and additions until the wine ran out. The time had moved on to 1:30am. Phil yawned and was beginning to look a little jaded. Wil was looking hungry again.

'I'm going down the road for a kebab. Want one?' Asked Wil standing up and stretching.

'Want me to come with you?' Phil answered with a nod to the kebab, but not making any perceivable effort to move.

'No PC. Travel alone. Travel Fast. Just relax I'll be back in halfa.' Wil said, then walked out the door into the night.

Phil sat and read through the notes with great uncertainty, then decided he'd come too far to waste time with uncertainty and pressed on. He added new concepts, and new reasons why, in his opinion, things must change. Maybe it was the dozen beers and half a bottle of vintage banana wine talking, but he was feeling like it was making sense.

Wil strolled through the door with heavy footsteps and poked his head around the corner.

'You're not asleep PC? Kebabs here. Beef with the lot, extra chilli.' Then tossed Phil the offering.

'Brilliant! Pity we don't have any more beers. The bacteria in your average Kebab can kill a sober man in under two days clinical studies have proven.' Phil said taking a big bite.

'Got it covered.' Wil said walking to his spot on the lounge, with a half-eaten Kebab in one hand and a six pack in the other.

'Captain fucking resourceful!' Phil said genuinely impressed.

'Where did you get that? It's 1 in the morning. The nannas that run the state don't trust the likes of us to get takeaway after 10. That's apparently when all decent people should be tucked away in bed.' Phil added trying

160

to look and sound like a wise old lady.

'Well, let me take you through it.' Wil lent back on the lounge, took a bite of his kebab and opened a beer. Wil loved taking the time to explain a successful plan.

'If you remember. I put my jacket on before I left, even though it's a warm night. Right?' He said.

'Right' Answered Phil taking another bite.

'I also put on my work pass.'

'You went back to work and nicked some from the fridge?' Phil said thinking he'd worked it out.

'Mate. I'm a professional. That's stealing. It would put my entire career at risk.' Wil continued. 'As I was saying, I had on my jacket and pass, then went to the kebab shop next to the pub and ordered three kebabs.'

'Three!' Phil said horrified.

'Yeah! Three. I ate one on the way back.' Wil remarked casually.

Phil, who had been rushing through his Kebab seeing a once in a lifetime window of opportunity open, suddenly slam shut. He eased off defeated.

'Well, while I was waiting. One of the doormen came over for a chat.' Wil said taking the last bite of his second kebab.

'Turns out, he used to work at the mall about 10 years ago. So, I told him. I work at the mall.' Wil said raising his eyebrows, holding up his security pass.

'Well. He started telling me all these stories, mostly bullshit I suspect, about huge parties they had back in the day. Mmm., I said.' Wil added for effect.

'Is that right I said. We're having our Christmas party tonight, and we've run out of beer. Christmas party a bit early mate! He said... Yes mate. Remember it's open 24 hours at Christmas, so we have it now.' Wil added.

'Well, he said. That's a good idea, wish we'd thought of that he said. Well, he couldn't have been more sympathetic, he then leaned over and whispered in my ear.' Will said leaning forward in imitation.

'Meet me in the alley in 5 minutes. Well, 5 minutes later I have three kebabs and half a carton.' Wil held his arms out emphasising the accomplishment.

'Of course, I had to listen to an impassioned speech about shift workers and how they are discriminated against with shopping, banking and the bloody lockout laws, so he got me half a carton as a way of sticking it to the man I suppose.'

Phil raised his hand in a fist and said, 'Solidarity brother. Fight the power.' And grabbed one of the beers. 'They're even cold.' He said surprised.

'To shift workers!' They both said holding up their beers.

'Add it to the list Wil. We still have time and now we have the supplies.'

Phil finished his kebab coming in a poor second, then chased it down with a beer, then started drafting the addition of Shift Work, which was mostly contributed to by Wil. Wil knew everything about shift work. He'd done it since he left school.

They edited the remaining topics, then took turns reading it out loud to see if it made sense. They agreed it did, and then on reflection it didn't. Perfect! The reason that was perfect was because it was about freedom of speech. Not about being right. It was about your right to be wrong, about your right to open discussion, not being bullied, ridiculed or censored into a preordained narrative.

Wil finished typing it up on his 17 inch laptop, which he managed to make look comically small.

They both decided the best marketing plan was total saturation, and they meant total! All social media sites, E-mails addressed to individuals. Not just any individuals but world leaders, industry leaders, leaders in social commentary, intellectual leaders. And of course, the mainstream media. Phil was hoping they would comically try to justify, or back pedal on their long and extensive catalogue of lies.

Wil, who had already collated a list of E-mail addresses', showed them to Phil.

'Are you sure about this mate?' Phil said, reading the

list through one eye.

'Yes PC. It's all about hitting the target. Addressing the right audience. Well, there's your audience.' Will said confidently pointing at the list.

'Yeah but... 'Phil looked down at the list. 'The Secretary General of the U.N., The President of the United States, the French President. Couldn't this get out of hand?' Asked Phil, staring down the reality.

'No chance mate. Let's just say one of these lazy pricks actually reads it, comments, and those comments cause some ripples. Isn't that kind of the point?' Emphasised Wil.

'Do you think we can talk Beccs into doing the social media stuff?' Phil asked as he had no clue about social media.

'Yeah. She has to manage all that shit for work. Does it all day.'

Phil took a deep breath to steel himself.

'Fuck it! You're right. Tomorrow, we publish.' Phil said out of commitment and exhaustion. He then promptly and uncharacteristically stood up, shook hands with Wil and went upstairs to pass out.

Wil, who was a stayer pulled out the sofa bed and finished making the document look professional, while at the same time maintaining the look and feel of something created in an isolated log cabin no where off the grid. When he was satisfied, he printed it out, which took him through to 4:30am and through the remaining beer. As soon as the sun started to rise and the birds started to sing, he was out like a light.

The house was bathed in sunlight. Phil, who had only just made it to bed before the night got the better of him, hadn't moved.

The clock in his bedroom ticked away peacefully.

He woke, suddenly with an undeniably urgent need to urinate. Slid off the bed backwards, then stumbled to the bathroom, relieved his urgency and stumbled into the shower. Today was the day. The work was done and if he knew Wil, the document would look amazing. Phil was excited about seeing Beccs again. This time he would have something to impress her with. He was feeling relaxed, in control, organised and only slightly hungover. Totally ready.

He got out of the shower, dressed and started to walk downstairs to see if Wil was awake, or even there. He stopped and walked back upstairs to get his phone, picked it up and stared at it in disbelief. 4:40pm.

How could it be 4:40pm. They were already 10 minutes late.

'Wil!' Phil shouted in alarm and rushed down the stairs hoping.

'Yes mate!' He answered.

Relief!

'Do you know what time it is?' Asked Phil sounding unsettled.

'Yes mate!' He replied. 'Relax PC. It's all sorted, I'm showered and ready to go. Even had breakfast. We'll be fashionably late. I think I heard your neighbour already leave. Excited PC!' Wil said smiling almost maniacally.

'It's going to be a fucking catastrophe. I can feel it. We're already late.'

The Fucking Catastrophe

Phil frisked himself for his keys and wallet as Wil walked past, carrying an impressive looking briefcase that looked new, while at the same time looking oddly familiar.

'What's with the briefcase? Haven't seen that before?' Phil asked slamming the door shut behind them.

'It's an executive document carrier. It's totally new tech.' Wil said enthusiastically. 'It's dust proof, fireproof, waterproof and lockable. It's more like a safe really.' Wil stated confidently.

Phil's question of who needed one of those briefcases was answered belatedly.

The walk to the pub was brisk. Wil was leading the way enthusiastically. Phil was following behind hesitantly. He couldn't get his mind off the tsunami of potentially catastrophic events looming on the horizon. Showing Beccs his work, meeting his psycho neighbour while standing up, meeting his what the fuck flatmate and sparring with his old nemesis Ryan.

Wil could sense Phil's hesitation and eased back to match his speed.

'It's gonna be a really fun night PC. Lighten up. Like Rod Stewart sang "Tonight's the night…." He sung in one of the worst impersonations ever. 'That's all I know… Anyway, you get my point.' Wil finished.

Phil didn't really get the point but was grateful Wil didn't know any more Rod Stewart.

'You're right Wil. Tonight, will be a turning point.' Phil said trying to convince himself.

'Today is the first day of your new life. Today is the day everything changes for you... I can feel it PC. Remember when I picked the score in the Grand Final. I have that same feeling right now.' Wil said waving his fingers at Phil spookily. 'It's going to be a really awesome night.'

Each step moved them closer to the pub and closer to Phil's destiny.

'Hey! Look! I can see Beccs in the smoking area. There're two drinks at her table.' Wil said pointing and squinting.

'Well, well. Beccs always said she was ambidextrous, now we have the proof.' He said holding up an imaginary pair of binoculars.

'No! Correction. One's a beer and one's something else, in a fancy looking glass.' Wil said adjusting the binoculars.

'Shit!' Phil muttered knowing only Ryan would drink something else in a fancy looking glass.

'Update.' Wil said making fine adjustments.

'She's holding up a coaster. It says...' He made even more fine adjustments.

'It says Umm'. Further adjustments. 'HELP!'

Beccs held up another coaster. Phil snatched the imaginary binoculars off him. He read it out loud, 'Get here now or I'll kill you, with a smiley face underneath'.

They looked at each other seriously. 'Standard Operating Procedures PC. I'll go to the bar. You run defence for Beccs. 10-4?' Wil said bumping fists.

'10-4.' Returned Phil.

Phil walked purposely towards Beccs, dodging bar flies with consummate skill. Beccs stood up and walked over hurriedly, gave him a quick hug and ushered Phil to her table, pushing him into the seat next to her.

'Hi Beccs.' Phil finally had time to say.

'Hi PC.' Beccs replied then leaned over to give him a proper hug taking him completely by surprise.

'It's good to see you. Are we all good? I hated going away before I had time to say sorry for the outburst.' Beccs frowned looking comically contrite.

'Apology not required Beccs! We're always good. You know that.' Phil said, reaching over to touch her hand, then hesitated. Beccs met him halfway. 'It wasn't an outburst.'

'Yes it was!'

'At best it was a message of chagrin... Which I needed.' Phil added sternly and truthfully.

'No you didn't, you're...' Beccs smile changed to an expression of exasperation. 'Christ! Here he comes.'

Ryan strolled in, nodding and smiling at confused strangers sporting what Phil assumed was a suit that cost more than his bathroom renovations. And that cost a fucking fortune.

'You're sitting in my seat old man?' Were Ryan's first words.

Phil started to stand, only to be dragged back down by Beccs.

'Sit on that seat Ryan.' Beccs said pointing to a seat at another table.

Ryan dragged his chair over to sit on the other side of Beccs, uncomfortably close.

Wil strolled back in with two beers, put them on the table and dragged his own chair over.

'Mate, did you bring your own glass. Or is that the lady's sampler?' All three laughed at Wil's joke that wasn't funny at all, or made any sense, but enjoyed leaving Ryan on the sidelines.

'So, it's Wil and Phil if I recall.' Ryan said rolling his eyes ever so slightly, but not unnoticeably.

'It's PC.' Beccs, Wil and Phil said at the same time, laughed, and raised their glasses together.

Ryan saw he was outnumbered and decided to just smile.

'So Beccs, how was the business trip? I hope not all business and no play.' Phil said winking at Beccs, who answered the wink with a death stare.

'Well, not entirely.' Answered Ryan. 'We had some fun, dinner, dancing. Didn't we Rebecca? Oh, can you pass me my brewed Kombucha Beccs dear?' Ryan said smiling, but still somehow looking condescending.

Beccs pushed Ryan's beer an inch closer.

'So, what's brewed Kombucha Ryan?' Wil asked leaning in feigning mock interest.

Ryan missed the mock and explained. 'It's a fermented Manchurian mushroom drink created around 200BC which…'

'Fascinating. Does it get you pissed? Did you say mushrooms?' Wil said with a horrified look. 'I'll stick to tap beer Ryan mate.'

'Tap beer! Do you know how long some beers stay in the taps at establishments like this.' Ryan said waving his arm around at the décor.

'Not long if we're here.' Answered Wil quickly getting nods of approval from both Phil and Beccs.

'Why are we even drinking in this…' Ryan waved his arms around again. 'Dump?' He added not bothering to put a spin on it. 'There's a charming Wine Bar just five clicks down the road.'

'A fucking Wine Bar?' Uttered Phil not that quietly. An uncomfortable silence fell across the table. They all let it linger.

'So, tell us how the dinner and dancing was Beccs?' Asked Phil breaking the silence, smiling and winking, fishing for more information.

Beccs glared at Phil with her "I'll get you later." look.

'Yeah, dinner was nice. Fortunately, Umm… Unfortunately. I sprained my ankle on the first dance.' she said going a bit red at the slip.

'It's looking better now.' Phil said leaning down to look under the table.

'Maybe we could hit the night club later, bust a move.' Wil said also smiling and winking.

'There is all too much winking going on today. Can we please stop with the winking?' Beccs pleaded.

'Ok but Phil and I will need to get it out of our systems first.' Wil said, setting both of them off on a winking frenzy.

'We're done now Beccs. Sorry Ryan do you need to have a quick wink, or are you good?' Phil said making Beccs snigger.

Another awkward silence fell across the table. Phil looked at everyone smiling. He was really enjoying this one.

'I think the bistro's open?' Wil said just long enough for everyone to enjoy it. They all stood up and walked to the bistro.

'There isn't a table for us.' Wil said a little edgy at the thought of dinner being delayed.

'Yes there is Wil. See the table with the reserved sign on it.' Beccs said pointing at a table.

Wil stared at the little sign with Wil #6 in disbelief. Someone had booked a table, and in his name. Most people forgot Wil was even present during dinner. He was genuinely touched and gave Beccs arm a squeeze.

'Thanks Beccs.'

Beccs looked at Wil sadly and gave him a wink.

'Let's not start that again Beccs. Phil and I are both completely winked out.'

'I'm sure Ryan could squeeze another one out.' Phil said snidely, overhearing the conversation.

Phil and Wil both pulled out a chair, sat down and picked up a menu. Ryan pulled out Beccs chair, dusted it with his handkerchief, which matched his tie, waistcoat, socks and glasses, and offered the chair to Beccs.

Beccs smiled too sweetly at Ryan and sat down.

'You're welcome, Rebecca.' Ryan muttered to himself.

'Please stop calling me Rebecca.' Beccs said sounding exhausted.

'But Beccs doesn't sound as classy as you are Rebecca.' Ryan said with Kombucha confidence.

Wil and Phil both smiled at each other. Phil leaned over to whisper in Beccs' ear. 'Do you want to swap places?' Asked Phil, Beccs smiled in reply.

'Couldn't do that to you on your birthday PC.' She said, then whispered in Phil's ear. 'But stay close in case I try to rip his ears off.'

Phil leaned back laughing and said, 'I'll stop you right after the first one.'

Ryan looked annoyed at being left out of another conversation and asked. 'So, who else is coming to your birthday Phillip?'

'Just my neighbour and flatmate.' Phil answered sharply, hating being called Phillip again.

Another awkward silence fell across the table.

'When's Chris getting here?' Wil asked excitedly.

'Who's Chris.' Asked Beccs which Phil hoped was in a jealous tone.

'You know. My mysterious flatmate.' Phil answered, then turned his attention to Wil.

'Not sure. She knew the time and the place. I assume she passed that on to whoever the fuck my neighbour is. Maybe they're both out buying me a present.' Phil said hoping he was right. Phil loved the mystery of presents.

'Hey PC. Check out the Hippy chick across the street.' Wil said pointing. 'She's coming this way!' He added with mock horror, knowing Phil's allergy to hippies.

All four of them gazed out at the explosion of tie dye billowing down the street, then heard the jingling of bells and bangles as she opened the door. Gazed around, stared at each of them in turn then squealed and jumped with delight.

They all stood up more from shock than politeness.

'Ravi Shankir.' Beccs said in amazement making Phil snigger.

'I think I can feel my chakras aligning.' Added Wil

Phil was too stunned to say or think anything.

She rushed up to Phil first and wrapped her arms around him in a violent embrace, let go, stepped back and then did it again, this time even more violently, let go, then took a few jingly steps back again.

'You absolutely must be Phillip.' She said and squealed again. 'I'm Chris your flatmate, slash life mate.'

'Phil umm, PC's better.' He said still recovering from the hug.

170

'Phillip. I feel like I've known you forever.' she said pressing her hands to his chest.

'That's weird. It feels like we just met.' Phil said, looking a little bewildered, then took a step back into the security of his personal space almost knocking his chair over.

Will reached out, saved the chair and grinned at the prospect of the unfolding evening.

Without any warning she launched herself at Ryan with the same vigour.

'You must be Phillip's best friend.' She said squealing again.

'Actually No. I'm Ryan, Ryan Knewarthe. The surname is French before you ask.' No one ever asked.

'I'm Rebecca's best friend actually.' Ryan said smiling and gesturing at Beccs.

Beccs dropped her head down wondering how much weirder this night was going to get, then looked up grinning at everyone and punched Ryan in the shoulder harder than could be considered friendly. 'Hi Besty.' She said with gusto.

Ryan smiled and rubbed his shoulder, then to everyone's amusement took Christine's hand and kissed it.

'It's an absolute pleasure to meet you Christine.' Ryan said, still holding her hand causing Chris to squeal again.

'You are a vision of loveliness.' He added making everyone grateful they hadn't already eaten.

That was too much for Wil who sniggered behind his hand, then froze as Christine's gaze turned to him.

Wil darted his hand out in front of him offering a hardy arm's length handshake. 'I'm Wil. Pleased to meet you Christine.'

Christine didn't seem to even recognise the offering and slid in under his arms and squeezed Wil in an energetic bear hug.

'I can already tell we're all going to have a super awesomely spiritual night tonight. Just awesome. Really awesome!' Christine let out another small squeal and sat in the chair being offered to her by Ryan.

'Hi Rebecca.' She said belatedly waving at Beccs.

'Let's all really get to know each other tonight. You know.' She said squeezing Phil's arm.

'Just say whatever you're thinking. Whatever comes to mind. A totally real and thorough exchange of our emotions.' Christine said smiling broadly looking at everyone in turn.

Wil's smile was so big now it looked like it might actually be hurting.

Wil looked at Phil squeezing his other arm. 'Told you PC. We're going to have a top night and your neighbour hasn't even arrived yet. Can hardly wait for that.' Wil rubbed his hands together gleefully.

'So, what's our neighbour like Christine?' Phil asked.

'Well, his names Bobo and ...'

'Bobo!' Phil interrupted nervously. Guys with cuddly names were always bad asses, probably an eastern European war criminal he suspected. Phil was sure there was one called Bobo.

'Yes. He's fascinating. I think he's from eastern Europe, definitely has an accent from somewhere anyway.' Christine elaborated unhelpfully. 'He's very sweet, and he's very eager to talk to you Phillip.'

Phil nodded more nervously glancing at Wil. Wil smiled broadly back and gave Phil two thumbs up.

'He said he wants to clear the air. So that will fit right in with tonight's theme. Awesome!' Christine beamed.

Phil raised his eyebrows sceptically.

'Hey everyone. Here he comes!' Enthused Christine jumping up and down rushing to the door greeting Bobo with a frenetic hug.

'How come you didn't get a hug Beccs?' Phil asked.

'Just lucky I guess. Don't you dare remind her.' She added.

Bobo, no longer obscured by Chris walked towards their table Sporting not double, but triple denim. And a moustache he'd obviously borrowed off John Oates circa 1982, a matching mullet, and an open neck shirt. So open it was practically open neck trousers. He stood at their table and nodded at everyone in turn.

'Bobo.' He said in an accent that Christine was right, definitely was from somewhere. Then fixated on Phil.

'Ah Phillip, it's nice to meet you socially. Will you be doing a lot of loud swearing this evening?' He said offering his hand.

'It's PC Bobo and we'll see how the night progresses. I don't want to commit too early.' Phil said reaching in to shake Bobo's hand.

Bobo pulled Phil in close jolting him forward and made uncomfortable eye contact. Phil wasn't sure if he was trying to hypnotise him, hit on him, or scare the shit out of him.

Will noticed the tension, jumped to his feet put his hand out grabbing Bobo's out of Phil's and shook it too vigorously. 'Wil. Pleased to meet you Bobo.'

'How's the anger management classes going?' Wil said winking at Phil.

'Have you been to one of my classes. I'm sorry. I don't remember you Wil.' Bobo said without any hint of sarcasm.

Beccs, Wil and Phil looked at each other uncertainly, then nodded politely in unison.

They all sat down and perused the menu.

Will and Phil made up their minds instantly. Mo Mo's for Phil predictably, a T-bone, chips and salad for Wil. Beccs ordered a grilled chicken burger, Ryan selected soft shell crab sauteed with lemon butter served on a bed of risotto with a side of asparagus, because it was the most expensive. Bobo ordered a steak, rare.

They put their menus down and looked up to see Chris staring at the back of the menu.

Phil watched her staring at the back of the menu and gave Wil a confused look, then turned over his own menu.

'Fuck me. I didn't know it had stuff on the back.' Phil said surprised.

'You're right PC!' Wil said picking up and turning his own menu over. 'Don't panic. It's only the vegan menu.' Wil said looking genuinely relieved.

Christine was still staring at the menu not moving. She didn't even seem to be breathing. Bobo was staring into the middle distance.

'Seen anything you fancy Chris?' Asked Beccs showing some female solidarity she thought.

'Yes Phillip.' Christine smiled still staring at the menu ignoring Beccs. 'I'm having the Baba Ghanoush.'

'Interesting choice Christine. Oh, and I prefer to be called PC if that's OK?' Phil said smiling politely.

'I never eat anything that has a face or eats anything else Phillip.' She said ignoring him. 'I think nick names are stupid.' She giggled.

'I did warn you. I would just say whatever comes to mind tonight. No offence Phillip.' she said in a sing songy voice while squeezing Phil's arm to his growing annoyance.

'I agree.' Said Ryan.

'I also agree.' Said Bobo.

Wil and Phil both looked at each other trying not to laugh.

The waiter arrived and took their orders. Their food arrived mercifully quickly.

Phil, Wil and Beccs ate theirs only occasionally stopping to talk between themselves.

Ryan, Bobo and Christine were laughing, talking loudly and generally drawing attention to themselves from every other diner.

When they finished their meals and loud conversations about their meals. The waiter moved in, cleared the table, suggested coffee, then offered the dessert menu.

Wil and Phil politely declined settling for another beer. Beccs ordered a flat white, 1 sugar. Chris and Ryan ordered a dessert to share, and two decaf cappuccinos with almond milk. Bobo ordered a double Vodka which didn't surprise anyone.

'Oh my God!' Squealed Christine startling everyone. 'We have so much in common Ryan.'

Beccs smiled at Phil looking relieved that Ryan had found someone else to annoy. She then made the mistake of smiling at Ryan.

'Don't fret Beccs, I'm just being friendly to our guest.' Ryan said as a reply.

'What! No Ryan, please keep being friendly I'm mostly here to celebrate PC's birthday, and their completed project.'

'What project?' Ryan said, with Christine looking at them fascinated, with a hint of vacuous.

Phil spotted the waiter walking over with the coffee's thankfully putting an end to the question.

Beccs, Wil and Phil watched them share the sickeningly sweet dessert, then watched them eat in an even more sickeningly sweet display.

'More coffee?' Their waiter said, clearing the table again.

Three no's, and an awkward pause followed, as the three of them stared at Chris and Ryan in hopeful anticipation that the dining part of the evening would be coming to a merciful conclusion.

'No. I think we're good Garcon. Cheque please.' Ryan said dismissively at the waiter.

PC mouthed a sorry.

Ryan took the check to inspect the bill. Phil saw an opportunity and jumped on it.

'Thanks Ryan. Nice of you to pay on my birthday mate.' Phil grinned.

Ryan was about to protest but noticed Christine slap her hands together excitedly and beam at Ryan. Ryan gave Phil a dirty look and said 'Of course. I'm known for my generosity.' Then smiled back at Christine.

Ryan put a gold Amex on the bill and handed it back to the waiter. The waiter quietly whispered in Ryan's ear that they didn't take Amex. He reluctantly got cash out of his wallet and more reluctantly, put it on the bill.

Phil often wondered why people had Amex cards. No one ever accepted them. He was thinking of getting one himself.

They all got up and walked to the bar. Phil lagged behind apologising for Ryan. The waiter winked in return, saying don't worry about it. He was used to corporate wankers. More winking Phil thought. Maybe it's contagious like yawning. He jogged out to the bar to catch up.

The Evening Continues

Ryan and Chris were now holding hands to everyone's utter astonishment. Phil, Wil and Beccs huddled together at the bar. Bobo stood in the center of the room staring into the middle distance again.

'Fuck me, wasn't that fun?' Wil said to distract them from another weird moment. 'I reckon Ryan's in tonight PC. I hope they don't go back to your place.' He said winking again. 'Sorry Beccs. Forgot the no winking rule.'

'No. That one deserved a good wink.' She said giggling. 'How thick are the walls at your place PC?' She said laughing loudly now seeing a panicked look flash across Phil's face, then winked herself.

'I think I'll sleep rough tonight. Maybe in the doorway at the library.' He lamented.

They walked to the table Ryan and Chris had selected with a view of the street and sat down. Bobo had apparently broken free of his stare and joined them. They all smiled at each other awkwardly.

Christine interrupted asking. 'So Beccs. What's this project Phillip and William have finished?' She beamed with an exaggerated expression of interest, at the same time finally acknowledging Beccs.

'Yes. Tell us lads. What is this big project. Planning a start-up?' Ryan said dismissively.

Wil and Phil were lost for words. They ummed and arrred attempting to describe what they had done, then looked skyward hoping Ryan would find someone else to pester.

Beccs saw they were lost and dived in 'Well, if I can speak for you guys?' She offered. Wil and Phil nodded eager approval.

'It's a work of modern philosophy detailing dynamic issues, and dynamic solutions for a modern society encompassing both social, economic and environmental concerns.' She said sounding impressed herself.

Wil was already jotting that down on the back of a coaster as it sounded better than their summary.

'So, you both study Philosophy.' Christine chirped back.

'Not academically.' Phil said looking at Wil who returned the look.

'So, what's the objective. What's the end game? What's the ROI?' Ryan said clicking his fingers both condescendingly and annoyingly.

'Not everything has to have an end game Ryan. Or a return on investment.' Phil said proving he knew what ROI meant.

'Not everything has to be profitable.' Beccs said trying to match his condescension. 'Some things aren't about personal gain. Sometimes it's about trying to make a change.' Beccs finished, as always ready to defend her friends.

Ryan refused to be shut down, and restated his stance with a series of practicalities, interspersed with tedious time is money analogies, before finally finishing with an exasperated, what's the point if it doesn't make any money, therefore boring the discussion into silence.

'What is everyone talking about?' Bobo interjected sitting in his chair the wrong way round, again not surprising anyone.

'Well Bobo. Apparently, William and Phillip.' Ryan said smiling at Christine, who smiled back approvingly at him for using their full names. 'Have come up with a philosophical document that will change the world apparently.' He finished with a smirk, and another dismissive wave.

Beccs could almost see Phil and Wil deflating.

'Shut the fuck up Ryan.' Beccs said finally sick of hearing him trying to demean everyone. 'Don't you get tired of being a dick all the time? It's PC's birthday.' Beccs said trying to make Ryan feel bad, completely wasting her time.

'That's not in the spirit of the evening Beccs.' Ryan said adding. 'And I don't think that's how a lady should speak, especially in front of another lady.' He bowed his head at Christine.

'No Ryan! That's the whole point of the evening sweet pea.' Christine said putting her hand on Ryan's face tenderly.

'Exactly Christine.' Phil said remembering to use her full name himself. 'So, what I'm hearing is that Ryan apparently doesn't get tired of being a dick.' Phil said making Wil nearly spit his beer.

Ryan glared at Phil. Phil glared back thinking maybe he'd pushed it a bit too far, or that's what he was thinking as a fancy looking glass of Kombucha beer sailed across the table connecting heavily with his nose.

'Fuck!' Yelled Phil already sounding nasally, and already bleeding.

Wil rushed to Phil's aid putting a napkin to his nose, then held his head back to slow the bleeding. Beccs reached over and grabbed Ryan in a headlock.

'Turn down the feelings guys. I think we've hit the red zone. It's getting pretty heavy.' Christine said moving her hands up and down in no way helping the situation.

Bobo sat there unsure who he needed to counsel first.

Justin arrived on the scene, also looking a little unsure of what to do.

'Hi Justin.' Beccs said tightening her grip.

'Hi Beccs. Haven't seen you for a few days.' Justin replied in a friendly manner leaning over to look at Phil's already swollen nose.

'I've been in Melbourne with my boss. Say hi Ryan.'

'Hi.' Ryan gasped.

'Hi PC, Wil. So, what's going on?' He smiled looking at all of them pulling out his walkie talkie to call security.

'Is PC alright Wil?' Justin said looking a bit concerned at the rapidly reddening napkin.

'PC! Do you know where you are mate?' asked Justin remembering that's what his football coach used to ask him after his many head injuries.

'Dapto dogs?' Phil said sounding even more nasally.

'See. He's fine Justy'. Wil said looking unconcerned.

'Yeah, he's fine.' Beccs said nodding, as Ryan's face was starting to change colour from red to purple.

'Beccs? Might be a good idea to stop strangling the Kombucha guy. He's the only bastard that drinks that shit.'

Beccs released her grip reluctantly. Ryan coughed, spluttered and gathered his composure.

'You know I could have got out of that hold anytime I wanted to Beccs.' He said smugly dusting off his lapels smiling at Christine.

'Really! Best out of three Ryan.' She said feigning to make another lunge at him.

Ryan leapt back knocking into Chris, apologised mocking exaggerated fear.

Two large, tall and intimidating security guards strolled over and spoke with Justin. Justin gesticulated wildly, made some other somewhat misleading gestures, and then mimicked the entire incident in slow motion in surprisingly precise detail.

The two security guards walked over to their table and pointed at Bobo intimidatingly.

'Thankyou sir for not getting involved tonight. Please move away from the table and enjoy your evening.' Said the larger of the two security guards.

Bobo stood up slowly, picked up his drink and moved one step back.

'Take him away and clean him up.' Said the other security guard pointing at Phil.

'Oh. And come back here when you're done. We may need to take further action.' He added as Wil and Phil walked off.

Christine smiled and waved at security like someone meeting an old friend at the airport.

'Hiiii.' She said waving and smiling in her increasingly annoying sing songy voice.

'I think I should be standing with Bobo. I mean I have a complete non-violence policy, and lifestyle, plus, and in addition to. I'm just getting a really bad spiritual vibe from this whole area.' she said waving her arms around the table they were sitting at, which was now dotted with Phil's blood.

Wil and Phil returned with tissues plugging both of Phil's nostrils.

'What the gnuck did I do.' Phil said looking at Ryan. 'You're a gnucking pbsycho Ryan.' He burst out.

'Sir.' Both security guards said. 'Calm down and tell us exactly what happened.'

Phil took a deep breath and explained. 'I was sitting here.' He said pointing at his chair. 'When this Wallstreet Psycho launched his Wankers Bitter at me.' Phil said imploring the more lucid looking of the security guards to take his side.

'I thought we were all friends here.' Christine said now crying on Bobo's shoulder, who patted her protectively.

Ryan was going to correct Phil and say Kombucha Bitter, then thought better of it.

'I inadvertently lost control of my schooner.' Ryan said holding his hands up innocently.

'That's not a schooner.' Wil muttered maliciously.

'That's a ...' The more lucid security guard wanted to say wine glass, then thought tumbler, then thought fuck it.

'That's a weapon sir. Hand me the ... glass please. You. Miss.' He said gesturing Beccs over with his finger.

Beccs who was over hyped, was now worried that being wagged over with a finger would push her over the edge, smiled sweetly and wagged her own finger back. The security guard walked over slowly and stood too close to Beccs towering over her. 'What's your story love? Why did you try to pull Gordon Gecko's head off?' He said smiling.

Justin moved in and politely pushed the gorilla back a few paces.

'Beccs. Tell me what happened?' Justin asked more politely. Justin had a soft spot for Beccs, after all she had to put up with both Phil and Wil.

'Well for no apparent rea…' Beccs started before being interrupted by Ryan.

'Quiet Gordon. We'll get to you soon.' Justin said shushing him.

'Ryan.' She said gesturing. 'Was being a dick, although that's not unusual. PC helpfully pointed this out, and then Gordon.' Beccs said staring threateningly at Ryan, liking his new nickname. 'Went Psycho and threw his glass at PC.' Beccs put her hands in the air to say that's it, end of story.

'It slipped.' Ryan restated.

'Thanks Beccs.' Said Justin ignoring Ryan.

Justin then walked the two security guards away a few paces to discuss the matter.

They all awaited the verdict.

Justin returned assuming the role of jury foreman.

'Well as far as I see it. I can take the easy way out and call the cops for the assault on PC and let them sort it out. That's up to you PC?' He said pointing at Phil who grimaced and shook his head in disapproval.

'Or you … Gordon.' He said already forgetting Ryan's name. 'Could apologise to Phil.'

'And buy me a few drinks.' Phil mumbled still holding his nose.

'And buy them all a few rounds.' Justin finished also putting his hands in the air to say that's it.

'Sorry Phillip.' Ryan said. Phil raised his eyebrows in reply. Ryan repeated with a sigh. 'I mean, sorry PC, sorry Beccs, and sorry Wil.' Ryan said trying to look contrite while rubbing his neck.

'All good PC. Guy's?' Justin said looking at the four of them. They all nodded ascension.

The security guards slumped away disappointed not to be throwing someone out.

'Ooo Kaay. Have a fun night.' Justin said smiling, shaking his head walking off.

Phil was still holding his dented nose.

They all stood up deciding to get some fresh air in the outdoor section. Wil carried Phil's beer out and put it on a table in front of him. Beccs pulled a chair out, and eased it in for Phil, whose face had now gone completely numb. He was thoroughly enjoying all the attention, and somehow also feeling heroic.

Ryan returned from the bar with a tray of drinks.

'Here's your drinks everyone.' Ryan said cheerfully putting the drinks down in turn in front of each of them. A schooner for Wil, a G & T for Beccs, a Vodka for Bobo, a Cocktail with fruit and an umbrella for Christine, and a middy for Phil.

'And I do apologise for all the fuss. I didn't mean to hit you with my schooner Phil.' Ryan added trying to look apologetic but not at all nailing the completely alien emotion.

'That wasn't a schooner.' Muttered Wil again.

'Fuss! I think you might have broken my nose you dick.' Phil said emphasising dick.

'And is that a fucking middy?' Phil picked up the middy sculled it angrily and put it back on the table.

'Can you go and get me a proper beer now please?' Phil said indignantly.

'I was worried you might have a concussion old man. You should probably ease up a bit tonight.' Ryan said trying to look concerned but again not quite pulling it off.

'Noted Ryan, truly touching. I think I'll risk it.' Phil said pointing at his empty glass with both hands open.

'And not another fucking middy.' Phil shouted at Ryan who was already heading to the bar.

'Having fun Bobo?' Wil said laughing noticing Bobo was now smoking a cigar.

'Yes. My new friend here got hit with some Karma.' He said slapping Phil on the back way too hard causing one of the tissues to fall out of his nose onto the table.

'Relax Bobo.' Wil said standing up smiling and getting very close to Bobo who took a few steps back, only to be pursued by Wil.

'Don't touch PC again.' Wil whispered reaching over pulling the cigar out of his mouth and crushing it in his hand, while not breaking his glare.

Bobo thought discretion was the better part of valour and sat down at a different table.

Christine could only see the back of Wil and smiled seeing then talking very close.

'It's sooo nice to see everyone has put their differences aside. If only the UN could see this. The world would be a super awesome happy place.' Christine said smiling at each of them in turn, as was her habit.

Beccs thought if she tried to start a group hug, she was going to punch her in the face.

'It's a pity that Phil is now disfigured.' Christine added.

Phil looked horrified and squinted at Beccs through his narrowing vision.

'Disfigured! How bad is it?' Phil asked. 'Be honest.'

'Well.' she said moving in to have a really good look.

'I don't think it's broken. Its stopped bleeding, but it is getting more swollen by the second. I can actually see it swelling up. You're going to have two raging bull black eyes by tomorrow morning PC.' Beccs said looking sorrowfully at Phil.

'I've had worse.' He said lying.

'Yeah. A few years, and a couple of dozen surgeries and you'll be as good as new PC'. Beccs added trying to lighten the mood.

'Makes you look hard.' Wil said helping.

Ryan arrived back from the bar, with Phil's schooner and put it down in front of him.

'That's better Ryan.' Phil nodded approval and held the drink in two hands protectively.

'You're about ten percent of the way through your apology now Ryan.' Phil said seriously.

Ryan put his own drink down and pulled his chair next to Beccs and smiled attempting to patch things up. Beccs wasn't buying it and turned her back on him. Ryan took the hint and decided to move to the table that Bobo and Christine were sitting at.

Beccs turned to Ryan, smiled sourly and said, 'Good idea Ryan, best keep at arm's length.' Then helped Phil pick up his beer and gently helped it to his lips for a sip.

Beccs, Wil and Phil engaged in some light conversation with Wil miming what Phil should have done to deflect the assault, while at the same time showing how he should have immobilised Ryan.

Phil was recovering rapidly enjoying Beccs' company and enjoying the anaesthetic effect of Ryan's free beer.

'So, you really finished. Did you bring a copy? Can I have a look?' Beccs said looking interested and genuinely impressed.

Wil reached down to pick up his briefcase then put it on the table.

Found a very small but sturdy looking key on his key ring, turned it in the lock, then fumbled with a combination lock. It opened with a satisfying and synchronised click, slowly on hydraulic hinges.

Beccs looked at Wil and smiled at the impressive looking briefcase. 'Nice briefcase James Bond.'

'It's cool isn't it. It's dust proof, fireproof, water...' Wil gushed.

'I saw the ad.' She interrupted. 'It's very you Wil.'

Wil pulled out a red manila folder from one of its pockets and handed it over to Beccs.

Beccs took the folder, opened it and flicked at the pages. 'Christ guys. Looks professional.' She then reached into her bag, got out her glasses, put them on, and laid the folder on the table reading the first page carefully. She looked up to see Wil and Phil staring at her intently.

'Guys I can't concentrate with you both staring at me. Go away and play with the greyhounds or go play with Justy for a while.' Beccs said shooing them off.

'Are you sure you'll be alright here with Ryan and Bobo, the probably on the run war criminal and the space hippy?' Asked Phil.

'Wow!' She said flicking through the very professional looking and quite substantial document again.

'Give me a while to have a good look and I'll let you know what I think.' Beccs said shooing them again.

'Here's a pen Beccs. We welcome feedback.' Said Wil with Phil nodding approval.

'Alright. Now shoo, shoo. Go play and I'll wave to you when I'm done. I can't wait to read it.'

'Are you sure you'll be OK?' Phil asked again pointing to the table that Ryan, Bobo and Christine were sitting at, who were now engaged in a deep discussion about God knows what. Whatever it was, Christine must have a very well disguised intellect, as both Bobo and Ryan were nodding approval, and making golf claps whenever she paused for breath. Either that, or one of them really wanted to get laid tonight.

Beccs then made a further shooing gesture, settled into her chair and started reading.

End of a Super Awesome Night

Beccs finished reading, put down her pen and turned over the last page, thinking. I can't believe he finished it. He really finished something, and it's not bad. It's actually good. At least it should get people talking, well arguing mostly. Typical PC she thought smiling to herself.

Beccs looked up to see both Wil and Phil yelling 'Go Bobo', and other encouragements until they both paused, leaned in unnecessarily closer to the massive screen, and simultaneously yelled 'YESSS!' nearly hugged, then looked around hoping no one noticed and punched the air in celebration.

She couldn't even begin to wonder what that was about, then saw Wil turning around to see if Beccs saw their triumph.

She waved for them to come back, but not before making the international sign for another drink, which was basically her holding up an empty glass with her tongue hanging out.

Phil turned to see where Wil was looking and smiled at Beccs, then saw her tongue hanging out. Was that her "This makes me gag face?" Phil walked out to Beccs prepared for the worst.

'It's rubbish, isn't it?' Phil said meekly.

'No. It's brilliant. Really thought provoking. I particularly like the E-protest. It would work if everyone did it.' She said, then looked at Phil more closely wondering how he could even see out of the tiny slits where his eyes used to be.

'Can you even see out of those? You look like you lost a fight with a football team PC. Let's get you home, I'll put some ice on it.' Beccs said looking concerned.

Wil returned looking a little wobbly with three drinks in hand and smiled at Beccs.

'What do you think Beccs.' Wil said eagerly.

'I think we should get PC home... With a few takeaways.' She added.

'Of course. But what do you think?' Wil asked again.

'I think you're both lunatics, and I think PC might have a concussion.' She said looking again at the puffy circles where Phil's eyes once were.

'I feel great Beccs. We just won a small fortune on Bobo's Girl, Dicks Revenge and hippy chick. We got the quinella, exacta and the trifecta at Dapto. If that isn't fucking serendipity, I don't know what is.' Enthused Phil.

'Just another piece of empirical evidence for our coincidental probability hypothesis PC.' Will said confidently.

'Exactly!' Phil agreed.

Beccs smiled seeing the unstoppable PC again. 'Let's get you home.' She turned to look at Wil. 'I'll walk him back Wil. You can head off if you like and start working on that hangover.'

'No chance Beccs. Besides it's Bobo girl's shout. And its PC's birthday, don't forget.' Will said smirking walking to the bar for the takeaways. He returned with two six packs of beer, and a six pack of pre-mix G & T's.

'Pre-mix spirits! You really did have a win.' Beccs said looking surprised.

'Oh yeah!' Wil said fanning a fairly thick wad of 50's. Looking at Beccs, then turned his attention to Phil.

'Put this lot in the wall safe PC.' He said handing Phil the cash. 'We'll invest in beer stocks over the coming weeks.'

'Always a sound investment' Phil agreed.

They finished their drinks, waved at Justy who was the only other person in the bar, with closing time rapidly approaching. Justin waved back and replied.

'Top night guys. Loved the show. Let me know when you're coming back for dinner again. I'll sell tickets next time?' Justin yelled from behind the bar.

Beccs replied with a thumbs up and a 'Will do Justy.' Then opened the door for everyone, as she thought her motor skills were in the best condition for the task.

'Oh yeah. I nearly forgot, where's Bobo, Ryan and Christine?' Phil asked who had completely forgotten about them.

They all shrugged their shoulders and walked a zig zag path back to Phil's house, stopping for Wil to pick up a pizza. Beccs gushed for the entire walk about some of the finer points, and about Wil's outstanding documentation skills.

'Seriously Wil. It looks like an annual report from BHP. Well done guys.' She added with exuberance.

'So, you really like it? Really?' Phil asked obviously fishing for another compliment.

'Yes! Really! I can't believe you finished it, and in a week. It's completely unbelievable, and it's gotta be what, 150 odd pages?' Beccs said pretending to struggle to lift the folder.

'It's a tome guys.'

'158 pages Beccs.' Will slipped in proudly before taking another bite of his pizza.

They all arrived at Phil's door. It took him a few stabs at the lock before finally landing the key at its destination. Then fumbled with the light and staggered over to crash land on the lounge. Beccs looked around at the house still impressed at its always now, but still totally unexpected tidiness.

'Place still looks great PC.' She commented thinking maybe Phil finally has got himself together. Then went to the fridge, opened the freezer and found it cavernously empty.

'Do you have any frozen peas I'm not seeing.' She said laughing. 'Maybe an ice pack PC?'

'No!' He said, which sounded more like Bo than No.

'Maybe I should just put my head in the freezer for a few minutes.' Phil said almost seriously, as his face was now beginning to hurt again.

'So, PC?' Beccs said on her way to the lounge passing a determined looking Wil on his way to the kitchen.

She looked at PC, who the light wasn't doing any favours and involuntarily put on her saddest sad face.

Phil didn't want to upset Beccs and said, 'It doesn't hurt too much anymore,'. He lied, 'and it was completely worth it. I shouldn't have to see Ryan again. Ever! You don't think he'll be upset you tried to strangle him though do you Beccs?' Phil asked mischievously.

'Nah. For Ryan, that's probably just Friday night I imagine. Shhhh!. Keep still.' She said quickly, but carefully, putting a cold beer against his nose.'

'It's a pity it's dented and not bent PC, then you could smell around corners.' Wil added.

'Don't worry PC. I brought you a drinking one too.' Wil said handing Phil a can, then dragging over Phil's red swivel high backed super villain chair that he found out the front of his house one day. Phil couldn't believe his luck that day, or even understand why anyone would throw a classic like that out in the first place. He loved that chair. Wil eased back and took a very serious sip of his beer.

'It's not finished you know PC?' He said swallowing seriously.

Phil and Beccs looked at each other and leaned forward.

'Are you going to kill Ryan?' Beccs said smiling giving Wil a thumbs up. Phil Owwwed through his laughter.

'May be.' Wil said raising his eyebrows at Phil.

'However. Right now, I'm talking about the publication PC? We didn't finish it for our own amusement. It's time to release it into the wild.' He paused for more refreshment and pointed at Beccs.

'That's where you come in Beccs.'

Beccs took a sip of her own drink, shrugged her shoulders, and said 'How?'

Phil felt like shouting "This has gone on long enough!" With another rogue wave of doubt washing over him.

'PC?' Beccs said looking at Phil.

Phil stared back, like he was staring off a precipice. Looked at Beccs and thought...Jump!

'Well. I think our best approach is total saturation. The mainstream media, politicians, political parties, global organisations, industry heavy weights, and of course the major villains in this story Wal, Adam and Clay. Basically, fucking everyone. Get it everywhere. Get it viral.' Phil said feeling awkward saying viral.

'Yeah. Give them the right of reply. You know, give them enough rope and maybe they'll hang themselves.'

A reverent silence fell across the room.

'Ok. It's time to get you on social media PC.' Beccs said breaking the reverence. 'Do you have a preferred social media handle guys?' They both shrugged in reply.

After a few false starts they all decided on "PCQuestions".

Beccs signed him up to HeadSpace first, which Phil insisted would condemn his mortal soul for all eternity, but decided to do it anyway because he was an atheist, and assumed the risk was minimal. She then signed them up to YouTube, WhatsApp, Instagram, Pinterest, TikTok, SnapChat, Reddit, X, Tumblr, Rumble, etc., the list was comprehensive.

Wil and Phil continued drinking, only occasionally stopping to look over Beccs shoulder to see how it was going. After a few hours she was finally finished.

'Basically, what I've done is publish the entire document where possible, in its entirety, or published a preface and a link to it on OneDrive giving read access to everyone.

Wil and Phil insisted on adding an alarming sub note mentioning that this is the last chance to reclaim freedom. To stop the global elites from transforming the world into an authoritarian dystopian nightmare.

'It always pays to frighten the audience.' Will said.

'Gaslighting always works for the nightly news.' Added Phil.

'See if you can work the words "Warning or Breaking!" in there somewhere as well.' Wil added. 'No, better still. Put a warning disclaimer on it, something like "The following content should not be read by anybody who feels threatened by having their belief systems challenged. Or doesn't want to participate in critical thinking, or any person or persons who accept the mainstream media as truth. The following content will cause you irreparable harm." Something like that Beccs.' Wil finished.

'Wil. Let's work on the warning then.' Said Phil trying to sound dynamic.

'I'll send the E-mail addresses to you Beccs.' Will fumbled with his laptop and sent the list.

'Who have you got so far?' Asked Beccs.

'Well. Who haven't I got would be a shorter list. Let's see.' He said scrolling through the list on his laptop.

'There's the Prime Minister of Australia, Great Britain, Singapore, Bangladesh, Soloman Islands, Namibia, Trinidad and Tobago, ...' Phil put his hand up to Wil to stop, signalling that he got the point.

'Oh, and Canada.' He said to finish.

Wil then moved on to Presidents, and other world leaders. He then moved on to the top 50 media outlets, along with any other industry group or international organisation that may have been mentioned at any point. The list was extremely eclectic and extremely long.

'You have thousands of E-mail addresses here Wil.' Beccs said.

'Yeah.' He agreed, then leaned over to whisper in her ear.

'I do have a bit of spare time at work.'

'Where did you get all these?' Asked Beccs flabbergasted.

'I got a lot of them from lists on the internet, you know amnesty, the UN, other crackpots that compile these lists. Anyway, the plan is for total saturation.' He reiterated.

'Ok. I'll send the blurb and the link otherwise we'll be here all night, and your router might explode.' She laughed. 'Oh, and I've already checked PC, your VPN is on.'

Becca spent the next hour tapping and swearing away at the computer before finally looking up flustered but satisfied.

'Alright your E-mail is on the way, and you're posted on all social media. Oh, your YouTube, Rumble etc., video is just a 30 second PowerPoint converted to a video with linked descriptions.' She stopped and put her hands out and said 'Finished!'

Wil, Beccs and Phil sat back in their respective places. Nobody knew quite what to say.

The silence continued.

The silence was then broken by a banging sound, and a few grunts from upstairs. It sounded like it was coming from the roof.

'Fucking possums.' Mumbled Phil destroying any chance of making any sort of lasting and profound statement.

Beccs stood up, went to the bathroom, returned, and offered to get more drinks from the fridge. Wil and Phil both took up the offer.

'Hey PC. Did you see Ryan, Chris and Bobo leave the pub?' She asked.

'No. I noticed Bobo's lights off, so he's definitely home. He has his lights off when he's home, and on when he's out. He is genuinely crazy I think.' Phil said a little concerned.

'Ryan probably got lucky with Christine. I think they left together. Probably rolling around on Ryan's waterbed by now. Can't be sure. I could really only make out shapes by then.' Added Phil.

'Why Beccs? Are you worried you missed your chance with Ryan?' He said and regretted it immediately as Beccs punched him hard in the shoulder.

'Nice punch Beccs.' Phil said pretending it didn't hurt.

The mood was now a celebration and a relief. They were all happy and relaxed. Phil decided to ignore the nagging little thoughts going around in his head, and the throbbing numbing pain in his face and just get drunk. Whatever the consequences were, they could wait for the morning. Most things fix themselves up by the morning anyway.

Part 2 – The End

Consequences

Wal Sletter was sleeping not very soundly at all in his magnificent four poster bed. It wasn't very comfortable, not that Wal would ever admit to that, and this wasn't just any four-poster bed either. This bed was once slept on by Louis XIV himself. In Versailles. In 1704. Well, he'd apparently slept on it in Versailles in 1704. Wal wasn't entirely sure if that was true or not. He didn't care. What he cared about was that it cost a fucking fortune, and everybody knew he bought it, and he fucking well slept in it.

Wal wasn't completely loaded. He was absolutely, completely fucking loaded! If Wal sold everything he owned and insisted on being paid in cash. Wal could just about insist on anything. Every tree on planet earth would need to be cut down, pulped, turned into paper, cut into little rectangles, and given to Wal. He was made aware of that titillating little statistic by Money Today magazine.

Money Today magazine was one of a new breed of tabloid offerings that thought the rich were gods, and we must all worship them. That was the only media offering Wal ever read. He owned a substantial share of the mainstream media but wouldn't be caught dead reading that shit. He created the news. He didn't read it.

The nearly imperceptible alarm cautiously trying to wake up Wal was specifically designed by a team of scientists, who no doubt had something better to do. The team was also specifically selected by Wal. He didn't know what he was doing, either about selecting a team, or any of the intricacies and nuances of alarms. But Wal absolutely insisted on being involved in all aspects of his self-designed estate house, which when finally complete, could only at best be described as an appalling eye sore.

The temperature started to rise by increments of exactly 1° every 10 minutes. A rhapsody of soothing music was gently introduced, subtly interspersed with the morning calls of woodlands creatures that Wal, in no small part was helping down the path to extinction.

The volume increased by precisely 1 decibel every 10 minutes in tender graduations. The tranquil milieu of soothing sounds produced by his all-round centuple phonic sound system was breathtaking.

Wal only stopped at a hundred speakers as he wasn't aware of a tuple word bigger than that. A gentle fragrance was added subtly to the air system. It wasn't air conditioning like a cheap hotel, or like normal people had. Wal had an air system, which he would point out boring shitless anyone unfortunate enough to be invited to Wal's estate house. Nobody ever refused an invitation from Wal.

After about an hour he would be ready to greet the day. Wal was never really sure what time it was. His specifically designed alarm was set to go off exactly 8 hours after he turned the lights off and laid down to sleep. What time it was didn't matter to Wal. People ran to his schedule.

He got out of his insanely expensive bed and walked naked to his en suite. Although, you could hardly call his en suite, an en suite. It was exactly 1000 square metres. Wal insisted on the square metreage of every room in his estate house ending in precisely zero. All this design effect achieved was to make every room in his house seem either unnecessarily too big, unnecessarily too small, or off-puttingly shaped.

He emerged from the bathroom in a lynx lined snow

leopard fur dressing gown and scrutinized the choice of suits now displayed on his suit display rack. Also personally designed by Wal. He chose the Alexander Amosu because he thought it was the most expensive. The rack immediately collapsed in a tangled heap with his unselected suits. Wal didn't care. He hadn't cleaned up his own mess in over 30 years and wasn't about to start now. He dressed and didn't bother to look at himself in one of the many mirrors in his bedroom. Wal knew he looked magnificent. He went to his 24/7 fully staffed gym about 4 hours a day, he had his hair cut by some French hairdressing artisan with nice tits he flew out once a week, and nobody would dare tell Wal he didn't look fucking magnificent.

He walked to the elevator and pondered the buttons, then noticed the boardroom button flashing ever so faintly. The reason it was flashing ever so faintly was because Wal didn't take orders. He accepted suggestions. Maybe!

Wal had probably had a good night, or possibly even a good day's sleep and was feeling pretty good. He pressed the boardroom button for the sheer hell of it.

The doors on the elevator opened instantly. He stepped in. The flat screen on the inside of the door was showing a live newsfeed presented by a newsreader with a really nice haircut. Wal made a mental note to get his hairdresser to give him one of those next week. The newsreader was talking very, very seriously about a cyber…, protest, e-protest, or something or other, while at the same time trying to look down his co-hosts top. Wal flicked it to the sports channel.

'Ping!' The elevator announced.

The doors slid open dramatically. Wal made sure he was always standing in the exact centre of the elevator, with his hands joined together at the fingertips. He hoped it would make him look like a super villain. It was meant to be a joke. Nobody ever got it. Nobody ever laughed. What made the joke not funny was Wal practically, was a super villain.

197

All twelve attendees in the board room smiled and greeted Wal with a series of 'Good Morning Sir', 'Thanks for joining us today Sir', 'It's an honour to see you today Sir', 'Good morning. Love that suit Sir', until Wal put up his hand mercifully putting an end to the sycophantic chorus.

A waiter dressed immaculately offered Wal one of thirty different types of juices, coffees, teas and assorted herbal supplements. Wal made the waiter describe each one in tedious detail. Wal liked keeping people waiting. He then made the same selection he always made. Four additional waiters arrived, with four separate food services offering Wal a selection of breakfasts, lunches, dinners, and snacks. Wal picked up a packet of peanuts off the snacks service and waved the rest away. He opened the nuts, took a sip of his instant coffee, then looked around the room at the sea of smiling and nodding faces. He waited for someone to speak. Wal knew that would never happen. All his board members were well trained, and well frightened.

Silence.

'Sooo. What's with the alert in the lift. Have aliens fucking landed?' Wal sickly smiled and put his hands out requiring an answer.

'No. Not exactly Sir. We've had an alert, well..., a major alert from our global distribution and sales sectors Sir.' Blain said, who had been a board member at TearDrop for over 15 years, but Wal could somehow, still never quite remember his name.

'Thanks Dwayne.' Wal said, then leaned forward impatiently waving his hands up and down frantically demanding more details.

'Sir.' Said a nervous looking woman unsurely sitting at the furthest point of the large teardrop shaped board room table. The table was made precisely to match the company logo. Wal of course was seated at the top, at the tear duct. He waved his arms more vigorously, getting even more impatient.

'It's been reported that most of our global systems are being attacked by a kind of denial of service thing.' She paused nervously. 'Kind of....Plus,' She added only to be stopped by Wal putting his hand up like a crossing guard.

'Stop right there. Why am I being blinded by the flashing fucking button in the elevator. Isn't this a problem for I.T. for buggering sake. Didn't I just spend...' Wal clicked his fingers at some guy he knew handled the numbers.

'10 billion Sir.' Said the numbers guy hoping that would be the only question he'd be asked by Wal today.

'10 fucking Billion! So precisely this sort of shit couldn't fucking happen. Anyway, big fucking deal. We still have sales coming in. Right? All will be forgiven and forgotten when the sheeple get their toys.' Wal said looking smug. Thinking they'll bitch, but they'll still buy.

'That was one of the things they guaranteed couldn't happen. Quarantining of business processes.' Wal said hoping that was a thing, and then somewhat composed himself.

'I checked it myself. Those systems just can't all go fucking down.' He added getting annoyed with why he was being forced to have this conversation in the first place.

'Quite right Sir. The Cyberattack is under control. However, it seems to have been part of a more serious attack Sir. One that's out of our control.' Said an older board member Wal thought was named Keith.

'Thanks Keith.' Wal said unsurely, then noticed a nod from Keith, and smiled. He always liked Keith.

'Alright then... Nothing is out of our control. Give it to Louie.' Wal said confidently half standing already losing interest, while at the same time thinking about breakfast.

'For a minute I thought one of those third world shit holes the Satisfaction Centre's are in,' Wal paused to smile.

He loved the spin he put on his sweatshops. The name created the satisfaction perspective. The customers were satisfied, the sweatshop workers certainly were not.

'Had a worker revolt, or something. Not that they'd have the fucking energy. Or the fucking time.' Wal laughed loudly at his own joke.

'Well.' Keith smiled politely. 'We do have a bit of a problem with sales Sir. Apparently for the last 12 rolling hours sales are down globally,' Keith swallowed involuntarily, and continued. 'Eighty five percent. That's globally Sir.' Keith finished and smiled again.

'You're fired Keith.' Wal said without any emotion.

Keith laughed then said 'But Sir...' Then stopped, knowing arguing with Wal was not only pointless, it could also be potentially fatal. He'd heard the rumours. Keith just stood up and walked out.

'Now that Keith the fucking comedian has finished his set. Great set Keith. Big round of applause for fucking Keith. Thanks, we've been a great audience. Don't forget, Keith won't be here every Saturday, or any other fucking day!' Wal shouted, clapping loudly hoping he was still within earshot. He never liked that guy.

'Who can tell me if, and why sales are down eighty five percent. That can't even be fucking possible?' Wal shouted looking around at the eleven remaining terrified board members.

The nervous woman who spoke first, stood up and offered a report to an assistant who jumped up and jogged it down to Wal, then scuttled away into a corner.

Wal sat down and read through all 30 pages carefully, folded it up calmly, then angrily screwed it up and threw it down the table. It only made it halfway, making him even angrier.

'It's not fucking possible! There must be some other cause. Are you trying to tell me that everybody has just stopped buying my shit?' Shouted Wal.

'Get me Louie on the Phone. NOW!' Yelled Wal as no one seemed to be doing anything quickly enough for his liking.

Ten seconds later a phone ring could be heard around the boardroom, it only rang once, then was abruptly answered by a gruff but alert voice.

'Yes Wal.'

'Louie. What the fuck is happening. Is it really fucking happening, and if it is fucking happening, fucking why's it fucking happening?' Wal said with barely controlled rage.

'Well, it's pretty weird. I've put IT under a bare bulb, it's not their fault.'

Wal suspected Louie wasn't exaggerating.

'I've checked all the search engines and we're still top of the redirects. Advertising, and marketing is pumping out, I've even created dummy purchases, and everything is running smoothly. It seems like almost everyone has just stopped buying our products.' Louie finished.

Louie was Wal's right-hand man. Louie always knew what was going on, and when he didn't know, he would find out. Most problems didn't even come to Wal's attention. When Wal wanted a problem fixed, Louie would fix it, whatever it was, whatever it took.

'Find out what the fuck caused it Louie. Fix it, then get back to me.' Wal slammed his hand hard down on the table, as he couldn't slam down a virtual phone. The line went dead. His hand started to sting.

'All right.' Wal said feeling a bit better. Louie would fix it. Louie always fixed it.

'I'm off for breakfast. Someone find me and interrupt me when Louie gets back.' He stamped out to the elevator, then stopped.

'And somebody come and pick up Keith's balls before someone trips on them.' Wal said laughing, inadvertently creating his best super villain improv yet.

The remaining board members sat in silence until Wal got into the elevator, they watched the doors close, then watched the numbers change indicating the elevator was moving. They all then started arguing loudly and violently about who would take on the near suicidal task of interrupting Wal.

The Morning After

The lounge room was silent barring the occasional snore coming from Wil, Beccs and Phil at disturbingly regular intervals.

Beccs thought she had a few too many drinks to walk home and decided to stay at Phil's. Phil insisted she sleep in his bed, and he'd sleep on the lounge. Wil insisted on walking her home through closed eyes, already half asleep on a chair. The argument started as a philosophical discussion, then finally degenerated into existentialism. At that point they both stubbornly refused to change positions based on existential freedom of choice, and freedom of movement, then fell asleep in their respective spots. Wil fell asleep when the discussion turned existential.

Wil was folded up asleep looking surprisingly comfortable in the chair, it was a skill he'd perfected through years of shift work. Wil believed he was well on his way to perfecting the much-revered art of falling asleep standing up.

Phil was asleep on the small part of the L shaped lounge still holding a beer. Beccs was asleep on the big part of the L shaped lounge with her feet balanced precariously above his head. A door creaked open upstairs. Beccs woke with a start causing her feet to slip off the lounge and hit Phil on the head, this caused him to yell 'We're under attack!', and throw his beer in the air, which woke Wil up who fell off his chair. They all looked around and pretended none of that just happened.

'Did you hear a noise?' Beccs said through a dry mouth.

'I thought I heard a creak.' Phil said rubbing his head. 'Have you got the spirit box on you Wil?'.

Wil looked around for his briefcase.

'Stand down mate. It's probably just Christine.' Phil said, still rubbing his head.

'She probably just crash landed from her astral travels, or something else fucking weird.' He said unconcerned, then said less unconcerned. 'I've got a hippy in the house. How did that happen?'

Phil didn't trust hippies, they were normally all about sharing and caring, mostly sharing his stuff, and not caring about it at all. But not so, all about buying food, or paying rent. He made a mental note to check his bank statements.

All three slowly began to move. Wil was making the best progress and walked to the kitchen offering everyone tea. The kettle started to hiss. Phil stood up, stretched like a cat, and headed towards the stairs muttering about a shower. A few moments later Beccs could hear the water running. Wil arrived back with a pot of tea and three cups ready to pour, only to be interrupted by a blood curdling scream, followed by an emphatic and disturbingly loud 'Fuck that!'.

Wil put the pot down.

'You OK PC?'. He said beginning to head upstairs followed closely by an anxious Beccs. They only took one step before being passed at cartoonish speed by a half stumbling, half falling, half naked Phil with a towel wrapped around himself dripping soapy water in torrents. He stood panting and pacing on the spot in the lounge room.

'Oh God. Oh God. Oh God. What the fuck was that?' He said now visibly shaking, and not from the cold.

'What is it PC? Wil asked concerned.

'It's fucking Ryan.' Phil said shaking his head in disbelief.

Beccs' jaw dropped open in horror. She got Phil another towel and a shirt from the laundry and put her arm around him, then poured a cup of straight black tea. He drank it down as quickly as he could. Beccs refilled the cup hastily.

'Here PC have more.' She said helping to hold Phil's cup. 'Is he still up there?' Asked Beccs looking equally concerned.

'Yes, he's still up there!' Phil yelled loudly at Beccs.

'Sorry Beccs. Still a bit shocky. There's no way out or in from the second floor. How did he get in?' Phil said, sipped his tea again, then indicated to Beccs for more.

'He was naked on the toilet when I got in the shower. I'll be in therapy for fucking years.' Phil said not unseriously. Beccs gave him a squeeze and a comforting smile.

'Did we leave the door open last night?' Phil said standing up to look around the corner to check that the front door was really closed.

'He must have been here before we got home PC.' Wil said looking alarmed.

'Jesus Christ. What do we do now?' He said looking at Beccs, who was now joined by Wil, also now looking at Beccs.

'Don't look at me. I'm not going up there.' Beccs said, then folded her arms adopting her absolutely no fucking chance pose.

'I can't go up. I'm still a bit wobbly at the knees.' Phil said exaggerating his voice to sound overtly nasally again. His eyes were not as swollen as last night but were turning some impressive colours. Beccs looked at Wil who simply shook his head no.

Beccs looked at Phil again, who now had two of the best black eyes she'd ever seen. Shook her head at him pitifully and said reluctantly. 'Alright, I'll do it.'

She walked cautiously and ominously to the base of the stairs. Grabbed the rail to steady herself ready to ascend, then changed her mind and yelled. 'Ryan... Ryan...... RYAN! Are you coming down? We know you're up there.' She said without humour and waited.

'We're on our way now Beccs. Did I hear you say tea?... Two coffees for us, milk and one sugar for both thanks.'

She heard Ryan say followed by a very girlish little giggle.

'How did you know Ryza? What are the odds?' A girlish little voice said still giggling.

'We have a connection, a common thought process Chrissy my love.' Ryan said followed by some disturbingly overt kissy sounds.

Phil didn't have coffee, and Beccs didn't make coffee. Not for Ryan anyway. Ryan had been trying to get her to make coffee for him for years now. Beccs thought it was time he let go of that dream.

Christine jingled her way downstairs in a dress that had at least ten different fluorescent-coloured layers. It appeared to be actually emitting its own light. It was not helping anybody's hangover. Ryan followed behind her wearing one of Phil's T-shirts, and not just any T-shirt, Phil's oldest and most precious T-shirt. The circa 1981 Danger Mouse BBC T-shirt. A classic.

Ryan pulled over a dining room chair next to Beccs, smiled and sat down. Then looked directly at Phil and burst out laughing, accompanied by Christine who didn't know why she was laughing, but always laughed when other people laughed.

'That's a nasty pair of black eyes you have their Phillip.' Ryan said struggling to speak through his laughter.

'Yeah. You do nice work Ryan.' Phil said throwing the last of his tea at him.

'See how that's done Ryan! You don't let go of the cup Dickhead! And give me back my T-shirt.' Phil said, annoyed that almost all the tea had landed on it, and almost none of it on Ryan.

'I found it on the floor beside your bathroom door Phillip.' Ryan said innocently.

'PC... Dickhead! When you're in my house Ryza. It's PC.' Phil said exaggerating Ryza sarcastically.

'And that's a Floordrobe™' Interjected Wil indignantly.

'OK, PC Dickhead.' Ryan said smugly, before being grabbed in yet another headlock by Beccs. She was beginning to like assaulting Ryan and decided to take advantage of every opportunity.

'OK PC...' Ryan said pretending to laugh. 'Now let go of me Rebecca before I demonstrate how easily I can get out of this hold.' Ryan wheezed, turning red. Beccs tightened her grip.

Ryan tried twisting, then turning, then tried dragging Beccs to the floor without any success. He then gave up and went limp. Beccs decided at that moment to let go.

'See Beccs, easy.' He said crashing to the floor coughing and gasping again.

'Guys! Settle down. Do I need to go and get Bobo? He could do an impromptu harmony class. Maybe some meditation, essential oils. That should help.' Christine said imploringly like she had all the answers. Why was no one listening. 'Should I get Bobo? I'll get Bobo.' She nodded heading to the door.

'NO!' All four of them shouted loudly. Beccs then helped Ryan up and smiled... They all heard the neighbour's door slam shut.

'See. Now we've upset Bobo.' Phil said. 'He's probably gathering up some yoga mats and scented candles right now.' Phil said laughing at his own joke.

'I'll get the door if it's Bobo PC.' Wil said, thoroughly enjoying how the morning was progressing, and fully intending on opening the door and letting him in.

Everyone sat quietly before Beccs finally broke the silence by going out to the kitchen and putting the kettle on, then yelling 'Ryan, kettle's on. That's as close as you get to having coffee made.' Ryan waited for Beccs to leave before going out to the kitchen with Christine.

'Where's the coffee Phillip?' Ryan asked from the kitchen. No answer was forth coming.

'Phillip?' Asked Ryan again. Still no answer.

'PC?' Ryan said finally working out why he was not getting any response.

'No coffee Ryan. Just Tea!' Phil answered spitefully.

Ryan made tea begrudgingly and returned from the kitchen accompanied by Christine.

'So. Top night last night everyone.' Christine said sitting on a chair next to Ryan smiling at each of them. 'Happy birthday again Phillip. How young were you yesterday? Did you get any good prezzies? Is anyone coming over to celebrate the big day with you?' She fired off seemingly losing the ability to stop talking.

'I think I really made a connection with Ryan. Sorry Beccs.' She said frowning sympathetically. 'The early bird catches the worm. No hard feelings sister?' Christine said reaching over to hold both of Beccs hands.

Beccs stared at her, then grasped what Christine was saying and pulled her hands away sharply.

'Oh God. No Christine. He's all yours, sister.' Beccs replied, causing Christine to let out an excited squeal, which caused Ryan to let out a nervous gasp.

Wil was having too much fun enjoying the banter and decided to get up and make another cup of tea and toast, so he had something to enjoy with the morning's unexpected pantomime.

When he returned, to his disappointment an awkward silence had fallen across the room.

Phil stood up a few minutes later, oddly not enjoying this awkward silence himself, and turned on the TV. He then went with Beccs to the kitchen to forage. They returned to see Wil, Ryan and Christine staring at the TV intently. Ryan looked around at Beccs and PC who were both walking back with some toast and cereal of their own.

'Seems like there's some big news today. Some new type of global protest happening. They're calling it an E-Protest Phil..., PC?' Ryan corrected himself nervously glancing at Beccs. 'You know about this IT stuff. Gotta stay on top of these things. They might need a corporate lawyer.' Ryan said instinctively thinking of his wallet.

'E-Protest?' Asked Phil who looked nervously at Wil and Beccs.

'Yes. An E-Protest,' Ryan said curtly, whatever that is. Apparently, someone has rattled the cages of all the activists with a rhetoric-based document doing the rounds of social media. Questions or something.'

'PCQuestions or something?' Asked Phil looking even

more nervous.

'Yes Phillip, PC.' Ryan said thinking, that's oddly coincidental, then dismissed the coincidence. He reached over testily and snatched the remote off the table and pressed the increase volume button vigorously, the lack of success made him press the button more vigorously. Beccs and Wil watched unhelpfully. Phil walked over and turned it up manually when he thought Ryan was running out of steam.

'Our leading story today.' Said the overtly cheery for a Saturday morning news reader. 'Is the Protest, or should I say E-protest.' She said to polite chuckles from her immaculately groomed, but vacuous looking co-host.

'Yes. I can see people now. Holding up placards to their web cams shouting slogans.' Interrupted the immaculately groomed, but vacuous looking co-host to even more chuckles coming from his colleagues off camera.

'Will the police be able to fire virtual water cannons, and virtual rubber bullets at them?' He added to even louder chuckles.

'The E-protest,' She continued trying not to giggle herself. 'has reduced the number of HeadSpace subscribers by over 40% and reduced the daily sales of TearDrop.' She said looking seriously into the camera. 'The world's largest e-commerce company by up to 85%. The stock market has responded by dropping its share price accordingly. Reports are also coming in that all sorts of other businesses are suffering negative effects. Those affected include industries ranging from air-conditioning right through to zoos, all suffering reduced sales, denial of service attacks, boycotting. It's a mess.' She said looking seriously disappointed down the barrel of the camera again. Clearly ready for her closeup.

'Disgraceful.' Said her immaculately groomed co-host frowning, trying very hard to look extremely concerned.

'Who would attack zoo animals.' He said frowning, shaking his head now looking down at his desk.

'Ok. More on that story later. Well, coming up after the

break Davey.' She said looking at her smiling co-host.

'We will be interviewing the leader of the opposition Stephen Faulkerl and asking him to explain his decision to back the current Governments bills.'

'Steevy, Stevo. Can't wait. I'm more interested to hear if he can explain the Demon's performance on Friday night.'

'We'll be back after these very important messages.' The host interrupted smiling broadly. The camera then panned back as some old disco music started to play loudly and the entire panel started dancing in their chairs. Phil stood up and changed the channel sharply.

The next channel's morning news crew were just wrapping up their ad break dance routines, with the camera zooming back in ominously to the talking head.

'More on our leading story today. Apparently, all the fuss about this E-Protest was started by a social media post from username PCQuestions, who posted what can only be described as a wide-ranging document on everything wrong with the world, and what needs to be done to fix it.' The female news reader said quizzically and dryly.

'I'm joined now by highly respected Psychiatrist, Philanthropist, and Social Commentator Franklin Parker the third. Good morning Franklin. How are you this morning?' She said smiling.

'Having just read through the entire document published by PCQuestions.' Franklin said ignoring the greeting then launching into one of his trademark tirades.

'Bullshit. He hasn't read it the lazy prick.' Wil muttered under his breath.

'You can read through the subtext that this has come from a frustrated, petulant and unintelligent adolescent mind, unfortunately trapped in a man's body I suspect.' He laughed at his own joke. No one else did.

'Is not!' Said Phil folding his arms petulantly, canvassing a smile from Beccs and Wil, and confused looks from Chris and Ryan. The news continued.

'Why do you say that Franklin? And the names

210

Jacqueline Albert.' She said smiling again.

'Well.' He said completely ignoring her introduction once again.

'The reason being the Protests, or "E-Protests" as these are so named.' He said using air-quotes.

'Are merely the petulant foot stamping of a spoilt proletariat child. What are they expecting to achieve? The reality is all they're achieving is some hippy feel good vibe that they are part of something bigger, when all they have done is cause a minor blip in the global economy which, if allowed to continue would hurt them most of all. They seem unable to comprehend that very, very important entrepreneurs, and great philanthropists aren't the only people being affected. This will affect all their futures.' Franklin said leaning into the camera almost threateningly, then leant back again.

'The mainstream media are also under attack Jacqueline. How is everyone supposed to get accurate up to date news. Who are they supposed to trust, get the truth from. How are they supposed to know what to think?' Franklin put his hands out in dismay.

'Maybe it's time the mainstream media listened, and started being bipartisan for a change?' Jacqueline said in reply, causing raised eyebrows from her own colleagues.

'News is not bipartisan Jacqueline,' He said very condescendingly. 'The truth does not need a second opinion.'

'And who are they trying to hurt the most? Adam Socclier, Clay Siliolvnee and Wal Sletter whom most of their misguided hatred seems to be directed towards. I know all these gentlemen personally and I am privileged to call them friends.' Franklin said nodding and leaning back to look relaxed and confident.

'Take Wal Sletter for instance. Who wouldn't want to work for a company like TearDrop, and work for a dynamic man like Wal Sletter.' Franklin said raising one hand motioning that he was about to start to refine his point further.

'Let me just interrupt you their Franklin. Wal Sletter's

business model has been accused of using practices comparable to slave labour, manipulating Governments to favour those practices, unfair employee quotas, it's quite a comprehensive list of accusations you'd agree. And that doesn't include some of his highly questionable philanthropic practices.' She paused, but not long enough for Franklin to interject.

'The World Catastrophic Event Authority, and I quote from their latest press release.' She said holding up a piece of paper 'Ask the question "How much money does Mr. Sletter need in his philanthropy fund before he starts to distribute it to people that are already in urgent need." It continues "Mr. Sletter's Philanthropic undertakings so far have been mostly directed towards endeavours, that will at some point supply a return on investment, such as monopolized farming, monopolized pharmaceuticals...' She was abruptly interrupted.

'Well, yes.' Franklin said rolling his eyes. 'But that's simply because most people can't see Mr. Sletter's vision of reimagining the entire concept of Philanthropy. Instead of it being an ongoing problem. It becomes self-funding and over time will be able to address the entire world's charitable needs without requiring further donations. The answer to the WCEA's question, how much money is needed. The answer is more.' Finished Franklin.

'Ok. That's an entire topic in itself Franklin. But let's discuss one of the main concerns of the E-Protestors and that is, censoring of free speech, manipulation of the media, particularly anybody speaking out against their current agenda, ...' She was interrupted again.

'Let's put this all into perspective, and let's not get overly emotional. The reality is that none of his workers are chained to their desks, his employees go home to their families after work. It's his work practices that allow him to employ more people, most of whom would otherwise be unemployed. And it's also what makes everything so cheap.' Franklin said smiling broadly.

'Who doesn't love browsing through TearDrop. I'm guilty.' Franklin added laughing with his hands up in mock surrender.

'Well, they may not be chained to their workstations Franklin, but not all of them go home to their families. Suicide rates among TearDrop...' She was interrupted again.

'I'm sure Mr. Sletter is very upset about that and is endeavouring to sort, that little problem out.' He paused, this time not being interrupted by Jacqueline Albert who was left completely speechless.

'If the market was concerned with that, then his business wouldn't exist. It's condoned by capitalism. Are you a communist Jacqueline?' He said, looking sternly at her through the monitor.

'No. But maybe the market is now becoming concerned. Just like they are now becoming concerned about the unelected influence of the World Treasury Forum. WTF! And the influence of Schultz Dauber their so-called puppet master.' Jacqueline said enjoying saying WTF on the news legitimately.

'Mr. Dauber is merely a guiding and benevolent father figure to these gentlemen and is always working for the greater good.' Franklin smiled innocently.

'His very, should I say colourful and controversial past...' Jacqueline was hastily interrupted yet again.

'The problem is, people have it too good. These people couldn't possibly comprehend the complexities of global agendas, and as such need to be looked after by the ruling class. Be they politicians, or major stakeholders like Wal, Adam, Clay or even Mr. Dauber for instance. They can't possibly be allowed to make decisions on their own. They should only ever be given the right choices, which is why we are all so heavily involved in stopping the dangerous flow of misinformation and disinformation, and so are you Jacqueline. People can't come up with their own opinions. That would be disastrous. We've all seen how effective global government mandates have been in the past, and recent years.' Jacqueline raised her eyebrows suspiciously at Franklin.

'The one thing that all stakeholders have in common,

and all agree on, is that if we left important decisions in the hands of the people, they would select. God help us, humanity over the greater good. Or worse individual choice… Freedom.' He threw his hands up with dread.

'These decisions must be made for all of us, and we all must comply to improve society.' He smiled terrifyingly down the camera.

'Ok.' She said throwing her hands up in surrender. 'Thanks, as always for staying on topic, and for your unbiased insight Franklin.' She said with poorly disguised sarcasm, crossed back to the main camera, looked down and muttered 'Wanker' which was unfortunately picked up by her mic.

'PCQuestions has certainly raised a lot of questions that's for sure.' Jacqueline said raising her eyebrows and shuffling uncomfortably in her chair.

'If you are one of the E-Protestors, please post your opinions on our news website, or if the E-protest is affecting you, we'd like to hear from you as well. And of course, if the person or persons behind PCQuestions is watching we would especially like to get your side of the story. Now over to …'. Phil changed the channel, checked around the other channels, which were pretty much covering the same story. He finally settled on a channel showing Pokémon Go.

'What did you do that for PC. I love the weekend news. It's less serious, but more inciteful than the weekday news. Plus, that Franklin Parker sure knows his stuff. His head is on the right way around. Always insightful.' Ryan said knowingly.

Phil hated the media, but he hated media pundits even more, and Franklin Parker was the worst of both worlds.

'Shut up Ryan. When are you leaving exactly?' Phil enquired, trying to comprehend what can't be happening.

'I have a vegan fridge upstairs Ryan, and a telly. We can have an indoor picnic.' Christine said and smiled, pointing to the stairs.

'What's a vegan fridge?' Wil asked immediately regretting the question.

214

'It's a fridge that doesn't eat meat silly.' Replied Christine not surprising anyone with the answer.

Christine and Ryan stood up and bade their farewells to a disinterested crowd. Phil opened his laptop and handed it to Beccs.

'Can you check my social media pages and see what's happening Beccs. Then tell me this hasn't got out of control, regardless of whether it has or not.' Phil said smiling with his fingers clasped together like he was preying.

'Ok PC. You make another pot of tea.' Said Beccs.

'I can't handle this on an empty stomach. I need to go for a walk, need to walk off a hangover. You handle the tea Wil. I'll head to the shops and pick up something for lunch. Any requests?' Phil asked, gathering up his bag, pen, and a list pad.

'Just some party pies, frozen chips...a big bag, and snacks.' Said Wil.

'And a bottle of champagne. You're a hit PC. Let's celebrate.' Beccs said hitting Phil on the shoulder.

Phil jotted down all the requests on his list and added a few things of his own.

'Wait, you can't go out like that PC. Put a baseball cap on pulled down, and some sunglasses. You look like an escaped convict. They are impressive black eyes.' Added Beccs shaking her head sympathetically.

Phil put on his disguise and left the house now suspiciously looking even more like an escaped convict and started on his trek to the shops.

No One Interrupts Me!

Wal finished breakfast and started walking to the gym, then thought, maybe play a round of virtual golf with Adam. Wal wasn't worried, Louie had fixed bigger and scarier problems than this in the past, plus his mind was preoccupied with the company he was expecting later that afternoon.

Wal had procured. Procured being the correct word in this context. Some eastern European company being flown in on his private jet, discreetly. What discreetly meant was, they didn't have passports, and they were all underage. Wal knew he was scum, but he didn't care, all his billionaire friends, mainstream media pals, high-powered politicians, and all the top shelf celebrities he knew were all scum too. Everybody knew, and no one really cared, besides he practically owned the media anyway, so no one could do anything about it to make anyone care. Symbiosis he thought.

'Time for a quick workout with Katarina, then slip in 9 holes.' He said out loud pleased with the day ahead.

Wal was walking down the unnecessarily too wide corridor, that had roughly ten billion dollars' worth of art hanging on its walls. You name the artist, they were there. He had Van Gogh, Rothko, Matisse, Turner, Warhol and even a da Vinci. They were all beautiful works of art, in their own right, but somehow, Wal had arranged them in a way that made them look tacky and talentless.

He was slowly closing in on his private elevator that he always wanted to be able to travel to every location in his estate house. You know, sideways, slantways, longways, backways and of course frontways. Just like the one Willy Wonka had. Wal loved Willy Wonka, he loved that he tortured children, and he loved that he had slaves. Willy was quite a role model for Wal growing up. However, Willy was an unrealistic engineer. Wal tried everything, and everyone to get it to work, but it wasn't possible surprising no one except Wal. He heard footsteps briskly approaching from behind him and turned sharply.

'Who the fuck are you sonny? And why are your footsteps affecting the ambiance of my artworks?' Wal said enjoying frightening a twenty something intern.

'Sir. I have a …' The terrified Intern started to say.

'Shut your fucking mouth son. And don't look at the fucking art. What I need you to do is turn the fuck around and fuck off before I put a Matisse over your fucking head. Don't say one more fucking word. Alright sonny.' Wal turned and walked off smiling with the beginnings of an erection. He hadn't frightened anyone in a few hours and frightening someone always pushed Wal's buttons. The intern stood there and cried silently.

Wal finished his workout and was playing his VR golf game with Adam who he was beating mercilessly as always. Wal hated Adam, but he liked beating him. He took off his VR headset, took off his golf shoes and glove, and turned around to get a drink.

'FUCK!!!' Wal scream recognizing the same kid from the corridor.

'No one interrupts me! And I mean fucking no one. Who the fuck do you think you are to be on MY!' Wal screamed, pointing at himself. 'Golf course?'

'CUNT!!' He added as a full stop.

'Now turn around and fuck off before I beat you to death with my four iron? And it won't be a virtual beating son.' Wal said drawing a four iron from his bag, knowing he could get away with anything.

The intern at that point involuntarily collapsed to the ground and started crying again.

Wal saw a weakness he could exploit and decided it would be fun to play the "Overworked, tough but fair, with

218

a heart of gold under his gruff exterior, good guy" routine. His last performance in the media, he thought was a little lacklustre. He could do with the practise. It got him some good deals, and sometimes it even got him laid. Although strictly speaking, now he only fucked his acquisitions. Acquisitions he thought sounded better than helpless underage children. It had been too long since he'd practised being nice.

Wal walked over, knelt down, and put his arm around the hapless intern.

'Sorry son. I just had a really bad round. Deep down I have a heart of gold.' He said moving his head in close. 'Tell me why you have interrupted me twice today son?' Wal said as the intern looked up.

'Well, Sir. I have been asked to...' He blubbered.

'Come on son.' Wal said holding out a very expensive silk handkerchief and smiling innocently.

'Sir.' He blubbered again, and gurgled his nose loudly into Wal's expensive hanky, making Wal smile with barely controlled anger. He then handed it back to Wal who politely took it and put it in his pocket, knowing he would never see this suit, or that handkerchief again. Hopefully not this snotty kid either.

'I have a phone call for you Sir.' He said, pulling a phone out of his pocket, looking at Wal with the most terrified and saddest eyes he'd ever seen, and Wal had seen some sad and terrified eyes in his time. He was getting incredibly aroused.

'Thanks son.' He said putting his hand out for the intern to give him the phone. He dropped it in Wal's hand smiling like someone who was just about to enter stage 4 Stockholm syndrome.

Wal picked up the phone. 'What is it Louie?'

'Ah huh... Really... I know that.... Who ... How the fuck should I know! ... Well find the fuck out ... mmm ... mmm .... mmm ... Who? The singer. What's she got to do with it. I thought she was dead. Check it anyway... Ok... Ok... Ok... Put out the usual media, and social media propaganda, and no fuckups! Threaten them so they

219

know who the boss is, and that I'm really fucking serious this time. Have this guy censored. Call Adam and cut the cunt off at the knees. Total censorship, not just him, but anyone who agrees with him, or doesn't actively disagree with him, cut them off too, and have them play an ad, or put up a message pointing to a government website with the facts about how bad this is for them, and how much worse it could get. Frighten the fucka's silly...Ok...Good idea Louie...How should I fucking know...Have our spin doctors make up some facts... The Government will post it or their biggest donors will withdraw their support...Ah huh...Ok...Ok...Ok...But remind everyone. Fear is the key. Fear always keeps the masses in line. Fear gets people to comply without question...Yes...Yes...Ok...Remember, if even one of those news reader pricks gives any airtime, or lip service to any other opinion that disagrees with the now new consensus, threaten them Louie. Kill someone if you have to. Yes, I'm serious...I'm working on something from my end.' Wal threw the phone against the wall. hard! Smashing it into small chunks. He stood still thinking. Then he remembered the annoying little prick on the ground, only snivelling now, and smiled.

'Hi son. Sorry you had to hear that. Been a bit of a hectic morning. You understand.' He said putting his arm under the intern helping him up.

'What's your name son?' Wal said smiling and frowning at the same time.

'It'ssss Butch Sir.' Butch said, now fully into stage 5.

'Hi Butch. Walter, Wal. Let's go have a drink mate.' Wal guided him to the virtual 19th hole.

Wal poured a couple of Scotches neat and handed one to his terrified drinking buddy.

'So, what do you do here at my company Butch?' Asked Wal looking remarkably like someone you could trust.

Butch took a tentative sip of his Scotch, grimaced and coughed. Wal did exactly the same thing. Wal was a master of the art of the psychological technique of mirroring.

'I'm a Social Media Liaison Officer Sir.' Butch said

unsurely.

'Call me Wal, Butch. A Social Media Liaison officer. So, what is it a Social Media Liaison officer does Butch?' Asked Wal slipping on his genuinely interested face.

Butch took another sip of his Scotch, proudly not grimacing, or coughing this time.

'Basically, what I do is reply to any posts that have been shared with you on all your social media platforms and like, or comment on them.' Butch looked unimpressed with his job now that he'd described it out loud.

'Wow.' Wal said putting his hands up whistling, he hoped in confused shock. 'Like, and or comment?' an even more confused look appeared on Wal's face.

'But I'm trained to be able to understand social media interactions. Get inside the head of the user collective.' Butch added trying to make his skills sound like something harder that what your average twelve year old does a thousand times a day.

'All that social media computer stuff is beyond me. You must have some education for that?' Wal smiled again wondering how far he could take this.

'I have a Diploma in Social Media Interactions. I hope to get a master's someday. With the help of the TearDrop scholarship program... Wal.' Butch said smiling appreciatively.

'Good for you.' Wal said thinking, what the fuck passes as a degree these days?

'Maybe you can help me with a little project?' Wal said.

'As you know here Butch, we're all about education and improvement.' Said Wal, thinking not money or control at all, and laughed in his head.

'You've probably seen the news today Butch.' Said Wal.

Butch nodded ascension. But he probably would have nodded ascension if Wal had asked him if he'd seen a unicorn today.

'Well, we have some poor misguided person who thinks I'm...' Wal said pointing too himself innocently. 'Some kind of boogey man, or worse.' Wal said laughing heartily looking more wholesome and innocent all the time.

'I'm not a monster Butch. I pay everybody's salary. I pay yours Butch. Is the money always in your bank account on time?' He said locking a steely gaze on Butch.

Butch was too scared to tell Wal that he was on an internship, and was basically only getting living expenses, discount vouchers and free food at the staff canteen. He just nodded.

'Right!' Said Wal.

'But apparently that's not good enough for some people. They don't like people who supply good, no! Great quality products globally at almost unbelievably low prices, and straight to your front door too.' Said Wal sounding like one of his own ads.

'That's where I think you come in Butch. What with your degree in Social Studies Interactions.' Wal said unsurely.

'Social Media Interactions... Wal.' Butch said thinking he may have just crossed a line.

'Exactly Butch. That's the sort of help I need. It's the details I'm lacking.' Wal said smiling like a used car salesman about to close a deal on a car that would have been lucky to make it off the lot.

'Now before I double your salary.' Wal said thinking this little prick can't be on much anyway.

'I want to know if I have your full commitment to the task ahead.' Wal said leaning into Butch and squeezing his shoulder almost too tightly.

'Yes Sir!' Butch said not knowing what else to say.

'Great news Butch. Really great news.' Wal offered his hand to shake on it.

Butch reached over and shook hands with Wal. Wal was physically repulsed by the limp sweaty handshake, but somehow managed to look pleased and smiled broadly.

'Fantastic Butch. Let me write something up for you to give to personnel, and I'll run you through the assignment.

'What's your last name Butch? It's not Cassidy, is it son?' Wal said pretending to use his fingers as imaginary guns, while lightly punching Butch in the arm. Really pouring on the charm, now just for the hell of it.

Butch took the note off Wal, folded it in half and put it in his pocket carefully.

'Right let's get down to business.' Wal said putting his arm around the diminutive Butch, then guided him to an adjoining meeting room.

Wal and Butch walked out of the meeting room about an hour later, both laughing like old buddies.

'Listen Butch. Mate. I've got to go to a board meeting.' Wal lied.

Butch smiled, gave Wal two thumbs up, and walked out the door with purpose. He then headed straight to the canteen. Today he was going to have two sandwiches for lunch.

The Afternoon After

Phil arrived back from the shops looking a little worse for wear but feeling refreshed. He packed everything away in the kitchen and walked out with three pies in a bag from the little corner cake shop. They all took one and started eating.

Tastes different. Did you get these from the little corner cake shop? The one that got caught putting something in them a few months back?'. Asked Wil taking another bite.

Beccs held her bite in her mouth and mumbled, 'What do you mean something else? What sort of something?' She asked refusing to swallow. 'A not meat something?'

'No. It was definitely meat.' Giggled Phil taking another large bite.

Beccs put down her pie after seeing what she thought might have been a claw buried just below the gravy, stood up, walked to the kitchen, and silently spat her bite into a napkin then rinsed out her mouth. She browsed the kitchen for something else and returned with more cereal.

'They're probably OK Beccs, they've most likely sold out the old stock by now anyway.' Phil said not reassuring her at all.

'They're not as good.' Wil added taking another bite.

Wil and Phil finished their pies, then cut Beccs discarded pie in half to share. Beccs scraped the last of the cereal from the bowl.

'Well PC. Good news, and bad news.' Beccs said collecting the discarded pie packets and bowls together to take to the kitchen, then remembered it wasn't 1950, and put them back down.

'You know I always like to finish on a high. Give me the bad news first.'

'The bad news is Ryan and Christine are still here.' Beccs said picking up the scraps again nearly forgetting again, then put them back down.

Phil picked up the scraps and took them to the kitchen before she made another play for them.

'If they're still here by 5, we'll smoke them out PC.' Wil said giggling. Phil looked at him not seeing the funny side.

'The good news PC is you now have two and half million friends on HeadSpace and rising. On YouTube you have over four hundred million hits and eighty million likes.' Beccs said.

'Each time I refresh, the numbers just keep going up.' She added smiling.

'Your file has been viewed on OneDrive over 700 million times. Social media, X blah blah it's been shared over one hundred million times. Pretty impressive PC.' She said.

Phil smiled unsurely.

'Nobody's worked out who I am, right?' Phil asked nervously.

'No PC. We had the VPN on, and I made up bogus details. The internet believes you to be a 58 year old spinster from Wyoming named Laura Branigan.' Beccs answered.

Phil leaned back on the lounge a little more relaxed.

'Laura Branigan.' He said, then started whistling Gloria, stood up and walked to the kitchen asking if anyone wanted a drink.

'What've you got?' Called out Wil.

'I've got Fanta, lemon cordial, Champagne, and water of course.' He called back.

'Fanta for me.' Said Wil.

'I'll have a strong cordial PC.' Answered Beccs, still somewhat tasting the pie.

Phil walked out with the drinks and sat back down on the lounge.

'What next PC?' Asked Beccs.

'Probably just have an easy day on the lounge I guess.'

Answered Phil sliding back to recline.

'No. With the document. The whole thing, you can't just leave it there?' Beccs said looking at Phil like he'd just picked 10 numbers at Keno and was going to wait until tomorrow to collect the ticket.

'It's time to make some comment about what's happening. We watched the news when you were out. Just about every group, everybody, every organisation you mentioned reacted. Both good and bad. The journalists are calling you a socialist, an anarchist, misogynist, some even a domestic terrorist, and a racist Nazi.'

'A racist Nazi. Isn't that a bit redundant.' Phil interrupted.

'I thought so. However, the internet is calling you a straight shooter, a visionary, the voice of the free speech oppressed. You have to post something PC.' Beccs said looking at him with eyes that Phil noticed, had a hint of respect he didn't see often enough.

'What do you mean reacted.' Asked Phil, with an unconcerned quizzical look he hoped.

'Well, from reading the mainstream media. You have successfully pissed off just about every celebrity, all organised religions, all cosmetic companies, all of big pharma, even mathematicians.' Beccs said.

Phil smiled at that one.

'Every single politician, sportsmen, the entire financial industry, garbage men.' She added.

'Garbage people.' Wil said opening a packet of Chips he found in Phil's kitchen.

'Airconditioning manufactures, and the zoo. Apparently, they have made a global pact to ban you from all zoos, when they find out who you are.' Beccs finished.

'I like the zoo.' lamented Phil. 'Is anyone happy.'

'Oh, and the major supermarkets have said they will ban you as well. Although most individuals seem happy, which is why we're seeing the E-Protest. So far TearDrop's share price has dropped further costing Wal Sletter 30 billion dollars so far. People are deactivating their HeadSpace accounts, and other social media accounts too. The mainstream news service has suffered a 50% traffic drop. There are protests in front of most charities including the Red Cross's head office, the Wal Sletter foundation, and the World Treasury Forum... WTF.' Beccs said making Phil laugh nervously.

'The list goes on. And today has been declared no shopping day. With a slogan inspired by you. "Let's stop buying garbage", or no consumption day or something apparently.' Beccs finished.

'Quite a list Beccs. Where to start?' Phil said, opening his eyes wide.

'Well, I suggest we work on a post thanking everyone. And give them some direction, or encouragement maybe.' Beccs said.

'You have an audience now PC. It's time to step up to the podium.' Wil said seriously, taking his pen and some paper out of his bag.

'I have a bit of a hangover. Don't you think I should wait till I'm a little more, clear-headed?' Phil asked.

'Nah!' Answered Wil. 'You wrote most of it when you were pissed. I feel it's appropriate your rebuttal should be born from a hangover. Don't you?' Asked Wil.

Phil saw just enough logic in there to get by on, and nodded agreement.

'Well let's start with Thanks, as Beccs mentioned.' Wil said nodding to Beccs.

'We should also remind everyone of the power that all people have over Governments, and Corporations, that are basically the same thing these days anyway. They only have the power because we gave it to them. If we all stop obeying their edicts and mandates, they have no power.' Phil said with Wil taking notes again.

'We should also focus on apathy. We don't want this to be a flash in the pan PC.' Added Wil.

'Exactly. It needs to continue until something gets done. We need to stress that. This isn't about making a statement. This is about making a change.' He emphasised. 'We can starve these bastards to death.'

'What's going on guys.' Said Ryan making everyone jump, who had emerged from Christine's room silently.

'Christ Ryan!' Beccs said, startled again by Ryan's unexpected presence.

'For fuck's sake Ryan, can you wear a bell or something. How long have you been there?' Phil said, also startled by his continuing unexpected presence.

'Not long Rebecca, Beccs. Christine and I are heading out for a late lunch, care to join us?' Ryan asked without any hint of sincerity, or enthusiasm.

'No!' They all replied in turn matching his lack of enthusiasm. The memory of their last meal together still fresh in all their minds.

'Come on guys.' Said Christine making everyone jump again.

'When the hell did you get there Christine? And how did you get there.' Asked Phil, pointing at the normally vacant corner of the lounge room sitting on a chair that Phil always assumed was only ornamental.

'I've been here for ages guys.' She said ignoring most of the question. 'What's going on? I thought you finished your philosophy paper yesterday?' Said Christine sidling over to Ryan and putting an arm around his waist nuzzling against his shoulder, making everyone feel uncomfortable, including Ryan.

'We have finished, we're just doing an umm... group philosophy workshop thing Christine.' Why don't you too love birds run along.' Said Beccs trying not to laugh at Ryan's predicament. Was he really that desperate for a root?

'Good idea Beccs. Let's leave Aristotle, Socrates,' he said, pointing at Wil and Phil in turn. 'and, ahh.' Ryan said pointing at Beccs, struggling to name a female philosopher.

'Hipparchia!' Beccs said to complete his sentence.

'Right Beccs.' Ryan said, like he knew exactly who she was talking about.

'Anyway, we're off. Might stay another night PC old man.' Ryan said more as a statement than a question, before walking out the door and slamming it behind him.

'Fucking awesome.' Mumbled Phil.

After several hours of discussion, some of it serious, they all finally agreed on a post. It offered thanks to all those that read and shared the document. It reiterated his belief that a real change can only be achieved by continuing the fight, continuing the E-protests, and by spreading the word. Don't let the media, social or otherwise censor you. E-mail it directly, post your disgust everywhere, stop watching the lying mainstream media. Bombard notice boards with the truth, not just electronic ones, actual notice boards. Get on a soap box in the park. It continued with more rhetoric and finally decided to end with a few quotes:

"It always seems impossible until it's done."
Nelson Mandela.

"You can't beat a person who won't give up."
Unknown.

P.s., You are the unknown. If you don't give up, you will win!

Signed
PCQuestions.

Beccs posted the message everywhere and almost instantaneously the replies, the likes and shares all started to flow in. Phil stared in disbelief.

They started to scroll through the replies starting with the first one. The timestamp showed it was posted 1 second after Phil's post. It was posted by username Victim_of_Wal. The post had a photo of someone in chains. It came with a plea for help. Beccs read it out loud.

'Hi PC. You are a real inspiration to me. The way you are not only fearless in your criticism, but fearless in sending it directly to who, or what you are criticizing.

Daring them to respond. Well, I'm as my username says, a victim of Wal, and the TearDrop corporation's ethos. There are probably some things I know that would even shock you. Please reply and friend me so I can help. Butch. Smiley face.'

'His name's Butch Smiley face?' Phil said seriously.

'No, his names Butch and he put a smiley face.' Fuck me thought Beccs. He can be so literal sometimes, it's a wonder he can function in society.

'What do you reckon? Friend him and get some undercover dirt?' Asked Phil.

'I don't know PC, looks sus.' Wil said.

'I think so too. You're not a freedom fighter, you're just raising issues of concern, making suggestions, and TearDrop is just part of a bigger problem.' Beccs added now totally committed again to whatever the hell was happening.

'Yes. That's how this whole thing may have started, but it's evolved into something bigger. None of us thought anybody would even read it, let alone give a fuck.' Phil said looking pleased with himself, at the same time daydreaming he would end up on a T-shirt like Che Guevara, or maybe even a Nobel Peace Prize nomination. Even a real statue of him in the park.

'Be careful PC. He could be an operative, a spy for TearDrop.' Answered Beccs suspiciously.

'An operative you say. Who's being paranoid now Beccs. And you thought we were the tin foil hat wearers.' Phil said laughing, then stopped, thinking that sounded a bit spiteful, and added. 'And you're right of course Beccs.'

'Listen PC.' She said, fiddling with her phone.

'As it stands, Teardrop's share price has dropped even further, and you just posted that everyone needs to hurt these fascist slave driving bastards more. Does that sound like something someone like Wal Sletter would not take seriously?' Beccs said rather sternly.

'We've all heard the rumours. All seen the conspiracy theories. That bastard and his sociopathic mates make more people disappear than the Clinton's.' Beccs said looking even more stern.

'Allegedly.' Phil and Wil said simultaneously and very nervously.

'I found his mobile in the profile.' Phil said, ignoring the warning. 'Don't worry Beccs, I'll private number, and put it on speaker phone. They don't know who I am, I have anonymity.' Phil said confidently.

He picked up his phone while Wil and Beccs looked at each other concerned. He hung up in a panic and then put private number on and pressed redial.

'Everything is under control.' Phil said, smiling confidently.

Anonymity

Butch had only been on his new assignment for a few hours when his 'burner' phone, as Wal put it so coolly started ringing. He stared at it in consternation. The call was coming from a private number.

Wal would be so pleased. This would definitely earn him a slap on the back, and a well done sport. Butch answered the phone.

'Hello.' Butch said trying to sound older and wiser than he was.

'Who am I speaking to?' Said the voice at the other end of the line authoritatively.

'Butch.' Butch repeated.

'Butch. Butch Who?' Phil said worried the phone call was about to degenerate into a knock knock joke.

'Smith. Butch Smith.' He said nearly saying Cassidy thinking of Wal, then settling on Smith immediately regretting it.

Christ thought Phil, "Smith, Butch Smith". Now I'm in a Bond movie. He regathered his thoughts as Beccs and Wil sniggered behind their hands, miming for Phil to hand up.

'Hi Butch Smith. It's PCQuestions here. So, you work for Wal you say?' Phil said almost accusingly.

'Yes PC. And I'm pretty annoyed with how he treats me, and pretty much everyone else here.' Butch said glancing at the notes he and Wal had made.

'And I'd really like to get even with him.' Butch added sounding nervous, and unsure of how his subterfuge was going.

'OK Butch. But how do I know you're the real deal buddy?' Phil said winking at Beccs, who rolled her eyes in reply.

'Umm. Don't know, what would convince you?' Butch answered.

Phil looked at Wil and Beccs sporting his best 'Beats me' face, not sure what to answer. Wil mimed putting on his lanyard and then mimed holding up his imaginary pass and waved it at Phil. Beccs nodded approval. Phil was absolutely shit at charades and thought they wanted him to offer Butch a medal or something and held his hands out looking confused. Beccs, who also knew Phil was completely shit at charades leaned over and whispered in Phil's ear, or they could have been there all day.

'He could send you a copy of his work pass... Butch?' Phil said confidently, in one of the most inconsistent verb tense sentences ever spoken.

Beccs simply stared at him in amazement.

'Umm OK PCQuestions.' Said Butch unsurely. 'So, I should send you a copy of my pass?' He said hoping for clarification.

'Yes, that's what I said.' Phil answered.

'No you didn't.' Beccs said laughing.

'But you'll have to wait, I've only got 3 minutes left on my break.' Butch said knowing his real pass had his real name on it. Butch Harmon. That didn't matter, Wal would fix it, and Wal would be really pleased. Gratitude was one of the coping mechanisms he was using to deal with his worsening Stockholm syndrome.

'He's such a bastard.' Butch said trying to sound really aggrieved, knowing Wal was probably listening, if not now, then definitely later.

'Yeah, a real bastard.' Butch added with a lot more feeling, and he hoped grit.

'Ok Butch Smith.' Phil said suspiciously.

'He makes me work late, so it'll probably be tonight... Can hardly wait to get the bastard,' Butch added thinking he'd probably said Bastard one too many times already.

Phil let the silence linger.

'You're a real inspiration PCQuestions.' Butch finally said to break the silence. 'Anyway, I have to go. I'm in the toilet right now. We're not allowed to use our personal devices in the office. What a bastard!' Butch said grimacing at saying bastard, yet again.

'Ok Butch. I'll wait for the post, and we'll go from there.' Poor bastard, working on a Saturday he thought and hung up not bothering to say goodbye. Phil thought that would make him sound shadowy.

'See easy peezy! No muss, no fuss, no problem.' Phil said looking at Wil and Phil nodding confidently. They nodded back unsurely.

Butch immediately sent an SMS to Wal, reading "Contact made. Need a fake office pass in the name of Butch Smith ☺." He didn't care how tough Wal thought he was. Everyone appreciates a smiley face.

Wal was in the middle of his underage orgy when one of his phones pinged a message. He unceremoniously pushed the girls aside and slid across the barbie pink TearDrop shaped, gigantic, was not a big enough word to describe it. Bed. Reached over and picked up the phone.

'What a fucking moron.' Wal said not appreciating the smiley face at all.

'Smith! For fuck's sake.' He said aloud thinking, I have to sack the asshole that hired this idiot.

Wal stood up, put on a dressing gown, and walked out without acknowledging any of his terrified company, then stepped into an adjacent room. He spoke with a large man who held the title of procurement officer. Wal wasn't comfortable with the word pimp or more accurately, people trafficker, so he used procurement officer instead.

'Get those little whores out of here. I'm finished playing with them now. Oh, and get rid of them. You know the deal.' The deal Wal meant was they were to be sealed in concrete and dropped in a deep part of the ocean.

'Which ocean sir?' Asked the procurement officer.

Wal answered by punching him hard in the face.

'I don't fucking care shit for brains, just so long as it's beyond the reach of James fucking Cameron's submarine.' Wal said angrily watching blood trickle out of the nose of the pimp who showed no emotion, or concern.

Wal walked into one of his many walk-in wardrobes scattered throughout his estate house and put on a fresh suit. He then picked up his tablet and clicked the tracker app.

Wal's tracker app showed the exact location of every employee that had ever worked for him at any time, and he meant at any time. He found where Butch was and had him summoned to his office.

No one ever knew when Wal was in his office. Wal had installed his own private entrance and exit for that very purpose. He liked to keep his staff guessing. Wal sat behind his giant Shell Cordovan leather upholstered chair behind an absurdly expensive Parnian desk, pressed a button and waited.

The doors to his enormous office opened automatically revealing Butch, who looked very small standing in the middle of the doorway smiling nervously.

'Hi Butch. Gee it's good to see you pal. I hear you've got some really good news for me?' Wal said smiling like a Cheshire cat. He really, really fucking hated Butch.

Butch walked the forty odd metres to a chair placed in front of Wal's enormous desk and sat down. Wal's visitor's chair was ergonomically designed to make his guests feel as uncomfortable as possible.

'I've made contact with PCQuestions. He seems nice.' Butch said with Wal gritting his teeth. 'And he wants me to show him a pass.' He added.

Wal pulled the "Butch Smith" pass out of his pocket and slid it across the table to Butch. 'That will get you into my offices at the industrial estate.'

'So, what else do you know Butch?' Wal smiled.

Butch steeled himself as best he could.

'Well not much. He has only posted twice to social media, and both posts are the same across all platforms. However, I did read everything, and I have come to the conclusion, it's the work of two, possibly three people, although I suspect only two. And both of them seem to be suffering from the Dunning-Kruger effect.' Butch stopped unsure whether he should stop to explain what that was.

'Fascinating!' Wal said already bored shitless, yet somehow looking totally fascinated.

'Explain to me what your understanding of the Dunning-Kruger effect is, just to see if we're on the same page on this one,' Wal said not realising he was one of the world's leading sufferers.

'It's a hypothetical cognitive bias stating that people with low ability at a task overestimate their own ability, and that people with high ability at a task underestimate their own ability.' Butch explained.

'Mmm,' Wal said absorbing the information.

'Sooo. What is it Butch. Are they Einsteins or Rosie O'Donnells?' Wal asked genuinely, as he hadn't even bothered reading the document Wil and Phil had published. Wal paid people to read for him, then summarise, and then reduce it to bullet points. That way it almost guaranteed he missed the point entirely.

'At this stage, I'm unsure. I think I'll remain nonpartisan.'

'Nonpartisan,' repeated Wal thinking, what's wrong with saying I don't know you little wanker.

'Ok Butch, thanks for the report, stick to the plan and let me know when you get any information at all about who this little,' Wal refrained from saying cunt, and instead just thought it. 'spark is.'

'Yes Wal.' Said Butch taking the hint, then left the office.

Wal picked up his desk phone and called Louie.

'Louie, it's Wal.' He said unnecessarily.

'Got any leads on who this cunt is yet?' Wal asked

impatiently.

'OK. Just keep digging. Don't stop until you get what I need. Did you check that singer isn't real...Kim Wilde or something...That's it Laura... Yeah... It's probably bullshit but check it anyway.' Wal slammed the phone down, then picked it up again and redialled.

'Call Adam and Clay's offices. Tell them we need a meeting.' He slammed the phone down again.

Wal didn't like Adam or Clay, and he especially didn't like meeting with them, but this was getting serious. Adam and Clay were both sociopathic bastards, which always made Wal nervous.

He preferred being the only sociopathic bastard in the room.

Sociopathic Bastards

A dam Socclier was another one of those billionaire bastards that publications like Money Today magazine try very, very hard to make appear human, but always seem to just fall short.

Adam made all his money from social media. Well, he made all his money from his now former best friend, who in reality came up with the idea, and did all the hard work creating HeadSpace.

Neither the friendship, nor his morals stopped Adam from stealing everything. He justified this to himself by saying his friend was far too honest, and he was just stealing it before someone else did. After all he was his friend. He didn't deserve any of the credit, and more particularly, he didn't deserve any of the money.

Adam looked up from his desk noticing someone standing in front of it out of the corner of his eye. This interrupted what he was doing, which was precisely nothing. He stared at one of the perky breasts of one of his perky breasted secretaries who was standing silently not making eye contact.

'What is it miss...' He trailed off as he could never remember the names of his secretaries. They were replaced as soon as he got tired of ogling them.

'It's a request for a meeting from Mr. Wal Sletter Mr. Socclier.' Said the perky breasted secretary still not making any eye contact.

'Thank you.' Said Adam taking the printed out E-mail handed to him. 'You may go now.' He said ogling her ass as she walked away. I think I'll keep her for a few more weeks, he thought.

Adam had all his correspondence printed out and handed to him. When he was finished with it, he'd put it in one of the two trays on his desk. The one labelled out, where it would be dutifully filed in an appropriate binder. He insisted it was a failsafe. The reality was Adam could barely use a computer. He relied on his former friend for that, but he wasn't talking to him anymore. Well, not since he jumped off his balcony anyway.

The lie that he was an I.T. genius had grown completely out of control. In the early days he tried using private tutors, in an attempt to at least give him some rudimentary understanding, but both he and his tutors soon faced up to the reality that it was totally pointless.

He was once snapped by the paparazzo holding a copy of "Social Media for Dummies" boarding his private jet. Everybody laughed. Really laughed. He even became a popular meme. Adam set his spin doctors on it to try and convince everyone it was a brilliant joke, showcasing the genius of his ironic dry wit. Nobody bought it. Instead, he had to purge it off the face of the internet. That took a lot of resources and cost him a fucking fortune. He wasn't taking any more chances, so from then on Adam always worked off paper.

He picked up his Montblanc diamond encrusted pen and wrote in rather childish handwriting. "Yes! When and where?". He put the piece of paper in a Clairefontaine Triomphe silk envelope and put it in his out-tray, then pressed another button.

A different perky breasted secretary walked into his office, again not making eye contact. Adam insisted all his secretaries were not to make any eye contact. That way he could really ogle them properly, without having to put up with their frightened and contemptuous glances.

She smiled into the middle distance, picked up the envelope and walked out. Adam watched her walk away feeling a bit unsatisfied. He'll need to replace that one soon he thought.

Clay Siliolvnee was a different sort of billionaire bastard. Not different in the fact that he too, also basically stole his money. He stole his money by selling something he didn't even own. Then subsequently looking so pathetic in both clothes and manner that when he got caught, they actually let him get away with it. Clay took that as a lesson to never let anyone else ever get away with anything.

Clay took theft to a new all-time low. Gave everyone a completely new definition for the expression 'biting the hand that feeds you'. Although laziness also played a big part.

Clay grew up in a rough part of town. He was born to hard working migrant parents, although nobody knew that as he disowned them as soon as he made any money. His family taught him and his brothers and sisters good moral values. They worked hard to make sure they had everything they needed. But that was not enough for Clay, he hated that he didn't get everything he wanted, and he resented his family for not doing anything about it.

Early on in his childhood his parents did everything they could to foster Clay's obvious genius in the hopes that one day he would metamorphosize from the grotesque foul-smelling venomous caterpillar he was now, into well, a butterfly was probably too high to aim for, a praying mantis would have been an improvement for Clay.

Clay's problem was that nothing happened fast enough for him. That was all about to change. At the age of 16 Clay was offered an internship with the number one software development company on the planet, MegaSoft. MegaSoft was one of a few of the remaining foundation companies of the software industry. Some could argue they invented the software industry. They were a socially responsible company based on innovation. They were also proud of the amount of people they helped get a start. Clay was destined to be one of those people.

He was their youngest ever intern, and as such, they treated him like someone they needed to nurture, look after, put a loving arm around if he made a mistake. It was a bit like the way the officers on Star Trek The Next Generation treated Wesley Crusher on the bridge of the Enterprise. The difference was, Wesley wasn't a sociopath.

Less than two weeks after he started, Clay had already stolen, and rebranded MegaSoft's latest software innovation, then had sold it to the highest bidder. Due to his Wesley Crusher status at MegaSoft, he was able to cover his tracks so well there was nothing anyone could do about it until it was too late. Clay stood on the corpse of his first conquest triumphantly. MonoTech was born.

Since then, he had successfully managed to change his image into that of a likeable nerd, while simultaneously fostering the notion that he actually gave a fuck about people. Clay used this image to allow him to siphon large chunks of his wealth into a dodgy charity he set up called the World Treasury Forum. Which nobody bothered to tell him, and that he figured out far too late had the acronym WTF. In hindsight it was apt. All his morally bankrupt buddies were also part of it. The charity only worked on projects that would make them all more money, or allow them to take control of an industry, and make them even more money later. The chairman Shultz Dauber was perfect for the job. He came from genuine Nazi pedigree.

It was getting late in the evening, and Clay was sitting up in bed playing the last level of a computer game he personally developed. The object of the game was to kill anything that moved. Clay had one of his adversaries pinned in a corner and was shooting off its limbs one at a time, laughing maniacally at the realistic screams. The best part about the game Clay thought, was that it was programmed so that nothing in it could hurt him, but he could hurt, torture, and kill everything else. He paused the game when his final adversary screamed its last scream.

He fiddled with his remote control that had more buttons than a standard keyboard and pressed the one that displayed his messages. He read through them without much interest, until he got to the one from Wal. 'What does he want?' Clay muttered to himself and read the message.

Clay replied to the message. He also sent an E-mail to Adam asking him if he knew anything. The E-mail was prioritised as very urgent. He liked sending very urgent E-mails to Adam, he knew he wouldn't get a reply until tomorrow. Clay knew Adam was I.T. illiterate and found it a constant source of amusement.

The wheels had now been placed in motion. These wheels were oiled with sweat and blood. Blood mostly. On three separate continents, Boeing 757's, Gulfstream III's and Learjet 75's, were being readied for their important cargo to board. Wal's Jet was the most expensive, the 757 which is why he picked it. He was departing from Sydney airport. Clay was flying in a Gulfstream departing from Heathrow airport because he thought it was the most technologically advanced. Adam was departing from JFK. He was flying in a Learjet because he thought it looked and sounded really cool.

Mission Accepted

When the call to Butch concluded. Phil, Beccs and Wil all burst into raucous laughter.

'Smith, Butch Smith. Fucking hilarious.' Phil said in a bad Sean Connery impersonation.

'Put on your psychiatric profiler's hat Beccs and share your thoughts on Butch.' Phil said resting his chin on the back of his hand reminiscent of Rodin's The Thinker.

Beccs assumed her serious countenance. 'Having watched nearly every episode of Criminal Minds. More than once!' She added.

Both Wil and Phil nodded at each other looking impressed.

'I feel completely and thoroughly prepared for the task.' Beccs paused and took the paper and pen off Wil and started to doodle on it absentmindedly. She continued.

'One. He clearly isn't one of Wal's "Operatives" as Smith is every body's, I didn't think I'd need an alias, alias.' Beccs said pausing her doodling, then raised two fingers.

'Two. He sounded a little young don't you think, a little unsure? Not really the hardened Wal Sletter type operative you'd expect.'

'Maybe he's just pretending to sound young. Maybe he's trying to put us off our guard.' Wil said nodding at both of them. Beccs gave that thought an asymmetrical smile and continued.

'Three.' Beccs said this time holding up 5 fingers, a classic running joke with Phil.

'Three.' Repeated Phil, holding up two of his own.

'Right, three. Why did he keep saying bastard? It just

seemed so rehearsed, so declamatory. And he just kept saying it. He didn't convince me. Totally weird!' She paused to wait for the reaction, but was encouraged on by Wil and Phil.

'And four. Anyone can make a pass genii.' She said to Wil and Phil who both missed the plural.

'Even if he comes through with the pass. The only way you'll know it's real is if you get him to use it. Show you it really works and gets you into one of TearDrop's offices.' Beccs leaned back in her chair.

'Butch sounds like an American name. I doubt he's in Australia anyway. Sounds like a dead end. My professional recommendation would be to drop the whole thing with Butch entirely.' Beccs said nodding a professional conclusion.

'I agree Beccs.' Said Wil. 'There's nothing really to gain from this. Maybe we should regroup on it later. See where things lead tomorrow.'

'I agree too.' Phil said, who stood up to click around the TV channels. He stopped on a channel where an old movie was just starting.

'I've seen this one Phil. It's good, 'Mrs Forsythe's Daughters', or something.' Wil said that way too excitedly for Beccs' liking. She'd endured Wil's movie selections before.

Beccs tried to make polite excuses to no avail and was forced to watch the entire movie. Thankfully it only went for a bit over an hour, to her considerable relief.

The early afternoon had gone on long enough, midafternoon had arrived, and Beccs, Phil and Wil were all looking a bit over the day. Beccs stood up and announced that she was leaving. 'I'm going home PC, Wil.' She said standing up and stretching.

'I'll walk you home Beccs.' Wil said also stretching and standing up. He'd been basically sleeping and sitting in the same chair for the best part of a day and looked like he needed some home comfort.

Phil politely offered another cup of tea, which they politely declined, then thanked them for coming over and helping with everything. He smiled a sincere and remorseful goodbye to Beccs. Beccs smiled sincerely back.

'It's not over yet. We're on the precipice of greatness PC.' Wil said walking away with Beccs.

Phil looked worried. He was afraid of heights.

'Hey PC!' Said Beccs turning around. 'Put some more ice on those eyes, maybe some tea bags. You're beginning to look like a malnourished Panda.' She said looking sadly at Phil.

'Call me if you want to talk later. I'm really proud of you. You've done something. Amazing! I don't mean it like that.' She giggled and rushed back to give Phil an unexpected, but very welcome hug whispering 'Impressive,' in his ear before running back to Wil to continue their journey.

Phil stood in complete shock. Could his relationship with Beccs have taken a new turn? Could the long running saga finally be about to approach a new page? Watching Phil and Beccs' relationship was like watching the long running Pitch Drop experiment. Like most things in Phil's life, they moved so slowly it was almost indetectable. This time he was determined not to miss the drop.

'SMS me in the morning. Let's grab a beer at the pub tomorrow. See if your 15 minutes of fame is over.' Wil yelled before they both disappeared down the driveway.

Phil waved goodbye unnecessarily, walked back inside and closed the door to settle in for a lazy afternoon of laying on the lounge with Saturday TV. He fell asleep quickly.

Phil woke in near darkness saved only by the glow of a MacGyver rerun. Why was it always the same episode? He then heard what woke him. It was the sound of a key scratching at the door before finally, clumsily, finding the lock. He heard some now all too familiar giggling.

'Fuck!' Muttered Phil who instinctively rolled off the lounge onto the floor, then started duck walking to the stairs.

The door opened with a bang followed by Ryan and

Christine falling through locked in an embrace indulging in a sickeningly sloppy kiss. Phil was too horrified to duck walk any further.

'Hey PC old mate. Are you getting shorter?' Ryan said noticing Phil squatting in the hallway and laughed loudly, followed by Christine who also laughed loudly because that's what she did.

Ryan then laughed even louder seeing Phil's blackened eyes again. Christine wasn't paying attention at that point and didn't laugh along. This disappointed Ryan terribly, who thought he'd been an absolute crack up all night. Phil stood up nonchalantly.

'Well, it's been fantastic bumping into you again Ryan. And I feel the last two....' Phil stopped seeing that Ryan had also stopped paying attention and simply said.

'Goodnight!' Turned, then started to trudge up the stairs.

'Phillip, PC, Phil, Philly.' Have a drink with us. You like conspiracies, well Chrissy-poo and I,' Ryan said, giggling at being poked at by Christine. 'Have a conspiracy theory we'd like to run past an expert.' Ryan said with unmasked sarcasm.

He threw a newspaper on the lounge and stumbled after it. Phil continued his journey up the stairs ignoring the request.

'Have you seen today's paper Philly. The first 10 pages are all about this Protest, E-Protest blah, blah, blah thing.' Continued Ryan. Phil turned the corner for the final ascent.

'And Christine.' He said talking louder. 'Thinks you're PCQuestions. The PCQuestions from the social unrest thing that's happening?' Ryan said, then finally shut up. Phil assumed because Christine had her tongue down his throat again.

Phil paused his ascent and wanted to say something that sounded dismissive, and disinterested but instead just said 'It's not me.'

'Yeeeesss Iiiittt Iiiisss.' Christine said in a sing songy voice that Phil had only heard a few times before but

248

already found intensely tedious.

'It's not me.' Phil said again, then muttered 'God damn it.' under his breath and headed back down the stairs.

'You mentioned a drink Ryan? Phil said causing Ryan to get up which allowed Phil the time to resume his place on the lounge grabbing the newspaper to have a look.

Phil looked at the banner headline. "PCQuestions False Prophet". Further down was an article referred to him as a "Devious Puppet Master", with a swastika silhouette. The next page showed a collage of protests happening in cities around the world. All the remaining pages right up to the sport section were full of gloom and doom articles about micro, and macroeconomics, trigger events, fiscal fallout and a whole lot of other newsy catch phrases that sounded highly technical and were specifically designed to convince us they know what they're talking about, while at the same time, scaring the shit out of you.

It was also smattered with pictures of angry celebrities, angry politicians, basically everyone they had an angry picture of. The pictures of angry sportsmen were in the sports section.

Every journalist wrote an editorial set to kill. Even the wine and gardening writer had a go. It was Government and corporate bought and paid for sponsored vitriol at its best.

'Fuck me.' Muttered Phil under his breath.

'Fuck me indeedy Philly.' Said Ryan smugly, startling Phil from behind the lounge handing him a Pineapple Cruiser.

'Fuck me.' Phil muttered again seeing the Pineapple Cruiser. He took it anyway.

'So, Phillip. You're a celebrity.' Christine squealed excitedly.

'Oh! Can I be your Media Liaison Officer...Please!' Christine asked in a pathetic pleading voice, pushing out her bottom lip. Phil decided her pathetic pleading voice had just edged out her sing songy voice as her most annoying.

'Obviously Christine. That would be just fantastic.' Phil

said, taking a sip of his drink making a grimace.

'However, I'm not PCQuestions, I'm just PC.' Phil said not liking referring to himself in the third person twice in the same sentence, at the same time glad Wil was not there.

'But weren't you guys writing a philosophical-socio-neo-economic-political document thingy yesterday?' Said Christine.

'No.' Answered Phil. 'Well yes, but no. It's just a coincidence. Like you two meeting.' Phil said hoping to change the subject, at the same time smiling sweetly at each of them.

'Hold on PC. It seems very coincidental don't you think?' Ryan interjected.

'On the surface. Yes... However,' Phil paused to take another tentative sip of his drink, stalling for thought.

'However, coincidences as you would know, are just a concurrence of events, or occurrences without any apparent causal connection.' Phil said hoping to at best convince them, or at the very least confuse them.

'That may be the dictionary definition Philly. But seriously. It's you. Admit it. It's too many... Causal connections don't you think?' Ryan said raising an eyebrow suspiciously.

'To the inexperienced, untrained eye. Yes. That may appear to be the case. Except there are only two causal connections Ryan. The first is that my nickname is PC, and the second is that I was writing an ... What did you call it Christine?' He said smiling at Christine.

'A philosophical-socio-neo-economic-political document thingy.' Christine repeated impressing everyone, including herself.

'Exactly.' Said Phil. 'How many of those are written each day?' He said trying to sound like he was making an obvious statement, and an obvious observation.

'Now if you weigh that up against the noncausal connections, like I don't use social media.'

'Beccs did mention you're a bit of a solitudinarian.' Agreed Ryan.

'And why would I spend time creating a document and not bother to put my name to it.' Phil added raising his eyebrows.

'And finally, and conclusively. It's NOT me!' Phil concluded.

'Ok Philly. I don't give a fuck either way. I just thought maybe you'd done something with your life. Maybe Beccs would take you seriously. That's what you want isn't it?' Ryan said insightfully finishing the last of his drink and walking to the fridge for another.

'Beccs takes me seriously.' Phil said petulantly, sculled the last of his drink out of spite, stood up, grabbed the newspaper and walked towards the stairs.

'Thanks for the drink Ryan.' He shouted as he walked up.

Phil walked into his room and closed the door. No good. He could still hear them giggling downstairs. God only knows what it will be like when they get upstairs. He decided to stuff all the clothes from his Floordrobe ™ around the doorsill hoping to baffle the sound. It helped a bit. He crash landed on his bed and put on an audiobook with some storm sounds hoping to try and drown out Ryan and Christine, then closed his eyes to sleep.

He didn't feel tired and could still taste the Cruiser. He reached over to get a sip of water and picked up his mobile to check the time. 9:05pm. He was surprised it wasn't later, although that assumption was based on how drunk Ryan and Christine were. Phil couldn't get the headlines from the paper out of his head. He needed to talk to Beccs. He started to compose an SMS when the phone pinged in his hand. He flicked at the phone and read the message, then dialled Beccs' number.

'What's up Beccs.' Phil said as soon as she answered.

'Have you seen the newspapers PC? Have you been watching the telly? It's everywhere. It's all people are talking about. Reporters doing on the street interviews are getting ridiculed. It's freakin' huge!' Beccs said.

'Yeah. I've got one here. I haven't read anything good yet. It's pretty bleak Beccs.' Phil said forlornly.

'You're getting to them PC. Your social media pages have exploded with likes and gratitude for finally saying what needed to be said. Here, I'll read you one from an obviously discerning gentleman named "RogerTheSystem". And I quote. "You fuckin rock PC!!! We all gotta stick it up the Man. We're all right behind you, smiley face, and what looks like a clenched fist".'

'Nice. Not sure I want someone named Roger right behind me with a clenched fist though.' Phil said laughing.

'That one maxed out the likes, you have freaking millions of questions, and millions of requests from everyone wanting to interview you. The most famous being from Franklin Parker.' Said Beccs.

'That wanker! There's no pleasing him. I wouldn't mind being interviewed by Jacqueline Smith though...She's more professional I mean' Phil said scrambling to try and not sound like a pervert.

'Oh yes. Those skirts and tops she wears are very professional.' Beccs said giggling feeling Phil blush through the phone.

'Anyway Beccs. Your message said you had some important news.' Asked Phil changing the subject.

'Well. You know our new friend Smith, Butch Smith.' Answered Beccs.

'Maybe he's related to Jacqueline Smith.' Asked Phil.

'Umm. Seems unlikely, anyhoo. I was apparently wrong, someone in Australia saw their baby boy and thought, he looks like a Butch. Yes Butch, that's what I'll call him.' Beccs took a deep breath and continued.

'Well, he posted again, maybe he is the real deal. He said he would like to meet you tomorrow.' Added Beccs.

'On Sunday?' Asked Phil.

'Yes, Sunday is tomorrow, at TearDrops Office at the industrial estate. It's about 20k's away. He said he wants to prove to you he is a real employee. He said be there at thirteen hundred hours if you want to meet him.' Beccs giggled, 'and wear a disguise that includes a white carnation, so he'll recognise you.' Beccs finished with another giggle.

'Fuck me. Smith, Butch Smith.' Phil said. 'I have the perfect disguise Beccs.' Phil added enthusiastically.

'Do you want to go? Sounds exciting.' She asked sounding enthusiastic herself.

'Do you want to go?' Phil would sit in front row seats at a Nickelback concert with Beccs.

'This guy sounds nuts Beccs. Total James Bond, shaken not stirred nuts. We should definitely go?'

'Definitely!' Answered Beccs. 'I'll drive. Do you want me to pick you up at about 12?' She asked.

'No. I'll meet you at your place. I have to pick up some snacks for the trip. It might turn into a stake out.' Phil said, sounding more excited.

'I assume Wil will be in?' Asked Beccs.

'I'll send him an SMS. He wouldn't speak to me again if he wasn't. He lives for things like this.' Phil said confidently.

'Ok meet me at my place... At twelve hundred hours. Should we synchronize our watches? I'll get the white carnations. Do you accept the mission PC?' Beccs asked in her best serious voice.

'Mission accepted.' Phil replied deadpan and ended the call.

The Mission

Phil woke up late, showered and dressed in what he thought was the perfect disguise. Obvious really. Opened his bathroom door cautiously and walked downstairs hoping to God he was alone. So far, so good, he thought seeing an empty lounge room, then walked to the kitchen to make his now customary breakfast. He hesitated thinking about cholesterol and wrote, 'Cereal.' on a list on the fridge. He finished making breakfast, walked back out to the lounge room, turned on the TV and sat down. The television glowed into life.

'It appears the E-Protest is really taking hold. Couple that with the disgraceful, no, appalling behaviour of in person protestors globally.' The newsreader said looking skyward, symbolically asking for help.

Phil thought his name was Oliver. He hated Sunday Oliver. Oliver continued.

'Who have now begun blockading government buildings, in an attempt to stop officials from entering their respective offices on Monday. That is until they release a quite comprehensive list of redacted documents, among other demands. They are also harassing the media who have had to withdraw from the protests due to the violent actions of these domestic terrorists.' Oliver paused looking sternly down the barrel.

'Truly appalling behaviour. How are the people supposed to know the truth if we are not allowed to tell them. PCQuestions' opinions will certainly not be up for discussion on this network, that's for sure. These sorts of opinions are dangerous disinformation.' Oliver nodded agreeing with himself.

Phil braced himself for the inevitable editorialising.

'Don't these people understand our elected officials, and our media have an important job to do. They can't be wasting their time dealing with issues the people want them to deal with. I think it's time to stop pussy footing around with these terrorists.' He said looking at his co-host, who was nodding like a bobble head in reply.

'It's just not good enough. Something has to be done! I've seen the behaviour myself Oliver. Journalists trying to cover the story are being ridiculed in the streets. Outrageous chants of "Tell the Truth." yelled at them...' The bobble head bobbled frantically at her own discourse.

'That's what we're trying to do people.' She paused trying to look angry but only achieved petulant.

'It's time to breakout the tear gas, rubber bullets and water cannons, in my opinion.' Oliver added laughing, while mock firing an imaginary weapon.

'Quite right Oliver. Everyone has the right to an opinion. It's just that these opinions are dangerously wrong, and as such need to be censored. Leave the big decisions to our elected leaders. People, please show some respect for the office at least.' Oliver's co-host said sincerely, pausing just long enough she hoped to take effect.

'Let us be your only source of truth.' Oliver added upping her sincerity.

'Well, I guess they'll get the day off on Monday, if we don't get this under control soon.' Oliver said smiling with perfect teeth, remembering it was Sunday and regardless of what was happening, he had to keep it light.

'It'll be well earned Oliver. Well earned.' She said, also remembering herself.

Phil struggled to keep his breakfast down.

'After the break we'll be talking to the minister for Energy and the Environment who will be joining us from deep, deep in the state. He's there this morning to open a museum showcasing all the artifacts that were recovered after that unfortunate surveying accident by the Goku mining operation.' The co-host smiled like a

Cheshire cat.

'Dreadful, dreadful accident. However, the company responsible has been forced to spend upwards of 10 million dollars,' Oliver said raising his eyebrows pretending to look impressed. 'On this magnificent cultural museum. Which is quite a win for the traditional owners.' Oliver said, leaning in smiling unbelievably broader.

'Yes, a great result Oliver. Can hardly wait to get a virtual grand tour with the Minister Peter Hughes. Hughesy. Should be quite something. As we know Goku mining are a very responsible corporation and were very happy to undergo the clean-up, and repatriation.' She said smiling, then bounced on her chair excitedly.

'And, as it turned out the area was rich with bauxite, so the entire museum paid for itself anyway,' She ended looking entirely satisfied with the result.

'Yes, and who wants to go into a smelly and probably dangerous cave to see these magnificent artifacts, when you can be in air-conditioned comfort sipping a latte.' Oliver added laughing then shrugged dismissively.

They both pretended to talk discernibly as the music started to play them to a break. Phil leaned over fast enough to turn the telly off before they started to dance, laugh, and gesticulate wildly. Or most likely. All three at once.

He finished breakfast, careful not to spill any on his disguise. Drank the last of his tea and started to make a list of materials and equipment needed for today's mission. He gathered up his keys, sunglasses, binoculars, put on his hat and picked up his backpack, then heard a door click open upstairs. Phil scrambled to check the time. 11:15. Close enough, then tiptoed to the front door leaving silently.

It didn't matter if he was a bit early, it would give him time to talk strategy with Wil. He walked down the street taking the back way past the service station to buy road trip snacks. He arrived at Wil and Beccs' apartment block, walked up the stairs to their floor, then knocked on Wil's door. A few moments later Wil opened the door.

'Come in PC. Nice ensemble mate. You look ready.' Wil said seeing Phil.

'Yours too mate.' Phil said equally impressed.

'Standard field work uniform, I would have thought. Want a beer PC?'

'No thanks. I need to keep my wits about me. I'm still a bit suspicious. What do you think he's going to do?' Asked Phil.

'Not sure. Tea PC?'. Said Wil. Phil nodded a yes in reply.

'Well, I think he'll show us that he can open the front door I suspect. He may ask us in. Which I would advise against. It could be a trap.' Will said pouring the tea.

'We haven't really broken any laws. I guess we could, if we entered the building though.'

'Not necessarily. Particularly as we were invited in by an employee. However, I agree with Beccs. I did some research last night and this Wal Sletter is a really sick nasty little prick. If you believe all the many and disturbing rumours. He leaves quite a trail of misery behind him. Probably a trail of corpses as well I suspect. I just don't think we should take any chances. Agreed?' Wil said stirring and bringing the tea over.

'Agreed. If Butch wants to talk. We'll meet him somewhere on our terms.' Phil said taking a sip of his tea, looking confidently in control.

'Oh. I didn't mention. Christine thinks she's worked out it's us behind this whole thing. I didn't think she had it in her.' Phil said surprised. 'I think I set her straight. But I'm a bit worried about Ryan. The devious prick is pretty convinced it's us.' Phil added taking another sip of his tea.

They both watched the TV still absolutely amazed at the sheer scope of everything that was happening. Completely wild.

The world to Phil always felt a bit like a movie, but he normally wasn't in it. Now he felt like everyone was anxiously awaiting his grand entrance.

They finished their tea, and both left to walk out the front to wait at Beccs' garage. About 10 minutes later she walked out, head down fumbling in her bag for her keys, found them and looked up stopping dead in her tracks. She suspected Phil's disguise would be interesting, and she wasn't wrong.

Phil was wearing a solid navy blue high waisted wool suit with a double-breasted peak lapeled jacket, a matching high button waist coat, a spread collared black dress shirt with a burgundy linen tie and matching pocket square. Completed with a matching banded black trilby, tilted on his head the way Humphrey Bogart wore his. His outfit also included a pocket watch on a gold chain, and a pair of wingtip shoes with spats. She barely had time to absorb the look when Wil walked around the corner wearing a black hat, a black trench coat over a black suit, and black shirt, with accompanying black tie, black studded boots and a black fedora hat. They both completed their looks with black dark sunglasses. Beccs stood speechless.

'You guys look great. Should I go change? I just have no idea what into though.' She opened the garage door, got into her yellow Cortina and backed out. Phil smoothly got in the front seat as Wil simultaneously got in the back.

'Hi.' Beccs said looking at Phil, then looked at Wil in the rear-view mirror. 'What's the plan today? Sam Spade, Don Corleone?' She asked giggling.

She checked her mirrors, put the car in gear and lurched off down the street wrestling with the gears towards their destination.

Phil watched in awe, he thought Beccs always looked like a sexy space pilot from a seventies sci-fi movie whenever she drove. Everything she did looked so technical and complicated, yet performed effortlessly.

'When we get to the old meat works. I'll direct you from there.' Wil said.

'I know the way Wil.' Replied Beccs reaching over to hand Phil his white carnation which he put straight into his lapel.

'Yes, but we're approaching it from the back, that way we have a direct line of exit.' He said holding up a hand drawn map, handing it to Phil who was already opening the snacks.

'OK. Ok.' Phil said perusing the map. 'How about you guys drop me here.' He said pointing at a spot on the map crunching some chips, then handed the pack over to Wil. 'And Wil approaches from this direction.'

'Mmmm. No.' Said Wil through a mouthful of chips. 'I think we should stick together and then fan out only if absolutely necessary.'

'How about we just drive in the front driveway and turn the car around, that way it's facing the exit.' Asked Beccs.

'It's a bit simplistic Beccs.' Wil said. 'However, having said that, it's probably the last thing they'd expect.'

'Who is this, they exactly? Aren't we just meeting some, most likely spotty little kid named Butch, who also most likely has to sit next to the photocopiers.' Beccs asked smiling.

'Wil and I are, you're staying in the car. We might need to make a fast getaway.' Said Phil.

'Keep the engine running.' Added Wil.

Beccs giggled and grabbed a hand full of chips to stuff in her face. Today was going to be a fun day, she could feel it.

The drive only took about 15 minutes in the early Sunday afternoon traffic. Beccs pulled into the driveway, turned around and parked. Wil and Phil each pulled out some very small binoculars and looked at the building.

'Everything seems clear.' Said Wil reaching into Phil's bag to see what other snacks he had.

Beccs started to giggle, which quickly became uncontrollable laughter. She finally got it under control.

'What are we doing guys? What is the purpose of this mission precisely? And the building is only twenty feet away.' She said laughing again.

'Reconnaissance Beccs.' Answered Wil still looking through his binoculars, not seeing what was so funny.

'And I've always wanted to wear this suit.' Added Phil.

They silently sat in the car now watching the driveway, waiting for someone to arrive. The time rolled around to

1 o'clock.

'Do you think we should get out PC and do a lap of the building?' Asked Wil.

'Why not. He could be waiting for us to make the first move.' Phil said. Beccs started to giggle again.

They put their hats and sunglasses back on, took a handful of lollies, and put them in their jacket pockets for the journey.

'Wait Sam, Don, someone's just got off the bus across the street.' Beccs said grabbing Phil's binoculars. 'It's a guy. A little guy. He's walking this way.'

Phil took the binoculars back and looked himself. 'You're right Beccs. And he's wearing a white carnation. That's got to be him Wil.' Phil said stating the extremely obvious making Beccs giggle again.

'Everyone, act nonchalant.' Wil said making Beccs laugh more. She was really enjoying the mission so far.

'We'll wait till he goes in, then get out of the car. That way he won't know what car we got out of.' Wil tapped his head knowingly.

Beccs put her head on the steering wheel laughing. 'We're the only car in the car park Wil.'

They were suddenly startled by a knock on the back window causing them all to jump in their seats.

Phil and Wil looked at each other nonchalantly, nodded and clicked their doors open, then walked around to the back of the car approaching from different sides. They stared at Butch suspiciously. Phil spoke first.

'Butch I assume. I'm PC. This is my colleague.' Phil said holding his hand out in Wil's direction.

Butch nodded at both of them.

'Don.' Said Wil.

Neither of them offered their hand to shake. Butch moved his hands around uneasily, then reached in his pocket and handed Phil a pass.

'This will get you into the building. It has my name and employee number on it. I do really work at TearDrop PC.' Butch said looking sincere.

'Ok.' Phil said, taking the pass and looked at Wil. They

all started to walk to the main entrance. They both pulled their hats down low over their eyes and raised the pass to the reader. The doors slid open. Wil and Phil walked in completely forgetting their earlier agreement.

'What now PC?' Will said pulling up his lapels.

'Do you want to see my desk?' Said Butch excitedly. 'I work from here three days a week. Monday Wednesday and Friday'

Wil looked at Phil, shrugged and said, 'Definitely Butch.' Offering him a lolly.

They used the pass to summon the elevator. Butch pressed 6 and the elevator ascended. The doors opened to a typical office scene. Butch jogged forward excitedly to a desk in the middle of the office right next to a bank of photocopy machines.

'This is my desk here.' He said pointing. 'I can see the whole office, and out all the windows. I'm kind of a hub.' He said exaggerating wildly.

'Niiice.' Wil said liking the easy photocopier access.

'Looks great Butch. You're right in the middle of things alright, next to the stationery cupboard too. Love the desk plant.' Phil said gently touching one of the peace lily's leaves.

'I like the feng shui.' Added Wil looking around, making various other complimentary comments about the office layout and decor.

Wil and Phil then talked amongst themselves, mostly pointing out other features of Butch's office space and generally pumping up the kid's tyres. They liked Butch, he seemed totally harmless.

'Ok Butch. It seems like you're the real deal. Have you seen enough here Don?' Phil nodded at Wil. 'We'll be in touch Butch.' He added.

They walked back to the elevator, pressed the button and got in. They descended silently, got out of the lift and walked out of the building.

'You're not going to plant some listening devices, a booby trap, a bomb, steal some documents or something?' Asked Butch looking confused, maybe even a little disappointed.

'No Butch. Change comes from ignoring these people, not blowing them up.' Phil said walking back to the car not pausing.

Butch stopped in his tracks looking more confused.

Phil took off his hat and sunglasses, opened the front door and sat in the car. Will got in the back, precisely at the same time.

'How'd it go? Did you get any juicy details? Did you find any bodies?' Asked Beccs smiling, eager to find out everything. 'Was I right about Butch?' She said pulling out of the driveway and into the traffic.

'You were right about Butch Beccs.' Said Phil. 'He is spotty, and he does sit next to the photocopiers.' Phil added laughing.

'All the photocopiers.' Emphasised Wil.

'You were also right about Smith not being his real name.' Said Wil more seriously.

'It said Smith on his pass. Shit! I've still got it.' Phil said reaching into his jacket pocket to get it out. 'It definitely says Smith, Wil.' Phil said reading the pass.

'The pass may say Butch Smith. But did you see his name plate? It read Butch Harmon.'

'So he's sus.' Beccs said holding her hands up briefly taking them off the wheel. 'Let's just drop the whole thing, as I think I originally suggested. Still. A great day out.' She said genuinely. 'Want to stop at that Russian place for lunch?' Beccs asked looking in the rear-view mirror smiling. 'You guys simply can't take those suits home yet.'

Harmon, Butch Harmon

Butch watched PC and Don drive off. He was excited, but a little confused. He expected hippy revolutionary types smelling of weed and talking about bringing down the man. Not early last century gangsters. He wasn't expecting that. And they were really, really nice. He wasn't expecting that either.

Butch was instructed by Wal, that these types would try to manipulate him. Turn him to their side. "You know, Stockholm syndrome." Wal had said. Butch didn't know what that was, but thought he should look it up when he got home.

He refocused again on his assignment, after all, Wal had said he could be one of his chosen ones. He was Special Projects Operative 'Agent Harmon, Butch Harmon' Butch said out loud getting a startled look from an old lady sitting next to him at the bus stop. She slid along the seat, further away.' There was still forty minutes until the next bus. The service on Sundays was terrible.

The bus finally arrived. Butch daydreamed all the way home about being one of Wal's chosen ones. The ones in the know. The ones that earned pornographic salaries. The ones that drove Maseratis accompanied by hot blondes who laughed a lot. He got off the bus and walked straight up the path to his studio apartment and then reached into his pocket for his keys.

'Crap!' He muttered, then frantically checked all his other pockets. 'Crap!' he repeated. He forgot to get the pass back off PC. Never mind he thought, he'd just tell Wal he refused to give it back. Butch was already beginning to think like a TearDrop executive.

He put the key in his lock and opened the door, walked to the fridge and got himself a can of drink, cracked it open and took a sip, then sat on his lounge feeling pleased with himself.

Time to SMS Wal about the meeting. Butch picked up his mobile and sent the following SMS.

'Contact made with PC at 1300 as planned. Entered the building at approx. 1304 using pass provided. PC refused to give the pass back. He and a colleague inspected the 6th floor and my desk, then left in a yellow car. Over ☺.' He pressed send.

Butch sat on the lounge now at a bit of a loss as to what to do next. Then he remembered, he'd look up what Stockholm syndrome was.

Somewhere Over the Pacific

Somewhere over the Pacific enroute to Japan in Wal's 757, a phone pinged a message in one of Wal's travel bags. His travel assistant opened the bag, picked up the phone, then nervously walked it down the plane to Wal's makeshift office. She'd also heard the rumours.

'Excuse me Sir. This phone I believe just received an SMS. Would you like it Mr. Sletter?' She asked politely.

'Yes. Thanks ...' He said holding his hand out looking at her name tag. 'Nancy.' Wal smiled, grabbed the phone and ogled Nancy as she walked away.

Wal opened the message, laughed loudly and disdainfully at the smiley face, or whatever the fuck that was and replied. He then picked up the phone and dialled Louie's number.

'Louie. Have you made any headway on who this PC prick is?... So, the VPN won't hand over the data?... Have you tried to buy them...Fuck!... Well., I have security footage of this PC walking into my building today at about 1... Yeah, the one in Sydney... Right.... Right... Well, find out what he drove there in, plates, rego, the works. I want to know exactly who this prick is, so I can see how fucking happy he looks now, then compare that to how he looks after we've dealt with him.' Wal ended the call.

He turned down the lights, pressed a button reclining his chair, seamlessly turning it into a bed and went to sleep confident that this, like every other hiccup in his life, would soon be forgotten.

Somewhere over a different part of the Pacific, Adam

Socclier was playing on a Gameboy looking very bored. He hated the Lear Jet III 75. Yes, it did look really cool. And it sounded cool. However, it was very, very small. He barely had room for two assistants, and they were beginning to look tired, having smiled continuously since take off.

Adam called out 'Take a break girls.' and waved them off to the back of the plane, which was not very far away anyway. But was at least behind a curtain. He decided to put his Game-boy away and look out the window. This too became boring.

Adam had his plane fly low over climate change conferences for his amusement, but apart from that, he was totally over flying, and totally over the window seat. The thought of another four hours on his tiny plane made him irritable. So irritable in fact, he decided to call his office and irritate someone there to make himself feel better. The phone rang once before being picked up. 'You've got HeadSpace. How can I direct your call?'

'It's Adam here. Get me the head of strategy.' The phone gave another single ring.

'Strategy. Simon speaking.'

'Adam here Simon. How is the response to the mature HeadSpace marketing going?' That was one of Adam's own ideas to try and increase his market share to the over 85 demographics.

He handed the whole thing over to Simon as he didn't really like the idea, and he didn't like Simon. He expected it would go badly and decided to place the blame on someone else. Besides, he hadn't fired or yelled at anyone for at least a day. Screw abstinence, it was time to get his hands dirty again. Get back in the game.

'Haven't had time to look at that Sir I'm very sorry.' Said Simon.

Adam was just about to do his now famous. 'Can you put me through to someone who works for me Simon. Because you sure as fuck don't anymore.' speech, only to be interrupted by Simon.

'The number of HeadSpace users has dropped by

another 40% Sir.' Simon paused waiting for the speech but pressed on through the silence hopefully.

'And the drop is steadily rising…We've checked the latency, outage logs, checked for ISP issues, global DNS server issues. Nothing.' Simon added nervously.

Adam had no idea what any of that meant but knew all his employees where too scared to make mistakes. He knew something big was happening. He also knew he would never be able to work it out himself. He decided to call Wal.

Clay Siliolvnee was somewhere over China. He thought he would find out exactly where, using the Gulfstream's state of the art technology. The exact map reference point appeared on screen and a camera installed on the plane showed a surprisingly sharp image of the ground, that is, it would if there weren't any clouds. Unfortunately, today there were clouds.

He had a few hours to kill before landing at Tokyo and was very curious about the cause of the meeting. Sure, the latest weird protest thing got his attention. It had a slight impact on his bottom line, but nothing really worrying. He was beginning to wonder why he was even going. Clay decided to check the news feed and see if anything bigger was happening that might have caused Wal to call the meeting. Nothing he noticed. He decided to turn his phone on and check his messages. Clay had been reassured many times that having a mobile phone on in flight wasn't dangerous, but regardless, he refused to have any devices on when he was taking off or landing. Why take the risk?

The phone turned on and pinged through a message. He opened the message and read it. What the fuck! He opened his laptop, turned it on and logged into his corporate network. The numbers were correct. The numbers of MonoTech licenses had dropped by 5%. It wasn't a dramatic, or even a noticeable drop as far as his shareholders were concerned, but for the first time in MonoTech's history his user base was declining. It was unprecedented. For the first time in years, Clay began to sweat. He didn't like things not being in his control. He didn't like it at all. He needed to find out what the heck was going on. It had to be related to this E-protest thing somehow. Wal would know what it was about. Clay decided to call him.

Wal's real mobile phone rang in his jacket pocket. Wal's real phone hardly ever rang. Only about half a dozen people had his real number. He looked at it relieved, it was only Adam. Adam didn't know shit, and as such, nothing he could say could upset him. Maybe he's finally worked out how to stop making so many air swings at virtual golf. Wal laughed to himself.

'Hello Adam. How's your swing?' He said not giving a fuck about Adam, or his swing.

'What? Oh great. Hey Wal. What do you know about this E-protest thing? I assume that's why we're meeting. I know your share price has taken a bit of a tumble. Nothing to worry about really though. So the E-pro..' Adam was interrupted.

'Shut the fuck up Adam. Don't pretend you give a fuck about my business. What's on your mind?' Wal said trying to stop Adam from talking himself to death. He had a tendency to just not stop when he was stressed.

'HeadSpace has lost another 40% of its user base in the last few hours.' Adam said anxiously.

The news shocked Wal out of his arrogance. 'Fuck me.' He muttered softly down the phone.

'What?' Said Adam.

'Sit tight Adam.' You useless fuck, he muttered under his breath. 'Meet me at the bunker in Tokyo as planned. Keep the press releases censorship and propaganda going. We'll get to the bottom of this soon.' Wal said about to hangup.

'But Wal, at the current decline, hardly anyone will be watching soon.

Wal hung up the phone thinking maybe this was a bit more serious than he first thought.

Wal's mobile phone rang again causing him to jump. Two calls in one day. Unprecedented.

'Clay, what is it?' Wal said gruffly recognising the number.

'MonoTech has lost 5% licensing in the last few days Wal. I've never lost licensing before. Not ever. Find out who is fucking responsible, so I can find them and do something really nasty. Like hand them over to you.' He said not as a joke.

'Relax. I have a lead, and I have Louie on it. Meet me at the bunker and do nothing until then. It will all be under control. He hung up.

For the first time in a long while, Wal felt like everything was not, all under control.

The Bunker

All three sociopaths arrived at a private airport in Tokyo within hours of each other. They were then subsequently whisked away in separate armoured Humvee's. The bunker was as advertised. It was deep inside a mountain hidden in the Hida Range, the security was impeccable, and the surveillance was thorough.

When all the necessary check-ins were completed, Adam and Clay each made their way to their private suites and settled in. After all this would become their home if the world found out what despicable deeds they were doing, and what despicable deeds they had planned for the near future.

Wal made sure he arrived last. He freshened up and was ready for business. Wal insisted his plane circle the airport until Adam in his tiny plane landed, and Clay in his enormous plane landed. This caused substantial delay in air traffic at nearby Tokyo airport much to Wal's delight.

Sometime later he arrived at the bunker, had his luggage moved to his private suite and headed straight to the crisis room.

The crisis room had been used only once before. That time it was used to formulate a flawless strategy they surmised would allow them to basically get away with anything. The plan was simple, and they had the resources to implement it.

Previously they had bribed governments, which only successful about half the time. The problem with that plan was governments come and go. Then they realised they'd been thinking about the problem too competitively. The solution was so simple. So obvious. Fix the game so they always won. Stop giving people a choice and simply bribe all major political parties.

Somehow nobody even noticed that all the major parties were now basically doing the same thing. They implemented the same policies. The same mandates. And everyone knew that not voting for a major party was a wasted vote, not the other way around at all.

It didn't really matter who you voted for anyway. Any differences were inconsequential. Nobody noticed because the media were dependant on government and pharmaceutical advertising dollars which comprised over half their revenue. Without that, they were out of business. The perfect trickle-down effect, and none of it could be linked to them. And if anybody did work it out, they had their own private army to crush any descent. Their private army supplied free of charge by all their bought and paid for governments. The police force, who also appeared to enjoy overreaching their powers without mercy, and particularly without thought. They believed the cycle would continue forever. Their grip would only tighten.

Wal walked through three blast proof mantrap doors and entered the crisis room. All the lights turning on automatically with horror movie like sound effects. He walked to a chair at the head of an enormous table, sat down and pressed a button to summon his sociopathic colleagues.

Clay was relaxing sitting at a computer doing some really complicated coding. He was distracted by a ceiling light gently oscillating alerting him the meeting would be starting soon. He stood up without alarm, stepped on his Segway and started segwaying to the crisis room.

Adam was watching repeats of Lingerie Football when the lights in his room started strobing violently. He fumbled at the light control pressing the off button repeatedly, each press making the lights strobe more violently. He put a pillow over his head solving the problem only briefly. An announcement came blasting over the speakers in a sycophantic condescending voice repeatedly announcing, 'Meeting Imminent, Meeting Imminent...'. Adam who'd had experience with Wal knew that things would only get worse, took the pillow off his head and started making his way to the crisis room.

Adam and Clay arrived at the crisis room, then sat at their respective seats.

'So, has the proletariat finally risen up?' Adam laughed, who knew that was not possible, he controlled and censored what everyone thought.

'Shut up Adam.' Wal hollered.

'The problem we have is that everyone has directed their anger towards us, instead of the fucking politicians, as they are told to do. This little cunt has figured out exactly what is going on. He somehow knows that if he can get every dumb sheeple to shut us down, the censorship stops, the consumerism stops, and as such gentlemen. The control stops.

'What we have here is a thought crisis. There is no point bribing, or should I say buying the political parties, the mainstream media, and social media Adam, if nobody is fucking watching.' Wal concluded his point angrily glaring at Adam.

'They'll still buy my software.' Added Clay.

'What the fuck ever Clay. You think you're safe. You're fucking not. The new freeware Operating System OpenOS does everything your Operating System does, shit for brains. And It's fucking free. The next E-Protest seems to be coming for you Clay.' Wal laughed nervously, knowing the numbers.

'So how do we fix it Wal?' Asked Adam a bit panicky, who had just received a message saying his user base has dropped another 5%.

'Well, I'm glad you fucking asked Adam, since people have lost all faith in HeadSpace because of your completely unsubtle censorship algorithms.' Wal said derisively.

'My algorithm's absolutely perfect. I wrote it myself.' Said Adam defensively, garnering a condescending smirk from Clay and Wal. They knew Adam couldn't write the code to say 'Hello World'.

'I have it under control. HeadSpace is censoring all speech about, or from this PCQuestions, and is putting out fake accounts with fake fact checking, linked to legitimate government website. We're also removing likes, and adding dislikes to his postings, bots are putting disparaging comments at the top of his comments section. It's all under control Wal.' Insisted Adam without any real conviction.

'Whoop di fucking do Adam.' Said Wal completely unimpressed.

'How is that supposed to help when no one is logging in dickhead! My sales have practically stopped. The third world cunts that work in my labour camps are actually having a fucking break.' Wal snarled.

'We need to find out who this PC is Wal?' Said Adam interrupting, stating the obvious as usual.

'We need to work out what to do, and when to do it.' Wal said somewhat composing himself.

'We kill him of course.' Said Clay snuffling and sniggering sadistically.

'Yes! We kill him of course.' Yelled Wal. Somehow annoyed by Clay's expected sadism. But we need to be discreet. We don't want to turn him into a fucking martyr.' Wal said shaking his head.

At that moment they all stopped as an absolutely terrifyingly looking man walked in holding a brief case under his arm. He held the brief case under his arm as he couldn't get his ridiculously sized fingers through the handle. He tried every briefcase available, and none of them fit. Adam fumbled for a panic button, while Clay simply looked at the man and swallowed.

'Gentlemen. This is my colleague, Louie. He has the answers to some of our questions. Hi Louie. How was the flight?' Wal said enjoying the fearful look on Clay and Adam's faces.

'I walked most of the way.' Said Louie who looked around the room for a response. None came.

'That's great Louie. Nice walk.' Said Wal, who suspected he did somehow walk.

'Yes.' He said putting the briefcase down on the table and opened it.

'I have the photos and details of the owner of the car he came in. These were taken earlier today.' He said, pulling out the photos and laying them on the table in front of each of them.

Wal picked up the folder and looked through it.

'Who is this, Rebecca Besnik? I thought we were dealing with Laura Branigan. Is she Russian? Is this whole thing Russian?' Asked Wal.

'No.' answered Louie. Pointing to a line on a piece of paper Adam was holding. 'She's from an island in the Pacific.'

'Australia. That's near you Wal.' Said Adam confirming his ability to state the fucking obvious again.

'Yes Adam, I'm aware of that.' Wal said not addressing Adam.

'So, is she PCQuestions?' Asked Clay.

'No. We don't think so, she has her own social media account and is not very anonymous. All her friends check out as well.' Said Louie robotically with no accent whatsoever.

'She definitely knows this PCQuestions asshole though?' Asked Wal.

'Yes. But we don't know who it is. It's definitely not one of her HeadSpace friends.' Said Louie pragmatically.

Louie handed each of them a series of enhanced photos of PC getting into a car taking off his hat and sunglasses.

'The girl Besnik. We scraped her image off HeadSpace and it's definitely her. The person beside her in the front is PCQuestions. It's the best photo we have. The ones from the building security are not good enough for our facial recognition software because he has a hat pulled down and sunglasses on.' Louie said pointing to one of the photos.

'Ok. So, who the fuck is he Louie?' Asked Wal getting excited.

'That remains a mystery. We scraped all HeadSpace images, and he doesn't exist.' Louie continued.

'Not possible.' Said Adam adamantly. 'We have 99.9999994% of the world's population in our database, either as users, or photos from users.'

'Guess what Adam? It looks like this guy is in the .0000006 percentile. Have you checked passports, driver's licenses, proof of age cards, library cards, everything Louie?' Asked Wal.

Louie looked at him with contempt and said nothing.

'Have you found out where she works?' Wal asked.

'It's Sunday, but we did hack her work computers, and they have a home phone number and home address.' Said Louie smiling.

'All right Louie.' Wal said returning the smile knowing Louie wouldn't let him down.

'It's time someone paid a visit to Rebecca Besnik. And ask her politely who her friend PCQuestions is.' Wal smiled.

No one ever wanted a polite visit from anyone that worked for Wal.

Beccs Gets a Visitor

It was getting late. She was just about to give up on Sunday night TV, make a cup of tea and go to bed. That's when she thought she heard the security door slam downstairs, then checked the time thinking it must be later than she thought. Only 11:35. Can't be Wil leaving, he never goes to work early. She thought nothing more of it and walked to the kitchen to put the kettle on.

Beccs stopped at the kitchen doorway thinking she heard something outside this time. Stretched her ears trying to hear what it was, then was stopped by the whistle of the kettle. She turned it off, poured the tea, walked into the kitchen, and listened again. Nothing. Picked up a packet of biscuits she found on the coffee table, tea table, she corrected herself, smiling thinking of Phil, then took a sip. She picked up her mobile phone and turned around to go to bed.

The door creaked open snapping her head around in alarm. Two men dressed in black loomed large, at the now open doorway. They moved a step closer coming into better focus.

'Who are you? Get out of my house!' She yelled dropping the tea and biscuits, stepped back and pointed to the door remembering what Wil had told her to do in this situation. Yell and give them plenty of room to leave.

Unfortunately, Wal's thugs, who were some of the best in the thug business, weren't aware of their part in tonight's performance art, and advanced on Beccs saying nothing.

'Get Out!' She yelled louder at the smaller of the two

who rushed at her smiling sickeningly.

They weren't even nervous, they were professionals. This was an easy job. Get the information they needed, through whatever means necessary, and leave. Too easy.

Beccs tried to run, stumbled falling in a panic. She then started to crawl her way to the bedroom only to be grabbed, picked up and have tape put quickly and efficiently over her mouth. She was then dragged roughly back to the lounge and pushed down. The two thugs smiled at her.

'We know you know who PCQuestions is. We need you to tell us his name and tell us his address now.' The larger one said sliding a pen and paper across the table to her. She looked up through teary eyes and just stared, not really believing this was happening.

Directly behind the two thugs Beccs saw another large dark shape looming at the doorway. She recognised this large dark looming shape and didn't take her eye contact off the thug who handed her the pen and paper, and shook her head no.

This made both men throw their heads back laughing like bond villains.

Beccs thought through the panic. That can't be spontaneous, they must practice that when they're alone together.

'You know that no is not really an option. We will break one finger and ask you again.' The smaller thug grabbed Beccs' hand who fought back futilely, then put her head down and started to sob.

Fortunately for Beccs, the two thug professionals weren't as professional as they thought they were. They forgot one important thing. They forgot to close the door behind them. A faint whistle from behind caused the larger thug who had his hand on the table to partly turn around only to be abruptly stopped.

The right cross that hit him next could only be best described as art. If a famous renaissance artist had been present, and subsequently painted the scene, the Louvre would have had to move the Mona Lisa to display this

280

painting in its place. Needless to say. it was a good punch.

Beccs looked up just in time to see Wil's fist crash into the side of her assailant's face causing it to distort unnaturally, followed by a spray of blood and teeth, shortly followed by his unconscious body crashing onto the table, then continue its journey to its final destination, landing limply on the carpet.

The smaller thug turned sharply looking confused. He was still holding Beccs hand. The last vision he had was of Wil's fist rapidly approaching. He too followed his friend to the floor.

'You Ok Beccs?' Said a very concerned looking Wil who stepped on one of the unconscious thugs and then put his feet on the other, taking a seat on the lounge next to her. He carefully removed the tape from her mouth.

'Jesus fucking Christ Wil.' She sobbed with Wil putting his arm around her.

'It's OK Beccs. I think they're both unconscious, maybe even dead?' Will said looking at his bleeding hand.

'Thank God you were here. They were going to break my fingers.' She said through sobs, then looked down at the little thug who was going to do it and stepped hard on his hand. A few satisfying cracks were heard.

'They're out for a while now Beccs.' Will looked down at his handy work.

'And it looks like they both need a hospital. I hope they both need a hospital.' Wil said looking at them with serious malice.

'Are you OK to drive Beccs? We should get out of here.' Wil said timidly. She shook her head yes, then looked at Wil.

'We should call the police.' Said Beccs anxiously.

'What did they want?'

'They wanted to know who PC was, and where he lived.' She said getting more composed, then decided to step on the little thug's hand again which made another satisfying crack.

'I think we should go now. Are you sure you're OK to drive Beccs?' Asked Wil seriously. She nodded yes again.

'I doubt they left anyone outside. These guys look like complete amateurs. Go to the garage, get the car, and meet me out the front. I'll get rid of them.' Beccs picked up her keys and left the flat. She stopped and turned around.

'Lock the doors until I get there.' Wil added.

'I'm in my pyjamas. I need to change.' She said walking back.

'No time Beccs. I don't know what's going on, but these guys were serious.' Wil said blocking her path.

'Ok.' She nodded and walked out again.

A few minutes later she saw Wil carrying the larger one of the two out in a fireman's hold, then unceremoniously drop him into the neighbour's hedge. He turned round, walked over to Beccs' car who unlocked the door and let him in.

'They're both over there. I closed your door. Drive to PC's Beccs.' Wil said looking very worried. 'They obviously don't know where he is.'

Wil called PC on the way, who had his garage door open for Beccs to drive straight in. He closed the door quickly behind them, nodded at Wil and walked straight over to open Beccs' door. She got out of the car and started to cry again.

Phil put his arm around her and helped her inside. Wil closed the front door and put the deadlock on. Beccs just sat on the lounge with her knees up sniffling and crying.

'You're OK now Beccs? Tell me what happened? Who did this?' Phil said quietly, looking seriously worried.

Beccs looked at Phil terrified. 'I don't know. They were going to hurt me PC.' She said and put her head on Phil's shoulder.

Phil was angry, really angry, really, really fucking angry. He started to shake not knowing what to do.

'Where are they now? Have you called the cops?' Phil asked Wil seeing him walk in with three cups of tea, and some peanut butter sandwiches cut into quarters with the crusts cut off. Wil was as good as the Country Women's Association when it came to what was really needed in a crisis.

'They're in the neighbours' hedge PC. It was lucky I saw Beccs door open and heard her yelling.' He said sipping his tea still a little shaky himself. 'They're both in a pretty bad way. Probably need an ambulance when they wake up. If they wake up. Beccs was really brave PC.' He added. 'She wasn't going to tell them anything.'

'Tell them what? What the fuck did they want?' Phil said looking even more worried and confused.

'They wanted to know who you were PC? Where you live?' She said a bit more calmly now, taking a triangle, immediately feeling a bit better.

'That's why we came here PC. They don't know who you are. Or where you are.' Added Wil.

'Good job Wil.' Phil said looking at Wil shaking his head with approval.

'Did they hurt you Beccs?' Asked Phil quietly turning his attention back to Beccs.

She shook her head no. 'Just a few bruises, but I'm OK.' She said and added. 'Great sandwiches Wil. Just what I needed.'

'Let me know if you need any more. PC is flush with condiments.' He said trying to lighten the mood. 'I can make you cheese and pickles if you like. He's even got chutney'

Beccs laughed, then started to cry again with delayed shock.

'They were going to break my fingers PC. What the fuck is happening?' She sobbed.

'You're safe here tonight Beccs. Ryan finally left with Christine.' Phil said. 'She was having a sleep over at Ryan's. Ryan didn't look as enthusiastic as Christine did.' Phil said getting a smile from everyone.

'I'll stay here tonight PC.' Wil said, getting a thumbs up from Phil. He then called work and let them know he needed to take a personal day.

They all sat quietly chatting, drinking tea, and eating cheese and chutney sandwiches. The time moved on to 1:30 in the morning.

'I washed the sheets, and the doona cover today Beccs, and I'm not even making that up.' He smiled.

'You sleep in my bed Beccs. Wil can have the fold out, and it's my turn in the chair.' He said giving his plan two thumbs up and a big smile.

'Can you sleep with me PC. I'm pretty freaked out. Do you mind?' Asked Beccs.

'Course not. Absolutely.' Phil said without any thought of impropriety.

'I'll guard down here.' Wil said confidently, closing all the curtains tight.

Phil helped Wil pull out the fold out, got him some blankets, and watched Beccs walk up the stairs.

'Have you still got that cricket bat PC?' Asked Wil.

'I'll get it. I've got a baseball bat as well.' Answered PC opening the cupboard under the stairs and offered either to Wil.

'I'm a traditionalist PC. I'll have the cricket bat. If anyone comes through that door, I'll cover drive them to hell.' Said Wil, practising the shot elegantly.

'Do you think they'll find us?' Phil said hoping for reassurance.

'Not tonight I don't think. But something serious is happening. They were pretty scary looking guys PC. Go keep Beccs company. I'll check the doors again and put the bars across the back just in case.'

Phil nodded appreciatively and walked up the stairs. Beccs was already in bed. Phil got in beside her and watched her sleep.

Outsourced

The meeting in the bunker finished abruptly. None of them could stand being in the same room with each other for more than an hour, at the most anyway. Wal, Clay and Adam all went back to their separate suites to deal with their growing list of tasks.

Louie arrived at his own suite. Louie modelled his suite on the less is more, Spartan interior design approach. It had only what he needed. Basically, one of everything. One chair, one desk, one pen, one knife, one fork, one plate, and so on. Nothing unnecessary would dare invade Louie's space. Needless to say, he didn't welcome guests often.

The phone rang, he answered it and held it up to his ear and said nothing. The conversation on the other end lasted about one minute. Louie ended the call without emotion. Pressed a button on the wall and waited.

'What is it?' Came Wal's voice from a speaker on the wall.

'The two operatives I sent to the girl's house have run into a problem.'

'They didn't fucking kill her, did they?' Wal said alarmed, preparing to be annoyed.

'No. They are both at a local hospital. A garbage person found them unconscious in a hedge at 4:30am this morning. Only one of them can talk. And he doesn't know much.' Answered Louie.

'Fuck! You said these guys were professionals. Did they find anything out at all? Apart from how to get the shit beat out of them by a little girl?' Wal said, glad now he took the time to prepare.

'No.' said Louie, not engaging. 'But it's apparent she has her own security. They didn't get a good look at him, but he took out both operatives with ease.'

'Send them a bouquet of fucking flowers Louie! And find out who this cunt is?' Wal said now losing patience. 'It's time to pay her employer a visit. This time send three guys. There definitely won't be any mistakes, will there Louie?' Asked Wal threateningly.

Louie didn't answer the threat or the question and ended the call.

Outside Ryan's office three large gentlemen were sitting in a very large car, that still somehow seemed a few sizes too small for them. All three got out when Ryan arrived and strolled up to the front door. He put down his brief case and fumbled in his jacket pocket for his pass, found it and swiped the reader. The doors slid open. He picked up his brief case and walked through the sliding doors followed by the three large gentlemen who tailgated behind him. Ryan turned around slightly startled, then smiled.

'Getting an early start on Monday boys. I bet you all work on the fifth floor. The dance studio.' Ryan said, sniggering pressing the elevator call button.

'Yes.' One of them said in reply with the other two nodding agreement. 'Do you know Rebecca Besnik?'

'Yes. Yes I do, quite well actually. Is she taking a class? I wouldn't mind seeing that.' Ryan said rubbing his hands together luridly. The three large gentlemen all responded with blank expressions.

The elevator arrived much to Ryan's relief. All four walked into the lift making it suddenly very crowded, then watched Ryan press the button for his floor. Four. None of the three gentlemen pressed any button and simply watched the doors close. The elevator pinged its arrival at the fourth floor. Ryan got out followed by his new companions. He ignored that, then fumbled for his keys, found the right one, put it in the lock and turned the key.

Before he had time to push the door open, a large hand beat him to the task and pushed the door open sharply. At the same time Ryan felt two large hands grab him under the arm pits guiding him in unceremoniously.

'Listen guys we had a really great time in the elevator. Absolutely fabulous, but I've had a very tough weekend, and you need to leave now.' Ryan said, trying to look forceful.

They ignored his request, with the two hands guiding him further into his office, picked him up, and sat him down hard on the reception desk, also unceremoniously.

'We will leave as soon as you tell us where Rebecca Besnik is, and where we can find one of her friends known as PCQuestions?' Their spokesman said without any emotion, leaning in uncomfortably close to Ryan's face.

'What's this about!' Ryan said leaning back on the desk taking charge of the situation he thought.

All that achieved was to trigger one of the thugs to pull Ryan back, lift him off the desk and punch him very hard in the stomach. Ryan buckled over struggling to breathe, then threw up coffee and banana bread on the carpet. He fell to the floor spluttering and kneeling on all fours in his own vomit. He shook the vomit off his right hand and made the sign for a pen and paper. One of the three gentlemen grabbed a drawer from the reception desk and ripped it out spilling the contents to the floor.

Ryan fumbled and scratched around the floor finally finding a post-it notepad and a pen amongst the debris. He wrote down Beccs' and Phil's full names and addresses on four post-its, stood back up, now finally able to breathe again, and handed the notes to the spokesman. He snatched them off Ryan and read the details.

'If these are not correct Ryan. We will come back. Are you absolutely certain they are correct? Do not play games with us.' Said the spokesman unnecessarily threateningly.

Ryan shook a vigorous series of nods and stood motionless holding himself up with the desk, looking terror struck.

'Ok. Then you should not see us again Ryan.' The spokesman said emphasising Ryan reading the post-its again. Then all three turned and started walking away.

'I won't call the police either.' Ryan said gasping and spluttering.

'We don't care.' One of them said as they walked away laughing.

Ryan rushed to the door and locked it. Then fell back on the floor and started to cry.

Wal's mobile phone rang in his Brunello Cucinelli tracksuit pants. He was jogging through a mountain pass around his secure compound, providing spectacular views of the villages below. He stopped and answered the call.

'Yes Louie…. Fan-fucking-tastic…. Send them to me. I'll call you in 10 minutes with Clay and Adam.' He ended the call, turned around and jogged back with added vigour.

A short time later they were all again assembled in the crisis room.

'So how should we play this. Just shoot him?' Asked Adam, with Clay eagerly agreeing.

'No. That would create a martyr as I said previously. In order to kill this cunt, we need to create enemies for him first. That way no one will be able to shine the blame spotlight on any of us. At the moment, we are the only ones that know who he is.' Wal said confidently.

'What are you suggesting Wal?' asked Clay not really concentrating.

'What I'm suggesting is, we find out everything we can about him, using HeadSpace while it still has some fucking users left that is,' Wal said looking at Adam acerbically.' and the mainstream media while anyone is still watching that shit.'

'Basically, let everyone who he's offended, or fucking adores him, know exactly who he is, and where he lives. It'll be a fucking circus.' Wal paused for dramatic effect.

'That's when amongst all the kerfuffle we send in some fucking neo-Nazi nut jobs, or someone equally as crazy to do the job for us. You…' Wal said pointing at Adam.

288

'Need to create a history for said nut jobs so when we find them, they'll already have a back story.' Adam nodded acceptance.

'That way, after the event, the mainstream can pump out a smear campaign about how dangerous these people are. Completely taking the spotlight off this PCQuestions, then demand more censorship to try and stop said nut jobs for everyone's fucking safety. You know, for the common good. Really pull at the people's guilt and fear strings. Even offer financial rewards for people who report someone they think might be a dissenter to our agenda. At the end of the day, we should have even more control, even more censorship than we had before. It's fucking perfect!' Wal finished fulfilling his super villain destiny.

Clay and Adam snorted with laughter.

They all agreed that outsourcing the problem to a vicious public lynch mob was the right idea. They were ready to light the flaming torches. Nothing gets the job done like a lynch mob.

An Aggregate Mob

The house was quiet. Wil was asleep on the foldout lounge still holding Phil's Gray Nichols Maax Strike cricket bat. Phil and Beccs were asleep in bed. It was about 10:30am on an overcast Monday morning. Wil stirred a little as a light thud was heard at the front door. It wasn't loud enough to wake him. A few minutes later a few more light thuds were heard, followed by some rustling and even more thuds. This time he opened his eyes and looked around the room cautiously, got up still carrying the Maax Strike, and walked towards the front door thinking he saw a shadow, then peered through the spy hole.

'What the fuck are they.' He muttered opening the door carefully.

A collection of parcels of varying sizes were strewn around. He bent down, picked up the two biggest ones, and walked back in the house. Then walked out again grabbing two more large packages and walked back in closing the door behind him.

Wil looked at the parcels all addressed to PCQuestions with concern. He thought briefly about waking up Phil and Beccs, then decided not to bother. They'd find out soon enough, that the cat was well and truly out of the bag.

Phil and Beccs got up about an hour later. They walked downstairs to find Wil already up, and the foldout folded away. He was peering through a tiny gap in the curtains eating toast.

'Morning Wil. What's up mate,' Phil said seeing him transfixed on his tiny view of the outside world.

'Morning PC. Morning Beccs.' He said not looking away.

'How are you feeling today Beccs? A bit stiff and sore?' Said Wil, still peering.

'Yeah. I've got a nasty bruise on my arm, and my shoulder is a bit stiff. But I'm Ok. Thanks again for being the hero last night Wil.' She said smiling at the back of his head.

'What are you looking at?' Beccs finally asked, after looking at PC quizzically who shrugged his shoulders in response.

'We have a bit of an issue guys.' Wil said finally turning around.

Phil walked over to where Wil was standing, peeked through the tiny gap himself, then opened the curtains wider.

A cacophony of clicks, shouts, whoops, cheers and boos were heard from people standing on his fence, sitting in trees. Placards were being waved frantically, questions were being screamed from people jumping up and down yelling, while simultaneously taking photos. It's a fucking circus he thought. Phil shut the curtains, just not quickly enough.

'Who the fuck are they?' Phil said totally freaking out.

'I think it's everyone PC.' Wil said grimacing. 'The media mostly.'

'Which media?' Phil said, looking confused.

'All of them. They started arriving about an hour ago. Oh, and you have about a hundred parcels out the front as well... And counting.' Wil said raising his eyebrows excitedly looking and pointing at the four he'd retrieved earlier.

'Parcels. They're not ticking, are they?' Phil said laughing nervously.

'Got a stethoscope PC.' Wil asked unnecessarily. Phil walked straight over to a drawer, opened it, and threw him one.

Beccs shook her head as Wil picked one up cautiously, waving his hand up and down demanding quiet, then listened carefully with the stethoscope.

Beccs grabbed another one off the floor laughing.

'Stand back. I'm going in!' She said clawing at the box.

'Noooooo...' They shouted in unison trailing off perfectly, then diving in slow motion behind the lounge. They'd been waiting a long time for that opportunity.

'It's got heaps of cool stuff in it PC.' Beccs said turning around to see them peeking over the lounge. 'It's got a card too.' She said picking up the card and reading it.

'Dear PCQuestions. You really speak to us man, and so does your philosophy. I have included a few essentials as I vibe life will be coming pretty hectic for you soon. Signed. Pandora.' Beccs finished, giving the peace sign, then handed Phil the card and turned the box upside down emptying the contents onto the floor.

'Thanks Pandora. What have we got?' Phil said throwing the card away, living for the moment as usual.

They all rummaged through the largess finding it was a literal Pandora's box of goodies. Canned goods, snacks, lollies, tea, coffee, scented candles, even wine.

'What a fucking legend.' Phil said excitedly. He loved presents.

'You should send them a card PC.' Wil said chewing some dried figs from a packet he'd found stuck to the bottom of the box.

'Does it have a return address Beccs?' Phil asked also opening some nuts he'd found.

She looked at all six sides of the box. 'Nothing. Don't know who sent it?' She said putting it down, trying to open a packet of very fancy looking biscuits.

Phil looked at the pile of goodies and then started to open the second one excitedly. It also had heaps of good stuff in it, that he added to a growing pile.

'Fucking Wow! There's still two more to go too.' Phil said more excitedly.

'Want to go get the rest?' Asked Wil eagerly.

'We can't hide in here forever. Let's see what else we've got. Play it cool Wil.'

They walked to the front door, looked at each other cautiously and opened it. They were greeted with flashes, and questions yelled from desperate faces craning over the front gate.

Wil who had done his fair share of crowd control was effortlessly able to block out the distraction.

'Not a bad day out today.' Wil said calmly looking around stacking and picking up the larger parcels, then putting some of the smaller parcels on top to carry in. Phil shielded himself from the flashes like a vampire.

'FUCK THIS!. THEY'RE LIKE A PAck of dogs. Let's go back inside...' Phil started shouting at Wil then reduced his volume dramatically when the noise from the crowd snapped into silence.

Wil and Phil stood in the silence for only a moment. Then the shouting started again. They both walked back inside with as many parcels as they could carry and closed the door behind them.

'A few feel heavy PC.' Said Wil putting the parcels down totally ignoring what just happened.

'What the actual fuck is going on.' Phil said now totally freaked out, then decided to put on the TV. Beccs and Wil got on the floor and started opening the bounty.

'The E-protest has not run out of steam as expected and is now pressing on to its third day. The impact on TearDrop, HeadSpace and MonoTech's share price has been substantial. In addition to the ongoing E-protest. In person protests are appearing at the strangest places.' Said Eric Petrovich who Phil recognised from blurred pictures of him in compromising positions with the weather girl, now third wife Petra.

'Yes.' Said Petra smiling, who had since been promoted to the news desk.

'Mmm...Inciteful Petra.' Eric said thinking, maybe he'd made a mistake. 'We will now cross live to the *Alleged* residence of PCQuestions.'

'Any news Rosco mate?' Said Eric leaning in to look concerned from his side of the split screen.

'Well, the perpetrator of this economic disaster has only had the courage to show himself once, then only to selfishly ignore all questions, and pick up some parcels which have apparently been delivered to him by misguided well-wishers.' Rosco said looking disgusted.

'I hope one of them isn't a bomb.' giggled Petra.

Eric laughed while at the same time hoping one of them, was a bomb, and was thinking about how he would react to that. Reaction was the most important thing.

'No, no. We don't want that.' Eric frowned into the camera unbiasedly.

'Imagine the terror of one domestic terrorist attacking another domestic terrorist. Total terror.' Chirped in Petra, nodding knowingly.

'Hold on. Rosco.' Eric said before Petra could say something else insightful. 'You say you have some footage now.'

'We have some footage *allegedly* of PCQuestions.' Rosco said, as some vision appeared on the screen.

'What do you mean you allegedly have some footage Rosco, you either do, or you don't wanker.' mumbled Phil.

'Some shaky footage appeared showing Phil shouting 'go FUCK! a dogs.' In an obviously put together sound bite. The video then paused on Phil with his mouth open looking obviously crazy.

'We have also found a security photo of the alleged PCQuestions shop lifting at the supermarket.' As a grainy photo of Phil pocketing a garlic appeared. Followed by another photo of him sitting at a bus stop reading "The Catcher in the Rye."' Rosco raised one eyebrow suspiciously.

'That supermarket should ban him for life.' Chirped in Petra.

'I knew reading that shitty book would come back to haunt me. How did they get that photo.' Phil raised his own eyebrow suspiciously.

'Scary stuff Rosco. Are you safe mate?' Asked a concerned looking Eric.

'For the moment Eric. But I feel a lot safer now.' He said smiling as sirens could be heard screaming down the street. I suspect PCQuestions will have some questions to answer himself soon.' Rosco added winking.

'Finally. I guess the community has spoken. They've

had enough and called for law and order.' Eric said knowing his producer had most certainly been the one to call the police.

'Not before time.' Agreed Petra.

Phil heard the sirens and turned off the TV, looked at Beccs and Wil and repeated. 'What the actual fuck is going on?'

The sirens stopped in front of Phil's house. Blue and red lights flashed across the curtains. They heard car doors open and close to a fairly even chorus of boos and cheers.

Phil, Beccs and Wil looked at each other in disbelief. They were then startled by a classic five knocks policeman's knock on the front door.

Phil smiled and said, 'I wonder who that is.' Stood up and walked to the door with Beccs inspired confidence and opened it.

'Hello Sir. My name is Officer Steve Broughton. Are you a resident of this house?' Said a policeman who looked like he'd shaved about three times in his entire life.

'Yes.' Phil said shielding his eyes from the ongoing flashes.

'We've had a complaint from someone about a disturbance.' Said the unnecessarily shaven policeman.

'Someone?... Who?... What disturbance?' Said Phil eyeballing the rather too young to be a police officer, police officer.

'Well, there's a lot of people here making a lot of noise if you haven't noticed Sir. They're even in the trees out the front. It's causing a disturbance.' Officer Steve said.

'What do you want me to do about it? You need to ask them to move along Officer.' Phil said looking both confused and annoyed.

'Can I come in where we can discuss this in private Sir?' Asked officer Steve.

'No.' Phil said closing the door.

Phil waited, expecting to hear a knock a few moments later, but instead heard nothing, walked back to the lounge and sat back down. They glanced around at each other giggling nervously.

'Nicely handled with the police PC. The law states that you don't have to ...' Wil was interrupted by another knock on the door.

'It's probably for me.' Phil said getting up again.

'Hi Steve.' Phil said opening the door again smiling.

'Hello Sir. I have spoken to the...gathering.' He said hesitantly.

'And the only way to disperse the crowd without making any arrests is for you to address them. Or address the media. Make a statement of some description.' Officer Steve said ambiguously.

'Why? I don't want to address the crowd. And, I definitely don't want to address the media.' Phil stated adamantly.

'Sir. It seems to be the only way. We don't have enough officers to deal with the crowd currently estimated at over two thousand. Can you meet us halfway on this?' Officer Steve said beginning to look desperate, hearing the crowd getting louder.

'Ok. Tell everyone to calm down, I'll be out in a minute Steve.' Phil closed the door and walked back to sit down.

'Did you hear... I have to talk to them.' Phil said gravely.

'I'll go with you PC.' Wil said.

'No. I'll do it ... I don't want to talk to the media. Those tellers of lies will chop me up and make me look like a psychopath.' Phil said stating the obvious.

'You have the upper hand PC.' Interjected Beccs. 'Who's that news reader chick you fancy?'

'I don't fancy her.' Phil said blushing.

'Jacqueline Albert. Ask her to interview you. Here, with us recording so they can't chop you up.' Interrupted Wil now excited by the prospect of being on TV.

'I don't fancy her. I just think she is at least trying.' Phil said again emphasizing that he didn't fancy her. 'But I agree. I'll go and let Steve know. He can address the crowd.' Phil said dismissively, getting up again.

Phil opened the door and yelled to Officer Steve who was standing vigil at the front gate to come back. He had a brief conversation, took a pen and notepad off him, and wrote something down, then handed it back and turned around to walk back inside closing the door.

'How'd it go PC?' Wil asked.

'I gave my mobile number to officer Steve to give to Jacqueline.' Phil said getting a raised eyebrow from Beccs.

'Officer Steve said he will let the crowd know.' Phil added.

'I'll close the kitchen curtains and make us some lunch.' They must surely have enough pictures of me by now.' Phil said, feeling quite the celebrity.

PC's Press Conference

Beccs looked at Phil with admiration. An almost reverent look. Was this really the same PC she'd known forever? How was he staying so calm in the face of a mounting number of surreal and unexpected happenings? Phil looked at Beccs thinking. I hope to God she can't tell I'm only one more surreal and unexpected happening away from a serious panic attack.

Phil stood up, walked to the kitchen and called out. 'Does anyone want a sandwich?... We suddenly have too much food in the fridge. Oh!... When do you think everyone will fuck off so we can get the rest of the stuff Wil?' Phil fired off calmly remembering he still had what he assumed was plenty of time to procrastinate. He was hoping it would all somehow simply, just go away.

'Yes please.' Shouted Beccs in reply. 'No thanks. And not sure. I'll have a peek through the curtains again.' Came back from Wil.

Phil prepared some sandwiches then took them out to the lounge room accompanied by a six pack. They were about to settle in for lunch only to be interrupted by yet another knock at the door.

'Want me to get it PC?' Asked Wil.

'Nah. It's probably just Steve again.' Phil said standing up to walk back to the front door to answer the knock.

'It sounds a bit quieter outside now anyway. Did you see anything through the curtains Wil?' Phil said, opening the door, looking back at Wil for an answer then turned around still talking.

'What is it Steve... Jacqueline.' Phil said in an alarmed

voice, then slammed the door shut.

'Guys, Jacqueline Albert the hot news chick from channel 6 is at the door.' Phil said too loudly cringing, then said even louder. 'Hot as I mean journalistically speaking.' He added cringing even more, then opened the door again to an amused Jacqueline Albert.

'I need to discuss something with my colleagues Jacqueline.' Phil said, closing the door again, then quickly opening it. 'Back in a few minutes.' He said closing it yet again then walked back into the lounge room with his mouth hanging ajar in shock.

'What should I do?'

Beccs and Wil were too busy crying with laughter, at what they believed was one of history's greatest faux pars to answer.

'You don't think she heard the "Hot" do you?' Phil said with tiny air quotes looking at Beccs, pleading for the right answer.

'Which one.' She answered not helping at all and not containing her laughter.

Phil waited until they both got themselves under control. It took an entire three minutes.

'What should I do? Should I do it?' He asked, hoping one of them would come up with a plausible excuse.

'Definitely!' Beccs said, now with total confidence in the new PC.

'You've come this far. It won't go away, you know. You always wanted to get your opinions across, get people thinking for themselves. Not being told what to think. I say you absolutely, definitely, have to do it!' She finished enthusiastically.

'I agree.' Wil agreed, also enthusiastically.

Beccs and Wil were already planning seating arrangements and lining up camera angles.

'I'll set up my phone here to record the entire interview. That way we have an unedited copy.' Beccs said excitedly.

'I'll take notes as a backup.' Will said cracking his knuckles, in preparation, reaching for his notepad.

Phil watched the whole thing happening around him

knowing there was absolutely nothing he could do to stop it.

'Are you going to do it with your pyjamas on Beccs? Do you want to borrow something off me? Maybe something from Christine?' Phil asked hoping that was somehow a possible out.

Beccs thought about the three alternatives and decided on her pyjamas.

Phil looked skywards, took a few slow steady deep breaths, then looked at Beccs who was smiling at him fondly. He was ready.

'Wil! Can you go to the front door and Tell Jacqueline that we'll be about 5 more minutes?... Beccs... Keep smiling and telling me I'm doing the right thing.' Phil said assuming leadership. 'I'm going upstairs to change.' They both put on a serious face, saluted, and got on with their tasks.

A few minutes later Phil walked down the stairs in his best suit.

'How do I look. Ready for the people?' Phil said pirouetting.

'Classy PC.' Whistled Wil.

Beccs thought Phil's best suit, a navy blue slightly too wide pin stripe made him look a little bit like Gomez Addams. All he needed was the cigar to complete the look.

She looked him up and down, nodded and said 'Sensational PC. You look totally ready.' Beccs added giving him an additional two thumbs up.

'You sure I don't look like Gomez Addams?' Phil asked unsurely.

'Not a bit.' She lied.

'Groovy.' Said Phil taking a seat next to Beccs on the lounge.

'See them in Wil. Then come and sit next to me on the lounge, I need the full brains trust assembled.'

Wil opened the door and asked Jacqueline and her accompanying camera man to come in. Jacqueline smiled politely, walked in, and introduced herself and her cameraman Colin. They all shook hands, which included roughly ten handshakes. Phil, Beccs and Wil then all sat back on the lounge crowded together.

'Hi PC, or should I call you Phillip?' Asked Jacqueline getting out a notepad and pen. 'Do you mind if Colin my cameraman starts to setup?' She asked. 'It's pretty dark in here. I guess you can't open the curtains yet.'

'Umm PC will be fine Jacqueline. Will this be a live broadcast?' Asked Phil.

'Umm No. We were going to do a quick Q & ...' Phil put his hand up stopping her dead.

'We have a problem Jacqueline. If it's pre-recorded, you can chop me up later. I know how the networks operate' Phil said sceptically.

'I assure you PC I will not be doing that.' Jacqueline said seriously.

'Yes, but can you guarantee your producer, or some other executive wanker won't do that?' Phil said matching her seriousness.

Jacqueline was going to give the official network response, of an uncategorical Yes! But just couldn't do it despite all her training. She should have realised, then and there she'd never make it in mainstream journalism.

'No. No I can't.' Jacqueline said looking down.

'It has to be live, or we'll have to say thanks, but no thanks right now Jacqueline.' Phil said, with Beccs and Wil nodding in agreement.

'I can phone the studio and see if they'll go for it. It's a pretty...HOT...Story.' She said smiling broadly. Wil and Beccs both giggled. Phil blushed.

Jacqueline walked out the front to make the call. The street was now nearly empty apart from some stragglers who were taping something to a telegraph pole out the front. She returned a few minutes later.

'Ok. They have agreed. They want to go live at 5. Give them time to advertise.' Jacqueline said excitedly.

Beccs. Wil. Can I see you upstairs for a moment?' Phil said picking up his laptop. They all went upstairs, walked into PC's bedroom, and closed the door.

'Beccs. I need you to post out everywhere letting everyone know that I will be "Live at 5"' Phil said in air quotes, nervously and smiling broadly. 'And this will be my one, and only mainstream media appearance.' He added seriously.

'Good Idea PC. Emphasize we are winning. Keep up the fight...' Wil added.

They all decided on a post quickly. Posted it and walked back downstairs. The room now had three large LED light panels, one large camera on an equally large tripod, three microphones and a snake pit of cables.

'PC, it's 2:30. We go live in two and a half hours, Ok?' Asked Jacqueline excitedly, knowing this could get her off location, and back in the studio. Maybe even doing her own report again. Of course, if it went badly, it could mean the weather.

Wil and Beccs answered 'Yes.' positively. Phil hesitated, then looked at Beccs smiling at him again and answered. 'Primed Jacqueline.'

'They want to do a split screen with Franklin Parker. He's one of your most vocal critics. Is that Ok with you PC?' Asked Jacqueline smiling, already beginning to like Phil.

'Do it PC. You always said you could rip that intellectual charlatan a new one.' Wil said making a tearing gesture with his hands.

'Oh, you've heard of Franklin PC?' Asked Jacqueline helping Colin the cameraman plug-in even more cords.

'Yeah. I've heard of Franklin.' Phil replied acrimoniously, then leaned over to turn the TV to channel 6 with the sound turned down, to make sure he really would be "live at 5".

'Well, I'm set up PC. My phone is ready to record when we go live.' Beccs said making some final adjustment to her phone sitting on the table, seeing a broad angle view.

'OK. I'll make us a pot of tea.' Phil said waving his head at Beccs to follow him into the kitchen.

'What the fuck am I doing? I'm sweatin' like a racehorse Beccs.' Phil said opening his jacket revealing two damp

303

patches under his arms that were rapidly threatening to overwhelm his entire shirt.

Beccs walked up to him, thought about giving him a hug, then thought better of it.

'You'll be fine.' She said reassuringly. 'Wil and I will be here. We'll help if you get stuck, and I can jab you in the ribs if you start to wander off topic. I've seen you argue with Franklin Wanker before. He doesn't stand a chance PC.' She said, squeezing Phil's arm. He knew he had to do it. Phil looked at Beccs with renewed determination.

'You're right.' Phil said and gave her a kiss on the cheek surprising both of them, mostly Phil who stepped back wondering where he found the courage to do that.

Beccs smiled, turned and walked back to the lounge room, a little surprised herself.

He arrived back from the kitchen carrying his best and only tea service. This one had matching cups and saucers if you didn't look too closely. And a tray of exotic goodies.

They nibbled and chatted the time away talking about nothing in particular, just enjoying each other's company. They were all interrupted by Jacqueline's phone ringing.

'Hello.' She answered with a smile in her voice.

'Don't talk just listen. For the last two days the networks ratings have been down over 90%. It's a total shit storm down here. Right now, we're rating at a 10 year high. Don't fuck this up Jacqueline. Just introduce the cunt, then hand him over to Franklin. If he starts to win an argument, or starts to make sense, cut him off. Got it. No fucking mistakes Jacqueline.' The phone went dead.

Jacqueline smiled nervously and looked at PC.

'All good Jacqueline? You look a bit pale. Do you need a glass of water?' Phil said, looking concerned.

'No... No. I'm always a bit nervous before I go on air.' She lied.

They all resumed their places and waited.

'2 minutes guys.' Announced Colin.

'Point the camera at me first Colin... Thanks guys...are you seeing and hearing me in the studio?... Great.'

Jacqueline asked.

'Under one minute.'

'How come you're here today? I thought you only did in-house, hard-hitting interviews?' Asked Phil curiously.

'I do...I did. I'm being punished for calling Franklin Parker a Wanker...Hi Franklin.' She said throwing her head back in disbelief noticing the red light on the camera indicating they were already live.

She paused and took a deep breath to compose herself.

'Good afternoon. This is Jacqueline Albert live from the residence of the author of PCQuestions. Thanks for giving me the opportunity to interview you this afternoon PC.' Said Jacqueline professionally. The camera swung away from Jacqueline and pointed at the three of them and then zoomed in on PC.

'It's a pleasure Jacqueline. I've always liked your forthright and honest interviewing style.' Phil said. Jacqueline smiled back politely.

'Never afraid to call out a wanker when you see one. On an unrelated subject, I see Franklin Parker has joined us. Hi Franklin.' Phil said smiling and waving into the camera.

Jacqueline fought back a giggle unsuccessfully.

Franklin nodded back curtly.

'I assume Franklin you are here today to try to defend the total corporatization of the mainstream news services. Can I save you the trouble of talking, and just tell everyone on your behalf to simply believe everything they are told without question, and to totally ignore any corporate bias and more particularly any censorship.' Phil paused happy with his first attack.

'Thank you PC. But I feel I can speak for myself.' Franklin said acerbically.

'That would be novel Franklin. You normally speak for the highest bidder.' Phil bit back.

'Now if you will let me speak...You say the media are to blame. They dictate the agenda of politicians, sponsored by big business, or worse, some globalist conspiracy.' Franklin said throwing his head back laughing. 'Oh, and democracy is an illusion created by both major parties, who are actually in collusion, and not in opposition at all. Alternatives are simply a pretext created by the media to simulate choice. I'm amazed you're not wearing a tin foil hat PC.' Franklin said, rolling his eyes like he was talking to a petulant teenager.

'The problem I have with you Franklin, as a media pundit. Is not that you have an opinion I disagree with, it's that you don't really have an opinion at all. You are merely a reflection of your benefactors. You are basically an infomercial for the elites. I'm normally taking a piss or making a cup of tea when you're talking. I suggest everyone should take the same opportunity.' Phil said eyeballing Franklin waiting to see how he reacted to someone not being forced, or paid to be nice to him.

'You don't have a lot of respect for journalists who are trying to keep you informed do you PC?' Franklin said, trying to look hurt.

'Respect is not handed out like a participation medal at a woke swimming carnival Franklin. You have to earn it.' Phil said trying to push as many of Franklins buttons as he could.

'Listen you proletariat...' Franklin said losing his temper not accustomed to being spoken to like that.

'Ok... PC... Franklin...' Jacqueline interrupted nervously. 'I'll stop you right there. The topic of the interview is the ongoing effect of the protest. Be the protest, E or otherwise.' Jacqueline abruptly interrupted.

Both PC and Franklin kept hurling insults at each other as Jacqueline was forced to interrupt again.

'I think what needs to happen is that in order to have a proper debate...'

'What the fuck do you think you're doing Jacqueline. We don't want a proper debate poppet.' Her producer screamed down her earphone, causing Jacqueline to rip it from her ear.

'Sorry gentlemen. Some technical difficulties.' She said putting the earpiece on the table.

'I'll ask you a question PC, as you are the one being

interviewed, and then Franklin, you will have the right of reply...Does that sound fair gentlemen?' She asked ignoring the angry buzzing coming from her earpiece.

'Fine with me Jacqueline.' Said Phil winking, earning him an elbow in the ribs from Beccs.

'Agreed.' Franklin said confidently.

Colin also agreed unnecessarily.

'OK. Firstly PC. Why did you create the manifesto, slash document, and why did you send it to, well everyone really,' Jacqueline said starting the interview proper. 'What do you hope to achieve?' She finished her question with the camera swinging back around to focus on Phil.

'Thanks Cameron.' Phil said acknowledging Cameron.

'Jacqueline. Firstly. Great question, I wrote this because it had to be written. It's how all sane people are feeling right now. Watching everything that's happening in the world. Watching, or should I say not watching all the censorship taking place. Watching unnecessary wars being promoted. Watching the government being corrupted by financial elitists who insist they know best. When what they know is how to serve their own best interests. I say turn these elitists off, stop watching them, stop buying their stuff, stop using their products, please stop listening to their paid stooges.' Phil paused to stare at Franklin. 'And they will go away. We have the power to take back control.' Phil finished off strongly to nods of agreement from Wil and Beccs. Even Jacqueline had to stop herself from nodding.

'But to answer your question Jacqueline. What I hope to achieve is to liberate everyone from the lying, the censorship, the manipulation by globalists who control the media, and now own most of our food and pharmaceuticals as well. We are at the event horizon here Jacqueline.' Phil finished.

'Very dramatic PC. Very dramatic.' Franklin said pausing for a sarcastic round of polite applause.

'What you're basically saying is that every major leader in the world is being bribed to do the bidding of these so called elitists or globalists who you can't name.' Franklin rolled his eyes. 'Phantoms so to speak.'

'No. I'm saying it's Wal, Adam and Clay, and Schultz Dauber of the WTF. Did you not even read the document?' Phil interrupted.

'PC. Please it's Franklin's turn to speak.'

'Thank you.' Franklin said still not addressing Jacqueline by name.

'By these gentlemen. I assume you mean Mr. Sletter, Mr. Socclier, Mr. Siliolvnee and Mr. Dauber. These people and organizations are involved in a great and all reaching philanthropic mission. Which you and your misguided, and misinformed followers are trying to disrupt, with catastrophic results I must say. Do you like to see people suffering PC? Is that what you're hoping to achieve?' Franklin sat back in his chair confidently.

'Of course not, Franklin. That's your job. These great philanthropists as you call them seem to be on a mission to implement as much censorship and control as possible, over both our mind and our body, while at the same time accumulating more wealth. Isn't the Wal Sletter foundation currently estimated to have roughly...' Phil paused to look at Wil who knew the answer to that one.

'1.4 trillion PC' Answered Wil.

'Thanks Wil...1.4 trillion. Couldn't they help a lot of people with that money right now Franklin?'

'In a short-term view. Yes. That may be true. But in a long term, more mature, more intellectual approach. No. That would hurt them even more. To stop the problems moving forward we need to implement a global solution, and that requires a lot of money, resources, and yes, censoring misinformation is a big part of that.'

'Censorship denies everyone their basic right to free speech. To be right or wrong. And who are these elitists to say what's right? Wasn't it Nietzsche who said "Everything the state says is a lie. Everything it has, it has stolen." He's one of yours isn't he Franklin. And if you're censoring something, doesn't that mean you're unable to defend it on a level playing field.' Phil ended confidently. 'No one good ever implements censorship.

Historically.'

'What are your opinions on censorship Jacqueline as a member of the free press, although I don't believe there is a free press anymore.' Phil finished with the camera now swinging back to Jacqueline.

'Of course, I believe in free speech.' Jacqueline said, taken by surprise.

'You have taken me out of context PC.' Franklin said, taking back the conversation. 'What I meant was some free speech.' Franklin's comment was greeted with controlled laughter from everyone.

'No I mean...' Franklin said squirming.

'What you are saying, is what I'm saying Franklin. You're saying you and your masters know best, and now you want to control what we think as well. And when they achieve that, they will eventually try to control everything they don't already have control over.' Phil said knowing Franklin was on the run. 'It will never stop.'

'That is completely untrue...Umm, Ummm, they do a lot, and they're not forcing anyone to do anything they don't want to do. People still have all their rights...'

'Certainly not their right to bodily autonomy, or their right to protest peacefully. Unless it goes along with your woke, divide and conquer agenda for increasing control, then it's OK. Otherwise. they're greeted with riot police, rubber bullets and water cannons by a police force ordered by politicians corrupted by globalists to make sure no one has the wrong opinion. How is that rights?' Phil said to nods of approval from Beccs and Wil again.

'I admit that the WTF, and their benefactors still have a lot of good to do, which is why they meet frequently to work out the best way forward.' Franklin was interrupted again.

'By meet frequently, you mean discuss how we should all restrict our carbon footprint, while they fly around in carbon spewing private jets pushing whatever crisis they are pushing at the present moment, in order to frighten us into compliance, at the same time flaunting their own double standards. How can you defend that Franklin?' Phil said, sensing blood in the water.

Franklin smiled stroking his beard nervously knowing there was not a lot he could say to that. He then felt his phone vibrate in his pocket and held it to his ear.

'Getting some advice from your overlords Franklin?' Phil said sarcastically. 'No comment Franklin. Normally you'd critique a eulogy.' Phil said seeing Franklin put the phone down looking paler.

'He's killing him.' Shouted Jacqueline's soon to be former producer. 'Get them off the fucking air now!'

'No! It will add weight to his censorship debate.' Interjected a senior network executive. 'Just make up an emergency. Say there's been an earthquake in Antarctica, of course caused by climate change. Run some file footage of icebergs falling in slow motion, penguins huddling together looking frightened. No fuck it, show a few dead penguins with a warning message. That should get the masses to forget this little cunt and shed a tear.'

Jacqueline, who was rapidly losing control of the interview, was interrupted by Colin whispering in her ear.

'Sorry to interrupt this debate gentlemen. We have to cross back to the studio. Apparently, a severe earthquake has been detected in Antarctica.' Jacqueline said taking the camera shot. 'Any final words PC before we cross back to the studio.' She asked seeing the red light on the camera still on, thinking she should fill.

'Jesus fucking Christ. Cut him off now.' Screamed the network executive at an empty chair. 'Where the fuck did he go?'

He looked up to see the console operator jogging back to his desk, just too late.

'My final words are to everyone who cares. Everyone involved in the protests. Don't give up. We're winning. If you starve them out. The truth, and a better world will emerge. Turn off the mainstream media now. Thanks Jacqueline.' Phil smiled, and the red light went out.

Celebrity Rising

The interview finished with Cameron the cameraman calling, 'That's it guys, we're apparently out.' He said shrugging, seeing the light go out and the feed go dead.

Phil looked up noticing the TV was now showing an advertisement for a pharmaceutical product as expected. He was then accosted with hardy congratulations from Wil, Beccs, and even Cameron. He took his tie and his coat off revealing a now completely sweat soaked shirt. Jacqueline's phone started to ring as soon as the interview finished.

'Can someone get me a beer. I think I'm dehydrated.' Phil said, seeing how wet his shirt was. Wil immediately pulled a cold one out of his jacket pocket, cracked it and handed it to Phil who took it appreciatively.

'Had it ready PC. Knew you'd need one.' Wil said, getting another two out of his other pockets for Beccs and himself.

'Can I offer you a drink guys?' Will said looking at Jacqueline who was slumped in her chair.

'Ummm. No thanks.' She said, not hearing the question.

'How come the interview finished in such a hurry. I was just getting warmed up Jacqueline. I think Franklin was enjoying it.' Phil said with amusement. You didn't even ask Beccs or Wil any questions?'

'Ummm well. That's great PC. We should pack up and head off. Thanks again for the opportunity.' She said on autopilot.

'What's up Jacqueline?' PC said, concerned.

'That was my producer. He said my format was all wrong.' Jacqueline said, paraphrasing her producer's expletive ridden rant.

'I gave you too much freedom, and...' And she burst into tears. 'And I think I just lost my job.' She sobbed.

Jacqueline picked up her bag and started to walk to the door not waiting for Cameron, who had taken up Wil's offer of a beer.

'Hold on Jacqueline. Come back and have a drink with us.' Phil said, holding out a beer.

'I can't. They said I have to get back to the studio straight away. Probably clean out my desk.' She thought in disbelief then squatted down in the hallway as the shock hit her hard.

'Jacqueline. I'm sorry... But what's the rush. What are they going to do. Sack you twice. I feel kind of, responsible. Sit and have a drink with us... Please.' Said Phil squatting down beside her.

Jacqueline looked up at Phil seeing genuine kindness.

'I'm not in a rush Jacks. They'll probably sack me too.' Interjected Cameron the cameraman finishing off what he hoped wasn't his last beer.

'What the hell.' She said taking the can off Phil and walking back to the lounge room to sit back next to Cameron.

'Fig Jacqueline?' Will said, holding out the figs he found earlier.

She took one to be polite and started to cry again.

Wil, Phil and Cameron all looked at Beccs who threw out both hands mouthing "What am I supposed to do?'".

All three then nodded in the direction of Jacqueline. Beccs got off the lounge reluctantly and knelt down next to her, put a hand on her back and said 'There, there...It'll be OK... Would you like some wine instead?' Beccs really wasn't very good at comforting.

'You know what will cheer you up Jacqueline?' Said Wil. 'A mystery present.' He said answering his own question, then handed a parcel to Jacqueline who took it with a confused expression.

'Yeah. We got heaps.' Phil said encouraging her to open it.

'I can't open your gifts.' Jacqueline said offering it back.

Phil pushed it back and said 'Go on. We've had some pretty weird stuff so far. It'll definitely be interesting. Think of it as a thanks for the interview.'

Jacqueline opened the parcel which contained a T-shirt that she held up laughing. 'Fcuk the MSM.' It read. She immediately put it on over her top. 'Hey, it even fits.' She laughed, actually feeling a bit better.

'You get one too Cameron.' Wil said handing one to Cameron.

He opened it revealing a pile of socks, undies, assorted chocolates, topped off with a PC monographed hip flask. He unscrewed the lid and sniffed. 'It's even got scotch in it. I can't keep this PC.' Said Cameron holding out the hip flask.

'Opener's keepers Cam.' Phil said with considerable regret. He always needed socks and undies.

Phil and Wil both stood up and went out the front to bring in the rest of the packages. All the protestors and well wishes had left. It was now eerily quiet.

'You can help us open these.' Wil said depositing the remaining parcels onto the floor.

'Do you play golf PC?' Said Wil looking in the first package.

'No.' Replied Phil grabbing a parcel to open himself.

'Well, if you ever take it up you've got plenty of balls.' Wil said tipping out a box full of golf balls. 'That's an odd one PC.'

A few hours later most of the parcels were open and sorted into piles. The first pile was clothes, T-shirts mostly, although he did get a set of fitted sheets. The second pile was food, lollies and snacks. And the third pile was miscellaneous, which included books, knives, scented candles, soaps, sunglasses, beer, wine, Champagne glasses, dinner plates with handles, and threats.

'That was fun. Wanna get a pizza? It's nearly 6.' Phil

313

said, finally sick of eating snack food.

'We really should be going guys. Thanks for the fun afternoon.' Said Jacqueline standing up and stretching feeling somewhat better.

'I'm really sorry again about the job Jacqueline.' Phil said accompanied by a chorus of sympathy from Beccs, Wil and Cameron.

'It's not your fault PC. I'll be OK. Regional TV, or the weather awaits.' Jacqueline said philosophically.

'Nice to meet you all. If it's any help guys. I agree with what you're saying. Something has to change. The media have to stop selling out to the highest bidder. Anyway. Good luck!' Jacqueline said smiling.

Phil, Wil and Beccs stood up to walk them to the door. They opened it only to be greeted by a grinning Warwick Simpson, the lead presenter for Sunday Night Insight, a weekly current affairs magazine style show, specifically designed to make people angry. Phil gave Warwick Simpson his TV's worst journalists award to, annually.

'Hi Phil, or do you prefer PC? Warwick Simpson.' Warwick said, taking a step inside holding his hand out. Then smiled sardonically seeing Jacqueline standing behind Phil.

'Nice T-shirt Jacky.' Warwick said.

'Warwick fucking Simpson. Why are you darkening my door?' Phil said standing in his way pushing his handshake aside. There were some people Phil refused to shake hands with.

'Phil. I'm here to help you. Give you the opportunity to be interviewed by a professional journalist. Not by some Jacky on the spot.' He said dismissively looking at Jacqueline.

'Provide you with a serious media platform.' He smiled and held his microphone out for Phil. Phil smiled, pulled the microphone closer and shouted. 'Fuck off Warwick, you bought and paid for hack.' Then pushed him out the door and slammed it shut.

All five walked back into the lounge room ignoring the pleas coming from Warwick. They all sat back down listening to Warwick now basically interviewing Phil's front door. Phil thought seriously about getting the hose out if he didn't go away soon.

'It looks like your celebrity statis is rising PC.' Beccs said grinning nervously.

Decision Made

Wal, Clay and Adam were alerted to the broadcast and watched it with abject horror. The unnervingly large screen they were watching it on showed each bead of sweat on Franklin's forehead form, then drip slowly down his face like it was on a slippery dip before completing its final journey to Franklin's already clinging white shirt.

Wal shook with near uncontrollable anger, not just because everyone, absolutely everyone fucking knows you shouldn't wear a white shirt at an interview. But mostly because Franklin was being a useless pompous prick as usual. He'd finally fucked up for the last time. Wal got his phone out of his pocket, found Franklin in his contacts, and dialled him angrily.

He stared at the television, saw Franklin reach into his jacket pocket on his side of the screen, which triggered Wal to start yelling.

'What the fuck are you doing you overpriced jack-cunt fuck bag.' Wal screamed down the phone. The angrier Wal got, the more non-sensical his swearing became.

'Get the fuck out of that interview now! You dog jerking dick pile. He's fucking killing you...' Wal hung up not waiting for a reply then dialled another number. He waited calmly for it to answer, then screamed. 'Get that fucking shit off the air NOW!!!'.

He didn't bother to end the call, instead just threw the phone smashing it into pieces as usual. Wal went through about two phones a week.

'Louie!' Wal shouted.

Louie turned his gaze to Wal without emotion.

'Kill Franklin tomorrow... Make it look like autoerotic asphyxiation. I want that cunt discredited and humiliated.' Wal said matter of factly, then took a breath and looked at Adam and Clay in turn.

'Well, that settles it gentlemen. Decision made. This annoying little prick PC must die.

'I'll do it.' Said Louie smirking psychotically making everyone feel uncomfortable.

'No! For Christs sake Louie. We don't want a mess, and we don't want anything that points any blame, even fucking remotely at us. We don't want a fucking martyr. Why do I have to keep repeating myself.' Yelled Wal putting both hands on the table leaning forward looking angrily for suggestions.

Clay leaned back in his chair and put his arms behind his head in his usual, I have all the answers pose.

'It's easy gentlemen. We've been setting up for this scenario for years. What do we do every time anyone wakes up to our conspiratorial plans? Clay paused to add melodrama. 'We use the Trudeau Technique. 'We get everyone. Politicians, sound bites from public service stooges, obviously all the MSM to label him extreme far right, white supremist, neo-Nazi, paedophile, anti-this, anti-that. Your average braindead slob watching or reading our mainstream media won't be able to get any other opinion anyway. They'll stop worrying about protesting and put all their focus on the scary labels.' Clay paused to take a sip of his coffee.

'Won't work!' Wal said nervously. 'The problem is Adam's user base has dropped to almost fucking zero, and the mainstream media just fucked up royally. Their viewers are dropping like fucking flies.'

'We wait.' Said Clay pausing for the drama again. 'The end game is to not just kill him. Not get even with him. But to make everyone glad he's dead. Happy even. And frighten them into only ever trusting our mainstream media again.'

'How the fuck do we do that Clay. Most people seem to

318

love the little prick right now.' Added Adam, not impressed by Clay's plan so far.

'I haven't finished Adam. We keep the social media censorship going. We might not have any users, or anyone watching the MSM at the moment. But when the news breaks he's dead, the sheeple will come back not knowing what else to do. Particularly the HeadSpace users, they'll all want to one up each other on how fucking sad they are. That's when we bombard them with, "the truth" about his links to the so-called nut bags we're going to send to kill him. We'll create an on-line tiff where said group claim he is not extreme enough, forgotten his white supremist, Nazi, Communist or somethingist roots.'

'Then we kill him.' Louie added liking where the conversation was going.

'But not before we send some actual nut-jobs in to work him and his friends over a bit.' Wal said sternly. 'That will get people watching the news again. Make it a real public scene. Can you organise it Louie?' Wal said unnecessarily, smiling at Louie, who smiled sickeningly in return.

'Not some prissy assholes who like to wear uniforms with embroider emblems on their khaki short sleeved shirts. Some really crazy pricks who like getting their hands dirty. Maybe hurt a few innocent bystanders on the way as well.' Wal said getting aroused.

Louie nodded confidently in reply.

'Ok gentlemen. Let's set the wheels in motion.' Finished Wal as they all stood up.

That went well Phil thought. He'd always wanted to tell Warwick Simpson to fuck-off.

'You guys can make an escape through the backyard if you like. You're welcome to stay. I'm sure an ambulance will go past shortly, and Warwick will involuntarily chase after it like a well-trained Pavlovian media dog.' Phil said hoping Warwick might get runover in the process.

'We're parked out the front of your place PC. Do you mind if we wait?' Asked Jacqueline, not wanting to get side walked by Warwick Simpson.

'Not at all.' Answered Phil rather too eagerly for Beccs' liking.

'Does anyone want another beer?' Phil shouted heading to the fridge returning with another six pack, closely followed by Beccs.

'You killed him PC.' Beccs said, getting back Phil's attention and giving him a very welcome hug.

'Thanks Beccs.' Phil said, looking into her eyes blushing.

The moment was broken by Jacqueline's phone pinging a message.

She took it out of her pocket, looked at it, and then started to shed more tears. An instant later Cameron's phone pinged. He looked at it and smirked knowingly. The messages were from the Dolos Media Group, which was not at all coincidentally owned by Clay through a series of untraceable shelf companies.

The message didn't contain any niceties, no thanks, no, all the best. Just notice saying their final salaries had been deposited in their banks, and that their personal belongings would be forwarded, and to not attempt to enter, or call anyone from the Dolos Media Group again.

'I wanted to be a sports cameraman anyway.' Cameron said putting his phone away, taking another sip of his beer. 'You get the best seat in the house too.' He added eagerly.

Wil worked out pretty quickly what the message was about, took the empty beer that Jacqueline was crying into, and replaced it with a fresh one.

'Right on Cameron. You're both too good for the mainstream media anyway. You're the only journalist we watch Jacqueline.' Said Wil kicking Beccs foot, who nudged Phil.

'Yeah! .... Yep! That's right Jacqueline.' Phil and Beccs lied with conviction.

All four of them sat in the lounge room running through reasons why everyone was better off without the Dolos Media Group.

They were all stopped in their conversations by a loud repeated beeping coming from the front of Phil's house.

Then the sound of a truck door opening, followed shortly by the sound of rattling chains.

'What's that?' Said Phil.

Wil and Phil both stood up and peeked through the curtains again. Then opened them back up.

'Did you guys come here in a blue Camry station wagon?' Wil asked turning around.

'Yes.' Cameron and Jacqueline both answered.

'I think it's being towed.' Wil said grimacing.

Jacqueline and Cameron stood up and looked out the curtains. They both ran to the front door, opened it and ran out.

Several minutes later they returned both holding bags. Jacqueline was holding her handbag. Cameron was carrying a backpack and a packet of cigarettes.

'What the hell. What am I supposed to do now?' Jacqueline said, then started to sob again collapsing on the lounge with her head in her hands.

Cameron was a bit more introspective 'Well, I don't have to drive anymore. Mind if I have a few more beers?' Asked ever adaptable Cameron.

'No problem. I'll get another six pack Col.' Phil said watching the tow truck drive off with Jacqueline and Cameron's blue Camry.

They all sat in stunned silence drinking.

'You know what Jacqueline. Have you ever thought about going freelance? I need a media liaison person apparently.' Phil said breaking the uncomfortable silence.

Jacqueline smiled appreciating the thought, I have probably flushed my career anyway. She also thought about some of the scurrilous things her mainstream masters had made her do. Decision made.

'I'll do it.'

Wheels In Motion

All three members of the sociopathic bastard's club disbanded leaving in completely different directions, but all with the same singular objective in mind. The wheels were well and truly in motion, and not just the wheels of their expensive jets, but also the wheels of their completely unstoppable, and completely merciless murder machine.

Less than 20 minutes later Adam was in his jet, taxiing for take-off. Already busily grinding his technocratic, propaganda propagating social media wheels.

Clay was grinding his monopolizing software wheels forcing updates making it practically impossible to view any other narrative than their own. Clay would deal with the consequences and the supreme court later. He'd bought off those guys before. He could easily do it again.

Wal requisitioned a "Truth Sheet" he arrogantly included with every purchase from TearDrop. Needless to say. The truths were completely provided by highly qualified and highly paid professionals. Their obfuscation skills were unquestionable. Each fact was then verified by government, or global organisations funded by Wal and backed up by the mainstream media. Also funded by Wal. Their propaganda machine was in overdrive.

Louie was sitting comfortably in Wal's 757 staring intently and unnervingly at nothing. He was flying with Wal back to Australia to recruit just the right kind of psychotic nut jobs for the job. Wal knew Louie would know where to find them.

Less than an hour after landing Louie was standing in an abandoned warehouse, on the outskirts of the city. The location of the 'Free the People' movement was remote, but not exactly secret. The police certainly knew about it, and where it was. The problem was they were too scared to do anything about it. These guys were the real deal. No matter who fucked with them, someone inevitably got hurt. The 'Free the People' movement typically and unsurprisingly were not about freeing the people at all.

Louie stood in the middle of a warehouse and watched two large and one small terrifying looking bovver boys dressed completely in camo gear from head to foot, faces adorned with swastikas and various other disturbing tattoos, all walking in unison up to Louie, stopping only half a metre short. Louie didn't break eye contact and simply handed them a briefcase.

'Here is a million dollars to listen to me.' They took the briefcase, clicked it open and looked in, unable to hide their stupefaction.

'Who the fuck are you? And what the fuck do you want from us?' Said the largest, and scariest of the trio, shutting the case to help compose his stupefaction.

'I'm Amon. That is merely a drop in the ocean gentlemen.' Louie said nodding at the briefcase.

'Ok. But what do you fuckin' want? I won't ask again.' The scariest looking one asked again, then pulled out a shiny new Glock pistol form his jacket pocket and pointed it at Louie aiming right between his eyes.' The scariest looking one was thinking a million bucks is not a bad day's work anyway.

Louie totally disregarded the gun pointed at him. He'd had guns pointed at him many times before.

'I want you to terrorise,' Louie said speaking like he was sitting in his lounge room. 'then kill someone for me... For this task you will get 10 million in cash.' Louie said matter of factly.

'20 million!' The smallest of the three said confidently.

'Ok, 20 million.' Agreed Louie, not changing his

expression. 'That also includes a cache of automatic weapons.' He knew he could promise anything. They would never get it.

'May I ask whom I'm making a deal with?' Louie said politely, yet also with terrifying menace.

'Psycho.' Psycho said pointing at himself. 'That's Mad Dog and he's Adolph.' He indicated pointing to his left, then to his right unnecessarily at a shortish man with a Hitler moustache.

'No doubt you've seen the news about the E-protests triggered by the so name PCQuestions?' Louie enquired.

'Yeah. So what. He's chump change. A pussy Amon.' Psycho said condescendingly.

'I was hoping you'd say the PM, or Franklin fucking Parker, the fucking third.' Added the diminutive Adolph scratching his name's sakes moustache.

'He's not chump change to the people who are intending to pay you 20 million dollars gentlemen. Now please put the gun down. You're not any use to anyone dead.' Louie said calmly.

Psycho, Adolph and Mad Dog all burst into exaggerated laughter, then stopped laughing seeing a series of red dots appear on their chests and between their disturbingly too close together eyes. Psycho put the gun down, and back in his jacket pocket.

'Ok. When? Where?' He asked more respectfully.

'When I tell you. And where I tell you. I will give you one million when I tell you, and the remaining eighteen million when the job is completed.'

Louie didn't wait for any acknowledgement of agreement, instead he just reached into his pocket and threw Psycho a mobile phone.

'I'll be in touch.' Louie finished and walked away. The red dots disappeared with him. Psycho, Adolph and Mad Dog all exhaled with relief.

They all finished the pizza's Phil ordered, then sat back satisfied in their chairs. An awkward contented silence fell across the room.

'Pretty wild day PC.' Said Cameron the cameraman. 'I've dismantled the equipment. I guess someone will be by to collect it.' Cameron shrugged, not really caring.

Jacqueline and Cameron stood up, then thanked Phil, Beccs and Wil for their hospitality, exchanged phone numbers, and decided it was time to get moving.

'How are you getting home?' Phil asked.

'We'll get the train.' Jacqueline and Cameron both answered.

'I'll check the timetable.' Phil said opening his computer being too helpful for Beccs liking again.

'Shit! The trains are out. Bugger!... All transports out.' Phil said looking at the timetable that had a red alert flashing across the top stating all transport was indefinitely delayed due to the on going E-protests. No one was quite sure how an E-Protest could stop the trains, but nonetheless, they'd stopped.

Jacqueline sighed, then pulled out her phone and dialed for a taxi. She paced around the lounge room for several minutes waiting for the phone to answer.

The phone finally connected. Everyone heard the one-sided conversation with the taxi company, which was apparently using the transport problem as an opportunity to change their business model to an extortion racket.

'Forget it.' She hung up angrily.

'They want $500 just to get in a taxi. Apparently, the transport outage has coincided with several broken water mains, a terrorist threat, and a climate emergency. Traffic is backed up for hours. What is happening?' Jacqueline said looking at everyone wanting answers that were not forthcoming.

Wil and Phil looked at each other concerned. Phil walked over to the window and looked out at the road in front of his house. The traffic was already bumper to bumper.

'Is there a hotel in walking distance?' Asked the ever adaptable, and ever cheerful Cameron.

'Only the Pub. They have rooms! If we're quick we might be able to get one, or you could stay here Jacqueline?' Phil said getting another raised eyebrow from Beccs.

'I'll sleep with PC again.' Said Beccs too quickly, and too loudly for her own liking. 'That way you two can sleep in the spare room, and Wil can have the lounge again.' She added clearly over thinking the situation and simultaneously making it worse, while also trying not to blush unsuccessfully. Quite a busy sentence she thought.

Phil picked up the phone with an involuntary Cheshire cat smile and said, 'I'll check first.'

He ran through the contacts on his mobile and called the pub.

'Hello.'

'Hi Justy, It's PC. Do you have any rooms available tonight?' Phil raised his eyebrows looking at everyone and waited.

'Just one. OK. Can you hold it. I have two VIP's coming down. Thanks mate. We'll be there soon.' Phil winked at Jacqueline and Cameron, then hung up.

'Got you a room at the pub. Unfortunately, you'll have to share.' Phil added.

'No problem. I'll let my flat mate know I won't be home.' Answered Cameron.

'I'll ask my neighbour to feed my cat.' Said Jacqueline nodding agreement.
. 'Thanks PC.' She reached over and squeezed his hand.

Phil smiled in return and then slapped his hands on his knees and stood up.

'Wil, will you stay with Beccs? I don't think you're up to leaving the house yet Beccs are you?' Phil said looking at her worryingly, not forgetting the previous night's terror.

'No. I'm fine.' Beccs said smiling not at all liking the look of that hand squeeze. 'I think we should all stick together. I could do with some fresh air.'

Celebrity Status Confirmed

They all left the house with Phil slamming the door behind them. Phil had a quick pocket panic checking for his keys, found them and ushered everyone on calmly. He checked to see if Warwick Simpson, or any of the other mainstream roaches were readying themselves to scuttle out from under some bins, microphone in hand yelling scripted questions, then saw the coast was clear. They commenced their journey to the pub.

Wal had uncovered the details of who PC was and had sent Butch where he and his heretical dissidents, as Wal described them would most likely be. Wal called it a field assignment and added a secret agent emoji. Butch smiled and replied 10-4, on assignment, and ended his message with a serious face emoji. Butch prepared for the assignment. Wal smashed his phone under his heel and vowed to kill that emoji using pathetic little cunt as soon as possible.

Butch's instructions were to monitor and gather information. He walked into the pub, chose a table in a corner, and waited.

The unlikely group, preceded by Phil walked into the pub sometime later. Phil introduced Jacqueline and Cameron to Justin, who attended to their check in.

The usual barflies were all present with one conspicuous addition. Sitting in the corner wearing a trench coat, dark glasses and a black hat was a small, but obvious looking Butch Harmon. Wil spotted him immediately, walked past and said, 'Hi Butch.' who replied in an equally obviously disguised voice. 'Who's Butch?'

'Nice disguise mate, coming over for a beer.' Wil said smiling, looking sympathetically at him. He liked this little guy, and he liked his office.

Butch stood up disappointed and walked with Wil over to their table, then sat down dejectedly.

'How did you know it was me?' Butch said looking genuinely surprised.

'Ummm. Years of training.' Answered Wil. 'Plus, I have the same disguise at home. What brings you here Butch?' Wil added smiling.

Butch didn't have time to answer before Phil leaned in trying to look intimidating, then asked intimidatingly.

'Who sent you?'. Classic good cop, bad cop Phil thought, then leant back with his hands behind his head.

'I can't tell you. Wal would kill me.' Butch said and dropped his head down into his hands. 'Oh God. Please don't tell him I said that.'

Phil laughed, then saw Butch looking totally terrified then leaned in again and said 'Of course not Butch. So, you know....' Phil hesitated trying to think of a horrible enough, or derogatory enough expletive, but couldn't think of one disappointingly, and finished 'Wal?'

'Yes. I work at the place where you met me, and sometimes even at Wal's estate house... As an intern.' Butch said smiling nervously.

'OK.' Phil said suspiciously, 'Tell me this then?' He leaned in even closer. 'Is his estate house as bad as everyone says?' Phil said, leaning back out raising his eyebrows up and down with curiosity.

Butch took a deep breath with relief. 'It's a complete nightmare. Nothing makes any sense. He has corridors that lead to nowhere, an elevator that opens to brick walls. He even has a room with priceless artworks, one of the Picassos, and two of the Rothcos are hung upside down. No one has the courage to tell him though.' Butch said shaking his head taking a sip of his beer.

Wil noticed three dangerous looking men walk

menacingly into the bar and take a seat at a table, then glare in Phil's direction even more menacingly.

'Hey Butch. Are those guys with you?' Wil said nodding in the obvious direction.

'No. I was told to come alone.'

'Mmm. Wait here PC. I'll do some reconnaissance, get us some more glasses, and a jug of beer. We might need it.' Wil said standing up looking at the three men.

Wil returned from the bar and walked up to their table and leant over. 'Nice day boys. Hey, you guys might be able to answer a question for me. When you get a tattoo on your face, aren't you supposed to wrap it in gladwrap for a few days?' He said smiling at each of them in turn. All three looked at him without comment.

'Do you find it hard to breath?' Wil said not happy not getting any reaction at all.

'Fuck off fat boy.' The largest of the three spat back.

'No need to get personal.' Wil said, holding his smile and holding three glasses in one hand and a jug of beer in the other. The tension was palpable.

The tension was then shattered by the doors of the pub swinging open with a large group of revellers pouring through, wearing T-shirts emblazoned with slogans like "Power to people, not elites.", "Fuck the MSM", with a picture of Warwick Simpson crossed out, and a lot of "Don't vote for a major party again", "E-Protests make a Difference", "Stop listening to the Mainstream" and even one with a picture of George Orwell with "I told you so!" written underneath.

About half of them went to the bar, the other half looked around, spotted Phil sitting at a table with Butch and Beccs, and started cheering loudly, then chanted "PC, PC, PC" and strode out to his table en masse.

Phil's celebrity status was now officially confirmed.

He stood up greeted with handshakes, hugs and slaps on the back (Phil seldom refused a handshake, regardless of Government restrictions). He was in his element. Wil walked back in accompanied by Jacqueline and Cameron who were greeted by even louder cheers.

They had all been at a rally that Phil was told was attended by between 1,000 and 1,000,000 people depending on how enthusiastic or drunk the person was who was doing the estimating. The rally targeted the media, big business, politicians, big pharma, charities, everyone. The point of the rally was to starve these manipulative bastards out, mostly the MSM. Their targets were also, not too subtly at all directed at the real puppet masters Wal, Adam, Clay and Schultz.

They showed pictures to Phil of the rally, which he had to admit was a pretty damn good turnout. Another rally was planned for tomorrow that he was promised would be even bigger. Phil also promised to attend.

'I don't like the look of those three seethers Phil. Nasty types I suspect. I think we should leave with the crowd PC?' Wil said eyeballing the three nasty types.

Phil paused now completely wrapped up in his own celebrity status and stood up.

'I'm going to ask them to join us.' Phil said to Wil's horror, who got up and followed him cautiously to their table.

'Hi guys.' He said, smiling offering his hand. They didn't offer theirs in return.

'I don't know who you are, or why you are pissed off at me. But if you come over and have a beer, I'm sure we can sort this out.' Phil smiled again.

'I'll tell you what our fucking problem is dickhead.' Said the scariest looking of the three.

'It's you arsehole.' Added the one with the tasteless moustache.

'Ok.' Phil said unperturbed, surrounded by Wil and a growing number of his followers who followed them out.

'Let's talk about that.' He said, sounding a bit like Bobo he imagined, now surrounded by even more revellers listening intently.

'If I've pissed you off. I'm sorry, but I don't even know you. What part of the document in particular bothers you?' Asked Phil leaning in with his followers doing the same thing.

'We didn't read your bullshit document dickhead!' Said tasteless moustache guy.

'Well. If you did, you'd read that I'm not against freedom of expression. Although I am against racism and violence.' Phil paused, leaning in even further nearly over balancing, gathered his balance choosing to ignore that, then continued. 'Someone is using you guys, and when it's all over, you'll be fucked.'

'No, you'll be fucked PC. Really fucked.' Said the other scary guy smirking, who up to that moment no one was sure could even talk.

'Ok. Can I at least know who is going to fuck me? At least tell me your names...,' Asked Phil. To agreement from the now intimidatingly large crowd.

'I'm Mad Dog, this is Psycho' He said pointing, 'and this is...'

'Let me guess, Oliver Hardy, Charlie Chaplin, Adolph...' Asked Wil who was interrupted by Adolph.

'It's Adolph. How'd you know.' Said Adolph genuinely surprised.

'Lucky guess.' Said Wil, as a smile broke out almost painfully across Mad Dog and Psycho's face.

'Come over to our table guys. Let's talk this through.' Phil said, enjoying the crowd who was nodding agreement with everything he said.

'Fuck off dickhead!' Said Mad Dog.

'Why? Tell me what I have done that is beyond any kind of discussion.' Phil said looking baffled.

'You friended and liked.' Said Psycho looking down at the table looking hurt. 'With a big fucking smiley face too. What that Jew loving cunt Franklin Parker posted on your HeadSpace page about the Free the People movement. He was really rude.' Psycho said looking genuinely hurt. 'You said we're all pampered fucking pussies.' He concluded.

'That really hurts.' Said Adolph, with Mad Dog nodding agreement.

'You're being played boys. I only used HeadSpace to get the message out, which was to basically stop using

HeadSpace. Although I do have to agree that Franklin is a prick, although I disagree with the antisemitism. That's so 1940's guys. You're sounding like troglodytes, elitist puppets.' Phil said calmly.

'We're not pre-historic cave dwellers, or puppets. You are.' Said Adolph, now hearing how childish that sounded.

'Shut up Adolph.' Mad Dog snarled, knowing his 'you are.' retorts were not adding to the argument. Adolph shut up and scratched his always itchy moustache.

'If you watched the news today, although God knows why you'd do that.'

'We don't watch that shit...' Interrupted Psycho.

'That's two things we agree on now..., but if you did watch, you'd have seen that I debated that posh pompous elitist prick, and I apparently won that debate.' Phil said, accompanied by loud cheering.

'But, so what guys. He's just a stooge for billionaire bastards like Wal and his cronies. They pay him to do their dirty work, and to manipulate everyone's opinion to their agenda. And that agenda includes manipulating people like you.' Phil paused to sip his beer.

'I bet someone has promised to pay you a truck load of money to fuck me up. Does that sound right?' He moved his gaze to each of them in turn, knowing things were getting serious.

'What if it is? That money could buy a lot of firepower. The revolution would begin. It would be a prudent investment to do you in mate.' Said Mad Dog leaning it to look directly into Phil's eyes.

'If you get it that is. Let me guess. He's even offered to get you the firepower too. Right?' Mad Dog nodded involuntarily.

'What makes you think whoever is behind this won't use them on you first. They probably already have their laser sights aimed at you.' Phil said, with uncomfortable looks appearing on Mad Dog, Psycho and Adolph's faces.

'The only people I have my laser sights on are the billionaire-controlled shadow governments, and their bought and paid for media, politicians, pharmaceuticals, and big money. How much have they promised to pay you? 10 million? 20 million.' Phil said just pulling a number from the air.

Mad Dog, Psycho and Adolph all looked at each other nervously, then decided to walk out to Phil's table to talk.

The discussion between Phil, Wil, Beccs, Mad Dog, Psycho, and to a lesser extent Adolph moved along with Phil artfully turning their anger towards their soon to be masters. Their conversation was interrupted by yelling and loud cheering coming from a crowd in the pub looking at the television.

'Turn up the telly.' Someone yelled loudly pointing at the TV showing some breaking news. The volume started to rise.

'The world is in shock today at the unexpected death of Franklin Parker the third who was found dead in his home by his 14-year-old Filipino house boy of suspected autoerotic asphyxiation, it is alleged. Franklin was a respected academic and philanthropist, who was an outspoken supporter of the work of Wal Sletter and the WTF.' The news reader said trying to look close to tears.

The rest of the editorial was lost behind a large cheer from the crowd.

Phil winced at the cheer from the crowd. Psycho made ominous eye contact with Phil, then raised his glass for a toast. Phil reluctantly touched glasses.

Out of Control

'FUUUUCK!' Roared Adam, then continued raging through the entire live stream of PC holding court to an adoring crowd. The videos bounced around HeadSpace and social media faster than his censorship bots could identify and delete them.

Clay was also fighting a losing battle against a tsunami of bad press flowing through uncensored and uncontrolled independent media. As fast as he could push out propaganda through the mainstream, the faster it was discredited. The lies just wouldn't hold up anymore. The MSM's viewership, and their credibility were circling the drain. Fast!

Wal's inserts were also being lampooned, or worse yet returned defaced, some quite creatively Wal noticed. But all arriving with a promise to never buy anything off TearDrop again.

Adam's social media apps were being abandoned nearly as fast as his stock price was dropping. Clay's software subscriptions were dropping even faster. Wal was even being advised by his board to cut costs. It was out of control. They were losing control. They couldn't let that happen, or everyone would find out what reprehensible manipulative scum they all were. They needed to put this bin fire out.

'Fuck Off!' Wal yelled as a reply to the cost cutting and then sacked the entire board. Wal hadn't had to think about what anything cost, little own cost cutting ever. And he wasn't about to start now.

They felt like they were watching a slow-motion car

crash. But this time, it was their car, and they were all in it.

'It's out of fucking control.' Yelled Wal down their virtual meeting.

'I can see that Wal. The question is, what are we going to do about it?' Clay asked, sweating uncharacteristically.

Wal, who had overcome many problems in his life somewhat composed himself and then sat back calmly. He knew a well tried, and well tested technique that had never failed him in the past, and it always made him feel better regardless. Murder.

'Gentlemen. It's time we remove PC from the equation.' Said Wal somewhat mischievously.

'Remove. What do you think we've been trying to do!' Protested Adam.

'Jesus fucking Christ idiots. Do I have to fucking spell it out. I mean murder the little cunt NOW!' Wal said looking frustrated.

'How will … removing him solve anything. It's the people who are doing this Wal. Weren't we going to discredit him first. Make everyone glad he's dead.' Clay said scornfully, never quite comfortable saying murder openly. Although he was very comfortable with it in private.

'If you cut off the head, the body dies gentlemen.' Wal smiled sickeningly. 'You two think you're so fucking smart, but neither of you, and your fancy degrees could find your way out of your own shitter in the dark. "The People"'. He said with condescending quotes. 'Will have no fucking clue what to do next. They'll tub thump for a while, then they'll mourn their lost fucking martyr and all sing Imagine in chorus while waving fucking cigarette lighters.'

'They wave mobile phones now Wal.' Adam interrupted, trying to be helpful.

'Thanks Adam!' Wal said sarcastically.

'People don't want a fucking saviour. They want a fucking martyr. Every major religion on earth proves that point…' Wal paused, then added 'Dickheads!' to emphasize his point.

'But you said we didn't want to martyr him Wal.' Clay interjected instantly regretting it.

'Shut up Clay.' Wal snapped. He never liked anyone reminding him when he'd changed his mind. He composed himself again, then continued.

'When he's dead. They'll all share their feelings. Set up sad and pathetic memorials on HeadSpace. They'll buy his fucking leather-bound memoir off you Clay! And put it on their shelves next to a copy of Stephen fucking Hawkins a Brief History of Time, which just like his book, they'll never actually get around to fucking reading.

Everything will go back to the new normal, and we can get back on with the agenda. Do we agree?' Wal smiled smugly at Adam and Clay knowing neither one would disagree with him.

Silence fell across the virtual room. They had never actually spoken of a murder out loud before. Wal could tell neither Adam nor Clay weren't enjoying it nearly as much as he was.

'We all need to be anonymously complicit. Plausible deniability.'

They all then got to work on their murderous plan.

Louie noticed Mad Dog, Adolph and Psycho amongst the crowd in the videos of PC at the pub. He also noticed they weren't assaulting him. Louie looked depressed, very depressed. Where had all the hard asses gone? Was he the last psychopath left? He had high hopes for those three. He even liked them in a contemptuous kind of way. Louie's phone rang.

'Yes Wal.'

He heard the plan from Wal, then told him of his disappointment in Mad Dog, Adolph and Psycho and apologized profusely to Wal. Wal was in a good mood for the first time in three days. The thought of murder always put Wal in a good mood.

'Don't worry about it Louie. You can kill them if it will make you feel better.' Wal said cheerfully.

339

'Thank you Wal.' Louie said, exhaling involuntarily.

'Don't let me down this time Louie. No more morons, just the very best.' He said and hung up, then immediately called back.

'Louie. Make that kid Butch go missing too. Not dead. Missing. Find somewhere really, really remote and just leave him there. Somewhere no one will ever find the little prick.' Wal hung up smiling at the thought of Butch terrified and alone.

The eventful afternoon at the pub had gone on well into the evening. Mad Dog, Psycho and Adolph all agreed to an uneasy truce. The crowd slowly began to disperse.

Beccs was still shaken from the night before's home invasion and decided to spend another night at Phil's. Wil went back to his place to shower, change and pick up some clothes for Beccs and himself. He also decided it best to stay at Phil's.

Phil and Beccs walked back up the street accompanied by a respectable group of his new entourage. They bade them all farewell at Phil's door to a series of raucous cheers, followed by some more chanting that faded as they slowly dispersed down the road. Phil hoped the ruckus would piss off Bobo.

Phil barely had time to make a cup of tea when they both heard a knock at the door.

'Must be Wil back already. That was fast.' Phil said walking to the door and opening it.

'Hi Christine.' Phil said with surprise, already completely forgetting about his newfound housemate.

'Hiiii.' Christine said in her now characteristic sing-songy voice.

'Couldn't find my keys sweetie. I saw you on the telly today. You were really, really good, although I think you might have killed poor Franklin.' She said with an exaggerated frown, then stepped in past Phil, followed closely behind by Ryan.

'Hi Ryan.' Phil moaned, unable to hide his disappointment.

'Eyes looking better Phil. Yeah, I loved your TV debut too. Be it a bit pernicious.' Ryan commented. 'Can't wait to see you at the rally tomorrow. Well done Phi….PC.'

'How'd you know I'd be at the rally?' Phil said aggressively just because it was Ryan.

'PC old man. Turn on the TV, well turn on anything really, you're everywhere, still.' Ryan said genuinely impressed. 'Great marketing PC.' He nodded approval.

Beccs switched on the TV and found the late news.

'Our leading story tonight is the potentially tumultuous rally tomorrow which is planned to start at Central Station at around 12pm, and then march to Parliament where PC, the catalyst behind this whole dramatic pantomime is scheduled to address the crowd. There is predicted to be somewhere between 100,000 and 2,000,000 people expected to attend.' Said Danny, the nervous looking news reader.

'Live at 5 will be covering the event on the ground, and aerially in our NewsCopter, proudly sponsored by MonoTech.' The scripted propagandist newsreader Danny added.

'Bullshit!' mumbled Phil. 'They know their clip show lies will not be welcome.'

'Let's cross to Gloria in the NewsCopter now. Good evening Gloria'. Danny said smiling and winking.

The screen split into three sections. The top two parts showed Danny beaming, and the equally beaming Gloria sitting in front of a MonoTech, and World Treasury Fund logo, both strategically placed. The bottom of the screen was a live feed of the street below.

'Hi Danny. I'm flying over Central station now and it appears that a crowd is already gathering. I'd estimate it at a few thousand misguided souls already. They're holding up signs that I can't make out. Maybe the NewsCopter MonoTech street view camera can get a closer look. It also appears that a gallows is also being built, presumably in an attempt to brutally hang some of our elected officials, and therefore destroy freedom of speech and threaten our democracy.' Gloria said, reading

341

directly from her script.

The street view camera controlled by someone in the studio zoomed in on the biggest sign, then zoomed back out quickly. Just not quickly enough. The sign read "MSM Sellout to the highest bidder." With "Liars Fuck off."' Written underneath that in red accompanied by some not to bad characterizations of popular news readers taking bribes from Big Pharma, Politicians, Wal, Clay and Adam.

'Thanks Gloria.' Danny said nervously, for the first time in his media career hoping no one was watching. His hopes were almost, but not quite met.

'I'm just flying over Parliament now and there is a small police presence overseeing what appears to be the impromptu setup of a podium. It has a banner hanging over the front, you could probably read what it says if you zoomed in.' Said Gloria squinting trying to read it herself.

'NO!'. Yelled Danny involuntarily and then collected himself. 'Don't want to spoil the surprise tomorrow Gloria.' He added winking.

'Well it seems like the lunatics are trying to run the asylum.' The news readers cohort said with a giggle.

'Yes. We live in uncertain times. I'm not entirely certain what they're really rallying against either.' They both laughed.

'Neither are they I'm guessing.' Said Danny's cohorts to more laughter from both of them, joined in by a dazed looking sports reporter, accompanied by the vacuously stereotypical weather girl.

Beccs checked the other channels which were also covering the same story not mysteriously at all, and also not mysteriously at all, pretty much word for word. They had all been given the same script. The unexpected death of Franklin Parker had now been reduced to a flash past on the news ticker at the bottom of the screen.

'It's everywhere PC. It's even being covered overseas. Not favourably, but covered, nonetheless. It's out of control.' Beccs said looking a bit frightened.

Phil smiled back trying not to look a bit frightened.

'Knock, Knock... Probably a good idea to keep the door

closed PC.' Will said holding a kebab in one hand and a carton of beer under his other arm, then kicked the door shut deftly behind himself with his foot.

'There are a group of about 20 people holding a candlelight vigil out the front taking selfies PC. One of them has a guitar. I think they're threatening to start a sing-along.' Wil said, raising an eyebrow with concern.

'If they start singing Imagine, I'll turn the fucking hose on them.' Phil said only half joking, getting a nervous laugh from Beccs.

'It's out of control PC.' Said Wil.

'I just said that.' Beccs said in surprise.

'I know it's out of control. But I can't back down now.' Phil said knowing it was totally out of control, but there was nothing he could do to stop it.

Wil and Beccs looked at each other concerned.

'Don't go PC. Let's just go to the pub instead. Call in sick. Do it on a zoom call or something.' Beccs asked almost pleadingly.

Phil looked into Beccs' eyes, smiled and shook his head no.

The Last Supper

Christine and Ryan were in an extremely buoyant mood, which was in complete contrast to Beccs, Wil and Phil who were in a less than extremely buoyant mood. Their mood was a mixture of, how the fuck is this happening disbelief, interspersed with a feint smattering of hope. It was Phil's feint smattering that somehow hoped everything would just blow over. Or at the very least he'd come out of it alive.

He glanced at Beccs then caught her eye. She smiled at him in that way she smiled at him.

Phil was jolted by a mind exploding, earth shifting epiphany. He didn't care whether he came out of it alive or not. What he cared about. Only truly, really cared about was Beccs.

Sure, he cared about the social media induced insanity. The censorship, the propaganda, the merging of Media, Politics, Big Business, Big Pharma. The erosion of freedoms. The false perception of democratic choice. But that all suddenly seemed to drift insignificantly into the background.

He'd had enough of his own lies. He'd had enough of his fear. He was going to tell Beccs how he felt. Really how he felt. The thought of tomorrow was not very scary at all anymore. He smiled back with genuine optimism.

Ryan absolutely insisted on ordering delivery to celebrate Phil's success. He also called Phil PC for the rest of the night.

Christine fussed around the kitchen knowledgably, opening cupboards seldom opened, finding bowls and plates never used. She then proceeded to set a truly magnificent table, resplendent with scented candles, crystals, incense, and an opulent centre piece.

'I've had this all tucked away you know.' Christine said coyly. 'Been waiting for just the right time... And just the right people.' She beamed and ushered everyone to the table.

Everyone complimented her on the display. Phil said it was good enough to win a gold medal at the table setting Olympics.

'That was an Olympic sport in 1896 I think?' He added.

'I think it was only a demonstration sport PC.' Said Wil with Phil nodding probable agreement.

They all sat down with Christine serving them all generous portions.

Christine then put her hands out waving her fingers frantically for everyone to hold hands. They all held hands accordingly, giggling and smiling in good spirits.

'Here's to new friends.' Christine said smiling at Beccs and Wil. 'Old friends.' She said smiling at Phil. 'I know we'll be friends for years more to come Phil. I have a sixth sense about these things.' Phil smiled back trying not to look confused. 'And special friends.' She said smiling in turn at Ryan.

'We should now all enjoy a proper sit-down meal. Like Jesus did when he had... "His last meal".' She said with reverence, then bowed her head.

'The Last Supp...' Ryan trailed off catching himself uncharacteristically.

Phil glanced at Beccs and Wil nervously and thought. He wasn't a religious expert, but he was pretty sure that it ended quite badly for the guest of honour.

Ryan had really gone all out. He'd ordered Italian, Moroccan, Chinese, Indian and a lot of other enticing dishes from unknown locations. It was all totally delicious. They even enjoyed each other's company.

Ryan mysteriously produced a bottle of very good, and very familiar looking wine, which Phil suspected he'd pinched from his fridge. But didn't care.

The conversations moved around the table freely. Ryan got a little drunk and had to admit Phil's exit from last year's Christmas party was absolutely priceless. The highlight of the evening. Possibly the greatest exit of all time. People are still talking about it! Phil blushed with pride. Ryan also insisted his office plant has never looked better.

Beccs told absurd stories about Phil and Wil's less successful concepts, which Wil and Phil defended energetically. Even Bobo dropped in to wish Phil all the best in a way only Bobo could.

The end of an absorbingly fun night was slowly beginning to approach.

Ryan and Christine said their good nights. Ryan shook hands with everyone twice tearfully apologising for being such a prick in the past, then put his arm around Christine affectionately and stumbled upstairs.

Phil, Wil and Beccs all looked at each other open mouthed waiting to hear the door upstairs click shut.

'Fuck Me! Is Ryan in the third stage of his life cycle. Finally coming out of his chrysalis and morphing into a human being?' Phil said.

'Apparently.' Said Beccs, looking at Phil smiling causing his heart to jump yet again.

'Quite the day guys.' Wil said interrupting a moment involuntarily, then fumbled noisily with the fold out lounge.

'We've got a big day tomorrow. Got to be in the city by 5. Any idea what you're going to say PC?' Wil said easing the lounge into place.

'A few ideas. It'll be totally fine. Tomorrow will be a super awesome day.' Phil said in his best Christine impersonation, hearing Beccs giggle, now totally committed to tomorrow. He didn't care what sort of world he lived in, or what happened tomorrow. As long as it was a world that still had Beccs in it.

Phil and Beccs said goodnight to Wil and walked upstairs to Phil's room, then changed awkwardly into their pyjamas with their backs to each other and got into bed.

347

Phil laid on his back looking at the ceiling in disbelief. Beccs rolled over, put an arm over him and gave him a kiss. Not a see you in the morning kiss, or a quick peck good night kiss, a proper kiss.

'You're going to be great tomorrow. The impossible is going to happen.' She said then spooned in behind him with her arm wrapped around.

Phil was the happiest he had ever been.

Mad Dog, Psycho and Adolph were sitting in a very expensive hotel room, in a very expensive part of town, each drinking their own very expensive bottle of scotch. The mobile phone Louie had given them long forgotten. They had also ordered very expensive room service. Pakistani, Indian (They couldn't tell the difference which inadvertently offended over one and a half billion people) Italian, Moroccan and Chinese. Their racism didn't apparently extend to culinary fair.

They'd decided to take the money. Forget all about the job. Forget all about Amon and have a holiday in the sun. At Amon's fucking expense. All three were in an extremely buoyant mood.

Their high spirits were heightened hearing a knock at the door followed by a call of. 'Room service!'.

'It must be the Cajun. I'll get it.' Adolph said struggling off the deep and plush lounge putting down his plate of biryani on an already overcluttered table. He then picked up his now half empty bottle, took a swig and walked to the door.

He opened it and saw a man, but no room service cart, then looked up and recognised who it was. 'Amon, what the fu...' were the last words Adolph would ever say. The gun had a moderator, the shot made a muffled sound loud enough to cause Mad Dog and Psycho to turn conveniently around to receive a bullet in the middle of each of their foreheads. The door closed. The job was done. Louie walked off feeling much, much better.

Butch arrived back at his apartment feeling a bit tipsy.

He'd decided that PC, Wil and Beccs were right. A normal job at a normal company did not include a no speaking day, tracking devises and dressing up like Humphrey Bogart. It also normally included being paid.

Butch did look up what Stockholm syndrome was, and didn't like that he was an acute sufferer. He decided to quit in the morning. Well, he wasn't actually brave enough to quit, he was simply not going to go back. He was just going to not turn up. He would buy a new plant and new troll dolls when he got a new job. Although he did like his plant. Maybe he would take Wil's advice and take his mother with him. Nobody can stand up to someone's mother. Not even Wal Sletter. Butch was feeling good about his future. He didn't want to work for a nut job like Wal anymore anyway.

Butch found the right key, then fumbled around the wall looking for, and finally finding the light switch. He turned the light on which illuminated his door for a brief moment. Then everything went completely dark again. The darkness was created by a very large hand roughly put over his face, accompanied by a feeling of weightlessness as he was lifted into his apartment. It was the last thing Butch would see today. The next thing he would see would be much, much more frightening than the dark.

Many hours later Butch woke up uncomfortably in a crate, looking up at a clear blue sky. He sat up unsurely and was relieved to discover he was alone. Butch would change his mind on that soon enough. He looked around and could only see ice, lots of ice, nothing but ice. It was then Butch realised he was freezing. He pulled his coat around himself, found his Humphrey Bogart hat, put it on and pulled it down hard.

He then saw what he thought was a small table on top of a very flat horizon. It was the only thing he could see that wasn't flat. Butch trudged up the slight incline through an icy wind until he was close enough to see that it really was a small table. He walked up to it optimistically. On it was a note held down by a large rock. The note read:

Dear Butch,

I was disappointed to see you buddying up to PC today. In case you're wondering where you are, apart from fucked! You're on Bouvet Island, which if you're also wondering is fucking nowhere. You have three choices. freeze to death, starve to death, or drown. The crabs, birds or sharks will take care of you whichever you choose.

Consider yourself fired.

Best Regards,
Wal. ☺☺☺☺
Ps.,
Your troll dolls and plant are under the table in a box.

Butch looked under the table, found a cardboard box and opened it hopefully.

Road Trip

The big day started inauspiciously. It was not only already getting hot. It also started with a tiny knock at the door. Wil stirred slightly. The tiny knock on the door repeated. He sat up cautiously and suspiciously, put on his pants and shirt, stretched, and looked towards the door with consternation. The knock repeated once again, this time accompanied by tiny whispers. Wil walked to the door and opened it sharply for affect.

'Who are you?' He said as intimidatingly as he could, then looked around seeing two craggy looking hippies staring back at him.

'It's him.' A shaggy bearded guy wearing frayed tie dyed everything said, standing a few paces back.

'It's Wil isn't it?' Wil heard from below his line of sight causing him to make a small high-pitched yelp and jump backwards.

A tiny elfish looking girl wearing red paisley dungarees and green pointy shoes smiled up at him making a peace sign with each hand.

'Chamomile tea?' Said the last of the trio holding out a thermos. He was a painfully skinny guy wearing a Muumuu, that he had to constantly adjust with his free hand to stop from slipping off. He poured Wil a cup, which he took quickly, fearing the skinny guy might not have the strength to hold it for very long. Wil sipped the tea tentatively.

'How can I help you?' He said enjoying and finishing the tea handing the empty cup back. Wil quite liked chamomile tea, despite Phil's fundamentalist beliefs.

'Firstly.' Said the elfish girl talking to Wil's stomach. 'We'd like to congratulate you all on...' Wil put his hand up to stop her, then put his hand down into her eyesight, as she continued talking.

'Would you all like to come in?' Wil said rubbing his neck which was already beginning to cramp up from looking down.

They all walked in with Wil leading the way. He folded the bed back into a lounge, then offered his guests a seat. The trio sat down smiling. An awkward silence fell across the room, Wil let it last long enough that he wished Phil was there to enjoy it with him.

'How can I help you?' Wil asked when he thought everyone had had enough.

'Firstly, we'd like...' Started the Elfish girl again only to be stopped by the Muumuu guy.

'Sorry Elfy. I think we should introduce ourselves first. Don't you?'

Wil frowned, trying not to laugh at what he would have correctly guessed was her name.

'I agree Aldrich.' Said the tie-dyed hippy.

'Thanks Basil. Do we all have a consensus then?' Said Basil with all three nodding agreement. They all then stopped for an impromptu hug.

'That's just super awesome.' Said Aldrich breaking the hug pointing at his forehead while making off putting eye contact with Wil. 'I'm Aldrich. Peace be with you Wil.'

'I'm Elfy.' Said Elfy pointing at her forehead, 'May the Goddess bless you Wil.'

'I'm Basil. May Light smile upon you Wil.' Basil said completing the redundant introductions.

'Nice to meet you all...' Wil stumbled, then thought of something. 'May you have endless blessings and good fortune.' He said quoting directly from a fortune cookie while at the same time wondering whether he'd made a mistake opening the door.

'Wow! Wow! Wow!' They all said 'Thanks for the blessing. That's just super awesome.'

'We all really appreciate you and PC's efforts to try and

set things right in a completely wrong world. And our friend Christine.' Wil nodded and smiled knowing they were obviously super awesome friends with Christine.

'Said you guys are going to the rally today and we'd like to offer you a ride in the Zombi Kombi.' Finished Basil.

'Thanks guys.' Said Wil smiling, nodding appreciatively. 'But we'll be Ok on the train.'

'The man has got to the trains man.' Said Aldrich. 'Christine. PC's Media Liaison Officer gave us the skinny on that late last night.'

'And the buses too Man.' Added Basil.

'They're trying to shut this thing down. But it won't work. The people are walking, cycling, riding, and hitching there.' Said Aldrich.

'Getting there any way they can.' Added Elfy raising a tiny but determined fist.

'Don't worry, the Zombie runs on hydrogen and methane gas created entirely from garbage. PC's fully committed no carbon policy will remain intact.' Said Elfy. 'He is such a Warrior.' They all nodded agreement.

'Ok. Ummm. I'm going to make a pot of tea. Who wants one?' Wil said leaving the room unsure if he really was awake. Wil was a very stoic individual but far too many weird things were happening lately, even for his steely nerves.

He returned with the tea and toast, then offered it to his guests who accepted it like a sacrament.

They spent quite some time discussing the finer points of PC's document, musing over its intricate inner meanings. Wil couldn't help but like his odd guests and was thoroughly enjoying his time being held in reverence. He then heard the door open upstairs.

'I think PC's on his way guys.' Said Wil eagerly returning a piece sign they all did frequently enough for it to almost be diagnosed as a Tourette's tick.

Elfy, Aldrich and Basil sprang to their feet and fussed with their clothes, not making any visible difference to their appearance at all.

Phil walked downstairs wearing a white suit followed by

Beccs dressed in light blue. They both stopped in their tracks seeing three hippies standing in the living room smiling all giving a peace sign. Phil looked at Wil who was also smiling and giving a peace sign just to freak him out.

'This is Elfy,' Wil said pointing at Elfy's forehead.

Phil stifled an involuntary laugh.

'Aldrich and Basil.' Wil finished the introductions. 'They're friends of Christine.'

'Really. That's super awesome.' Phil said, smiling, acknowledging his guests.

'Long story short. The trains and the buses are out. They are our only way to get to the rally, and they have wheels that run on garbage called the Kombi Zombie.'

'Zombie Kombi.' Corrected Aldrich, simultaneously apologising.

'Sorry Zombie Kombi, and this support team was organised by Christine, your Media Liaison Officer.' Finished Wil raising one eyebrow.

This time last week an unexpected event like this would have at least garnered a confused look from Phil. However, last week seemed a very normal, and very, very long time ago. Instead, he just said. 'Cool. That'd be great. Nice to meet you Elfy, Aldrich, Basil.' Then walked out to the kitchen trailed by Beccs.

'What's going on? Who the hell are they?' Said Beccs looking confused and slightly amused.

'Keep up Beccs. That's my support team Elfy, Aldrich and Basil. Organised by Christine, my Media Liaison Officer.' Phil said matter of factly.

'Well, that clears it up.' Beccs said with cheerful sarcasm.

'That's the spirit Beccs. I've never travelled in a garbage truck before. I bet you haven't either. No, wait I have once, anyway. Seems fitting... Toast?' He said getting the toaster out and turning it on.

Beccs and Phil returned with tea and toast.

They all sat in the lounge room with Wil, Phil and Beccs talking about the kind of things people talk about before they go to a rally. Elfy, Basil and Aldrich hung on every word.

A loud squeal startled everyone announcing the arrival of Christine.

She skipped down the stairs and immediately bounced into a group hug with Elfy, Basil and Aldrich.

'Come on guys, don't be shy.' Christine said enthusiastically separating her arm from around Elfy's head to her visible relief.

Phil, Beccs and Wil started their own group hug out of fear.

'PC. It's almost 12 o'clock. Wanna go to the pub for lunch, some refreshments.' Wil said separating from the hug feeling a bit hungry.

'I'll stay here guys if you don't mind. Ryan's a bit, under the weather.' Christine said, frowning looking sad.

'No worries, Christine. I hope he feels better soon.' Phil said without any scorn.

'Hey guys. Do you fancy taking the Zombie Kombi for a spin? See what she can do.' Phil said rolling with whatever the hell was happening. He looked enthusiastically at Basil, who appeared the most capable of driving.

'Yeah man.' Basil gave Phil two thumbs up, and then two peace signs. 'It'll give you a chance to check out some of the features before we take it on tour.' He said excitedly.

They all stood up and walked out the front. In front of Phil's house was what could only be described as a multi coloured garbage bin on wheels. It had so many dents, it had lost any of its original discernible shape. As they approached their transport Phil wondered why Basil bothered to mention it ran on garbage. The smell was a dead giveaway.

'Check this out guys.' Basil said, waving enthusiastically for Phil, Wil and Beccs to come over for a better look.

'It fits three in the front. If Elfy's one of them. It's manual, but it only has three gears. Sometimes I go a whole day without changing.' Basil said proudly. 'And it fits six in the back in complete luxury.' He swung the back door open revealing the luxury.

All three peered in to be confronted by a tie dyed, shag pile carpet interior, a fibre optic lamp hanging off the roof, and an assortment of dream catchers and other hippy bric-a-brac distributed about the interior.

'Ta-da.' Said Basil with unmistakable pride.

'Super awesome.' Wil said after a few moments' pause as Phil and Beccs were clearly rendered speechless.

'Under the seats on this side.' He said pointing to the left lifting up a cushion. 'Is some space to put any stuff you want to bring, and on the right is a cooler with refreshments.' Basil said leaning in to slide open the cooler door revealing the snacks.

'We have edamame and sea salt, Gochujang bean balls, spicy quinoa sticks and some Doritos. Oh, we also have iced green tea.' Basil finished closing the cooler.

'It's all vegan, organic, and it's all homemade.' Added Elfy popping up from nowhere startling Wil yet again.

'Jump in guys.' Said Aldrich pulling some stairs out from under the Kombi.

All three got in the back and had to admit it was quite comfortable. Apart from the smell.

'It has slide open windows behind the curtains. You might want to open them when we get moving. It helps air out the organic aroma.' Aldrich said nodding knowingly.

He closed the door behind them. They heard Basil release the hand brake and silently rolled down the driveway over the gutter and onto the road spluttering the Zombie back to life.

'Sorry, about the bump guys. Reverse isn't one of the Zombie's gears.' Basil said over the crunch of it being put in one of its two other gears.

'I think it's making a statement.' Added Aldrich.

'Hey guys.' Interrupted Wil. 'I don't see Elfy.' He said with some alarm, fearing they may have just run over her.

'I'm here.' She said springing up from the middle front seat startling Wil, now almost predictably again.

The Kombi sounded like it was genuinely in pain. It also

seemed to have a top speed of about 25kmph.

They had only just gone around the block, and around the corner when it pulled over to the side of the road and parked.

'That's as far as we can go. I need to park on a bit of a hill. Get a running start'. Basil said opening the back door.

Wil jumped out and stretched unnecessarily. 'Thanks guys. That's a real time saver.'

'I can still see your house PC.' Beccs said pointing and laughing.

They all strolled down the hill to the pub with Wil offering around the apparently homemade Doritos. They arrived at the pub and walked in.

'Hi guy's.' Said Justy smiling at Wil and Phil who walked up to the bar. 'Been a big couple of days. Who's your friends?' He said looking amused. 'Peter, Paul and Mini-Mary.'

'That's my support team Justy.' Answered Phil.

'Great looking team PC.' Justin said. 'Aren't you supposed to be at a rally? Addressing the masses.' He added.

'Yeah, but I'm not due until about 5, I think. I've still got a couple of hours.' Phil said sipping his unordered, but most appreciated beer.

'I think we should allow at least an hour to get there. You know, in case we run out of garbage.' Wil said taking his beer.

'Hi guys.' Said Jacqueline surprising both Phil and Wil.

'You're not still staying here, are you?' Phil enquired looking a little shocked.

'No. Checked out this morning. I called in at your place, but you weren't there. Your flat mate said you'd be here. Cam picked up the camera in case we bumped into you. Oh, I think you forgot to put the garbage out last week PC. There's a funny smell around your house.' She added waving her hand around comically.

'Coming to the rally Jacqueline?' Asked Phil not bothering to explain the smell.

'No. Dolos took my car remember, and the trains and

buses are out. The traffic is also pretty bad apparently.' She added.

'As you know, I'm between jobs at the moment.' She said, 'And I hoped I could interview you after the rally...An exclusive. You would have total control over what goes out, and what doesn't...' Jacqueline smiled hopefully. 'Start my freelance career.'

'Sounds good.' Said Phil. 'You can come with us to the rally Jacqueline. We've got wheels.'

'That'd be brilliant PC. I'll let Cam know.' She said pointing at Cameron who was out the front smoking, trying to look cool.

They ordered and ate a light lunch as the time drifted towards 3.

'Time to get moving everyone.' Phil said finishing up his third beer.

Their party had now expanded to seven. They all then walked back up the hill and stopped at the Kombi to Jacqueline and Cameron's horror.

'Is this your transport!' Said Jacqueline hoping there was some kind of mistake.

'Yeah.' Said Aldrich adjusting his Muumuu. 'Impressed? It's totally eco. It runs on garbage.' He added, again completely unnecessarily.

Wil, Phil and Beccs resumed their seats, with Jacqueline and Cameron climbing in reluctantly. Basil released the handbrake and rolled downhill kicking the Zombie back to life again. The traffic was already heavy and moving slowly. The Zombie struggled to keep up with it.

Phil regretted putting on a heavy white linen suit. He was seriously sweating.

'I'm sweating like a fat kid at a sports carnival.' He said taking off his jacket first, then taking off his pants and hanging them up.

It was a slow and uneventful trip apart from when Basil yelled 'gear change!' Which caused the Zombie to come to a complete stop, then lurch forward abruptly.

Phil and Wil spent most of the trip running through the broader points of what he was going to talk about. Beccs,

Jacqueline and Cameron spent most of the trip sampling the edamame and sea salt, Gochujang bean balls and spicy quinoa sticks.

After about an hour in the traffic and five gear changes later, they eventually arrived at their location driving past a huge all-encompassing crowd. Basil slowly circled around until he found a hill to park on.

As soon as the Zombie ground to a halt, and they heard the handbrake applied, they opened the back door, and all got out. Phil put his jacket back on, then started to reach in to get his pants only to be engulfed by a crowd chanting 'PC. PC. PC...' By the time he had time to turn back around to reach back for his pants, he saw the Zombie Kombi driving away with Basil yelling.

'I can't park here PC. I'll have to sell the Zombie if I get a ticket. I'll park as close to the podium as I can. See you there. Good luck.' He yelled and drove off taking Phil's pants with him.

'That's just fucking awesome.' Phil said looking down at his boxers.

He looked skyward as the crowd enveloped him further. They were all then ushered on towards their destination surrounded by an eclectic, chanting and sign waving crowd. The rally was about to begin.

The Rally

Cameron was filming and walking backwards through the jostle of the crowd with manifest skill and consummate ease.

'Can you take me from the waist up Cam?' Phil shouted gesticulating upwards with both hands over the throng of noise and movement, smiling and waving enthusiastically at the seemingly never-ending crowd. Deciding to really enjoy the moment.

'Can do PC. I'm live streaming.' Shouted Cameron back and gave Phil a confident thumbs up, lost his grip on the camera which slipped down below Phil's waist revealing his boxers, socks and bare legs. Cameron lifted the camera back up and gave Phil an even more confident, thumbs up.

Phil sighed, then noticed some of the crowd discarding their pants in solidarity and smiled a beaming smile at Beccs.

'It's going really well isn't it.' Phil shouted over the ever-increasing sound of the crowd, then involuntarily held her hand.

'You're a sensation PC. This is completely crazy!' Beccs shouted back, while also smiling and waving at the crowd herself.

They walked slowly through the crowd that moved aside at their approach. Phil felt like Moses parting the red sea.

Wil tapped Phil on the shoulder pointing and laughed at a thin and very nervous looking line of police skirting buildings desperately trying to look inconspicuous. The size of the crowd was totally overwhelming.

They approached their target, greeted by a cacophony of noise. Trumpets being blown, someone always brings a trumpet Phil thought. People shouting through bull horns and even a few bands, mercifully drowning each other out.

Phil was guided to a very rickety looking podium, then cautiously walked up some shaky stairs, then ushered to a makeshift lectern. The noise of the crowd slowly sank to a few whispers interspersed with some now unwelcome whoops. The bands played on for a few bars, then stopped realising the silence was not for them.

Phil waved to the crowd flanked by Beccs and Wil. An excitable guy who was previously addressing the crowd dropped the microphone upon seeing Phil. It made a loud crunching sound accompanied by screeching feedback. The excitable guy bent down, picked it up, bowed, and presented it to Phil like a sceptre. Phil smiled back, said thank you, took the microphone and shook hands with its previous custodian.

Phil looked as serene as a swan drifting across a mountain lake through a misty early morning sunrise. Barely a ripple. Underneath, his legs were flailing like a dog about to do its final paddles.

Phil could only remember one thing from his two-day public speaking course, and that was to take your time. He put his hands on the lectern making another crunch with the microphone and looked around at the enormous crowd. He saw several jumbo-sized screens and made eye contact with himself in one, then decided to not do that again. He looked down at a large group of the assembled mainstream media, located directly in front of the podium yelling questions, all holding up microphones and cameras badged with logos that people were beginning to trust in less and less. They were surrounded by police forced to listen to a chorus of merciless heckling.

Phil waved and smiled broadly, then waved his hands up and down in a hushing motion bringing a breathtaking silence. He brought the microphone to his lips.

'Good afternoon.' He muttered quietly. A few muttered

362

good afternoons were heard in reply, then quickly silenced.

'Thank you.' Phil looked down humbled.

'Although thank you is not what we are here for today.' He said, looking up sharply.

'We are all here today to say. No thank you!' Phil said pointing down to the assembled mainstream media, which was greeted with deafening boos.

'Today... Today.' He repeated. 'Is the day you reclaim your freedom. The day you say we've had enough of their immoral paid for pandering and lies. Their mainstream manipulation. Today you say no to the Censorship Industrial Complex.' Phil paused hearing a huge roar erupt from the crowd.

'Today is the day you tell big Tech, big Pharma, the Military Industrialists, HeadSpace, TearDrop, MonoTech and all the other unelected elitist supervillains of Klaus Dauber's World Treasury Fund that you have the power, and you are about to take it back. You're not going to listen anymore.' Another huge roar burst forth.

'Today we all make a commitment. Today we turn them off. We say no more to their fear mongering, their bought and paid for deception, their clouding of the truth through misinformation. Their censorship. Their one-sided reporting. Their lies by omission.' Phil paused for an even louder cheer to ripple through the crowd.

'Today we turn off social media and say no to their nefarious globalist agendas. No to their government and business complicit manipulation. No to their cancellation and suppression of contrary opinions and debate. No to their labelling of any other opinions as hate speech.' Phil paused again.

'Today we say no to the major political party cartels, who are conspiring to make our life harder. Conspiring to send us to die in pointless wars and conspire to take away our freedoms, while at the same time gorging themselves at a trough filled with, our money.' Phil paused and waited for the thundering explosion of approval to abate.

'Today we reclaim our freedom. We reclaim the truth.

363

Today is the day you realise you have the power. You don't need to be told what to think. You don't need to be censored. Bullied into doing what they want you to do. You can say no! Your future! Your destiny is in your hands. It's within your control. You gave them the power. You are the only ones who can take it back.' Phil heard agreement surge through the crowd.

'Today is the day we all become critical thinkers. Free thinkers.' Phil turned his gaze now to Cameron filming the live stream.

'Everyone watching through HeadSpace. Disable your account now. Uninstall the app now!' Phil pointed at the cluster of cameras filming from the mainstream melee below and fixed his gaze on the biggest one.

'Do not watch any mainstream news again! Turn off your television now.'

'Challenge your assumptions.'

'You don't need to be told what to think.'

'Question everything.'

'Don't vote for a major political party again.'

Phil turned around gesturing to the Parliament offices behind him.

'Let them know we are no longer scared sheep. We are lions! We are free thinkers. Their corrupt monopolies time is up!' A chorus of near ear-splitting cheers exploded from the crowd.

'Say no more to their collaborative, coordinated weapons of fear and mass deception.' Phil stopped to wait for the crowd noise to abate again.

'Thank you.' He finished abruptly.

Leave them wanting more he thought, then handed the microphone back to the excitable guy. He took it tentatively and stood speechless.

Phil stepped back from the podium, turned and smiled at Beccs and Wil. Beccs looked emotionally at Phil and smiled and nodded approval.

Wil simply said. 'Nice one PC.'

They all descended the podium followed by Cameron still filming. 'You can turn that off now Cam, and so can you.' Phil spoke sternly into the camera again.' Cameron turned off the stream and pointed the camera down.

'Hey, the trains are back on PC.' Beccs said, excited at the thought of not having to make the return journey in the Zombie Kombi. She reached out to hold Phil's hand again, which he took greedily.

'Perfect. Let's hang around for a bit, let the crowd thin out.' Phil asked as they all walked through the parting and still chanting crowd.

'Any sign of the mystery machine Wil?'

'I can't smell it PC.' Wil answered, sniffing the air.

'Let's just get the train home.' Beccs said imploringly.

'I'll call Christine and tell her to let my support team know we won't need the trash can mystery machine to pick us up.' Phil said to Beccs' relief.

They all walked following the train stations watching the crowd thin out at each one. They walked past another one, then rounded a corner.

'PC! Look it's the Zombie.' Wil said, indicating about 50 metres ahead. 'It's getting away...very slowly.' He sniggered, then sniffed the air again. 'It's definitely it.'

Phil laughed, then said with alarm. 'Christ! They've still got my pants.' He remembered and sprinted after it.

'You're making ground PC.' Wil shouted encouragingly.

They all watched as the comedic scene played out. Just as it appeared Phil's pants were going to make a successful getaway, Aldrich changed gears causing the Zombie to stop, giving Phil the time to catch it, open the door and scramble in. He turned around and held up his pants in triumph. The Zombie's gear then ground back into place, lurched ahead at top speed over a hill causing the doors to slam shut.

Wil, Beccs, Cameron and Jacqueline watched the whole scene playout in disbelief. It all happened so quickly.

'That's just ridiculous.' Beccs said who had started to run after him, then returned looking annoyed and worried.

'Quite the exit though. You have to give him that. I'll give him a buzz.' Wil said as always, the calm one, then pulled out his phone to dial.

Wil looked at his phone disappointed, then re-dialled.

'Not contactable. Try yours Beccs.' Wil said optimistically.

Beccs got out her phone and tried a few times getting the same result.

'What do we do now?' Beccs said holding her hands out perfectly communicating her total lack of ideas.

'Well. PC's plan, if separated, is return to base. So, I guess we go back to PC's.' They walked on to the next station which seemed to have thousands of people crowding around. It was thousands less than the previous one, which lifted their spirits a bit. They added themselves to the crowd.

'Guys. Can I borrow one of your phones?' Phil said sitting down composing himself to his fate. 'Mine has turned on that feature where it won't make calls when it's absolutely essential.' He laughed and waited for a response.

'I can, but it won't make any difference. None of us can make or receive calls. The Zombie is a kind of natural faraday cage, plus it has at least six coats of lead paint. Cool huh. We're off the grid man.' He said and ground into another gear.

Phil slumped into his seat and looked out the back window pointlessly.

Adam, Clay and Wal were in freefall. The sheeple, as they belittlingly referred to people, were no longer watching or reading their mainstream lies. No longer logging into HeadSpace. No longer buying from TearDrop. They thought things were bad before, now things were incomprehensibly bad. They could actually lose some serious money, but much, much worse than that. They could lose control.

At this stage of the game, they decided to forget about caution, forget about careful planning and kill PC as soon as possible. They tripled their already outrageously hefty bounty.

A non-descript man checked the message he just received, smiled to himself, picked up a large briefcase, his car keys and left his hotel room for the last time.

The trip home for Beccs, Wil and Jacqueline was painfully slow. It took an hour to just get onto the platform. Cameron at some stage also went missing in action.

When they did eventually get on a train it only went a few stations before they had to get off and do the whole thing again.

Jacqueline got off at a station nearish to where she lived. It was too late for an interview now anyway, plus she'd lost Cameron and was beginning to look and feel a bit fragile. This left Beccs and Wil to travel the remainder of the trip alone. Beccs kept trying Phil's number. They finally arrived at their station.

Phil's trip home was also painfully slow. The cause was not the traffic, which was practically non-existent. His problem was that the Zombie coughed, spluttered and wheezed to a complete stop roughly every few kilometres. Each time it stopped it sounded terminal. But each time Aldrich was somehow able to get it going again.

The Zombie finally limped its way to within a kilometre or two of its final destination, then stopped one last time. This time it stopped with a bang, accompanied by smoke billowing from under the hood.

'I think this is far as she'll go tonight PC. I'm going to have to overhaul the motor. Might take a few hours.' Aldrich said while climbing out. Basil popped the hood, then Elfy hit it with a fire extinguisher.

'Thanks guys, this is close enough anyway. Really appreciate everything today... Sorry about your car.' Phil said leaping out, stretching then bowing his head respectfully.

'It's OK PC. I've brought the Zombie back to life before. It's not as bad as I thought.' Aldrich said waving the smoke away to look at the engine which caught fire from the fanning. Elfy hit it with the fire extinguisher again.

Phil was eager to get moving and call Beccs. He was unsure what to say now but settled on 'peace out!' accompanied by two peace signs.

They all rushed over to Phil and gave him a smothering group hug and each said their emotional goodbyes.

Phil waved his final wave, turned towards his destination and pulled out his mobile. It pinged acknowledging 31 missed calls. Phil dialled Beccs' number. It rang only once.

Requiem

'PC. Where are you? Why was your phone off?' Beccs said not caring now simply relieved.

'I'm about 10 minutes away from the station. I was off the grid in a lead coated Faraday cage...Don't ask.' Phil laughed, the long trip and equally long and difficult day now completely forgotten.

'Should be home in about 15 minutes. Where are you Beccs?'

'We just got off the train a minute ago. What a trip. Do you want us to wait?'.

'No......Yes... I want you to wait for me Beccs. I want to talk to you.' He said nervously. 'Just you.' He added.

'Meet me at the park Beccs. Near the fountain...Where we first met... OK!'?

'OK. I really need to talk... To you.' He knew he was ready. Phil said goodbye and ended the call.

Beccs said goodbye to Wil. Assured him she'd be fine and that they'd call when they were on their way. Beccs was beginning to like Wil's mothering.

Phil was filled with his own words. 'Today is the day.' he said out loud. He was going to do it. He was going to say it. He was going to tell her. He was actually going to do it. He picked up the pace.

Beccs arrived at their park first. Walked up to the gate that was almost always stuck and stepped over it without thinking. She walked over to a bench under a light near the fountain. A few other people were walking around enjoying the warm evening. She sat down and waited.

Phil could see the park in the distance calling to him like

a siren's song. He started to run without noticing. Then he saw her, her silhouette. He'd recognise it anywhere.

His lungs were burning. He paused to catch his breath then walked on calmly. He then started running again. Fuck it! This is not the day, or the time to be calm. 'Today is the day!' He gasped.

Beccs saw Phil running, rapidly closing in. She waved. Phil's head was full of things to say. A clever quip, ask her how her day was. Fuck all that, he could see his procrastination approaching and decided to kick it in the balls. His procrastination could go fuck itself today.

He slowed down to a stop just before the fence. She waved and smiled. Phil approached the small fence, put his hands on it and jumped over landing in a perfect commando roll that would have got a nod of approval from both Starsky and Hutch. He heard Beccs giggle and give him a polite round of applause. Everything was going his way today.

Phil walked a few steps closer until he was out of the shadows, stopped and smiled. Beccs was now about 30 feet away, she stood up and smiled back. He threw his arms out wide, Beccs thrust her arms wide to knowing it was time for a slow motion run up and hug. He was going to whisper it in her ear. That's how he was going to do it. Perfect! They both slowly started running.

He only took one step when everything instantly stopped. Total nothingness. Phil crumpled to the ground dead.

The sniper shot that killed Phil was called "The Apricot". It was the perfect sniper shot, delivered by the perfect killer. He had already finished packing away the gun that killed Phil and was about to step into a car to be spirited away to the airport and gone forever. Easy money. No one would ever know who did it, or who he was.

Beccs had collapsed on the ground next to Phil's body. The scene was illuminated by the flashing of ambulance and police lights. The sound of frantic calls on police radios shattered the night. Wil squatted down on the ground next to Beccs and cried. They sat like that until the police told them they were taking Phil away now.

The dawn light was beginning to mark the arrival of a new day. They stood in the park and watched as Phil was carried away on a stretcher and put respectfully into an ambulance. They watched as it drove off into the distance. The police politely ushered them away and started putting up crime scene tape.

Beccs and Wil stared at each other not knowing what to do. 'Let's go back to PC's' Wil finally said.

They arrived back at Phil's as the sun rose. Wil and Beccs tried to make a cup of tea, tried to function to no avail. Phil was everywhere, his books, his clothes, his really bad paintings, his crazy ideas running wild through everything. They sat silently sobbing.

A phone rang next to a sleeping Wal. Wal didn't normally sleep with his phone on, but he wanted to know exactly when the job was done. He just couldn't wait. He picked it up.

'Louie.' Wal said knowing only he would be calling.

'It's done.' Is the only thing Louie said.

'Fucking awesome. Pick yourself out one of my luxury cars. Any one. Well done mate.' Wal hung up and slept like a baby.

Clay sniggered when he got the news and asked for details. 'How did he die? Did he suffer?' Louie hung up.

Adam received the news with a smile. Thanked Louie and hung up.

Christine and Ryan both came downstairs a few hours later in tears. The news had made it to the media. Ryan was being stoic and made everyone a pot of tea and some toast. Christine just made whimpering sobs.

Ryan brought out the tea.

'How are you doing Beccs? Feeling better?' Said

Christine still whimpering. She just stared at Christine. 'It must he hard on you losing a pub friend. But I lived with him. I lost a house mate.' She broke down crying loudly now.

'Shut up Christine.' Ryan said sternly. Christine actually shut up for the first time in her life.

They sat in silence drinking tea and eating toast. No one knew what to say.

'Can I put the TV on. Maybe they've caught the bastard.' Ryan said.

'No worries.' Wil said, not hearing the question at all.

The TV glowed into life. The news was on.

'The lead story today is the murder of PC. Real name Phil Collins. Not the singer,' She smirked. 'The social activist. Mr. Collins was gunned down in a park near his home late last night. He was on his way home after today's polarizing rally. Police are investigating.'

'Yes well, that was a wild ride while it lasted.' Her co-anchor said smiling. 'Seriously, it's a dreadful shame and it highlights the danger that celebrities, especially politicians take every day. The Prime Minister is joining us now. Prime Minister. Good morning.'

'Good morning Davey. You're quite right. Although the tragic death of Mr. Collins is… tragic. Ummm, it highlights a real need to ramp up security for all MPs and obviously increase gun control. Which is why I have vowed to increase spending on parliamentary security immediately. We're not going to wait for the budget on this one. This is something both sides of parliament will agree on I'm sure. Police are working around the clock, and hopefully we catch this killer soon.'

'Common sense government.' Was all the talking head had the time to say.

Beccs who had been staring blankly at the screen finally heard through her fog of grief what they were saying. She picked up her teacup and threw it at the television hard. The television screen cracked, then mosaiced and finally made a loud bang, then went silent. Wil walked over, pulled out the plug, picked it up and threw it out the back door smashing it loudly into the back fence.

'Thanks Wil.' Said Beccs. Wil nodded back.

'They don't even fucking care. PC was right, they are all sociopathic bastards.' She sobbed.

Beccs and Wil talked amongst themselves about Phil and his enthusiasm for life, reminisced about all his endearing idiosyncrasies, how terribly unfair it was, and cried throughout the morning. Ryan nodded in agreement and told Beccs to take off as much time as she needed. Christine sat quietly and kept the tea and toast coming.

Beccs and Wil decided they'd go to the pub. Phil would have definitely wanted that. They walked in and saw Justin standing behind the bar with red eyes. Justin said how sorry he was, barely holding it together. Wil thanked him, ordered two beers and a Vodka and coke. Justin reached for two beer glasses, stopped and looked at Wil. They were both hit with the full reality. PC was really gone. Justin pulled a single beer through tears and made Beccs a double Vodka and coke. And waved Wil's money away.

'Everything's on the house today guys.' He said with tears running down his face.

They drank through the afternoon and into the night. They both had Mo Mo dumplings for lunch.

In the background the television was droning away unnoticed, with the lead story whose narrative had been changed from the death of Phil to gun control. The government had found a scapegoat. Adam Soccliea held a press conference saying how sorry he was and that to commemorate his life he would make HeadSpace a better place. He would personally drive the change. He said a HeadSpace page was now available for people to post their tributes. To reach out to each other. The sociopathic bastard even had the audacity to put in a plug. Now is not the time to disable or disconnect from friends, he smiled, almost successfully.

Wal issued his own statement and his own product, which was a leather-bound edition of PC's musings. Of course, all proceeds would go to charity. His charity. It was heavily edited, but he knew in a few years, it would be the truth.

Clay decided to keep a low profile. He knew only too well that his boyish charm had long since left him. He knew that every time he appeared on the news his stock price went down. He knew he wasn't a likable guy.

Beccs and Wil decide to stay at Phil's house. When they got home, they noticed a pile of flowers and packages in the lounge room with a note on the table.
'Hi Guys. The flowers and packages came for PC. Ryan and I have gone back to his place. Call us if there is anything we can do. Love,
Christine and Ryan.
Ps., The biggest bunch came from Bobo.

They sat on the lounge and stared at a new TV. It had a note stuck to it. 'Dear Wil and Beccs. I bought you a new TV. It was my fault it got broken anyway. I suggest you don't turn it on for a while.
Ryan.

Over the next few days and weeks, the story slowly died down, Wal had setup a fund - The PC Free Speech foundation. Phil's HeadSpace memorial was beautiful, his YouTube testimonial touching, the production values were flawless. It already had nearly as many views as Phil's original document. Adam, Clay and Wal's stock values were recovering. Unlike Phil, they had dodged a bullet. The world that had briefly stood up, sat back down again and made itself comfortable. Wal, Clay, Adam and the WTF's grip tightened. The new normal would soon begin.

The End.

Author's Note

Dear Reader,

I hope you enjoyed my story. This apologue is meant as a warning. Remember, the people who want to censor your speech, are always telling the biggest lies.

If you liked my book, and even if you didn't. I'd really love to hear from you. Email me at: wayne.baker4242@hotmail.com

Thank you so much,
Wayne.

www.ingramcontent.com/pod-product-compliance
Lightning Source LLC
Chambersburg PA
CBHW051443260626
47162CB00001B/233